Promise Me Heaven

"My God, madame, I can assure you I have shown more restraint than any unfixed man in the entire kingdom!"

"No more restraint than any lady of the ton must exercise on a daily basis!" she retorted.

He reached out reflexively, catching her shoulders in his grip. His anger and frustration immediately died. He knew he had lost. He was incapable of resisting her. Smiling bitterly, he cursed himself . . .

"Play on, then," he challenged in a low, mesmerizing whisper. "My body is at your disposal. Go on then, seduce me." He pushed back the loose cloth of his shirt, baring his heaving chest. "Touch me." He reached down, pulling her trembling hand up, and gently pressed her palm over his heart. "Take from me . . . my heat." He bent his head down toward her. "My breath . . . my virtue . . ."

His lips were a feather's breadth from hers. Without volition, she moved to touch them . . .

Promise Me Heaven

Connie Brockway

AVON BOOKS ⬥ NEW YORK

PROMISE ME HEAVEN is an original publication of Avon Books. This work has never before appeared in book form. This work is a novel. Any similarity to actual persons or events is purely coincidental.

AVON BOOKS
A division of
The Hearst Corporation
1350 Avenue of the Americas
New York, New York 10019

Copyright © 1994 by Constance Brockway
Published by arrangement with the author
Library of Congress Catalog Card Number: 93-91663
ISBN: 0-380-77550-6

First Avon Books Printing: February 1994

AVON TRADEMARK REG. U.S. PAT. OFF. AND IN OTHER COUNTRIES, MARCA REGISTRADA, HECHO EN U.S.A.

Printed in the U.S.A.

RA 10 9 8 7 6 5 4 3 2 1

In Memory of my brother, Mark S. Howard

I couldn't stitch a quilt,
so I wove some words

Chapter 1

July 1814

Lady Catherine "Cat" Sinclair was hot. The heavy blue worsted habit she had donned in hopes of making a good impression had dark, wet rings beneath her arms. Her hair hung in a dusty, fast-uncoiling knot on the damp nape of her neck. Sweat trickled down her back.

She was also lost. After two days of listening to her great-aunt Hecuba read "bowdlerized" Defoe, Cat had escaped their shabby hired coach. Commandeering a sidesaddle from the last posting house, she had lit off on one of the outriders' steeds, only to find herself wandering the high Dover moors without any clue as to where she was. Now her London-bred horse was skittering nervously away from yet another group of blasted sheep emerging from a break in the hedgerow.

No one appeared to live on this high, windswept land. No one, that is, until she saw a lone herder half-buried in a nearby thicket. With a sigh of relief, Cat spurred her mare toward him. She was a third of the distance before she discovered he was half-naked. Quickly she reined in her horse.

Cat had seen men without their shirts before. She was, after all, the eldest in a family of three brothers and three sisters. But her brothers' slender torsos in no way prepared her for this man. His was nothing like their slight adolescent forms.

He was simply enormous. He was tall, broad, and deep, from his impossibly wide shoulders to the long, thick thews of his thighs straining the fabric of his workman's pants. Cat wondered how his wife found cloth to fit all of him, even as she called out. His back, gleaming with sweat and streaked with grime, bulged with muscle as he attempted to pull a large, anxious ewe from the thicket of briar in which she had entangled herself.

Cat called again. And waited.

And the huge, overgrown beast she had now spent the past ten minutes hailing still remained oblivious to her presence.

"Fellow! You there!" She called, louder this time.

Certain he would have answered had he heard her, Cat edged the mare closer a few yards, shouting down at him once more. He must hear her. God knows, she was making enough noise. He did not so much as turn his head. Abruptly Cat realized the brute was deliberately ignoring her.

"You there! Man!" *Mongrel, jackass, toad*, she added silently. "I'm speaking to you, fellow!"

She was quite close now. Close enough to see that his hair was shockingly long and black, sprinkled with dust—or gray—and curling damply on the wide nape of his neck. Still he continued to ignore her, linking his arms around the girth of the ewe and heaving against the purchase her front quarters had gained in the ground.

Angry with the brute's intolerable rudeness, and determined to be dismissed no longer, Cat stretched out an elegantly booted foot and nudged him with her toe in his sweat-slicked side. At the same moment the ewe lost her foothold in the thicket, and with a grunt, the giant wrenched her free.

The momentum threw him backwards against Cat's mount. It was too much for the poor mare. She reared back in panic, pitching Cat forward in her desperation to flee the terrifying woolly thing. Cat grabbed for the reins, yanking them back to bring her mount's head down. The horse lunged, kicking her hindquarters out, flinging Cat halfway out of the saddle. Her hat, and her hair, tumbled down over her eyes as she clutched fistfuls of mane, fighting to regain her seat. As suddenly as she had startled, the mare went still.

Gingerly Cat edged herself back into the saddle and, with a shaking hand, adjusted her bonnet. The brute was holding the reins tight up under her mount's mouth.

His face was as bold as his figure: a squarely cut chin, cleft and darkened nearly blue by what looked to be several days' growth of beard, wide lips set in a hard line, and black eyes gleaming dangerously from behind a fringe of blacker lashes. Looking into his angry face, Cat felt a frisson of fear.

"Now, what the bloody hell do you want?" the man shouted at her. The mare shied, but a mere flex of his huge wrist quieted her.

His tone stiffened Cat's back. She raised her chin and glared at him through lowered lids.

"You will inform me as to the whereabouts of the Montrose estate."

"The what?" The man frowned.

"The Thomas Montrose estate."

"Estate?" the great beast of a man asked, so slowly and in so perplexed a manner that Cat wondered if he might be mentally deficient.

"Yes," she said in measured tones. Thomas Montrose. Lives somewhere hereabout. In a big house. A nice house. Do you know where the nice, big house is?"

"Why?" the man snapped.

"Why?!" Cat asked. Whether he was mentally deficient or not, Cat had had just about enough. Her temper, suspect at best and tested by her journey, was stretched beyond its limits.

"Because, you great unwashed Vulcan, you Minotauran horror, I wish to go there!"

His gypsy dark eyes became shuttered between his lashes. "Why?"

"Oh, bloody hell! Because I am . . . I am his, er, niece. *Now* do you understand?"

His scowl was slowly replaced by a sneer, and he turned the mare's head so Cat's foot was caught between the wall of his hard chest and her saddle. Even through the leather of her boot she could feel his heat. She attempted to twist her leg free from the disturbing contact, but he only grinned wickedly up at her and reached his other hand out to capture the lip on the back of her saddle. Her leg was trapped, bracketed by the long, oiled bronze sinews of his arms. She refused to amuse him with her discomfort and defiantly glared down into his dark face. His teeth gleamed white in a feral smile of derision.

"Thomas Montrose does not have any nieces, you little baggage," he said in a deep, velvety bass. "I should know, for you see, *I* am Thomas Montrose. Now who *the bloody hell* are you?"

Thomas Montrose released the mare's reins, stepping back. The young woman with the tumbled russet hair and peculiar gray-green eyes was looking at him with something akin to horror. She did not even seem to notice he was no longer imprisoning her leg. It was a tact that had done much to quell the imperious manner in which she had spoken to him, as though he should have just dropped the confounded sheep and scuttled to her knee, doffing an imaginary cap as he awaited her command.

She was eyeing him now with distinct distaste, and Thomas was uncomfortably reminded that he was not only unclad but also filthy. His embarrassment irritated him, and he inhaled deeply, marshaling his temper. That he had to marshal his temper at all further angered him. He had spent the better part of the past year successfully maneuvering the most difficult of Russian, Austrian, and Prussian political adversaries. And he had done so with characteristic aplomb.

Now, with a few vitriolic gibes and a lift of a dark, arched brow, this haughty, tousled wench threatened his much-vaunted composure. It was intolerable. And who the devil was she at any rate?

When she had first stuttered out her ridiculous claim at kinship—and, to add to her faults, she was a terrible liar—he had assumed she was attempting to pass herself off as his by-blow by one of his former mistresses. He was grimly amused she would have thought it could work. She was twenty at the least, which would have him bedding wenches at—what? 13? While his reputation amongst the *ton* was unsavory, even he was surprised society had endowed him with such precocious tendencies.

But the look of genuine astonishment that had widened her incredible eyes had disabused him of that idea. In spite of her heightened color, she regarded him with the uninvolved gaze of an observer, objective and detached, not the knowing look of an adventuress. He waited for her to speak, the notion that she would shortly demand he produce birth records to confirm his claim causing his lips to curve ruefully.

She appeared to come to a decision, one that did not make her happy, though she managed to summon up a half smile. She inclined her head in polite recognition—for all the world as though they were being introduced at some fashionable town house fete rather then on the moors of Devon, he half-naked and she with her long, burnished hair falling about her shoulders.

"Thomas Montrose, sir. I am Lady Catherine Sinclair."

"Yes?" His tenuous hold on the situation dissolved further. Was he supposed to know who the hell Catherine Sinclair was?

"Your half brother, Philip, has these last four years been married to my mother. Lady Ringtree."

Philip's wife! The beautiful and much-married Lady Ringtree. He had known she had children. Lots of children, if his memory served him correctly. By lots of different fathers. That fact had not deterred his older brother, who had taken leave of his scholarly senses and proceeded to shock established society by marrying one of its brighter stars. And not with the discreet rectitude one might expect when the bride was embarking on her fourth trip down the aisle, but with all the bells and whistles. It had been an elaborate, sumptuous affair. And yes, Thomas did seem to remember several skinny girl children flitting about. This must be one of them. Who would have guessed that such unexceptional scrawniness would have erupted into such lavishness?

"And what might I do for you, Lady Catherine?" he asked.

She drew in a deep breath. "I have come on an important mission, sir. I have brought something of value to you. Not only to yourself, but to the literary world at large. Indeed, its value is so great, I felt I could not entrust its keeping to just anyone and have brought it to you myself. I have found your brother's opus." Though she seemed to be trying to engender a tone of breathless awe, the words came out as if by rote, trailing off in an increasingly unconvincing tone.

"Yes?" he prompted, intrigued in spite of himself. This must be some ploy to appropriate money from him. Philip never wrote about anything but birds. Yes, the chit was undoubtedly going to ask him for funds. From the preamble he had no doubt the touch would extend into many figures. He acquiesced silently, if cynically. His sense of family was strong, and Philip, his half brother, was his closest living relative. Thomas loved him deeply and loyally, even if he, too, had looked askance at Philip's chosen bride. If Philip's adopted family was in dun territory, Thomas would rectify it.

"Yes, I have no doubt," her voice lowered to a mumble, "I have acted for the best. I know my unannounced visit might seem a bit precipitous, but . . ." The gel was coloring delightfully now.

Thomas watched her fade off into obvious embarrassment and found he would, indeed, have to take pity on her. Perhaps asking for handouts on the merit of a trumped-up relationship and suspect manuscripts was as onerous to her as it appeared to be.

"This must be a matter of some import. Being so, it deserves more than a discussion amidst a flock of sheep on an open moor," he said.

She came to with this abrupt reminder of their bizarre circumstances and gazed at him helplessly.

"See here, Lady Catherine. My 'estate' is just down this lane, over the next rise. A harridan shall greet you at the door. That is my housekeeper, Mrs. Medge. Ignore her. No, you'd better tell her you are expected, but you must also inform her promptly—before she even opens her mouth—that you are my, er, niece. She is very circumspect. To have a young woman appear on my doorstep will no doubt excite the most disgusting—"

"I *do* have a chaperone, sir. I am not blind to the proprieties of an unaccompanied—"

"Merely uninvited," Thomas interjected. That bloody, haughty tone of hers could set his teeth on edge just in remembrance. "And who is this estimable individual?"

"My great-aunt Hecuba."

"Hecuba?"

"Lady Hecuba Montaigne White."

"Hundreds Hecuba?" An abrupt bark of incredulous laughter escaped him. Thirty years ago Lady Montaigne White, or 'Hundreds Hecuba' as she was better known, had been the most notorious grande dame of a notably lax society. Her liaisons were legion; her escapades were recounted in scintillating detail by the boys at the school where he had boarded. Quite a chaperone this lovely little beggar had brought.

"While I do not understand the appellation, sir, I can surmise its reason. I look forward to your meeting with my great-aunt," Cat said.

"No more then I, Lady Catherine. Her visit alone is worth any inconvenience. Why, the stories she must have to relay! I quite look forward to dinner. It may prove worth its cost."

The moss-eyed beauty frowned in perplexity before nodding and turning her horse's head. Thomas could not quite make out the words she uttered as she trotted off, but it sounded oddly as though she were saying, "Catherine, you ass, you fool, you dolt . . ."

Chapter 2

That could not be Thomas Montrose! That huge behemoth. That monolithic *male*! Impossible!

Cat was no green girl. She had made her come-out four years ago and traveled in the more exalted circles. While her personal concourse with rogues was slight, she knew their attributes: a pale countenance, a bored mien, drawled bon mots, and studied ennui.

How could *he* have garnered such an unlikely reputation? Thomas Montrose was the stuff of legends among the beau monde. His notoriety was nearly mythic. How often, when her friends had discovered her tangential relationship with him, had Cat watched their eyes grow round with titillation? Too many times by half.

There has to be some mistake, she thought. She could not—no, she simply could not—conceive of that much . . . *masculinity* lounging about a fashionable London drawing room, delivering beseeching, yet discreet, asides.

She could, however, easily imagine him stomping up to some poor woman and throwing her over his huge shoulder, grunting, "You be my woman now!"

Well perhaps he wouldn't grunt, she amended fairly. He did have a lovely, deep, cultured voice.

But nothing else about him was the least bit refined.

Well, she sighed, now she had met the legend. As she rounded the corner leading to the front of his house, her eyes widened with further disappointment.

Thomas Montrose's "estate" was a small country house made of local stone; its mullioned windows were covered by encroaching ivy, its front door bare of decoration. A large, crumbling fieldstone stable stretched out behind, flanking one side of the house. A paddock of ill-repaired raw timber held several bellicose-looking rams and a few scrawny chickens. It looked impoverished. It looked like her home, like Bellingcourt.

It was hardly the sumptuous den of iniquity Cat had imagined. It was unlikely there would be any French ladybirds in amongst the chickens, delivering smoldering come-hither glances at the rams. No, she thought as the odor of sheep wafted to her nostrils, it wasn't a den of iniquity at all.

A stableboy beshook himself from a midafternoon nap to take her horse. Before Cat had even begun to mount the steps, the door swung open upon the grim visage of a middle-aged, tight-faced hornet of a woman. Mrs. Medge. Cat picked up her skirts and approached her.

"Who are you?" the woman demanded.

"I am Lady Catherine Sinclair. I am the guest of Thomas Montrose," Cat said with dignity.

"Master Montrose doesn't have any 'lady' guests," the termagant announced as she started to close the door.

"Mrs. Medge," Cat began, "would you be so kind?" She started forward. The older woman stood her ground, looking Cat up and down with a notable lack of respect.

Cat sighed. Disappointment had been heaped

on disappointment. Just at the moment she was incapable of trying to charm anyone, particularly not this dragon. "You know, this grows tiresome in the extreme. Have the Americans lately annexed Devon? Because this local custom of democracy is most wearing. Or is it only Mr. Montrose who allows his servants a vote in whom will be allowed in his home? Mrs. Medge, let me make myself clear." She fixed the woman with a glare. It was returned balefully. "I am Mr. Montrose's . . . niece."

Mrs. Medge drew herself up, her black bombazine bodice puffing out like a spruce hen's. "Humph!"

"I was invited," Cat said.

"Humph!"

On a sudden impulse, Cat slid her foot past Mrs. Medge's dark skirts and gave the door a kick, sending it banging open. Calmly she slipped past her.

The entry was spotless. The flagstones shone with wax, and the unadorned walls, painted a silvery blue, were clear, light expanses. There were none of the dusty deer heads, antlers, or other dismembered pieces of animal anatomy Cat had half anticipated, and none of the field mud she had fully expected. It was a simple, clean, and well-maintained structure.

"Seeing how you're in, you'll be wanting to tidy up, I suppose," Mrs. Medge grumbled.

"Yes. Yes, I suppose I shall." Cat paused consideringly. "I may be staying the night. You best have a room made up for me."

"Oh, aye. A room," Mrs. Medge said grimly, and then, under her breath, but loud enough to make sure Cat heard, "I thought he was through with all that whoring around."

Cat drew herself up. "Mrs. Medge, I am not that

kind of guest. I am, as I have gone to pains to inform you, Mr. Montrose's niece."

"Mr. Montrose doesn't own a niece, 'Lady' Catherine," Mrs. Medge said triumphantly.

"Mr. Montrose will substantiate my claim." *I hope*, thought Cat. "Would you really like to wager your undoubtedly superior knowledge of his family against his own?"

Mrs. Medge pursed her lips in consternation. A wicked gleam suddenly kindled in her dark, raisin-like eye. "Shall I put you next to the master's room?"

"No! All the proprieties shall, of course, be observed!"

"Like unchaperoned girls gallivanting about the countryside, dropping in out of the clear blue to stay with bachelor 'relations'? Lah, proprieties have surely changed."

"I am not staying here alone, Mrs. Medge. My great-aunt, the dowager duchess Hecuba Montaigne White, will be chaperoning me," Cat said with chilly formality.

Her bravado did not last long. Mrs. Medge's mouth quivered open. She shook her head and began emitting a peculiar noise. It took Cat an instant to recognize it as laughter. Mrs. Medge's face grew red, and her beady eyes pooled with water.

"Oh my, yes! Oh, this is too much!" She gasped for breath, pressing a hand to her stomach. "Hundreds Hecuba! A proper chaperone she'll be!"

Catherine sputtered. "Mrs. Medge, my room, if you please."

"But where is Lady Montaigne White? Don't tell me she's already found the stables . . . and the stable lads?!"

Cat gritted her teeth. "My aunt will be arriving shortly. Now, my room, if you please."

Mrs. Medge moved off, cackling to herself while Cat took stock of her not completely unexpected situation. Even here, in the wilds of Devon, her great-aunt's history was still very much alive. Alive and capable of robbing her relations of that finishing touch of respectability. *Well*, thought Cat grimly, *wait until Mrs. Medge meets the formerly libidinous duchess.* It was Cat's turn to smile.

The lower quarters of the house owed nothing to current trends in interior decor. There were no Continental, Oriental, or classical influences. The furnishings were simple. The two pictures hung on the walls were landscapes unlike any Cat had ever seen, painted in an entirely haphazard manner by some person named Turner.

Other than Mrs. Medge and a young girl scrubbing assiduously at a pair of andirons, there appeared to be no one else about. The small size of the house was further evinced by the paucity of its bedchambers, a mere six. Such a house did not offer separate wings for lady and gentlemen visitors. All the suites opened upon the same hall. Cat was ushered into a corner bedroom and left with the grudging promise of hot water. She wandered around, noting the same dearth of ornamentation that marked the rest of the house, until the young maid she had seen earlier appeared, lugging a basin of water.

"I be Fielding, ma'am," the girl said, her freckle-dusted cheeks dimpling in a grin. "If you be wanting anything, you just goes round that wicked old b . . . biddy and asks me. We hadn't ever had a lady staying here," she finished wistfully, and bobbed a curtsey before leaving.

Cat combed out her thick hair and washed her face and hands before shaking the dust from her riding habit. No extra housemaid came to help her with her toilette. Luckily, Cat was unused to a chambermaid's attentions. Bellingcourt finances didn't extend to such niceties. Bellingcourt's finances didn't extend to any niceties at all. Apparently, neither did Thomas Montrose's estate.

Poor as a church mouse, thought Cat. *Poor as my own family. Maybe poorer*. That must be why Thomas Montrose, once the reigning prince of London's rakehells, had quit his throne and left for the Continent. More than one pink of the *ton* had been chased from society by a pack of creditors. The Beau himself was rumored to be nearly done in. And yet Thomas Montrose had chosen to return here after his supposedly scandalous sojourn, even if only as a shepherd, Cat thought with certain admiration. Unfortunately, she had no need of a shepherd. She needed a rakehell.

Even physically he was not at all what she had expected. The snippets of conversation she had heard from the older women during her four seasons in society had prepared her for the usual fare in roués. A rake was a rapier-slim, elegant, shining, and lethally charming man, in all, a "blade."

Thomas Montrose was more a bludgeon: big, heavy, towering, dark. As for all the scintillating, irresistible women she had assumed would be littering his decadent hallways ... Well, Fielding was a pretty enough girl, but she hardly qualified as a *femme fatale*.

How is one to study the mannerisms of courtesans when there aren't any courtesans around? Cat wondered.

From what she had seen thus far, Thomas' present situation was so far removed from his former one that Cat would wager everything she owned that his usefulness in the capacity of "rake" was nil. Unluckily, she had already gambled away everything she owned on the opposite wager. She might as well turn back home this instant and save them both the trouble of explanations.

She wondered how she was going to disinter her second cousin Emmaline from Bellingcourt. She had promised her elderly relative a fortnight of free lodging if she would act as surrogate guardian to her siblings. Emmaline had been coerced into accepting Cat's offer by her own poverty and the promise of a tenure that made the uncomfortable trip from Wales worth the effort. She would be most unhappy to quit Bellingcourt after less than a week.

Cat would have to pass that hurdle when she came to it. Her most pressing concern was coming up with some plausible excuse for her presence here. Her concept of a rake as being a buffleheaded fribble had also been overturned. There had been no want of intelligence in Thomas' pitch black gaze. He would never believe she had hauled herself and her great-aunt all the way from York to deliver his brother's treatise on the habitat differentiation of common British field birds.

It had been a hare-brained scheme, she thought miserably: thinking she could just arrive at Thomas Montrose's house, surreptitiously pick up a few pointers on seduction from the myriad glamorous men and women posing in his corridors, and hie herself off to London to captivate her would-be suitor. And it had seemed so reasonable a course! So clearly focused and astute! Damnation!

Well, she would just have to think up another plan. But first she must extricate herself from the situation, and the premises, as soon as she possibly could. And she must do so without ever, ever disclosing to Thomas Montrose the reason for her imprudent visit.

Cat thought of his swarthy face, the sweat drenched, graying black locks, his immense size.

Still, he must have his pride, and Lady Catherine Sinclair understood pride only too well. He must never know she had come to Devon precisely because of his past glory. It would be too lowering for him.

Finished gathering her hair into a twist, Cat took a seat on an overstuffed chair. She spent the remainder of the afternoon pondering credible reasons why a young woman would visit a man she didn't know and wasn't related to. She couldn't come up with many.

Chapter 3

Cat's gowns, and her aunt, had not yet arrived by the time Thomas seated her for dinner. She was uncomfortably aware that coming in to dine in one's traveling attire, particularly when that garment was in fact a riding habit, was unforgivably vulgar.

Thomas Montrose did not appear to notice. Indeed, he was not a great deal more appropriately dressed than she was. He wore black, form-fitting trousers tucked into dull Hessians. His shirt, a simple whitish linen, was topped by a hastily knotted cravat. He had pulled on some sort of jacket but neglected to don a waistcoat. He was entirely casual . . . as was his manner.

Not that he was forward or coarse. The black-visaged workman of the moors was gone, and in his place was an open-handed country squire, attentive to her comfort, chatting on about crop yields and the new weaving machines. He recommended each one of the simple dishes with a good-natured eye to her pleasure and kept up an erudite, if not exactly current, conversation. Occasionally she caught a speculative gleam from under his soot-colored lashes. And yet whenever she cleared her voice to confront the issue at hand, he summarily dismissed any conversation regarding her "mysterious tome" until he had seen her "properly fed."

He voiced a mild concern—it could hardly be called a rebuke—after she lost count of the number of times the poker-faced footman, Bob, filled her wineglass. Cat smiled, acknowledging her appreciation of his misplaced concern, and held her glass out for a refill. Her uneasiness seemed dispelled by quaffing wine so excellent as to be rare in her limited scope.

At least, she thought, *he has maintained the palate of a connoisseur. And it really isn't his fault his circumstances in the world have come down so much. One must remain compassionate, regardless of one's own misfortune.*

For his part, Thomas was completely confounded by his uninvited guest. She was lovely. Extremely lovely. But he had seen lovelier. She was poised and graceful. Again, gratifying but unexceptional. She was a pleasant dinner companion. And that was all.

Thomas had expected to be "captivated" by his young female petitioner. He had expected a wondrously—and scantily—clad vision to hang on his every word, to dart languid glances between demure, if drawn out, sips of wine, to laugh at his most feeble sallies and find some excuse, any excuse, to lay beseeching hands on his person.

Seeking to save himself the embarrassment of such a tawdry scene, Thomas had adopted his most bucolic persona. He had dressed with such carelessness that his valet had vowed to kill himself if Thomas took one step outside the confines of the house. Thomas expounded, ad nauseam, on every rural invention of the past decade. He exuded avuncular bon homie. Only to find that he needn't bother building walls. *She* already had one firmly in place.

Lady Catherine Sinclair had come to dinner, not in provocatively draped satins, but in her dusty riding habit. Her lovely, aristocratic visage was stamped with a decidedly doleful expression. She fixed him with a candid, gray-green stare when she spoke. She drank her wine as though she needed it. And she never came closer to him than the width of the table that separated them.

" . . . at a rate of yield exceeding four times the expected," Thomas finished saying.

Cat calmly cut in. "Apparently the Tories' proposed Corn Laws will soon be instituted. I cannot help but believe such measures can only prove provocative."

Aware his mouth was in the process of dropping open, Thomas snapped it shut.

"What with land rentals escalating so during the war, I realize some aid must be given to those producing our crops," she was saying, "but to impose a tariff on imported grain would have economic repercussions we can ill afford. Industry increasingly becomes an international arena in which England must be competitive. Raising wages to laborers so they might afford English grain does not seem to be the best means to insure our success in that area."

"How would a young woman know about international markets and Corn Laws?" Thomas asked.

Cat waved a hand dismissively. "I have read the text of all speeches pertinent to the problem. As for international markets, it is an interest of mine. What do you, as a landowner, think?"

He did not know what to think. Young women of his acquaintance usually had different interests. Very different.

She answered his dumfounded silence with a sigh and blithely steered the conversation back to more conventional grounds. Thomas was acutely aware of having further disappointed her. She made little attempt to conceal it; good manners demand she ignore it.

As the evening wore on, he felt sure her request for funds must be imminent. But each time she appeared to be coming to the point, she would fix him with that absurdly level gaze and waver.

Perhaps pride forbade a direct request, he thought, trying to make her as comfortable as possible. He was fast becoming impatient to have it out and over with. Having recognized the time-worn ploy of fortifying oneself with liquor, he was concerned the chit would slide senseless beneath the table before ever having the chance to divulge the reason for her visit. In some concern, he finally dismissed the footman that he might regulate her consumption himself. She was watching him now, a disheartened expression on her face, before she sighed yet again and peered at him speculatively. He felt the moment ripe to draw her out. But she spoke first.

"You do have a great deal of bald-faced charm," she said thoughtfully, her voice husky, slurred with alcohol.

"Thank you," he said, wondering if, from her tone, he should be thanking her at all.

"No, really," she said quickly, trying to interject an enthusiastic note. "I can see, I really can, how at one time you would be quite pleasant company for a lady."

"At one time?"

"Yes. I'm sure you were a very nice escort," she said.

"Oh, I see," he said. Polite understatement. She was obviously aware of his sordid reputation and was seeking assurance that those past transgressions would not be reenacted here. "Let us be frank, Lady Catherine. You have heard the rumors—"

She cut into his disclaimer. "Yes. Yes. Let us be frank." She slapped her open palm on the tabletop. The china danced. "I have heard the rumors. Lah, sir, we were more or less weaned on them. People could hardly wait to tell us of your . . . escapades, seeing how our mother had married your half brother."

"I am sorry . . ." he said. Indeed, he was. Some of the stories that could have reached those innocent ears were unfit for even the most sophisticated and jaded of listeners.

"So am I," she lamented woefully. "I shouldn't have been so naive. I, of all people, should have realized how one little transgression, oft-repeated, snowballs into fantastic proportions. My great-aunt, you know."

Montrose let his breath out, unaware he had been holding it. Obviously she had taken it upon herself to exonerate him of culpability. *He* certainly wasn't going to inform her that, in all probability, what she had heard had been the truth. He regretted the licentiousness that was the hallmark of his youth and was profoundly grateful some disease had not been his just reward.

"I should have known," she was saying, almost to herself as she stared into the wineglass, "that a reputation as a heartbreaker of almost mythic proportions could only be manufactured. No one could possibly live up to that reputation."

"Indeed, yes," he said with relief.

Encouraged by this understanding and rustic giant, unable to hide the disappointment of watching her carefully laid plans dissolve into nothing, Cat continued. "I mean, look at you! Even taking for granted that your . . . bulk . . . has increased somewhat in the past years, and your manners are very nice . . . for the country . . . you are hardly the . deadly combination of sensuality and suavity a rake is reported to be."

"My bulk?" Thomas asked, arrested in the act of lifting his glass to his mouth. But Cat was beyond watching her pleasant rural companion, being well launched into her theme.

"Aye," she said blithely, "your mass. Your size. You are huge. Why, just the thought of you doing the pretty at some crush is enough to bring tears of laughter. Don't you agree?"

"Quite," Thomas said.

She should have listened. Had she not been fou r sheets to the wind, she would have sensed the import of that telling softness.

"I mean really, can you imagine yourself swinging some fair thing in the waltz? I can. You'd probably launch her out a window during the first turn!" Here Cat had the misfortune to giggle, but, remembering her manners, was instantly contrite. "Not so many years ago, when you were more concerned with the fribbles of the *ton* . . ." she added hastily.

"I remember. 'Tis a bit vague, being so many years back, but I do seem to recall carrying a bit less . . . mass," Thomas said.

"Exactly!" she exclaimed, relaxing. "And I'm sure your manners were wonderful and that a great number of women found you the best of company. Some of them probably really *did* pursue you."

"I have decidedly fond memories of one or two," Thomas said sardonically. "But it was so long ago, one wonders if one is merely rewriting history to warm one on a dull evening."

"Oh, no," said Cat, "I'm sure there were. Really."

"How good of you to see back to the days of my long past youth and surmise, from this countrified hulk you have seen fit to dine with, the dim shadows of my insignificant career as a rake."

"You are too modest. I'm sure it wasn't altogether insignificant. My, what an easy man you are to talk to."

"It did much to further my reputation."

"I'm sure it did," she agreed, drunkenly polite.

"And since I do listen so well, perhaps you will now tell me the reason for your visit."

"Well, I don't know. I spent all afternoon trying to come up with some plausible excuse for coming here. It wasn't your brother's bird book." She stared at him with an equal mixture of candor and contrition.

What a confoundedly forthright woman, thought Thomas in exasperation. *Mayhaps now we can dispense with all my amusing shortcomings and finally come to the point.* "I rather thought not," he said. "Why don't you tell me the real reason you are here?"

"Should I?" she asked brightly, "Well, perhaps that's best. You'll think it rare amusing, no doubt." She dimpled at him. His face remained a smooth mask of polite interest.

"No doubt."

"All right then. I came precisely because of your past notoriety as a rake."

"Pardon me?" Thomas asked incredulously. He had anticipated a request for money. He had even prepared to grant it. Even now. But what his past had to do with her visit was beyond his comprehension.

"Yes. It was all rather silly, I'm afraid," she hurried to explain. "But, you see, I came out a good four years ago. Yes, I'm quite long in the tooth myself, if the truth be known." She smiled companionably. He glowered. "And I have had it in my mind to alter my current state by marrying."

"My best wishes," Thomas said, fervently wishing her intended the best of luck. "And?"

"Well then, there's the rub." Cat scowled, her dark brows drawing into an angry line. "The man I've selected won't come up to scratch."

"He won't?" asked Thomas, feigning surprise. Silently he congratulated the unknown fool on his good sense.

"No. No, he won't," said Cat, bright spots of color high on her cheekbones, again surprising him. He would expect her to be sad, or upset, or woeful, but not angry.

"You see," she continued, "the gentleman I have decided on is currently acquiring the reputation you had—or rather, the reputation that history has written for you. He's not quite achieved the name. But it is not for want of trying. I'm afraid, given time, he really *may* become a rake. He's quite, quite irresistible to females. Quite handsome—no, gloriously handsome—and very, very wealthy. And he's taken to using these attributes quite shamelessly in pursuing . . ."

"Pleasures of the flesh?" Thomas suggested.

"Exactly!" Cat said. "But, in spite of that, I feel we would deal well together. He's the perfect height to partner me in a dance," she stated with alcohol-imbued logic. "Besides which, I could make good use of his fortune and his position. And it really is past time I marry. I have quite set my mind on it."

"And your heart?" Thomas prompted, unsure why he asked.

Perhaps she did not hear the query in her current state, or simply chose not to answer it. She fluttered her fingers impatiently.

"And what was my role to be in this little tale of intrigue?" Thomas asked.

"Well, that's the laughable thing. I had formulated a sort of a program of study to advance my goal. It seemed a sensible sort of thing . . . before I met you. I heard you had returned from the Continent, and I thought you would come back surrounded by all of your type of friends."

"My type?"

"Yes, you know. Absolutely irresistible rakes and even more irresistible cypri—er, ladies. I thought if I could just stay here, I could sort of hang about the fringes of your house party and, well, pick up a few pointers. Learn by studying what a rake finds enticing in a woman.

"You see, Giles likes me well enough. He always seeks me out in polite company. But I haven't yet really captured his full attention."

"You mean his heart."

"No," she said in genuine surprise. "His attention. Fix his interest. Just that. I am not so green as to have romantic, ridiculous notions about his heart. As if one could study how to make another love one. What fustian!"

"Forgive my naivety," Thomas said.

She ignored his irony, continuing, "I thought if I could just learn what devices, what attitudes, to adopt in order to acquire a patina of . . . naughtiness? I could bring him up to scratch. Nothing too outré. The object is, after all, matrimony. I guess, in short, I thought you—you!—could inadvertently teach me how to be scintillating." She giggled, looking to see if he shared her amusement.

Apparently he did not. He was regarding her stonily. She caught a glimpse of something banked in his black eyes. A nerve twitched in his lean, hard jaw. But this couldn't be. Not from the kindly, fatherly host of just minutes past.

"And you don't think I'm up to the challenge?" Thomas asked.

She twirled the stem of her wineglass, tilting the cup toward him invitingly. He ignored the unspoken request. "Well, I'm sure you could teach me very pretty manners. But I already *have* very pretty manners. I had been thinking along the lines of something more explicit," she said, attempting to cajole a smile from him.

Thomas was not going to be cajoled. In the past half an hour, he had been taken down more pegs than he had in his entire thirty-three years. All from a lush-figured, basilisk-eyed, politically canny hoyden. A hoyden who went to no pains to conceal that she considered him an ancient, hulking . . . has-been!

All the feelings of remorse over his ill-spent youth, all the malaise of spirit that had ridden him since his return from France, evaporated in the face of this frontal assault on his male pride. His amorous conquests, which had only engendered in him a vague sense of self-disgust, now seemed like diamonds in a masculine crown, and she . . . *she* was questioning not only their number, but whether they even existed!

He would teach the hellish imp a thing or two about infamous rakes and their even more infamous desires. By God, he'd take the chit on!

"I don't think you have the raw materials," he said.

Her head snapped up, the smile vanishing with laughable alacrity. "What?"

"I simply don't think you have the necessary components to become the sort of woman who captures and maintains the interest of a man of the world. You certainly won't have caught mine."

"Yours?" she asked in offensive bewilderment.

"Yes, mine. I do not wish to elaborate on it unduly, but while I am sure much of my unsavory reputation is, as you so kindly surmised, a matter of historical embellishment, I was, to put it bluntly, a rake of no mean accomplishment."

"You were?"

"Really, if you are to become enigmatic, you will have to train your countenance into keeping secrets.

Right now it all too clearly registers disbelief. Yes, I was. And I daresay I could remember enough about what I found appealing in a consort to provide you with some direction."

"You could?"

He nodded his dark head. "But, I feel compelled to reiterate, I do not know if the basic elements are in you."

Cat's confusion was replaced by indignity. She drew herself up haughtily and said with admirable, if slightly slurred, outrage, "I can but try."

Montrose surveyed her languidly. He allowed his gaze to touch her face, frown at her hair, move slowly down the length of her neck and rest on her bosom before traveling to her waist. Cat felt a quiver stir in her beneath his lazy perusal. She hastily ascribed it to the wine. She was too warm. Still, a suspicion that she had just entered unplumbed depths nagged at her. Pride alone made her hold herself still beneath his regard.

"Mmm . . . perhaps," he said. "Well, it's as well the lambing is done and I have energy to devote to this project. Still, we can use all the time we can get. How much do you say we have?"

"The season begins in earnest one month hence," Cat bit out.

"A month. Well, 'twill be a challenge, perhaps not impossible," Thomas murmured. "But then, there is the question of propriety. We can hardly manufacture a scintillating little virgin only to have the gossips get hold of your unchaperoned position in my household and ruin the invention, can we? And as your great-aunt has chosen not to grace us with her presence, it is a matter we need address."

Cat opened her mouth to speak, but at that moment a series of crashes and angrily raised voices shook the outer hall. The door burst open. A small figure, swathed in layer upon layer of thick, black wool, stood quivering victoriously in the doorway. A huge, iron crucifix swung from an enshrouded throat. Green eyes, of amazing beauty and fierceness, impaled them from a perspiring, wrinkled visage. The tiny figure raised an ebony cane with one hand and with the other produced what appeared to be a well-worn Bible. She held both aloft as though warding off some despicable demon from below. In the dead silence, her voice hissed forth with sepulcher condemnation. "Evil!"

Cat turned calmly to Thomas. "My chaperon has arrived. Allow me to introduce my great-aunt, the dowager duchess Montaigne White. But I believe *you* know her better as 'Hundreds Hecuba.' "

Chapter 4

"**D**amn and blast the chit," Thomas muttered. He swung his long legs over the side of his bed, stifling a groan as his overworked muscles protested their cavalier treatment. He wondered darkly where *she* was now. Sprung, no doubt, fully clad and alert from the deep sleep of innocent youth. She probably did handsprings down the hall on her way to breakfast. After, of course, stopping for an edifying spiritual consultation with Hecuba Montaigne White.

Thinking of Hecuba, Thomas shuddered. Thus are the mighty tumbled. Or rather, thus are they *not* tumbled. A convert in the grip of religious mania. Thankfully, he'd not yet succumbed to a similar fate. Thomas only hoped that if in his dotage he should start collecting saints' knuckle bones, someone would do him the kindness of placing a bullet 'twixt his eyes.

Luckily, Thomas assured himself, his dotage was some years hence. In spite of what that "Catherine" person said. He was sure he had never been more fit. But, honesty compelled him to admit, while he may well be fit, there was no denying the silver streaking the hair at his temples, or the stiffness that was, even now, greeting his first moments of wakefulness. It made no difference that yesterday he had labored harder than the most stalwart farmhand. At least five years ago it would have made no difference, he amended. The chit had merely pointed out a few unassailable facts, the foremost being he was no longer a youth. What a confoundedly rude thing to do!

Ever since selling his commission a short while after the battle at Salamanca, and returning to England, Thomas had flirted with depression. He had forced himself to become involved in the estate, even though his interest was feigned and he often did little more than go through the motions.

This morning, however, the apathy he had tried so hard to combat had evaporated. This morning he wanted a spot of revenge.

He had spent hours last night wondering what to do with his unexpected, and unwanted, houseguest. This morning, images of her flitting about at the crack of dawn, concocting some syrupy tisane for her aged host, decided him. He would take her up on her outlandish proposal. He would turn the little shrike into a midnight swan, instruct her in the ways of a rogue, tutor her in the language of dandies, make her familiar with the ways of rakes and libertines. Begad, he'd win her respect, he thought angrily.

With that, Thomas rose with determination, if not grace, from his bed, all the while making plans for his new protégé.

"Ah!" Thomas began enthusiastically, rising from the breakfast table with flattering alacrity upon Cat's arrival. His gaze dropped to her gown. His "ah" trailed off.

"Is something wrong?" Cat asked worriedly, looking down to inspect her pale blue, sprigged frock for any undone fastenings.

He sighed. "We might as well begin immediately, don't you agree? But first we must set some ground rules."

She nodded gingerly, the motion causing her head to throb.

Cat had not sprung from her bed. She had crawled from it. Her pounding head failed to dim a horridly clear memory of the preceding evening's debacle. She had called her host "massive." She had laughed at his past conquests. And somehow, somewhere, she had been maneuvered into outlining her ridiculous plan. Worst of all, she had at some point agreed—God, had she even suggested it herself?—to a preposterous scheme whereby she became Thomas Montrose's pupil! If her head didn't hurt so much, she was sure she could have fathomed the reason for his readiness to fall in with her plan. It certainly couldn't have been her charm.

"Good," he was saying. "First, you must promise to put yourself completely in my hands. I will not have you continually doubting my judgment on these delicate matters, and I can assure you, with the utmost confidence, that I am remarkably knowing on the subject of seduction. Ain't I, Bob?" he cheerfully inquired of the dour-faced footman.

"Regular libertine," acknowledged the footman in a sad monotone.

"So, are we agreed?" Thomas asked politely.

"Ah, yes, sir," Cat answered, wincing.

His dark eyes flashed for an instant. "I realize that as your elder, and in view of your exquisite manners, it will be hard for you to do so, but considering the proposed nature of our relationship, I think you might call me Thomas."

She lowered her eyes. Nodding hurt too much.

"Good. And I shall call you Catherine."

"Cat."

"Excuse me?"

She reddened. "My family calls me Cat."

"A nickname? Famous seductresses usually forswear nicknames as juvenile affectations, but seeing how your appellation has certain . . . connotations . . . I believe it may do very well. Cat." The word on his lips became a caress, and she looked up to find him smiling at her, obviously amused.

He waved her to a seat across from him. "Do sit down, my dear. The fish is delicious. I believe Lady Montaigne White enjoyed quite a healthy portion earlier, didn't she, Bob?"

"Has a taste for the heads, does her ladyship," Bob agreed.

Fish! Oh, God, Cat thought miserably, please let him not uncover the fish! Again, Thomas grinned, a wicked contortion of his wide mouth. She felt the blood flee her face, and she covered her lips with unsteady fingertips before taking her seat.

"Now, as to the matter of your attire. If this is an example of your most seductive gown, I begin to suspect the cause of your lordling's disinterest. Who the deuce is the fellow, anyway?"

"He is the Marquis of Strand, Lord Giles Dalton."

The smile died on Thomas' mobile lips as his eyes focused intently on her. An odd silence ensued while he studied her.

"Strang, is it?" he finally asked, idly chasing a piece of sauced mushroom around his plate. Cat felt a new wave of nausea. "No matter. All the young pups who are presently cluttering London drawing rooms were in leaders the last time I was there. About your gown—"

"It is 'Strand.' And this is not my most seductive gown. Why would I wear my most seductive gown to breakfast?" Cat was dismayed to hear petulance creep into her voice.

"Ah," Thomas intoned. "A seductress does not own anything other then 'most seductive gowns.' Do you understand?"

"I think so." Cat squeezed her eyes shut, but the lights swirling dizzily on the back of her lids persuaded her to open them again.

"Good. Well, immediately after breakfast go change into something you consider alluring and we'll critique it, shall we?"

"Whatever should I deck myself out *for*? To entrance the local cows?" she asked, miserably aware she was being disastrously rude but unable to ignore his deliberately provoking tone.

"My dear," Thomas said with exaggerated kindness, "to the connoisseur, seduction is a life-style. You don't go out for an evening and suddenly become a siren. You have to work yourself into it. Take on the trappings and slowly, surely, hopefully, achieve your ends."

"Since we are rusticating here, perhaps I should clothe myself in a page's garb and cut my hair short like Lady Caroline Lamb. She is accounted something of a siren, is she not?"

"Lady Caroline Lamb is mad. Or as close to being there as makes no difference. Her relationship with that poet fellow is merely a prime example of self-indulgent histrionics. At one time, she might have been considered alluring, but there is nothing in the least attractive about mental instability."

Cat stared at him with wide eyes. It suddenly reoccurred to her that Thomas actually knew the figures of social legend; that he might have met Byron, flirted with Caroline Lamb, sat at the Bow Street window of White's with Brummell, Avonsley, and their ilk. How incredible! This great, muscular man with his casually tied neckcloth and plain white shirt, his comfortable old Hessians, his hair curling over his collar . . .

The rest of the meal passed with Thomas as friendly and even-tempered as last evening. But once or twice Cat caught glimpses of the rogue who had whispered her nickname, who had discomforted her with his perusal.

Afterwards, Cat went upstairs determined to make a success of her schooling and vowing to impress Thomas. She spent all morning toward this end, rifling through the dresses hanging in the armoire. The gown she finally chose was more suited for a Covent Garden entertainment than a morning in Devon. It was a mauve and white striped muslin with a décolletage well beyond the accepted bounds of provincial propriety. The skirt was caught up in a brilliant green silk ribbon tied beneath her breasts, pushing their ample fullness higher. Wondering what a siren did with her hair, Cat finally decided to twist the thick mass into waves, catching it loosely at the nape of her neck, like her mother's Dresden shepherdess. She had once heard one of her mama's husbands remark that the statuette "looks a wanton little thing." She smiled into the mirror, well pleased with herself, secure in the belief she would quite turn Thomas' head.

When Cat descended the stairs, it was with confidence. She stopped at the bottom, lifting her chin regally as her host approached.

Thomas did not fall over himself in eagerness to gain her side. He did not even reward her efforts with an appreciative gaze. He merely took her arm and wordlessly escorted her to the drawing room. Only after they had entered and he had shut the door did he turn and say, "I thought you were going to wear something alluring."

Cat blinked at him.

"This is alluring," she said.

"No. It's certainly very pretty. And it's very charming . . . for a young matron."

"A young matron?" she asked, her voice rising.

"Yes. A young matron. A married member of a conservative family of some means with a desire to appear fashionable but not forward," he instructed her. "Is this really the best you can do? Because this evening we begin the game in earnest. And be assured that is precisely what it is. A game. I shall be the accomplished rake and you must try to be the accomplished flirt."

"I shall do my best," she said quietly, lowering her eyes so he would not see the battle lights gleaming therein.

"Now, is this getup really the best you can muster?"

"Yes," she answered tightly.

"Well." He sighed. "There is nothing for it but that we go to Brighton to see about your wardrobe."

"I can't afford a new wardrobe." She cursed the blood she could feel staining her cheeks.

"You can't afford not to have one. Besides, I will find the ready to lend you until my brother returns. *He* can well afford it. We shall go in a fortnight. In the meantime, we shall see about your other accomplishments. You must spend the afternoon reviewing your repertoire. I regret I cannot take luncheon with you, but other, more pressing matters require my attention."

"Wrestling more sheep, no doubt?" she asked sweetly.

"No. Actually, Lord Coke has written me an interesting missive concerning the uses of manure. I intend to put his theories to the test." He allowed himself to smile only after he had seen the ill-concealed grimace on her face.

*   *   *

"Damn!" The door swung shut behind Cat. She stood quivering with suppressed ire in the small antechamber to the library.

"Profanity!" Her aunt Hecuba rustled in the depths of a damask-covered chair. She squinted around the corner of the winged back, hastily concealing a small book in the folds of her black dress.

"Yes, Aunt Hecuba, profanity. And where the deuce were you this morning?"

The old lady looked up guiltily, her glance darting to the book on her lap before she regained her composure. "Having risen with God's own creatures, I partook of a crust of bread and then, of course, spent the remainder of the morning on my knees, praying for the heathens of the world. And for you."

Cat suddenly laughed. She sank down beside her aunt. "I could use more than your prayers, Aunt Hecuba. I could use your instruction."

"Eh?" Hecuba asked, disarmed as usual by Cat's infectious good humor.

Cat cocked her gilt head. "You could help me, Aunt Hecuba. You have so much knowledge to bestow. You were the reigning queen of the *ton* for years. Your information in certain areas must be well nigh omniscient."

Hecuba scowled and plucked at the black tatting on her half-mitts. "And just why should I help you? So that you might marry some wealthy ne'er-do-well? For what? To have pretty dresses, houses full of servants, jewels, and all the other material snares with which the devil catches the unwary?"

"You know me better than that, Aunt."

"'Course I do. Always had more sense then all your brothers and sisters put together. Until you took on this rattle-pated notion, I would have said too much sense. Always formulating some scheme for increased poultry production or some such economic mathematics."

"I find it interesting." Cat shrugged. "And as there was never anyone else about to see to Marcus' lands, it was necessary."

"Your brother should have been the one seeing to the needs of that infernal estate he inherited. How in Go—in heaven's name he ever came to the title, I will never know."

"Third cousin once removed," Cat answered glibly before continuing softly, "and he was only thirteen."

"And you were all of what? Seventeen?"

Cat sighed. It was a long-standing source of contention between them. Hecuba had never understood one simple, glaringly obvious fact. Cat liked managing things. Although Hecuba certainly didn't want for those tendencies herself, thought Cat . . .

"You have asked for my help," Hecuba finally said. "You must give me a good reason if you expect me to ally myself with your delinquent scheme."

"And what's so delinquent about it?" Cat asked in genuine surprise. "If I manage to contract a marriage which will provide my family with the means to better themselves, garner myself an undemanding spouse, and secure a position of some influence in society, it is no more than myriad others have sought to do."

"I doubt very much whether a union with a fast-developing womanizer is going to make you happy."

"Happy?" Cat threw up her hands. "When did happiness become a requisite for marriage? Mama was constantly falling 'happily' in love. Four times she tripped 'happily' up the aisle to the altar!"

"Every union your mother engaged in was of a decidedly genial nature," Hecuba said primly.

"I don't deny it. But her continued 'happiness' has left the products of her conjugal rapture paupers! Simon can't borrow the ready to purchase a commission. Timon hasn't a prayer of entering Oxford, though he could well teach half the courses. Enid should have made her bow a year ago, and poor Marcus suffers the agonies of the damned over an inherited estate whose population is starving. Only Marianne hasn't felt the pinch of our circumstances, and she will in another year when she is due to come out!"

"You mustn't blame your poor mother for—"

Cat threw up her hands. "I don't blame her, Aunt. I merely seek to allay the effects of her 'happiness.' We all assumed our troubles would be over when she wed Philip Montrose. Indeed! Mama herself was promised handsome settlements once she and Philip returned from their honeymoon. But, Aunt Hecuba, they left on their honeymoon *four years ago*! And, save for the occasional extravagant—and useless—gift, we are still ruinously poor. It is time someone affected some changes before we all end up in debtors' prison. And I intend to do so in the most practical manner possible. By marrying Lord Strand."

Hecuba narrowed her eyes. "Why Strand?"

Cat shrugged. "Strand is wealthy. He is pleasant. He is a pragmatist. He is old enough to have outgrown the tiresome need to constantly pester a woman for her undivided attention. He is intelligent enough to have good conversation when we should happen to cohabit. And he has political and social associations which would assuage the boredom of the matrimonial state.

"I have studied the matter in depth, Aunt. I have spent a considerable amount of time and effort compiling a list of candidates and interviewing various sources as to their suitability as a spouse.

Not merely their social attachments, either. Their political, business, and family connections have been thoroughly investigated. Lord Strand quite tops the list." Cat, looking well pleased with herself, patted her skirt pocket.

Hecuba appeared dazed. "You actually have a list in there?"

"Yes!" Cat answered. "Not that I have need of it anymore, but one cannot be too careful."

"No," mumbled Hecuba. "Can't be too careful."

"You see, Aunt?" Cat said triumphantly. "There is nothing in the least reprehensible about my motives or my schemes. I assure you I have not made a frivolous choice."

Hecuba shook her head. "No, no one would *ever* call you frivolous, Catherine. And you really think you might come to love this man?"

"Love? A most modern notion, Aunt Hecuba. One which, in my opinion, is overrated. I have never been infatuated for longer than a dance or the dessert course at dinner. I would not like to base my future on so labile an emotion."

"I will think on this, Catherine," Hecuba said, shaking her head, watching her great-niece with a bemused expression. "In the meantime, I shall lend you my most recently acquired tract, 'The Lady's Manifest of Maidenly Virtues.' It is truly inspired."

Chapter 5

By midafternoon, Cat was impatient for company. Her aunt had retired to her room for "spiritual refurbishment," a phrase that usually meant she was going to take a nap. Or perhaps Hecuba was reading whatever it was she had so discreetly hidden in her skirts. Mrs. Medge avoided Cat, disappearing through the door opposite whichever one Cat entered. Hours earlier, Cat had seen Thomas stride off toward the stables. She had penned a few letters to friends in London and a few more to her siblings in York, but quit when a cramp set into her fingers. She was bored. Seldom had she experienced enforced inactivity. It was not an enjoyable experience.

She glanced out of her bedroom window overlooking the kitchen gardens. Several scraggly children were running after a harried-looking cat, pitching overripe fruit at the poor beast as it frantically sought to escape. Finally, in desperation, the motley creature fled up an old apple tree, only to have the hooting, ragamuffin lot encircle the tree and commence hurling rotten apples at it. Cat bristled visibly, turning and stalking from the room. On seeing the narrowing of those green eyes, anyone who knew her would have immediately fled for safer climes. Unfortunately for the children, they hadn't yet the pleasure of making Lady Cat Sinclair's acquaintance.

Rounding the corner leading from the stables to the back of the house, Thomas wiped the dust from his brow, kicking his bootheels against the slate path. Mrs. Medge had convulsions if "stable dirt" besmirched the blameless splendor of the front entry, and dirt was the least offensive element he carried on his boots.

Thomas stopped short in his tracks at the tableau before him.

The afternoon sun slanted over the old fieldstone wall, glazing with golden light the woman seated beneath an ancient apple tree. Her striped gown billowed about her legs. A battered straw bonnet hung from a green ribbon tied about her lovely throat. A group of urchins, most of them the estate manager's brats, lay in rapt attention at her feet, their small chins cupped in their hands, their faces intent. She was illustrating something she said, her slender hands held aloft.

She made a charming picture sitting thus, Thomas admitted to himself, her expressive features as absorbed as the children's. Undoubtedly she was telling them a fairy story, and soon would commence to making daisy chains for the two dirty little girls leaning against her. Very pretty, very tranquil, Thomas thought before cynically wondering why the deuce young women always supposed an ability to charm children with a story immediately convinced potential suitors they qualified for motherhood.

As he approached, Thomas wondered what tale she was relaying . . . Red Riding Hood? Too grisly. Puss 'n Boots?

" . . . and once you have him in your sights, you must draw your arm back ever so slowly, so as not to alert him, before launching your projectile. Aim for his body. They always jerk their heads around quick, and a moving target is hard to hit."

"Go on wid ya," said an openly doubtful young voice. "You never kilt no rat wid a rock."

"No? Were my brothers Simon and Timon here, they would attest to my abilities with a projectile," Cat said, her grin answering some wicked recollection. "And Enid, my youngest sister, is quite a dab hand, too. Not so handy as myself, but good enough." She sat back and dusted her skirts with her hands.

"How many rats has you snockered, Lady Cat?" asked a redheaded lad, idol worship clear in his hushed query.

"A few, a few. But I must say, I never managed to dispatch as many of the horrid little beasts as the kitchen cat. She averaged two a week."

"Ah," chimed in another boy. "That ain't so great. Blather there catches that many on some *nights!*"

Cat leaned forward and fixed each of the avid, dirty little faces with a glare. "And a fat lot of thanks it gets her! No, indeed! You show your appreciation by chasing her up a tree!"

"We wouldna hurt her, not really. We's just havin' a bit of sport," someone said.

"Some sport. Sport of fools to chase off a helping hand. Now, pitching rocks at rats—that's sport!"

"We won't do it no more," promised a reedy voice.

What an extraordinary little beauty, thought Thomas, leaning his forearms atop the wall, entranced in spite of himself. And she had set her cap at Giles Strand. And why not? If the occasional rumors Thomas had heard from his London correspondents were correct, his friend and onetime fellow officer was well on his way to enjoying the notoriety Thomas once had. Maybe Cat's plan had some merit, for Giles as well as for herself. Maybe she was just the woman who could save him from the spiritual degradation Thomas had courted. Looking at her, Thomas could well believe it.

If his ears didn't deceive him, she was now instructing the brats on the finer aspects of weed control. She had picked up a slender branch and, with near military authority, was directing the movement of her diminutive troop.

"Careful there, Jack, strawberries have notoriously shallow roots. Tansy, thinning a row is not the same as decimating it." She shook her leafy baton at the girl.

Thomas could hold his tongue no longer; the contrast between her polished elegance and her pragmatic supervision was simply too appealing.

"There are gardeners I pay rather well to do that," he said.

"It's 'im!" the urchins called out in unison, fleeing over the wall and around the corner, dispersing like a pack of the rats they had just been discussing.

Cat shot to her feet, feeling foolish. Thomas Montrose was leaning over the half wall, grinning, his strong white teeth making a wolfish contrast to his sun-darkened face. His shirt sleeves were rolled up over his muscular forearms, his jacket hooked on a finger over one broad shoulder. He'd obviously been standing there for some time. Once more she had amused him with her ingenuousness. He looked as though he considered watching her more entertaining than attending a farce. She simply had to learn to control these unrefined impulses or he would never take her seriously.

She really was very pretty, thought Thomas, even when she was turning three shades of red. He wanted to tell her not to be embarrassed. Her uniqueness was an enticement no one could teach. She started to leave, but he was suddenly loath to let her go. He wanted to hear what other singular thing she might have to say.

"You like children?" he asked casually.

Cat stopped and looked over her shoulder, studying him. Did sophisticated beauties admit to liking children? She didn't think so.

"Not at all," she said, turning to walk through the kitchen door. "I like cats."

Cat hated sitting here, waiting for Thomas to return and "critique" her evening attire. The more she thought of his barely masked amusement at her feminine wiles, the more determined she became to make him grovel, preferably in abject worship, before her. Only pity for his much-reduced circumstances and a tiny bit of embarrassment over her last night's social transgressions kept her from being packed and gone by now. Only Christian compassion, she thought, feeling much maligned, kept her here at all. How dare he not recognize that fact? By the time the door to her bedroom was tapped and Fielding had entered to offer her assistance as a lady's maid, Cat was in fine, militant fettle.

"Fielding," she said, "I have been issued a challenge." Cat started to unlace her bodice.

"Yes, ma'am."

"Mr. Montrose," Cat paused and pushed her skirts down over her petticoats. "Mr. Montrose believes my wardrobe sadly lacking in feminine appeal."

"He does?" The little maid's mouth dropped open.

Cat kicked the dress away and strode to the armoire. "Yes."

She rifled through her clothes, her green eyes gleaming as they fell on a particular dress. She took it from the hanger.

"Fielding, do you think any man has the right to decide what constitutes 'feminine' apparel? Of course you don't. What right-thinking woman would?" She marched with the dress to the vanity and sank down, holding the luscious ivory silk puddled in her lap.

"But, Fielding, we must learn—indeed, it is in our own best interest to do so—to acquiesce to this nonsense in order to achieve our own ends. It is not a noble thing, Fielding. But we have been robbed of direct recourse. No, not noble . . . but bloody well effective! So, Fielding, pull the stays!"

"Yes, ma'am." The girl approached and gave a tentative yank on Cat's lacings.

"Harder."

Fielding grabbed hold of the stays and pulled back tightly.

"Harder."

Fielding frowned over Cat's shoulder. "You won't be able to breathe, ma'am," she said in some exasperation.

Cat's answer to this obvious statement was to suck her breath in deeper and growl, "An alluring woman doesn't breathe, Fielding. I have it on the best authority. Now, pull the damn stays tighter."

"Any tighter and your bosom's going to heave up right over the top of your chemise," Fielding muttered, but she set her foot to the back of the vanity's stool and hauled back as hard as she could.

Cat's chest swelled over the top of the delicate lace edging. She surveyed her flushed countenance with bleak approval before shooing Fielding off to fetch the thin muslin petticoat. While she was waiting, grimly watching the blood recede from her face, the door to her room suddenly swung open and Thomas, work-sullied and coarsely garbed, strode into the room. With a gasp, Cat snatched her dress up in front of her.

"Ah, Cat. Good. I was hoping you would be taking more pains with your appearance for this evening's meal. We dine in—" he checked the mantel clock—"a little less then three hours. You should be able to do something with yourself in that time," he finished dubiously.

"Just what do you want, sir?" Cat sputtered.

He looked at her in surprise. "Why, I wanted to clarify the purpose of our role playing this evening."

"And you don't think you could wait until after I was decently dressed for this conversation?" she asked through stiff lips.

"Why, Cat, you aren't . . . Why, yes! You're embarrassed! How perfectly charming!" Thomas laughed in delight.

And then, as though he'd just had an unhappy thought, he added, "But charming isn't exactly what we're after, is it? No, Cat. 'Twon't do. You will simply have to forgo embarrassment. A sophisticated beauty is never embarrassed. She takes any uncomfortable situation and turns it to her advantage.

"For example, your maid is present." Thomas waved a hand at Fielding, who snorted in reply. "Your aunt is in the next room." He nodded to the open door from which issued Hecuba's gentle snoring. "And you should be thrilled to be able to present a man with a provocative, yet still sanctioned, view of your charms."

He looked her over, from her face to the dress she held to her bodice, and his expression grew doubtful. "Although why, in God's name, a woman trussed into layers of plain linen and metal bands is considered provocative is beyond me."

"Whalebone," she hissed.

"Whalebone?" He shuddered slightly. "Even worse. Anyway, Cat, we can't have you clutching cloth to your chest as though your worst fears were about to be realized. It reeks of prudishness."

She went from delicate rose to fiery red before mustering what dignity she could and saying, "Just what is it you want to instruct me on?"

"Oh, that. Well, you see, I wanted to give you more of the flavor of what you wish to accomplish. Because that's really what it's all about. Flavor, nuance, innuendo. You wish to titillate your victim . . . er, pigeon, er, intended." He smiled. Cat scowled.

"Titillation," he continued in that odious, instructional manner, "is the art of making someone want something he's not sure he'll get. Next, you make him think he not only wants but needs this thing until, finally, it becomes an obsession driving him to a final capitulation. He'll do anything to secure the object of his desire. In your case, I believe that the moment of capitulation is called a marriage proposal. Am I correct?" he asked cheerfully.

"Well," she said, "it's not quite that cold-blooded."

"Oh, but it is, Cat. It's merchandising in its highest form. There's nothing wrong with it. Perfectly acceptable as long as both the purchaser and the seller know what they're about. You do know what you're about, don't you, Cat?"

His rich, melodic voice lowered. Cat was disarmed by his sudden concern, and with her confusion, anger erupted. Surely this was just another means to punish her for last night; the worry he affected was feigned. Well, she wouldn't play into his hand.

"Aye, I am very sure of what I want," she said.

"Well then, set about it properly and we'll see what we can do about you, come dinner," he said, returning to his infuriating insouciance. He left Cat plotting revenge as Fielding approached, wielding a brush and a fistful of what looked to be grape leaves.

"I must confess the foliage dripping from your hair took me back at first, but now that I have gotten used to it, I find it quite original. Rather enticing after the usual knot of primroses one sees stuck atop most women's heads." Thomas nodded his approval.

He was rewarded by an unaffected laugh from his guest.

"I, too, had certain reservations. But I agree. They are unique. Fielding, I believe, has taken your challenge personally. She is determined to make me *à la mode*." Cat smiled broadly.

They had gotten along remarkably well throughout the meal. There had been a few moments at the onset of the evening when Thomas had wondered if he'd pushed her too far. But teasing Cat was simply too delicious to resist. He had even felt a twinge of guilt, which he had quickly smothered, at his cavalier treatment of her. It was obvious she had taken the bait and dressed to impress him with her sophistication.

She had removed the lace inset from the bodice of her gown. If the fabric's straining seams were any indication, she was trussed so tightly into the thing that a deep breath threatened to spill her over the top. She had further abused the poor gown by liberating it of such niceties as sleeves and hauling what little material was left down about her shoulders, a blatant bow to his remarks about prudishness. She'd allowed the heavy mane of her auburn hair to fall where it may down her back.

Thomas found himself wondering whether his

restraint was to be tested by this sudden, over-whelming display of feminine attributes. But her manner, after that first triumphant assessment of his unprepared reaction, had been all that was pleasant and friendly. Her astute observations on the problems of Lord Eldon's proposed Corn Bill had afforded some stimulating and informative conversation. If her grasp of the French situation had been as learned, they may well have spent the entire evening arguing politics, for God's sake! Instead, he had asked her to join him in his library for an after-dinner libation.

She was sitting in the small velvet chaise before the hearth, where a fire chased away an unseasonable chill. Hecuba had sent a terse note explaining that the rigors of prayer, which had kept her at her knees all afternoon, had exhausted her. Though she was obliged to absent herself for the rest of the evening, she wrote, she knew that *all* proprieties would be satisfied. Thomas nodded for Bob to deposit the decanter and glasses.

"I'm afraid Aunt Hecuba is set on rewriting her history as one of virtuous restraint," Cat said, wondering what her great-aunt could have written that would cause Thomas' lips to curl in that wry manner. He crumpled the paper, flinging it into the fire.

Thomas lifted his dark gaze to her, the injunction of Hecuba's note effectively forgotten as he waved his hand, dismissing Bob. "Why does she wear black? Surely if your family had lost a member, I would have been informed."

"No, we are a ridiculously robust lot," Cat said, laughing. "I suspect that my great-aunt is in mourning for the very past misdeeds she now claims to abhor. Oh, the sermons we have heard on the evil nature of men and the foulness of base physical unions!"

Thomas grinned, infected by her good humor. "I daresay she's an expert on the subject," he allowed.

"Oh, no doubt. But surely she can't have indulged in so many liaisons without having at least some kind memories?"

"Perhaps they weren't of a kind nature," he murmured, shifting his long legs and staring broodingly into the fire.

"Oh, that, I refuse to believe," Cat said with self-assured naïveté. "Then again, I am, as you have been at pains to point out, eminently unsuited to make such a judgment, being so sadly lacking in a knowledge of feminine allure."

"You put me in the unenviable position of either having to say only a tart would be qualified to make that judgment or agreeing with your unflattering opinion of yourself."

She smiled innocently. "Oh, I didn't mean to make you uncomfortable. I merely await your opinion as an expert on any matter of abandoned behavior."

"I see," he said. And he did. The pleasantries were over.

Rising, Cat went to stand a moment before the fire. She turned slowly, looking at him with soft eyes and a warm smile. "Now, on with the lessons."

There was an edge of steel in her soft voice. "I have a few questions I would like answered, if I might."

"Ask away," Thomas said warily.

"First, if a woman is to capture the interest of a rake, I assume that subtlety is not her chief concern."

"It depends on what one calls subtlety. If you mean scribbling frustrated longings in a diary, or whispering them to another country miss in the hopes that they will eventually reach the ear of the rake, you assume correctly. On the other hand, going about in red satin with your hair undone might be going a bit far."

He regretted the words as soon as they were spoken, having honestly not considered that her hair was, indeed, undone. But she merely colored a bit, returning her gaze to the fire. The flesh of her shoulders glowed amber in the soft light. Thomas had never taken Giles Strand for a fool, but if he had overlooked this woman, he was worse than a fool.

"So it's a matter of compromise? An attempt to capture the attention of this one man without the censorship of all others?" she asked.

"A fast pupil. That's it exactly."

"And as far as your discourse on titillation—how does one go about engendering this desire without being obvious?"

"You might make the availability of the goods known but leave doubt as to whom they are being offered."

"Oh, surely that won't do. Why, any female in London, unmarried and in society, is assumed to be available," she protested. "We are reared with the express purpose of making ourselves available."

"Yes, but available for what? That's the key. True, most any female is available for the honorable estate of marriage. But is she obtainable for anything else? As I see it, it is your task to make a sufficiently vague offer to Lord Stand to pique his interest." His voice sounded terse to his own ear.

"Strand," Cat corrected him, her eyes narrowing suspiciously before continuing. "Yes, but how am I to do that?"

"Well, that's what we're here to do, isn't it? Instructions in titillation."

"Ah, yes. The art of making a man want something . . ."

" . . . without being sure he's going to get it," Thomas finished.

"I think I see." She turned from her perusal of the flames, regarding him speculatively. She raised one arm above her head to draw her fingers through her hair in a seemingly unconscious gesture of concentration. Her pose threw her into a sculpted silhouette against the dying fire. He could see the rise and fall of her breath catch and release the light on the soft mounds of her breasts. Suddenly, unaccountably, his throat went dry. She stood thus for a long heartbeat before crossing the room to the sideboard and pouring a glass of sherry.

"Let me see if I can illustrate," she said, coming to his side. Silently Thomas watched her.

"Let's say you are a man who would like a drink of sherry." She considered the wineglass in her hand. "And I have the only glass of sherry around."

Cat drew a long, elegant forefinger in gentle circles around the rim of the crystal glass. "Let us say you have not had sherry in years. Madeira, ratafia, burgundy—yes . . . but not sherry."

Dipping her finger into the amber fluid, she raised it to her mouth. Her tongue peeked out and slowly licked the moisture from the tip of her finger. A smile of appreciation curved her lips. He watched her in wry admiration, feeling his pulse quicken in the face of the picture she presented.

"And now, this sherry is within reach," she continued softly. "But you don't know its price."

Rewetting her finger, she slowly took it into her mouth and sucked gently on its tip. He was riveted by her performance.

The silk of her gown rustled and settled over his boots as she leaned so close, he could see the blue veins in her breasts, feel the warmth emanating from her, the silken brush of her hair on his face as it swung over him. For a third time her fore-finger dipped into the sherry. This time she raised it slowly to his mouth, brushing his firm lower lip with butterfly lightness. He felt the muscles tighten in his jaw, his cheeks, his chest.

Teasing his lower lip, she stroked the slick inner flesh with languid care. "And now you are tasting that sherry. But is a taste enough? Won't a sip be more satisfying? Isn't that what you really want?" Her voice had become a husky caress.

Raising the delicate crystal glass, Cat slowly took a small sip. The liquid shimmered on her lips, the firelight outlining their budding fullness.

She lifted her hand toward him again and he knew with awful certainty that her revenge was complete. His restraint had been pushed to its limits, and while he was no randy young buck lusting after his first maid, the sensation was startling in its intensity. He wanted her. It had been years since he had wanted a woman like this. Simply. Elementally. Without hidden motives.

The little fool did not even know how far she tested him. Like a kitten first unsheathing its claws, she was delighted they had drawn blood, unaware her prey might be dangerous when provoked. He would allow this to go no further. He caught her slender wrist inches from his face. For a second their eyes locked, his in hotness, hers in open triumph. A second later her gaze fell confused before that heat. He drew in a ragged breath, mastering the desire that had exploded.

"Touché," he congratulated her.

"Truce?" she whispered.

"Truce."

Chapter 6

Brighton

"No, no, no," Thomas said in exasperation.
"Shhh," his pupil implored, "you're going to wake Aunt Hecuba, and then we'll be in for it."

Cat smiled fondly at her great-aunt, who was snoring softly in the corner of their coach. The trip to Brighton had been tiring for Hecuba, warranting, as it did, lengthy discourses on Sodom, Gomorrah, and Babylon. Conversely, her dire warnings about the road to perdition were littered with clumsily veiled, if pithy suggestions for Cat's transformation into a temptress.

This afternoon's excursion was to procure Cat some "suitable garb." Fielding, pressed into service as lady's maid, had volunteered to save Hecuba the nuisance of having to accompanying Cat and Thomas by going with them in her stead. The three of them had held their breath as Hecuba squinted at them before pronouncing Fielding's suggestion most unseemly. They'd expelled a collective sigh, Thomas and Cat's of resignation, Fielding's of disappointment.

Consequently, they were all three ensconced in a coach with Hecuba, rolling through the sunlit streets of Brighton. Her pose of vigilant suspicion had finally exhausted her.

"You two go on with your conversation," she had at length said, her eyes fluttering shut. "I shall just meditate a moment on the fate of fallen women. Women who pinch their cheeks to put color into them, moisten their lips with tallow, and don't wear gloves when dancing."

Thomas looked over at the small, heavily swathed figure. She looked like an untidy pile of clothes dumped into the corner of the landau. In the two weeks he had known Hecuba, Thomas had discovered her facade of religious zeal hid a still naughty wench with a weakness or two; she fell asleep anywhere, at any time, and she drank like a fish. Hecuba had "fortified" herself for their shopping excursion with liberal amounts of ratafia.

"I begin to suspect that your aunt's reputation owed less to a natural wantonness than to a proclivity for the vine," Thomas said.

Cat regarded her aunt with clinical interest. "You might be right."

"Tell me, is she often in this state at Bellingcourt?"

"Well, no. No, most often she's berating some poor housemaid for her supposed moral laxness. But then, Bellingcourt hasn't boasted a wine cellar since we moved there."

"Hmm, these things seem to be hereditary. I suggest that you, m'dear, stay firmly away from the bottle lest you end up giving away your trump card before even playing the hand," Thomas said.

Cat snorted companionably. "Not likely, sir. I shall guard my suspect tendencies till after Strand is firmly delivered to the altar. Then, no doubt, I shall fall into a perpetually disreputable state. But a happily wedded one."

"Just so," Thomas answered roughly. "But you will never reach that state unless you improve your skills. Now, don't fly into the boughs, Cat. We've dealt well enough together these past weeks. Too well to ruin all the groundwork we've laid just so you might teach me another well-deserved lesson."

It was true. Thomas treated Cat with a fond, if sometimes exasperated, familiarity. It was a course far more comfortable then the scene they had played out in his library. Cat should have been distinctly relieved. She had no desire to fall again into his dark, burning gaze. Having always prided herself on clear thinking, that not unpleasant but decidedly unfamiliar sense of imminent abandonment had shaken Cat. This friendship was far better, she told herself. She simply could not account for her feeling of dissatisfaction. It was ridiculous, particularly since they got along famously, laughing over their shared taste in the absurd, discussing various subjects, sometimes quite heatedly.

Thomas had become the perfect companion. She was surprised his declaration of truce had been earnest. No other man of her acquaintance, including any of her proud brothers, would have been capable of acknowledging a woman had bested him in a game of seduction. They would have sought to repair their damaged self-image, no matter what the cost. But truly, Thomas was unlike any other man.

He had apparently had some sort of military or diplomatic career after his brief, though brilliant, one as a London rake. He spoke French with a perfect accent, indiscernible from the haughtiest Parisian aristocrat's. He was willing to converse on any topic, from the inflammatory subject of home rule, to the explicit one of animal husbandry. And he honestly appeared to take pleasure in her opinions, and even more pleasure in their disagreements.

Once, after reviewing a treatise on rotating crops in a scientific publication he subscribed to, she had been so excited by the implications that she had hurried out to the field to enlighten him. She had found herself standing beside him, ankle deep in loamy soil, before realizing she was inappropriately dressed in a gauzy morning gown.

Thomas had not seemed to mind. He had listened to her excited litany with an earnest expression before swinging her high up in his great, powerful arms and striding with her back to the house. His embrace had been matter-of-fact, his clasp of her light; her heart had unaccountably quickened at the knowledge of his unusual strength, of how carefully his arms held her. The next day he had commenced to having his hay field turned over to barley.

And then there were the "lessons." Except for that one evening, their adopted roles were strictly as mentor and pupil. The art of seduction, Cat found, was ample ground for amusement when dissected in Thomas' wry, sardonic manner. Even here, bumping along on the way to the famous modiste, Madame Feille, the lessons continued. Thomas was attempting to teach Cat how to flirt with her eyes.

"The idea, Cat, is to send out covert messages of invitation, not to appear as though a swarm of gnats have just pelted you in the face."

"I was fluttering my eyelashes."

"No. You were trying to dislodge a field of sand. All that rapid blinking and squinting . . . The only man you'll attract with that behavior is an ophthalmologically oriented fellow who'll offer you a salve."

Cat giggled and fixed her mentor with a wicked grin. "Well then, if you're so expert at it, why don't you demonstrate?"

In reply, Montrose assumed a mask of weary dignity and pronounced, "You ungrateful baggage. It is only through a growing desire to see the population of London saved from your flirtatious exhibitions that I proceed with these lessons at all. However remote our connection, I do have family pride to consider, and the thought of you making those grimaces all over the city in an attempt to lure some poor fool to the altar pricks my conceit. To have it come out that we are related, however tangentially, is beyond enduring."

"I understand, Thomas," Cat said soberly, her eyes shining. "You wish to foster the notion that the entire family is irresistible."

"Exactly. Now lower your eyes slightly. No. Don't squint. That's right. Now look at me without moving your lids. Better . . . Now, maintain eye contact a second longer than is seemly . . .

"No. No, Cat!" he said in disgust. "You don't fix the poor swain with a basilisk stare. You dart a glance at him. Make him aware that your interest is piqued but not set. All right, we'll continue later. We have arrived."

Cat straightened, looking out of the coach's small window. They were near the Steyne in a fashionable side street close to Prinny's ongoing debacle, the Marine Pavilion.

"I do not feel right about this, Thomas," she said, her expression anxious.

"Nonsense. I was, in fact, sincere in my estimation of your wardrobe, Cat. It simply is too ingenuous. Don't worry, I have no intention of decking you out in wet muslin and red sãtin."

"Oh, I know. I trust your taste in these matters implicitly."

"How gratifying to know that I have a future as a lady's maid should the crops fail," he said teasingly, but her answering smile was still a distracted one.

"I cannot help but feel that I presume too much in having you incur the cost of my clothing. It doesn't seem . . . seemly," she said, her gaze on his rough, outdated garb.

Thomas apparently couldn't afford to purchase himself a simple wardrobe, and yet here he was, planning to spend an immense amount on her clothing. She simply couldn't allow his fields to lay fallow just so she could have an ermine-trimmed cloak or a satin petticoat. Loath to injure his pride, Cat cast about for some excuse he would accept, finally saying, "Aunt Hecuba would simply convulse if she knew."

"Aunt Hecuba, I'll warrant, has a shrewd idea of how matters stand. She has chosen ignorance. I take that as a sign of concurrence. As to the money, I firmly intend to recoup my losses at your marriage to whatever the confounded fellow's name is, or on the return of your parent. Consider it in the way of a loan."

"I suppose," she said, vowing to repay him with interest once she was a wealthy matron. Thomas would have his fields planted *and* a new coat. She had to start seeing his expenditures as an investment in not only her family's future, but his own as well. As Thomas handed her from the carriage she said, "And, Thomas?"

"Yes?"

"I am not at all averse to red satin."

"Witch," he replied equably.

Cat surveyed herself doubtfully in front of the long mirror. The gown she modeled was an emerald green silk worked with amber beads and garnet-colored ribbons. It nipped in tight beneath her breasts, falling in sheer folds to her ankles. Long, close-fitting sleeves extended just beyond her wrists. The front rose to a high, prim neckline, again figured in the amber beads. On the whole it was tasteful, elegant, nearly severe in the simplicity of its line. From the front. It was only when Cat turned to survey the back that she caught her breath. There was no back. She was entirely naked, the gown exposing the column of her spine, the flare of her shoulder, the white flesh over her ribs. It was beyond daring. It was scandalous.

"Are you sure, Thomas?" she asked.

He had stretched his giant's frame out in a ridiculously dainty love seat, causing the abused furniture to protest with an audible groan. There was a closed expression on his lean countenance.

"Sure of what? That it is as alluring a gown as you're likely to find? Or that I would have you wear it?" he asked with maddening ambiguity.

"Are you sure I won't reap the censure of all of London if I appear in public in it?"

"Vain little beast," he murmured, his tone indulgent. "I assure you that 'all of London' isn't likely to care what you wear as long as you publicly behave yourself. No, Cat. There are many fashionables clad in a good deal less cloth, displaying a great deal more flesh, who don't excite the least comment. The appeal of this gown lies in its contradictory nature. So innocent from the front, so wanton from the back. Does the wearer know it is so? Which is she? That is the sort of contradiction that excites the mind, stimulates the jaded interest.

"No," Thomas continued, his voice a low drawl, "it will do quite well for your designs. We'll take it."

He nodded to Madame Feille, the proprietress. Immediately she started to drag the pins from the materials, all the while barking orders to her attendants to fetch other gowns.

Cat stood still for their ministrations while watching Thomas in some concern. He was acting strangely. All his banter had left him. When they had entered the shop, there had been a few moments of comic disapproval from Madame Feille. Thomas had dressed himself not with the elegance Cat had secretly hoped he would drag out of mothballs, but with his usual disregard: dark worsted, white linen, dull Hessians.

Madame Feille had thought to make a quick sale of a cheap ready-made. She was soon disabused of that notion. Thomas' bearing marked him for a nob.

His speech too marked him as a peer. His tone was urbane, even suave. And he had displayed a sure and intimate knowledge of fashion. Madame Feille mentally rubbed her hands together as he demanded more of her skill as a dressmaker. Gown after gown was purchased for the statuesque young woman.

The auburn-haired beauty must be his mistress, she concluded, and he so careful a protector! Nothing too outré, too shameless. All tasteful and yet, at the same time, intensely provocative. Why, the gown of bronze and black silk tissue alone would make any impure's reputation. And it appeared he was going to escort her amongst the *ton* itself!

The eager modiste foresaw a windfall of orders from this unlikely source. She redoubled her efforts to provide just the flavor the huge gentleman seemed to want.

However, with each gown, with each creation of restrained enticement, the black-eyed giant became more withdrawn. The beauty's teasing comments provoked less and less of a response until finally, as she modeled a gown of ruby satin that displayed to full advantage her remarkable endowments, he rose and said, "This grows tedious in the extreme, Cat. And no doubt Hecuba is bestirring herself in the coach, interrogating poor Bob about his love life. Buy whatever else a lady needs to act as foundation for these fripperies, and I will see you presently."

"But won't you stay for the petticoats?" the young woman asked, surveying herself in the mirror. Her tone seemed to Madame Feille a genuine display of confused innocence.

Apparently the big man thought so too. He looked at the beauty with such a sudden flare of ill-disguised longing that Madame Feille caught her breath. But the girl had turned away to pluck a pin from her waistband. Unfortunate for her, thought Madame Feille; the beauty might have made good use of such knowledge. Another dozen gowns at the least.

The dark man collected himself and said in bored tones, "Oh, I think I can leave that in Madame's capable hands. Just stay away from the coarse linens, do."

But his eyes, Madame Feille noted with interest, still burned.

The man was waiting in the suite when Thomas returned to the Old Ship Hotel. He sat on a chair pulled up toward the window, his hands folded in his lap, his expression one of infinite patience. Though far from old, he was a seasoned man, a contemporary of Thomas'.

He had a military bearing; his slender physique was rigidly attentive, his dark blond head held at a proud angle. But his trappings were that of a gentleman: the ebony cane, the conservatively tied cravat, the dark coat and top hat.

"Damn," said Thomas, "I must speak to the management about allowing uninvited chits to wander into private rooms."

The man rose, shrugging with Gallic indifference. "But, Thomas, management knows nothing about it." His voice held a trace of a burr in its careful pronunciation.

"Of course not, Seward," Thomas said before running a hand through his thick black locks. His eyes suddenly looked older, weary, a hint of dismay clouding their obsidian brightness. "It was too much to hope that I had seen the last of you."

"Entirely too much," Colonel Henry Seward agreed politely. "Comes of making yourself too useful. Sir Stuart would never happily let go his premier—what shall we say?—consultant?"

"Say spy. It's what you mean," Thomas said tersely.

Seward continued as though he hadn't heard Thomas. "Not with the conferences in Vienna going on. Not with Napoleon plotting away on his little island."

"And whose fault is that?" said Thomas, suddenly angry. "I advised, repeatedly, against furnishing Napoleon with a fortune and a pet army."

The blond gentleman raised a hand. "And there were some who listened. But not enough, Thomas. And those who did weighed the benefits of this fine, diplomatic gesture against potential public outrage. Censure the populace, Thomas, if you must. The *ton* itself has made a darling of the little emperor.

"And who is to say the decision was not justified?" Seward continued. "Nothing has come of it yet. There are only rumors, after all. And London, Thomas! Have you been to London? The entire city is celebrating."

"I did my celebrating after Salamanca."

Colonel Seward's cold eyes met Thomas' steady gaze. "Yes. That's right. You purchased a commission shortly after that unfortunate affair with the Leons woman. Her son died, didn't he?"

An awful silence met his soft query.

"I'd heard you were with Wellington in Spain," Seward continued. "Your friend, Lord Strand, was there, too. Tell me, did fighting help assuage the guilt you felt over the boy's death? You blamed yourself entirely too much, you know. It was as much her responsibility as yours. He was, after all, her son."

He was a little boy who'd died because his mother had had information Thomas had wanted. "You overstep yourself, Seward. What do you want? I can hardly believe you have come to deliver an invitation by hand to one of Prinny's debauches." He gestured toward the folded paper Seward was holding.

"In fact, it is an invitation. To the Friday evening affair at the Pavilion. Many dignitaries will be there, many of your old friends, including Prinny himself. He misses you now that Brummell has alienated himself."

"In Paris I always reported to Sir Stuart. I was never a confidant of the Prince Regent's, nor a member of Brummell's circle."

"Ah, but you had just as distinct a reputation when you were first recruited." A hint of bitterness surfaced beneath the even timbre of Seward's soft voice. "I was there, if you recall, and you thought it all very intriguing and not a little amusing to be enlisted by Sir Charles Stuart himself, the English ambassador to France, as a spy. At what point exactly did you lose your sense of humor, Thomas?"

The flesh around Thomas' mouth grew white.

Seward smiled, a slight stretching of his lips. "But they all do, all the fine young blades. You weren't the only one, only the best. Even better than your friend Lord Strand. And success always has a price. You have made yourself invaluable, Thomas. Sir Stuart has need of you."

"Seward, I am here as escort to a respectable young lady. I have no intention of once more dancing on the end of your leash."

"Ah, yes. The beauteous Lady Catherine. The favor Sir Stuart begs should not interfere with your other obligations," Seward said, a note of entreaty barely discernible in his urbane tone. It was this that prompted Thomas to reply. He had never before heard it in Seward's voice.

"What is this favor?"

"Merely meeting with an old acquaintance, exchanging information, pleasantries."

"Who?"

"Daphne Bernard."

"What is she doing here?"

"She has taken the opportunity afforded by Napoleon's exile to leave Paris and come here to visit her sister and her husband, Viscount Addler. You remember. That is why she was originally induced to betray her French military lovers . . . her familial ties to England."

"English gold is the only thing that has ever had any influence over that woman."

"Whatever her reasons, they need not concern us. We need only know that her latest lover was a commander under Napoleon's regime. She claims she can deliver reliable information about the number of troops still loyal to the 'Little Emperor.' "

"Anyone can get the information from her. Why me?"

Seward shrugged. "How am I to know? She heard you were in Brighton and demands you be the courier for her information. Maybe she has fond memories of earlier meetings. Perhaps she is, after all, sentimental."

Seward's mouth tightened as he noted the expression of disgust that Thomas quickly conquered. He stood up. "I will extend your regrets to Prinny and Sir Stuart."

"You finally have justifications for your pitiful bigotry, haven't you, Seward?" Thomas said.

The expression of surprise on the other man's features was genuine. "Justification? Before I ever met you, I had justification for my 'bigotry,' Montrose. I knew you before I ever set eyes upon you. Eight years ago you were a cocksure hell-raiser. Untitled, true, but still a pink of the *ton*, as easy with a cyprian as a duchess. For whatever reason, whatever ennui that particular season had induced in you, you chose to make yourself useful to us. And you were."

Seward dusted an imaginary speck from his coat sleeve, controlling the anger that had uncharacteristically erupted. When he looked up, his expression was once more carefully bland. "It was amusing, wasn't it? All the intrigue, the French mistresses, the dark lure of danger. What happened? A friend died? Was tortured perhaps? And then it was not so amusing . . . and finally, not fun at all. And now you have adopted this provincial moral rectitude . . . because it isn't fun any longer. Or," he said, his eyes narrowed thoughtfully, "is it Lady Catherine?"

Seward cocked his head, noting the flare of Thomas' nostril, the unnatural stillness of his body. Seward shrugged.

"You take exception to being used," he said. "Well, there it is. Of course, your sudden attack of conscience might prove unfortunate for those to whom this is more than a game to assuage boredom. But it is no more than I expected. I am only surprised that it has taken so long for you to cry off. But it is, of course, your *privilege*." He sneered the last word and bent to pick up his hat and walking stick.

"God damn you, Seward," Thomas said dispassionately.

"Quite likely. Good-bye, Thomas."

"Leave the message," Thomas said in a danger-ously soft voice as Seward passed him. "I make no promises. I will consider it, that is all. But know this. I am not drawn into this business by any need to elevate myself in your estimation. Your antipa-thy is a matter of indifference to me. I consider your self-satisfied superiority and social prejudices a handicap to any natural intellect you might pos-sess. A shame. I am not manipulated in this by you, Seward."

Seward dropped the missive on a small table by the door. He turned only after he was standing in the hallway. "Of course not, Thomas. I may not like you, but I have never underestimated you."

Chapter 7

The biweekly affair at Brighton's Old Ship Hotel, sponsored for its guests, had begun in earnest. Most of the members of the aristocracy in residence at private homes or as guests of the hotel were present. Swarming the room in their elegant silks and brilliantly colored muslins, they were avaricious and bold, with the license of the Prince Regent's alternate society.

Thomas had dressed in an outdated blue evening coat, a remnant of the last season he had spent amongst the English *ton*. His usual black French attire would have stood out too blatantly in the room full of the more colorfully clad English dandies.

He looked around the room. He was familiar with these people. They represented a sybaritic faction of society of which he had been a penultimate example. There was nothing they would not dare, no lengths to which they would not go, in order to stimulate their jaded senses. Cat would become one of them. Thomas felt his jaw tighten painfully even as he spied her exchanging pleasantries with another woman at the top of the staircase.

If she pursued the proper course, Cat could eventually reign supreme amongst the *ton*. She would never be a classic beauty. She simply wasn't beautiful enough. Her eyes were that bizarre color.

Her hair was neither titian nor ginger but an odd nutmeg. Her features were regular enough, but her figure was all wrong. She was full-breasted, with a small waist which flared into a decidedly round, compact bottom—not at all the current fashion.

Proper beauties had white, soft, sloping shoulders and long, narrow forms. Elegant trifles best imagined at a dining table or in an assembly room. Cat . . . A man looked at Cat and could only see her tousled, warm, and welcoming in his bed. Thomas, his body reacting to his thoughts, raised his eyes to her face. When he did, he was forced to reassess his opinion.

There was nothing commonplace about Cat. She displayed none of the nervousness one would expect of a young, unmarried woman entering a crowded ballroom. She was completely self-possessed. Her head tilted slightly forward on her long and slender neck. Her eyes traveled the room, bright with curiosity. She had all the attributes of a social hostess, but none of the singleminded ambitions that often went with it. Cat was autocratic, imperious, regal.

Thomas had watched her intimidate, order, and high-hand his own small staff in just such a manner. And yet no one displayed the least reluctance to serve her. She commanded with complete equity. The lowliest stableboy was domineered with as much impartiality as the toplofty Mrs. Medge.

But to Thomas more important still was her sense of humor. Many acknowledged toasts sprinkled their conversation with clever bon mots, but these women could seldom take what they dished up, being too concerned with their own consequence to appreciate another's wit. Cat reveled in wordplay. A well-delivered quip brought a delighted glow to her eyes. When she was the object of teasing sallies, she was the first to dissolve into throaty laughter, acknowledging a "palpable hit." Cat appreciated her own consequence, thought Thomas, but she appreciated others' more.

Ah, he thought, she has spied "the green man," an inhabitant of Brighton who forswore wearing or eating anything that was not some shade of green. The corners of her eyes tilted up. Her sense of the ridiculous had been provoked. He alone saw her mouth curve before she managed to suppress the impulse to laugh.

And then she saw him. Damn her, he thought dispassionately, she is so very easy to read. Her face lightened with delight and she cocked a dark brow at him as she turned her palms outward at her side.

Cat had a right to frame her silent, teasing question. She looked elegant, lovely, happy. She was dressed in an awe-inspiring creation she had managed to bully Madame Feille into having ready this evening; the bishop's violet and jade affair set off the deep amber highlights in her hair and acted as a foil for the brilliance of her moss green eyes. Her shoulders were bare, a single emerald pendant encircled her creamy, slender throat.

She descended slowly, fully aware of the picture she made. But not, he'd wager his last coin, on the effect she had on him.

It was tantamount to madness, this captivation. He was too well versed in matters of the flesh to discount his feelings as pure lust. Too old, too knowing, certainly too worldly, to find himself so eager for her words, her laughter, her insight . . . her. He had forced himself to play the avuncular host. But each day the masquerade grew more strained.

He had returned from the Continent hoping to reacquaint himself with decency, having grown as familiar with deceit as he was well versed in baseness. It was laughable, really, that a woman who applied to him to teach her artifice should have set fire to his long-chilled blood. It made him nearly believe in a God, and one with a wicked sense of humor. For Thomas did not want only to physically possess her—and God help him, he did—he wanted a great deal more. He wanted her to be Cat: to run thoughtlessly out into muddy fields because an idea appealed to her, to bully ragged brats in a kitchen garden, to tuck her inebriated great-aunt in bed at night with a gentle kiss. He wanted to keep her from all the influences that would twist her spontaneous, practical, intelligent spirit into a societal caricature. God yes, he wanted her. In all ways.

But honor, Thomas conceded wryly, born late blooms strong. For too many years he had bartered himself "for the good of the empire." In too many instances, his flesh had been at the disposal of the crown, to whomever the crown offered it. Two nights hence, the crown planned to offer it to Daphne Bernard.

Bile rose in Thomas' throat. He would call out any man with his history were he to so much as dance twice with Cat. Besides, he reminded himself brutally, she had set her sights on Giles. A wise choice.

Giles had enough experience to appreciate her, but not so much as to preclude a decent union. No, Thomas had to remain detached from her. By God, he thought as she finally gained his side and placed her fingertips lightly on his proffered arm, her heady fragrance invading his senses, he must.

"Am I not grand?" she whispered teasingly.

"Don't beg for sweets."

"Lah! 'Tis a rhetorical question, Thomas. I *am* grand. And I owe it all to you, kind sir."

"Beware of kind sirs who tog you out in expensive finery, chit."

Cat looked at Thomas in surprise. His tone was sardonic, his wide mouth derisively curled. "Thomas?"

He relaxed under her concerned query and offered her a slight smile. "Ignore me, Cat. These affairs bored me eight years ago. They bore me more now. Now, smile, m'dear. Prepare to scintillate, but do so covertly. Aunt Hecuba approaches."

Hecuba tottered over with imperial disdain, and as she wordlessly passed them, she pointed her black lorgnette toward a large chair to one side of the room. With a grin, Thomas leaped gallantly forward to escort her. Once interred, the old dame fixed the amassed company with a deadly glower. Cat took up a standing position at her side, her fan flashing as she casually studied the room. Within a short time, several splendidly clad young bucks were bending over Hecuba's hand while their eyes sought the enchanting creature beside her. Finally Hecuba snorted an introduction, and the first of many led Cat out onto the dance floor.

Thomas stepped back and watched, crossing his arms over his broad chest, his black eyes hooded. More than one beauty cast interested glances his way, but he was blind to them.

Cat declined a second dance with a military-looking fellow before he reluctantly returned her to Hecuba's side. Cat motioned for Thomas, and he pushed himself off the wall he'd been supporting to prowl over to her.

"Won't you dance with me?" she demanded saucily.

"What? And risk hurling you through yon balcony windows? I should say not. No, no, you run along, little Cat. I shall critique." He turned before seeing a wistful expression steal over her face.

Soon she had whirled in the arms of any number of gentlemen. Taking her mentor's words to heart, she played the role she had set out to learn and discovered, with no little surprise and a great deal more delight, that she was quite good at it. No fewer than five men had sworn to quit Brighton and follow her to London.

And Thomas watched.

He saw her, her waist captured in the clasp of some would-be dandy, the pup's yellow head bent too close to the gleaming waves of auburn. He saw her, her head thrown back, the lights playing havoc with the color of the chestnut tresses, as she played havoc with the heart of the boy who held her. For Cat was laughing; her lips just parted, her color high. And then, quite suddenly, the smile died on her face and her color drained.

Thomas was by her side in a trice, suavely cutting in on the young fool, who mustered a complaint. The look Thomas sent the poor, besotted idiot was such that the boy's protest sputtered to a halt and he fled.

"Well, m'dear. Do I have to call that young ass out or shall we let him continue to draw breath?" Thomas asked.

"What?" Cat asked distractedly. "Oh, Thomas, can we please sit this one out? I really don't feel much like dancing."

"But of course," he said, leading her to a chair. "A punch perhaps?"

"Oh, for heaven's sake, Thomas, you don't have to hit him."

"I was inquiring as to whether you would like a libation."

She colored becomingly. "Forgive me. I thought . . . that is . . ."

"I know what you thought, Cat. And you were quite right. I am only wondering what punishment to mete out. But since I do not yet know the crime, it makes just recompense rather hard to determine."

"I just want to leave, Thomas. Please."

"Cat . . ."

"No. Please accept that nothing was said or done that would cause the least amount of offense. I beg you to take Aunt Hecuba and me in to dine."

"Of course. Hecuba, however, has already gone in to the buffet. She was thirsty. Her parting remarks were to exhort you to ladylike behavior. But we aren't finished with this, Cat," he added softly, offering her his arm.

He tucked her hand into the crook of his elbow as she looked up at him. But there was nothing on his dark countenance to betray any further interest, leaving her to wonder at the hard tension she felt beneath the light touch of her fingers. They passed Hecuba coming through the double doors leading to the dining rooms. She beckoned Thomas close, whispering something into his ear before leveling Cat a stern look.

"I retire," Hecuba told Cat. "I have put about the information that you are here with your uncle. No one would dare question my veracity. Still, you'd best come up as soon as you have eaten. Fielding shall be waiting for you."

"Yes, Aunt Hecuba," Cat replied obediently as Thomas drew her after him.

Cat spent most of the meal attempting to divert Thomas from trying to discover what her young, foolish dance partner had done. That it was something relatively inoffensive was suggested by the ease of her recovery. Still, though he replied in kind to her quips, he was not to be dissuaded from his goal.

She surmised this by the half smile curving his large, mobile mouth and the narrowing of his lavishly lashed eyes. Their gleam betrayed the direction of his thoughts. Toward the end of the meal, he raised a glass of sherry and viewed her through its amber hue.

"I think we must have a garnet-colored dress made for you, Cat," he said, as though he was thinking aloud. "Yes, a ruddy one so that when you feel overset, as you do now, your complexion can borrow its color from the dress. Or so you might claim. It's a dead giveaway, m'dear, that too thin flesh of yours. Now, desist with this mindless chatter . . . I'm sure it's all very charming to the local swains, but I have grown to know you better and am accustomed to your conversation having a bit of pepper in the broth. Out with it."

Cat squirmed uncomfortably beneath his too perceptive gaze. "I would really rather not say, Thomas. But since you shall undoubtedly bully me until you are satisfied, I at least pray you withhold your lowbred curiosity until we are elsewhere."

"Ah, there's my Cat. Come all over proper, she do, whenever she ain't gettin' her way," Thomas replied in fond and patently rustic tones.

Cat fought down an unexpected wave of happiness upon hearing Thomas say "my Cat." She fixed him with what she hoped was a quelling look.

" 'Tis low."

" 'Tis low I am. And if I leave off 'bullying you,' will you satisfy my 'low' curiosity?"

"I suspect I shall have to." She sighed before realizing her unfairness and laughing. Thomas narrowed his eyes even further, and had the lady been listening, she could have heard the sharp hiss of his indrawn breath.

"Well, mayhaps you wouldn't bully me," she owned.

"Badger?" he asked, eager to have her laugh again. He was rewarded.

"Pester, harass, annoy, distress ... persecute? Aye, I like persecute the best. Puts me in mind of Dumas. Only you'd swathe me in yards of red silk instead of an iron mask. Wouldn't you, Thomas?"

"As you say," he replied smoothly.

"I say it's time I resign myself to a stroll to my room, during which you will, no doubt, use all the diabolical methods at your disposal to have from me what you will," she said lightly.

"Really? I am agog. All I had expected you to give me was the answer to a question, and here I am to have all my dark desires granted. How munificent of you, Cat."

She had learned in the last short weeks. And she smiled at him, playing the game she thought they played, unaware of how the rules were changing all the while. "You can but try, sir," she said, a sudden low huskiness to her voice.

He reminded himself just in time to smile. Rising, he held her chair for her, quickly cutting off a hovering young lancer. She strolled from the assembly rooms at his side, conscious of how comfortable and safe she felt dwarfed by his gentle strength. They did not speak until they stopped outside her suite.

There was no sound other than the hushed click of a softly closing door. Thomas' face was inscrutable in the dimly lit hallway. As he stepped forward, the door at Cat's back and his body before her, Cat was jolted by an awareness of Thomas as a purely physical presense. His breadth blocked her view of the hall. He loomed over her. She felt the warmth rising from him and, closing her eyes, swayed slightly toward it.

"Well?" The word was a gruffly spoken intrusion. Her eyes flew open.

"Well?" he asked again, more gently.

"I won't even attempt to fend you off, Thomas. The whole thing is of such little consequence. I realize that. But indeed, I find that I do want to tell you . . . for you see, I am uncertain of what happened."

Lifting her hand, Cat forestalled his protests. " 'Tis true, I swear it. I would not dissemble. Not to you. But it is a bit embarrassing. How foolish of me. You who are my kind friend, my mentor. I would tell you anything. Yes," she said softly, as though she had answered some question to herself, "anything. And so, here it is in all its simplicity: He looked at me. That's all, and yet it doesn't say enough. It frightened me. It made me feel unsafe. After he looked at me like that, I turned to go, feeling uncomfortable, unpleasant. Thank heaven you were there."

"And what was this 'look' that so unnerved you? How did it transpire?"

"Oh, 'twas from flirting," Cat said artlessly. "I was doing it all evening, with everyone. The manner, the eyes, the smiles and pouts, the conversation . . . you know, Thomas, as we have practiced.

"And it worked, Thomas! And while I am conscious Brighton is not London, it was a heady experience to so enthrall men. And they were, each and every one, enthralled." She laid her hand on his forearm, tilting her face up toward his.

"They played the game far less adroitly than you. From which, by the way, I begin to suspect there is some validity in your claim to fame."

"I appreciate your newborn confidence," Thomas said wryly. "Pray go on."

"They were, as I have said, all charming until the last. I don't even know his name. Greenfield, Grenfeld? And he was playing along nicely himself." Her brow knitted in consternation.

"I don't even remember what I said or what he had said. I looked up at him from under my eyelashes—Thomas, you know the pose—and he was staring at me so fixedly. And he looked . . . he looked as though I were a sweet just placed on his plate. He looked frantic and greedy and . . ." She reddened and raised her hands, palms up. "You see? How silly I am."

But Thomas had raised his head from his intense study of hers, turning his face from her. Except for a small muscle working in his long, lean cheek, his face was expressionless.

He finally looked down at her, sidelong, without moving his head, and gave her a half smile. "Well, the young ass was, after all, young. What did you expect of him? You were more than he had ever experienced, and it seemed for one bright moment that you were within reach.

"He was too young to hide his feelings, Cat. The poor fool is no doubt headed for a lifetime of misery if he allows himself to be read by any lady, no matter how lovely or appealing. But he was young and untried, and you undid him."

Her anxiety was clear for him to read. He sighed.

"Don't worry, Cat. Most men you meet aren't going to be so blatant in their feelings," he said. "But it is going to happen again . . . and again. And by far more than raw boys in evening dress at Brighton assembly balls. And these men shall not be caught looking at you. They shall allow you only a glimpse of their intentions. They shall want to . . . to test you. To see if you do run away. And you, Cat, must meet the challenge of those men or be immediately discovered as a fraud."

He stepped back from her, and Cat was aware of the chill of the night hallway from which his warmth had protected her.

"It is the starting point of the games you would play, Cat. The opening move is languid unclothing with the eyes. The knowledge that the temptress knows of and enjoys that perusal but is, perhaps, not ready to acknowledge it."

He suddenly wanted to scare her away from her proposed scheme. To make her see how unsavory, how dangerous, the game really was. To let her experience, firsthand, the undisguised carnality of a rake's purpose.

He allowed his gaze to go hungry, to devour her face, to commit to memory every lovely feature: every sweep of lash, the curve of cheek, the suddenly trembling billow of her under lip. His gaze fell lingeringly down her throat to rest at the swell of her bosom, rising and falling rapidly under his hot stare. He allowed her to see want in that look. And need. He was suddenly all lupine appetite, all stalking desire, and she quivered uncertainly beneath his expression. And then the fire was abruptly banked. He offered her a casual smile.

"No," she said softly, placing a supplicating hand on his broad chest. She felt the heat of him through the fine lawn, the hardness of his muscle.

Thomas looked down at her long fingers splayed there and wanted to rip open the cursed shirt, to feel her hand upon his flesh. Instead, he merely reached behind her to the door of her suite and pushed it open.

"Yes," he said, knowing full well that if he were ever to witness a man looking at Cat as he had just done, he would certainly injure him.

He bowed, keeping his eyes firmly fixed on the floor until he saw the swirl of a silk hem and heard the click of her closing door.

Chapter 8

Thomas waited for Cat in the sumptuous lobby of the Old Ship. Chandeliers dripped crystal prisms above the pale Aubusson rugs, scattering rainbows of color over the hushed room. Only a few of the hotel's guests were up and about. Most, having extended their festivities well into the dawn, opted to stay in their beds well into the day. Those members of the beau monde who were present were disposing themselves in deep leather settees, looking fashionably exhausted.

Eight years before, Thomas had been but another one of their numbers. There had been no amorous challenge he'd ignored, no rule he had not bent to his will. Bored with the posturing, the carefully orchestrated seductions, the rejoinders and the lies, he paused in his pursuit of pleasure long enough to see the outcome of his chosen path amongst the enfeebled ruins of aged roués. With each affair, not only was he floundering for want of direction, but gambling with his physical well-being. He had nothing to show for all his town bronze; he had acquired no wealth, no pleasant memories, no particular skills, and no insight.

He'd been prime pickings for Lord Stuart and his agents, Thomas wryly conceded, notably Colonel Henry Seward. They'd approached him obliquely; a friend of a friend had casually mentioned that

81

his impeccable French might be put to better use than whispering graphic suggestions into willing female ears. Seward was right, damn him. At first it had been amusing, infiltrating the demimonde of French society, seducing the mistresses of French military advisors. But the role had subtly changed over the years. His political acumen was honed, his information-gathering abilities broadened in scope and depth, until his counsel was sought on all delicate matters of French foreign policy. Thomas had become a spy. And within the same breath he was made to understand that his information was no longer "useful" but "vital."

During his last year as Sir Stuart's agent, Thomas had seldom been called upon to act as a simple messenger. His talents were too great to waste on such elementary transactions. But occasionally a lonely woman whose husband was consumed by affairs of state, a woman starved for some fondling, any endearment, could not be made to divulge her particular information with a bit of "persuasion."

Or, as now, a woman like Daphne Bernard bartered her knowledge.

What could he say? That he no longer "did that sort of thing"? Impossible. He understood too well that such details as she might have to share were often responsible for saving countless lives. This knowledge, however, did not go far to lessen the self-loathing he felt.

He'd thought himself inured to this feeling; in the past, he'd been careful to keep himself separate from the functions of his body and, even in physical acts, had remained detached, a performer.

And now there was Cat. Cat with her well-laid plans, her faultless logic, and her perfectly ridiculous, but oh so rational, request. Thomas had admired such clear-sighted reasoning. He'd seen no reason why her machinations should not work in a society where many much more calculated matrimonial schemes had been played out. No reason except that he loved her.

Thomas stared out at the calm vista of sun-dappled sea. He would affect disinterest. He would not look at her when she made her entrance. Why should he? Already he knew every line. With disturbing clarity, he could imagine the texture of her satiny flesh. He even knew the rhythm of her breathing . . . It was all etched with acid brilliance in his mind's eye. Well, he'd be damned if he knew what to do with this emotion he felt.

Tied by constraints he could not break, and desires he could not ignore, he could do nothing but continue the game. He taught her what she wanted, all the while greedily hoarding their moments together: their conversation, their laughter, his intimate knowledge of her. He didn't know what else to do. She would run screaming from him were she to suspect the great, aging rustic she had asked to instruct her in the art of seduction had come to love her with all the decades of yearning, and hope, and hopelessness a past such as his could engender.

Thomas shut his eyes and found, to his grim amusement, that she waited even there, behind his eyelids, to further beguile him.

Thomas was still sitting thus when Cat presented herself a quarter of an hour later. She draped the full, amber-colored hem of her riding habit over her arm and walked forward to where he waited. As usual, he was dressed as a provincial, the heavy chambray shirt knotted at the collar by a linen scarf, his serviceable trousers bagging about the heavily scored leather boots. He opened his eyes and stared at her a moment before breaking his steadfast reverie, his mouth bowing sardonically.

"Well, you look like a veritable heartbreaker, m'dear," he said.

"That's an unfinished statement if ever I heard one," she said, arching a brow.

"Exactly. If it were looks alone that made a heartbreaker, you would already have achieved the most lofty position in society."

"How gallant, sir," she said. "And I am confident that my equestrian skills shall do nothing to tumble me from your high estimation."

He offered her his arm, escorting her to the front of the hotel, where he had arranged to have two horses waiting.

Cat felt a moment of delight; she was a fine rider, and she appraised the horses worthy of her talent. One, a large black gelding, was full-chested and thick-limbed with a massive, well-shaped head. The other was finer-boned, a dappled gray dancing at the end of his lead as a stable lad cooed softly. The boy grinned up at Cat.

"You be riding the sweetest-going horse in five counties, miss. I knowed 'cause me own da bred him for stride . . . not speed, mind you. Though he goes well enough if pushed. Name's Karl."

Cat, having grown used to the catholic conventions of Thomas' home, nodded politely and said, "How do you do?"

The boy's freckled face split into a wide grin. "Not my name, miss. The lad here. My name is Valentine. Ma named us all, horses and kids. Has a bit of book learning, she do, and Da dotes on her 'cause of it," the boy said, rolling his eyes as though his father's indulgence of such nonsense was beyond comprehension.

"Enough, Master Valentine," said Thomas. "Throw the lady up and buy yourself a sweet while you wait." He tossed the boy a coin and mounted the black. "And you, Cat, lead out. 'Tis a pretty ride outside of town."

Cat trotted the gray down an avenue of tall poplars, skirting the fashionable areas of town until they found themselves on a crescent of coastal lands above the sea. The sky was a clean wash of azure. The breeze gently fluttered her mount's pale mane. She enjoyed the brisk morning, the salty tang of the air, the bright sunlight glinting off the waves on the horizon. But most of all she enjoyed the company of the man who rode silently behind her.

Wondering if Thomas was assessing her ability, Cat straightened confidently in the sidesaddle, alive to each nuance of the gray's movement. Turning to accept Thomas' compliments, Cat found him staring not at her, but out over the sea. His forehead smoothed of lines, his mouth relaxed, he looked as though he were enjoying the day quite as much as she. Cat knew the request she was going to make was bold. Nearly as bold as asking Thomas to teach her how to be a seductress.

She coughed, attempting to draw his attention. "Thomas?"

"Hm?"

"Thomas, have you ever been to the Prince's Marine Pavilion?"

"Not when it was so named," he answered.

"I hear it is a wonder of the artisan's craft, filled with priceless treasures, masterpieces from all over the world."

"So they say."

She had his full attention now. "I wish I could see it," she said wistfully.

"Oh?"

"Thomas, I have heard that you were invited to dine there tomorrow."

"Who told you this?"

"Fielding heard it from Bob. But that makes no matter. I was wondering, that is to say, well . . . I thought perhaps you might like to escort me there." He was silent. She continued in a rush. "I dearly would like to be able to see all the—"

"No."

The single word was low, emphatic. Immediately color flooded Cat's cheeks. Well-deserved mortification caused her next words to trip huskily over one another. "Of course, forgive my audacity. I am terribly sorry to have put myself forward in so rude a manner . . ."

Thomas forced the tension away, unable to let Cat think he did not want her with him, though that course would undoubtedly have been the wisest.

"Leave off the self-recriminations, Cat. You might ask of me anything you like without standing on ceremony. I won't take you to the prince's fete because it will be peopled by a particularly unsavory lot. Boring, too. I'd cry off myself were it possible to do so. Prinny takes that sort of thing personally, and believe me, he can make life hell for anyone he considers unappreciative."

"I see," Cat answered quietly.

"No, you don't. The Prince Regent's crowd is not a nice group of people. I am not talking about rakish dandies, warm conversation. These people are ruthless."

Her pride stung, Cat said, "I can handle myself."

Thomas laughed bitterly. "The answer is no, Cat. I simply will not expose you to them, m'love."

His offhanded endearment caused her heart to unaccountably skip in her chest. Her eyes flew to his, but he was gazing out toward the pastures at a small flock of sheep.

"Really, Thomas. How are you going to free my potential when your mind is on those dirty beasts?"

"What? Oh. Sorry, Cat. I was just wool-gathering."

"Very amusing," she said severely before a wicked glint appeared in her eye and she continued, "Now, stop grinning so sheepishly."

She wrinkled her nose but burst into laughter when she saw the disgust momentarily twist Thomas' mouth.

He allowed his pained expression to disappear. Her fine features were animated. Her russet-sparked locks glinted beneath the brow of her ridiculous straw hat. He urged his horse up beside hers.

"Very good," he said, dragging himself back to the purpose of the ride. "You look very . . . appealing laughing like that. Not the controlled giggle of most women but that full laugh of real amusement. If you can do that on cue, I swear our task is all but complete."

"Oh, you haven't begun to appreciate me," Cat replied happily. With that, she moved her horse smoothly forward into a canter. For a few brief moments she seemed to fly in effortless movement over the ground.

"Oh, he does go lovely!" she called over her shoulder.

The gelding misstepped, stumbling. Coupled with her sudden turn, it was just enough to cause Cat to lurch forward over the horse's withers and slide toward the ground. For a brief second, she frantically scrambled to regain her seat, but her fall was inevitable. Kicking free of the stirrup, she felt the ground skittering beneath her boot. She pushed off the saddle and staggered an instant on her feet before her ankle buckled beneath her forward motion. She stumbled and fell in the weeds, flat on her rump.

Thomas was beside her in a trice, looking down

at her, saying with a casual interest at variance with his tense posture, "Fine in the walk. Questionable at speed. No, no, Cat. Falling off one's mount is all very good and fine if one can do it with grace and elegance . . . which you don't. You put me in mind of a wad of bread dough being dumped from a bowl."

Placing her hands on the ground on either side of her, Cat attempted to heave herself up. It hurt too much. She sputtered. Her pride, as well as her ankle, throbbed.

"I cannot . . . No, I absolutely cannot imagine, for one moment, that anyone as patently ungallant as you could ever have been a serious threat to a lady's virtue!"

"Fortunately, Cat, this aspect of my personality has never been put to the test. I have never before seen a lady dumped from so easy a gait. I cannot seriously consider you to be in much trouble . . . are you?"

Frustrated, Cat spat, "Yes!"

Immediately Thomas was kneeling beside her, a look of gratifying concern displacing his previous insouciance. "Where are you hurt?" he asked.

Embarrassed, Cat shifted beneath his regard. "It's nothing much really. I just turned my ankle."

"Is it broken, do you think?"

"No, I'm sure it's not. Really, Thomas, I'm fine."

He bent down beside her and lifted her foot to rest it against his hard thigh before unlacing her boot. She couldn't suppress a small shudder as he loosened the laces and found herself looking at him. His brow knotted with concern.

She attempted a smile. "Really, I'm fine."

" 'Really' you are becoming redundant, my love," he replied. His fingers moved gently about her fine-boned ankle. His eyes sought hers as his hands soothed over her, touching the arch of her foot, encompassing the thin ankle, searching farther up her calf for the source and extent of the damage.

"Where does it hurt most?"

"It doesn't hurt anywhere most," Cat replied quietly.

A sudden, unbidden memory of Thomas as she'd first seen him unfolded with startling explicitness. Naked to the waist, his broad shoulders strained with effort; the muscles of his chest stood out in sharp relief, glistening with exertion, his stomach shingled with hard sinew under smooth, tanned skin. She closed her eyes but could still see him thus, huge and perfectly formed. Her eyes flew open and she had an overwhelming desire to touch the long hair at the nape of his neck where it lay curled in silver-kissed darkness.

She felt the rock-solidness of his warm thigh beneath her foot, his hands gentle upon her skin, and was too aware of the hardness and steel of him countered too provokingly by the tenderness and care of his concern. He looked up at her, and their gazes held for an instant; his eyes were alight with warmth, concern, and humor. He smiled, and she found herself answering the irresistible lure of his personality with her own foolish grin. Thomas would always draw her with his offhand tenderness, his unbiased receptiveness, his understanding. He bent his head once more to his task.

Oh my God, she thought with sudden clarity, *I love him. God help me, I have, all unsuspecting, added myself to his list.*

With something akin to horror on her face, Cat stared up at Thomas, unable to deny the swell of attraction. This could not be! Would he laugh at her or pity her if he knew she had succumbed to the compelling lure of his magnetism? Which would be worse? His sorrowful understanding or his horrified concern that she would hound him as any number of tarts last evening had done? If he knew, would he be all sweetly understanding or would he run?

Oh God, Cat thought miserably, *and what difference does it make, anyway*? She *needed* to make a brilliant match. Her *family* needed her to make a brilliant match. It was the most logical course open to her. She would not follow her mother's lead, sacrificing family for personal gratification. Cat was responsible, practical. She simply would not entertain rattle-pated notions about an impoverished roué. A handsome, virile, muscular roué. A considerate, intelligent, perceptive . . .

She placed her foot against his stomach and shoved. He fell backwards on his rump, his long legs splaying out on either side of her, a look of stunned incredulity on his face.

"Why don't you cut your hair?" Cat demanded. "Just because you must rusticate in the middle of nowhere doesn't mean you need look like the farmer you play at being!"

He watched her warily, as though he feared she'd just lost her mind. "What?"

"I said, 'Cut your hair.' 'Tis shamefully long." The knowledge she was acting like an idiot only fueled Cat's ire.

"I find," Thomas said calmly as he rose, "that when one is 'playing farmer' and spending a great deal of time in the out-of-doors, a longer length of hair keeps the sun off one's neck, thus safeguarding one from an unnecessary and painful burn."

He dusted his trousers off before continuing, his voice rising to a low roar. "Now, what the bloody hell is this all about? Or did the fall so jar your brains that you are, in fact, ranting?"

"Never mind," Cat said sullenly. "I told you I was fine, and I am. Now if you would be so kind as to catch my mount, we can return to town."

She bit down on her lip to keep it from trembling. Thomas was standing over her, his feet spread in a belligerent pose.

"You can't possibly ride, you little fool," he said. Only Thomas, with his immense size and tremendous breadth, would ever call her "little," Cat realized. She was overwhelmed by her newly discovered weakness, by her attraction to this self-confessed rake and profligate. To him, she could be no more than an amusing diversion. Distressed, she turned her head.

"I most assuredly can," she said.

He answered her with an exasperated sigh and, with no warning, bent and scooped her up in his great arms. She felt the even rise and fall of his chest pressed close to hers. It was a delicious sensation. Too delicious. He adjusted her with a little bounce in his arms.

"This would be a trifle easier if you were to put your arms around my neck. You are a rather healthy armful," he said.

"You can put me down."

"Yes, I could. But try to regain some of the common sense that I have come to expect from you, Cat. If you walk, or strive to ride, you run the very real risk of further injury. Then how will you be able to dance?"

He smiled, attempting to win back her good humor, his black gaze inches from her face. Cat could delineate each of his thick, impossibly long lashes. "And I swear to you, Cat, a true seductress must, simply must, be able to dance the waltz. So that great oafs such as myself might better fling them from windows and thus have the pleasure of disentangling them from the shrubbery."

"Have you had the pleasure of disentangling many ladies from shrubbery?" Cat asked, annoyed when the words sounded waspish even to her own ear.

His face went blank. What the duce was she rambling on about now? Shubbery? Women? Why, Cat was acting jealous! The absurdity of his one love being jealous of the faceless women from his past overwhelmed Thomas, and he laughed. Cat sputtering ineffectually in his arms, he strode over to his horse and lifted her up onto its broad back, taking the reins of both steeds in one hand to lead them.

The walk back to the hotel was a silent one. Every now and again Thomas would cast a verbal gambit, which Cat ignored. There was more than the sharp prick of jealousy here, Thomas thought. Cat was glaring at him with such disapproving intensity, he wondered if he had ripped the seam in his breeches when she had kicked him backwards. And "kick" is exactly what she had done, he thought with no small degree of perplexity.

At the front of the hotel, he tossed the reins to the boy and, with cheerful disregard for her protest, swung Cat up in his arms, carrying her to her suite.

Cat held herself rigid, obviously afraid he was going to drop her. Hoping to reassure her, Thomas tightened his hold, only to be greeted by a look of increasing panic on her lovely features. Arriving at her suite, Thomas kicked the door open and strode into the room, deposited Cat on the slipper chair, and summoned Fielding.

While Fielding fluttered dramatically about Cat's swollen ankle, Thomas asked, "Can I do anything more?"

Cat merely lifted her grave countenance to his and tonelessly thanked him for his help.

He walked back to his room, damned if he could figure out what deviled the chit. Such moodiness was uncharacteristic of her. No one who engineered her own successful debut, was the recipient of the condemning comments of an antiquated religious fanatic, and single-handedly led a family of eccentrics could be subject to fits of pique. Raking his memory, Thomas searched for some clue of where his own conduct was lacking. He had treated her with a studied casualness and friendly disregard that challenged his playacting ability. And she had always laughingly accepted him.

He had disguised his interest, clamped down firmly on the attraction that haunted him with the passing of each restless night. She did not suspect the tightening in his loins when she appeared in some new gown, the constriction of his lungs as she laughed at his feeble sallies. He did nothing, he would swear it, nothing, to give her a clue as to his feelings.

His hunger was well disguised. He was good at this. He had, after all, made a career of it . . . and if he was a stranger to unsatisfied longing, by God, he would learn that role too, rather than frighten her from him. His jaw tightened with his determination.

"Over there . . . there. Not there!" Fielding directed the doorman with disgust.

The young man, unrecognizable under assorted bandboxes, cartons, and wrapped parcels, groaned and dropped his burden on the bed, then beat a hasty retreat, pausing only to wink at Fielding. She beamed even as she muttered, "Well, I never!" and set to work untying the strings that held the packages together.

"Oh, milady!" Fielding cooed, hauling out a pretty confection of lace and satin. "I never seen such a beauteous thing! Swear to Gawd, I haven't. A chemise, ain't it?"

Cat looked at the garment without interest and nodded. Immediately Fielding was solicitous.

"Hurts awful, does it? Perhaps we just ought to have the local leech look at it? Or maybe take a restorative in the seawater? I heard that Lady Renville—"

"No, Fielding. My ankle is just fine," Cat said dispiritedly.

"It's brave you are, milady."

At this, Cat finally smiled. "On the contrary, Fielding. I am the rankest coward."

"Coward? Who's a coward?" Hecuba said from her adjoining suite. She entered, stopping as Fielding pulled up a glittering bottle green silk dress overlaid with amaranth-colored netting.

"How very fetching!" Hecuba breathed.

She lifted her chin at Fielding, who was staring at her in amazement. "I meant but to say, 'tis a pretty piece of workmanship . . . though entirely unsuitable as garb." Hecuba darted a glance at Cat, continuing casually, "Though were one to wish to draw attention to oneself, this would do the trick. What other snares of the devil have you secreted in there, Fielding?"

Needing no further encouragement, Fielding proceeded to rend packages with enthusiastic fervor. Hecuba's eyes narrowed on Cat's unnaturally quiet figure.

"Fielding, take these dresses down to the laundry and have them pressed immediately. And don't you dare show your pert face up here without them. If you aspire to being a lady's maid, personally supervising your lady's gowns is of the utmost importance!"

"Yes, mum!" Fielding said, dutifully gathering an armful of brilliant-colored silks, satins, muslins, and lace.

As soon as she had left, Hecuba took a seat beside her great-niece. "It's Montrose, isn't it?"

"I don't know what you are talking about," came the quavering reply.

"Fustian! I may not approve of the conduct of your generation, but that does not mean I have turned blind. I have seen this coming for days."

Cat turned toward Hecuba, animation flooding her patrician features. "Seen what coming for days?"

"Your infatuation, Cat. Don't bother denying it." Hecuba held up her hand. "What else could it be? Off you traipse, unchaperoned, with one of the beau monde's most notorious blades—very foolish, most unwise—only to return a few hours later in the arms of a now thoroughly perplexed rake, your face a brown study and some Banbury tale on your lips.

"What has happened to our two cozy coconspirators?" Hecuba asked. "I will tell you! For I . . . I once had a . . . friend who entered into a similar 'platonic' liaison with just such a man. She, too, finally succumbed to a one-sided infatuation."

"What happened to her?" Cat asked.

"Well, *she* didn't sit about in a consumptive stupor waiting for the lad. *She* was proud. *She* ascertained the uselessness—and unattractiveness—of pining and set her sights on other, more appreciative suitors!"

"Oh, Aunt Hecuba!" Cat covered the older woman's hands with her own. "I am so sick of schemes! I am tired of being vivacious, amusing, and unattainable. I *want* to be attained!" she suddenly wailed, tears coursing down her face.

Hecuba pulled Cat's head onto her plump shoulder, patting her.

"It makes me so angry! All the plotting and planning and *work*! It's so bloody much *work* making oneself agreeable to men!" Cat said.

"Except with Thomas," Hecuba said quietly. Cat nodded.

"And yet, Aunt Hecuba, he's the worst of the lot! He's so attuned to all this ridiculous posturing that he gives lessons in it!"

Hecuba lifted Cat's chin with a single finger and gazed steadily into her red, bleary eyes. "You must keep your pride, Catherine. It is ultimately all we are left with and therefore sacrosanct. Even if it needs be manufactured, it is essential. There now." She patted Cat on top of the head and rose. "I'd better see how Fielding is mismanaging the ironing."

She squinted down at Cat, who was smiling up at her with watery, grateful eyes. "Leave off blubbering too, Cat," she said curtly. "You always look horrid after you've cried. Your nose runs."

A burble of laughter escaped Cat. Hecuba smiled and started for the door.

"Aunt Hecuba?" Cat called.

"Yes?"

"Your friend . . . the one with the unrequited attachment?"

"Yes?"

"Did she find a replacement for the unappreciative rake?"

Hecuba's nose rose in the air. She sniffed.

"Many."

Chapter 9

Resolving to put their relationship back on safe ground, Thomas strode through the anterooms of the hotel, looking for Cat. She was not in her suite. Hecuba's answer to his query as to her whereabouts was terse.

"Though she was not gravely injured, I adjured her to rest. The girl never listens to me, though. She has taken herself off somewhere to pout. Fielding here"—Hecuba tilted her black-turbaned head in the maid's direction—"has strapped her up. So she isn't very quick, Montrose. You should be able to run her to ground easily enough. Any more than that, I will not say."

"Fielding," Thomas said in exasperation, "where is Lady Catherine?"

The maid looked disapprovingly at him. "Why?"

"Cat is right," Thomas muttered. "I have been far too lenient in my expectations of my staff. 'Why,' Fielding? Because I wish to have my way with her, or perhaps to beat her, or merely to devour her. *Where the bloody hell is she?!*"

Fielding's mouth dropped open. She had never seen Master Montrose lose his temper before. While she suspected there was more aggravation than anger in it, it was still a formidable sight.

97

She hastily sought to recoup her situation; it was a good position she had in Mr. Montrose's household, in spite of Mrs. Medge.

Hecuba tottered over to Fielding and patted the maid's hand consolingly. "He's a wicked man, m'dear, evil black-eyed womanizer that he is. I shouldn't answer if I were you."

"Fielding . . ." Thomas ground out.

"She went to the conservatory, sir. Sorry I am for my impertinence, sir. I'm hoping you'll mark it down as the sap-skulled rattling of a feeble mind under the influence of—" here Fielding paused and narrowed her eyes on Hecuba, who was still patting her arm "—her betters." Before she had finished the sentence, Thomas had strode from the room.

In answer to Thomas's inquiries, a porter finally directed him to the conservatory at the east end of the hotel. He stepped from the dark hallway into the sunlit expanse of a greenhouse. Someone had transformed the alley running behind the hotel into a glass-encased fantasy. Brick paths wound between tall palms and figs; a miniature brook gurgled in its diminutive bed before disappearing under dense ferns; sun filtered in from between the lacy tapestry of vines hanging high overhead.

His entry amongst the lush green vegetation was masked by the sound of running water so that he spied Cat before she was aware of him. She was studying some flowering bromeliads. As he watched, she lifted her arms and stretched them high above her. Yawning hugely, she tilted her head back, closing her eyes to the warm touch of the sun on her face.

"How incredibly gauche," she heard a deep, familiar voice say in amusement. Pride, she reminded herself.

"Very. So please spare yourself more of the same by taking yourself off to where you will no longer be subject to witnessing such unladylike gestures," Cat replied without opening her eyes.

"Dear me, no! I am all eagerness to see what further examples of unfeminine behavior you might exhibit," Thomas said, dragging forth a chair and perching himself on its edge in an attitude of dramatized expectation.

"Perhaps I shall burp," she suggested, opening one eye.

He snorted with disgust. "Not unfeminine . . . merely coarse. *I* do not burp."

The other eye flew open so both regarded him balefully. "Hm, well then, I shall swear. Certainly that is a masculine habit."

"Only amongst common males."

"All right. I shall smoke a pipe. I shall ride astride and I shall wear breeches like Lady Skeffington is reputed to do!" Cat said in exasperation.

"Why do you insist in seeking out the most thoroughly unfeminine women in the realm as your examples?"

"Better to follow a woman's example than mindlessly heed the dictates of men."

Thomas considered her statement. She took his momentary silence as disapproval and, already tense, warmed to her discourse. " 'Tis true! How patently ridiculous you men make us! How unfair you treat us in your paternal assurance you know best what is feminine, as opposed to unfeminine, behavior."

"Ridiculous? How so?" he asked, genuinely curious.

"Take, for example, popular fashion." Cat gestured down at the gown that covered her in a snug sheath of cream and saffron striped silk.

"You look delectable," Thomas assured her with a grin.

"I expect I do," she countered. "And to what end? I am told to wear these . . . garments which only an idiot or a blind person would say does anything other than attract the eye to certain salient points of my anatomy. They assuredly are not comfortable! Have you ever tried gracefully proceeding down a crowded promenade, mincing in a muslin cylinder? I should say not! Their sole purpose is to draw attention to my figure."

"For the sake of argument, let us say you are correct," Thomas conceded.

"I am correct!" she said. "Here I sit, ensconced in a pretty prison of provocative attire, looking 'delectable.' I have become bait, Thomas! I am *supposed* to offer a gentleman temptation so great as to be irresistible. And yet, and yet, *Mr. Montrose*, when you gallants come to the point of taking the bait I have so graciously angled, it is your edict that I am at this point to say, 'No, no, Lord so-and-so, mustn't touch!' Who but an idiot or a perverse demigod would contrive such an affair?"

"I believe you overstate yourself. To attire oneself attractively is not the same as being wanton."

"Oh, pish! I'm not talking about morals! I'm discussing bribes!"

"Bribes?"

"Yes, sir! Bribes! I allow you to view what marriage buys." Though her lips trembled with the force of her feelings, she held her pale chin up, daring him to argue her claim.

"And what would you suggest?" Thomas asked, leaning forward and bracing his long forearms on his knees, his hands dangling between his legs. "Would you really attire yourself as a male? And where then are the boundaries drawn? Would you like to work as the manager of an estate, argue politics, be responsible for an entire population? And, if so, to whom does this leave the rearing of the young?"

Cat grimaced at Thomas in distaste. "Women already influence politics, manage estates, and are responsible for the population of their households. And—by the way—still produce heirs!"

He was silent a moment, apparently pondering her statements. It was a heady sensation for Cat. As an unmarried woman, her view on this particular subject had never been heard, let alone considered, beyond the boundaries of her immediate family.

"You may be correct, Cat," Thomas finally said. But his tone made it clear he wasn't going to cede her the point completely. "But given that your intellectual abilities are already engaged, I fail to see the reason you take exception to the manner of your dress."

"It is not the dress, Thomas. It is what the dress represents. The fashion which commands me to be a bizarre mixture of siren and religious novitiate. Somehow less accountable than males, and somehow more. It is a schism most uncomfortable to live with," she said heatedly. "I take exception to the supposition that merely because I am a woman, I do not harbor the same curiosities as a man. Particularly when the manner of my dress stimulates those 'curiosities'. The same 'curiosities' which, when aroused in the male, by a manner of dress which *he* has decreed, it is then my responsibility to discourage!"

"Perhaps the matter of sexuality—for we are speaking plainly, are we not, Cat?—is best left to men, who may be more adept at controlling their base tendencies?" Thomas suggested.

"Pish!"

"Really, Cat! Your fondness for that particular

expletive is irksome . . . particularly as I seem to be the one you most favor it with!"

"Pish!" she exclaimed again, pulling back from him in frustration. "If you men have so much greater restraint than women, why are we the ones who must always say 'stop'? I'll warrant *you* wouldn't have the moral fiber to withstand the siege of a determined suitor."

Thomas snorted. "In your own words, pish!"

In the ensuing silence, Cat's teeth could be heard grinding together. Thomas calmly maintained eye contact, but Cat knew his own temper was being tested by the telltale flare of his aristocratic nostrils. The silence stretched on.

"Would you care to make that a wager, Mr. Montrose?" Cat finally purred.

"I would be delighted, Lady Catherine," Thomas immediately snapped back. "And how would you go about proving your theory?"

"First the rules, then the ante."

"And they are . . . ?"

"First, you must be guided by the rules which govern women's behavior. You must not use your strength, or size, or masculine proclivities in any instance—"

"Agreed," Thomas clipped out.

"And the ante shall be this. Should I win, you will agree to escort me to the Pavilion tomorrow night."

"Now, Cat—"

"What? So certain of defeat? And with ample cause, I am sure," she said smugly.

"Agreed!" he said through clenched teeth.

"Where are you going?" Thomas asked as Cat jumped up.

"To lock the door." She turned the key in the latch before pocketing it.

"Cat, should anyone try the door, your reputation will be in tatters."

She eyed him, bracing her hands behind her, leaning against the carved panel. "It is well into the afternoon, a highly *un*fashionable time to be viewing the flora and fauna. Besides, any potential gossip will only know there are some persons in here, not who they are . . . Thomas."

She smiled at him as his eyes widened in surprise at the husky accents with which she caressed his name. Slowly she sashayed toward him, her hips undulating in a thoroughly provocative manner as she approached. Inches from him, she stopped.

"A woman," Cat said, reaching out to lightly brush his collar, causing him to go instantly still, " . . . a woman on the marriage mart would never be seen so bundled up."

Slowly she worked his cravat free. Letting the snowy silk ripple to the ground, Cat stood back and frowned.

"Still much too prudish. You do want this to be an accurate enactment?" She did not wait for an answer but set her hands to the pearl stud at the top of his white linen shirt. He felt his chest muscles leap painfully as her slender fingers brushed the heated flesh at his throat.

"Are you not afraid you are playing too deep a game?" he asked in a low growl.

She threw back her head, her teeth gleaming white as she laughed. "Not at all! Why, we are just begun, not even that! We are but evening the odds as yet. And besides . . . you are a model of masculine restraint."

She popped another stud free and, feeling him tense, smiled. Stepping in front of him, between his knees, she slid her hands beneath the superfine of his waistcoat, easing it off his shoulders. She paused only once to look down into his eyes.

They were midnight black, his features hardened into stone. His jaw had gone dusky red beneath the blue-black tint of his incipient beard. Cat hesitated a second, caught by his gaze, but tore her eyes from his to concentrate. It was nearly impossible. Her fingers wanted to linger in their task. His coat had trapped his body's heat, and he was warm beneath the thin cloth of his shirt.

"Almost at the disadvantage a woman finds herself," she murmured. Suddenly Thomas surged upward, towering over her. With an inarticulate growl he wrenched his coat off the rest of the way.

"Is there any other article of clothing I might oblige you by removing?" he demanded.

"Your vest."

He fairly ripped the stays free and then, at variance with the angry gesture, turned and casually tossed it onto the chair. He lifted his arms high, raising his palms upwards, and turned slowly, mockingly, in front of her. "Have I disrobed to your satisfaction?"

"Not *my* satisfaction. It is the unspoken law of men which govern what is worn; or rather what is not worn," Cat threw back. She had his measure now. He thought to shame her into stopping. Or anger her, or himself, to the point where his righteousness would shield him from her challenge.

Cat smiled at Thomas, who was glowering tall and imposing over her, his arms still spread wide for her inspection.

"Come," she said, "I have not asked you to do anything a woman does not do. Surely a few articles less clothing cannot be so awful a price to balance the contest? Look here, the conservatory is lovely, is it not? I would we just walk. Just a stroll through a hotel conservatory on a mild day. What harm is there?" she asked.

"Oh, for God's sake!" Thomas said, abruptly lowering his arms and planting his fists on his hips. "You do this so badly!"

"I do not!" Cat shouted, her decision to be leeringly conciliatory forgotten.

Thomas grinned, well pleased to be dealing once more with the predictably temperamental Cat. "Horrible. Quite awful. Your imitation is far too exaggerated, m'dear."

"You aren't allowed to say that!" Cat snapped. "An unmarried woman would never call an eligible man ridiculous! He would bandy her name about until she became a byword for harpy, were she to so much as giggle at him. No matter how idiotically he behaved!"

Thomas sobered, but a smile still played about his mobile lips. "Quite. What was it then? A stroll? I'd be delighted, Lady Catherine."

Somewhat mollified, Cat seized his forearm and would have dragged him forth had he not weighed nearly twelve stone. She looked up into his devilish, handsome face. The expression he bent on her was warm and open, tender and smiling. She mentally shook herself, reminding herself he was an expert at dissembling.

"Come along, m'dear," she said. "There is a particularly lovely plant in bloom, just around the corner here."

She patted the arm she had secured next to her side and set off at a leisurely pace along the bricked walkway. Her sprained ankle slowed their progress, but she took advantage, pointing out some of the more choice blooms in the collection, pausing to allow him time to appreciate their unique characteristics, nodding encouragingly and inwardly grinning as his smile slipped into an expression of bewilderment.

Whatever Thomas said, Cat smiled and agreed. If his comments held no botanical merit, she adopted an attitude of amusement. If they did, she acted surprised and congratulated him with disproportionate enthusiasm on his insight.

They finally gained the corner of the path and turning, found a wrought-iron love seat nestled in a small alcove hung with ivies and trailing flora. She led him there, motioning him to rest, as though their brief walk had been an arduous trek and he a valiant invalid. Glowering at her praise, Thomas acquiesced as she slid in next to him.

Her thigh pressed lightly through the layers of fabric against his, but once settled, she did nothing to remove herself from that intimate touch. Instead, she turned full toward him and casually reached up to touch his temple.

Thomas jerked his head back. Unprepared for her touch, he could not feign indifference. His eyes flew to where she held a leaf dangling from her fingertips, a wicked, knowing grin playing over her lips.

"Excuse my forwardness, Mr. Montrose." She did not sound the least sorry. "But you seem to be sprouting no end of greenery. May I?"

Without waiting for a reply, she once more reached up, lightly plucking another frond from where the dark locks grew overlong and curled upon his collar. But this time she lingered in her task. The cool brush of her fingers winnowed through his hair and tested the skin of his neck with delicate, insubstantial caresses. Thomas held himself motionless under that hesitant exploration, as loath to allow it to continue as he was to have it end. He was transfixed by her touch; never had he been the recipient of such gentle play. He had always purchased the touch of experienced women in one form or the other, whether with money, gifts, or merely his own much-vaunted experience.

Nothing had prepared him for his gut-wrenching response to this light stroking.

Fixing his gaze forward, like a man facing a firing squad, Thomas cursed himself for a fool, to be so mesmerized by such minor contact. But the caress changed, the featherlike movements becoming firmer as Cat grew bolder. She measured the tightening swell of biceps beneath his shirt sleeve, trailed a hand with heart-stopping deliberation down his long arm, pausing only when she reached his wrist. She turned his much larger hand over as he forced his fingers to uncurl.

His hands were large, strong but not as callused as she would have imagined a farmer's to be. His fingers were long; dark, downy hairs were sprinkled along their backs. Placing her palm against his, she compared their relative sizes, and smiled. She gave in to a sudden impulse and, bending her head, turned his hand and laid her lips gently on the ridge of his knuckles. Her hand was bruised in a sudden convulsive grip.

Gently she loosened herself, reaching up to his neck and sliding her fingers beneath his collar. She curled them over the muscle that ran thick atop his shoulders. And then her palms were lying flat against his naked skin, and he sucked in his breath as she rubbed them downward, lingeringly, over the top of his pectoral muscles. She left them there. He did not allow himself to look at her.

Cat had never had such license. The sensation was headier than that which the strongest wine could impart. To look at a man until sated, to study his form, his movements, his gestures. But this was beyond even that! This was the liberty to touch a man without fear of repercussions or reprisals. And *this* man, who constantly occupied her thoughts.

Her fingertips seemed abnormally sensitized to the texture of his flesh: warm, dense, and supple. The muscles, which leapt beneath her slightest touch, turned the velvet skin to hardness, as though granite had a chamois sheath. A vein stood out along the side of his neck. She could see the dark stubble of his beard on the hard angle of his jaw. He was so large, so appealing in his masculinity.

Cat could not stop herself. Seeking more of his heat, she stroked the hard curve of his chest. More of his shirt studs loosened, working free, and she saw the ladder of ribs, followed their curves to the satiny smooth skin stretched taut across his chest, down to where the muscles on his flat stomach stood out in ridged relief. Her hands, following her eyes, rode the dip and swell of sinew, tendon, and thew in artless urgency. She caressed him, petted him, searching farther back until her arms encircled him beneath his shirt, her hands mounting the hard bulge of his shoulder muscles. Her gaze fell between them and she saw her own white skin, exposed by the low-cut bodice, pressed lightly against his. Her own warmth merged with his, her over-stimulated nerves dancing at the contact.

She felt him shudder. Still, he did not move, and now—abandoning all thought of games, or roles, or contests—she pressed her lips to the hollow at the base of his strong, tanned throat and caught the heavy pulse beneath her partially opened lips. Breathing deeply, she inhaled, catching the unique combination of heat and scent that rose from his skin. He was hot, and the flesh here was thinner and silkier than the plush density of his chest. She was fascinated by the endless textures of his male body. Wrapping her hands more tightly about him, she rested her brow against his exposed torso, unsure of what to do next, only certain she did not want to draw away, and, somehow, wanted a great deal more. She lay pressed to him and listened to the heavy drumbeat of his heart, felt him drag in his own deep breaths.

Cat might have stayed thus, been content with this, but Thomas knew he would not be. And so, after a long moment, he lifted and set shaking hands upon her upper arms. Slowly he pushed her back from him and looked down at her flushed countenance.

Her lips were parted, her breath coming unevenly between their plump curves. Her eyes were brilliant, luminous with awakened sensuality. Unaware as yet of her own state, she gazed at him with undisguised desire. It was enough. His hands tightened on her, crimping the soft silk of her sleeves. He saw her flinch. Immediately he let her go.

"Am I expected to slap your face now?" he asked tersely. "Well, is that not my part? Have I not executed the proper maidenly restraint? My God, madame, I can assure you I have shown more restraint than any unfixed man in the entire kingdom!"

She was confused by his venom, frightened by the wantonness a modicum of liberty had inspired in her. "No more restraint than any lady of the *ton* must exercise on a daily basis!" she retorted.

His eyes narrowed to ebony slits. "I can personally vouch for the fact my restraint has far exceeded that exercised by any number of *tonnish* ladies."

Stung by the blatant reminder of his experience, she reacted without thought, wanting to wound him, as the sharp prick of jealousy wounded her. "You may be sure that the provocation I have teased you with is slight compared with what I *might* do!"

He reached out reflexively, catching her shoulders in his grip. As instinctively she raised a warding hand and placed it upon his still naked chest. His heart thundered under her palm, and she looked up into his eyes, her anger dissipating with the contact.

His own anger and frustration immediately died. He knew he had lost his private bid for integrity; he was incapable of resisting her. Smiling bitterly, he cursed himself for his failure to deny himself this, the sweetness of her voluntary touch.

"Play on, then, or lose," he challenged in a low, mesmerizing whisper. "My body is at your disposal, and I am as biddable as a lamb. Go on then," he said in a low voice, "seduce me." He pushed back the loose cloth of his shirt, baring his heaving chest. "Touch me." He reached down, pulling her other trembling hand up, and gently pressed her palm over his heart. "Take from me . . . my heat." He bent his head down toward her. "My breath . . ." She felt the soft air sluice over her cheek and closed her eyes. "My virtue . . ." His lips were a feather's breadth from hers. Without volition, she moved to touch them in the gentlest of meetings. They were dense, soft velvet. She brushed her lips tentatively over their warmth until her mouth tingled, demanding a firmer contact. She deepened the kiss, her mouth opening to more fully encompass his.

His sigh was more a growl; but other than that one sound, he was true to his word, neither encouraging nor directing her. She bracketed his face with her hands and tilted his head to afford her better access to his mouth, catching the fullness of his lower lip between her teeth, running the tip of her tongue along its satiny contours.

His lips parted, and she hesitantly outlined the widening seam. Instantly his mouth opened beneath hers. Without conscious choice, she took advantage of the access he afforded her and she lapped her tongue into the warm sleekness, feeling the ridge of his teeth, the inside of his cheek, the roughness of his tongue.

An urgent sound rasped from his throat. She was snatched abruptly to him, his arms lifting her onto his lap in a powerful, crushing embrace. Her head was bent over his arm. His tongue came alive beneath her own, demanding entry to her mouth, to caress, to fill with deep strokes. He caught her very breath, sucking in each exhaled bit of air, licking with explicit hunger each virgin crevice, each untouched recess. She lay back, overwhelmed by his passion, intuitively aware of the restraint that tested him, causing his great body to tremble, dimly conscious of his great size, the width of his chest, the depth and breadth of him enfolding her, all but enveloping her. She received the potent hunger of his lovemaking with equal ardor, holding her arms tightly about his neck to keep his head bowed to hers, to keep his mouth alive on hers, to compel him to continue drowning her in erotic sensation.

And still something in her wanted more, though her hands roved without restraint upon his body, though he held her as close as he could, pressing her thigh to his thigh, her hip to his hip, her breast to his breast. There was more her body instinctively sought, and though she was not aware of it, in her need she made soft whimpers of demand.

But Thomas heard and recognized the source of that sound. He tore his mouth from hers and pressed her face against his chest, nearly undone by the exquisite feel of her mouth against his chest. His body was rigid with urgency. He steeled himself with the need for self-control, even though her arms were still wrapped about his neck, and her body was warm and vibrant on his lap, and her lips were now damply on his throat.

He had not been aware he possessed such restraint. Part of him was grimly amused. Ten years prior, he would never have considered letting her go. But ten years ago she would not have been lying in his arms, panting in her first discovery of passion. Of utmost import was the simple, undeniable fact that she was Cat, and, being Cat, was in all probability the one woman for whom he would need to exercise this near self-abuse. And while he was able to keep from actively encouraging her passion, he could not bring himself to discourage it. And so, stretched on a rack of need and want, honor and desire, he closed his eyes, clenching his teeth as he endured the sweet abandonment of her exploration.

Slowly Cat became aware that Thomas was not returning her kisses and, while she was still being held tightly against him, he had raised his head. Confused, she shifted. His involuntary groan alerted her to the wantonness with which she lay pressed to him.

Her struggle warned him of her realization; he knew her horror was inevitable. Still, he could only look with a sad smile into her clouding eyes and say, "I am completely undone. Your reputation as a roué is confirmed. You have proven your point, and any further demonstrations shall leave my reputation in shreds, m'dear. So I must humbly beg you to have mercy on my overtried body . . . but see? I haven't the strength of will even to put you from me, let alone say you nay."

Cat bolted upright on his lap, and he was startled to see her lovely face go white. Her lips, swollen with his kisses, trembled.

"You needn't mock me!"

He wanted nothing so much as to take her once more into his arms, to smooth her furrowed brow with kisses and enfold her in his clasp. But, though he was no stranger to passion, he judged her to be, and therefore uncomfortable in its wake. She had read his response as simple lust and had not yet recognized the depth of emotion that had compelled him to act.

He was a fool, he acknowledged to himself, but not so much a fool as to allow himself to be flayed beneath her tender pity.

"Not at all," he said. "I congratulate you. I concede your victory. Stramp does not have a chance should you choose to utilize this . . . gift."

"I never would!" she said. "And his name is *Strand*!"

Quivering with fury, Cat bolted out of his arms, rising to stand over him. Thomas relaxed against the wrought-iron seat and stretched a long arm along its back. The act cost him much, but at least she would not see his hands shaking. Cocking his head, he looked up at her.

"Whatever," he said, relieved to hear that the tones so closely impersonated normalcy. "And now, how do you intend to cap the afternoon's instructions? Shall we go a bout of fisticuffs or try our hand at a round of intensive petit point?"

"Thomas, you are insufferable," she sputtered. "As far as I am concerned, the afternoon's instructions are at an end! I leave you to find your own way out."

"Not very gallant. *I* never seduced a lady and left her to her own devices after sampling her gifts. What? Leaving so abruptly? I shall be here to collect you, that you may collect my forfeit, at five o'clock. Did you hear me, Cat? Five!" he called after her.

Chapter 10

It meant nothing. She was making herself ill, needlessly. To Thomas, her extravagant reaction to his lovemaking must have seemed a tepid entertainment. And, truthfully, it was not *his* lovemaking at all. *She* had incited, then orchestrated, the entire scene. Yet she could have sworn her breath mingled with one nearly as ragged as her own.

And his casual teasing—for it was only that— must have been his way of extracting himself from her embrace. Why else would he have pulled away from her with such gentle determination?

She would retreat into the absurd charade of friendship. She must allow him to dictate the parameters of their relationship, or risk losing him altogether. And that, Cat would not do. If only she could forget the awful, wondrous sensation of being in his arms, feeling his fine-textured skin, his mouth open over hers.

Well, she must.

And Lady Catherine Sinclair always did what must be done.

Thomas and Cat approached each other warily when he arrived to take her and Hecuba to the Pavilion. Answering his impersonal greetings with monosyllables, Cat was unable to meet the gaze she knew was unwaveringly on her. Finally, defiantly, she looked directly in his eyes, only to find to her relief and irritation that he was not staring at her at all but nonchalantly studying his Hessians.

"What do you think, Cat?" he asked in a patently normal, friendly voice. "I hied myself off and acquired this entire getup just that I might not embarrass you. Though I must say, these boots are deuced uncomfortable. Am I not grand?" He quirked a black brow, blatantly imitating her words of the previous evening.

She could not fail to respond to such a good-humored overture.

"Don't beg for sweets," she said, answering his boyish grin with a girlish one of her own.

He looked magnificent. The dark broadcloth stretched across his shoulders, emphasizing their great breadth; the black trousers could not disguise the long muscles of his thighs and calves; the shirt was a flawless expanse of snowy linen. And his roguish, charming smile lit up his gypsy-dark eyes.

What had happened, anyway? She had kissed him. A simple, momentary diversion for a man like Thomas.

He was well used to that type of play. Indeed, it must have seemed a callow, impromptu pleasure. But there had been nothing green in her response, or in the tactile memory of his bronzed chest, muscular arms . . . She *must* put those memories firmly aside.

Taking his proffered arm, Cat was surprised by the flash of relief that had preceded his casual pat of her hand. By the time the carriage deposited them at the Pavilion, they were once again friends.

Stepping inside the Prince Regent's newly begun fantasy Pavilion, Cat felt her eyes grow wide. She had heard of the plans to renovate it, and the Prince Regent's new enthusiasm for anything Oriental was well-known, but this! Faux bamboo furniture, dragons, papier-mâché, and red lacquer met, mingled, and fought for attention in dizzying opulence. Carved wooden lotus blossoms, heavily gilded, acted as light fixtures. Palm leaves had been pressed into wet plaster, their pattern repeated in the bejeweled border of a table scarf. Huge pots of Chinese porcelain held enormous stands of flowering jasmine. It was overwhelming now; when completed it would be garish, gaudy, blatantly extravagant.

Hecuba peered through her lorgnette with ill-disguised disdain. "The lad has never understood the meaning of restraint."

Cat had to hide her smile behind her silk fan. Thomas grinned openly.

There was a small group, forty or fifty of Brighton's best, assembled. Though Cat did not personally travel in their circle, she had met most of those present: Lord Mansfield, the Creeveys, Sir John Lade and his wife, Letitia, the Canfields, and the Earl of Barrymore, "Hellsgate" Barrymore.

At the sight of Hellsgate's pale, lined face, Cat shuddered. She had crossed his path once before. He had fairly oozed dissipation. When she had been introduced, he'd grabbed her hand. His was hot. Dry, tensile strength lay in his long, bony fingers. She had to forcibly remove her hand from his prolonged grasp. He had flung back his head and laughed.

He saw her from across the room. Raising two fingers to his lips, he kissed their tips lingeringly, his eyes bright with sarcasm. She turned her shoulder to him, looking for her host, the Prince Regent. On the far side of the room, she saw him.

Ornate, overtight evening dress bedecked Prince George's stocky figure. He was bending to capture the words of the diminutive beauty next to him. She was fashionably pale, tendrils of black hair framing a piquant, angular face. Her eyes were dark, huge, their color indiscernible from across the room. Her mouth was a startling red bow.

The woman tilted her head, her eyes gleaming up at the Prince Regent. The crowd of people in the room shifted, and Cat could see her gown. It was pearl-hued, a shimmering, clinging fall of the sheerest muslin. There was no doubt in Cat's mind that the undergown had been damped. Cat had heard of the style but had yet to see any lady adopt it. The woman's small, pointed breasts were apparent under the moist, molded fabric, her fine-boned ribs and narrow waist clear to see beneath the all-but-transparent material. Cat beckoned Thomas near. He bent his head.

"Who is that extraordinary woman?" she asked.

"A whore," Hecuba answered loudly.

Thomas, his eyes bright with amusement, looked over Cat's shoulder. She saw the nearly imperceptible flare of his nostrils. An odd tension stiffened his body.

"Her name is Daphne Bernard."

"The name is French, is it not? You know her?"

"Yes."

"But how . . . ?"

"There are many people I have met over the course of the years. Don't forget, Cat, that I have led a much longer and infinitely more varied existence than you. *I* shan't." His tone was laced with a bitterness at odds with his casual words. Cat frowned.

"You have more honor than sense, Montrose," Hecuba grumbled.

"As always, Lady Montaigne White, you are correct," Thomas said stiffly. "His Highness always demands a near infernal climate and far too much food, so I suggest we find ourselves a window to wrest open when his royal back is turned."

It was overwhelmingly hot. The ladies were already vigorously fanning themselves, and the gentlemen, in their high collars, vests, and jackets, were glistening with perspiration. Thomas led them to a window and was in the process of heaving it open when the Prince Regent saw them. His face beamed with delight as he led the petite Frenchwoman through the brilliantly colored throng, which parted, fluttering like disturbed butterflies, in his path.

Hecuba, seated on a chair behind Thomas, snorted.

"Montrose!" Prince George exclaimed. "How pleased we are to see you! We insisted Seward bring you to us that we might convey our appreciation."

"Your Highness is far too kind. Any small assistance I have been privileged to offer is my duty." Thomas bowed and than, noting the shadow of petulance on the royal face, he added, "And, of course, my pleasure."

The Prince Regent's face immediately brightened. His sharp little eyes slid to Cat.

"May I present to Your Highness, Lady Catherine Sinclair?"

Cat dropped into a deep curtsey before her future king. When she rose, he was smiling at her in open admiration.

"We are delighted to have you with us this evening, Lady Catherine. We know your mama. Delightful woman. Delightful. Do you enjoy music? But of course you do. We have arranged a minor entertainment after dinner." He drew forth the Frenchwoman at his side. "And see? We have found an old friend of yours, Montrose! Madame Daphne Bernard, may we present Lady Catherine Sinclair?"

The woman's dark eyes locked on Thomas, a slow smile bending her bright red lips. Her glance flickered an instance over Cat. "*Bien*, Lady Catherine.

Bonsoir, mon grand raffin," she said, caressing the last word.

A disgruntled cough came from behind Thomas. Hastily he stepped aside to expose the seated form of Hecuba, her lorgnette raised to her eye, her head at an imperious angle. She did not rise. "Your Highness." She inclined her head fractionally.

The Prince Regent went pale. He cleared his throat and fidgeted nervously with his collar under Hecuba's hooded glare. Hecuba sighed, raising her eyes heavenward before allowing a slight jerk of her head in Daphne Bernard's direction.

"Oh, yes, yes indeed," muttered the discomforted Prince Regent. "Montrose, we were not informed that you would be escorting Lady Montaigne White, as well. A gross oversight on our secretary's part. A gross oversight! But a delightful one!"

He did not look delighted. The Prince Regent was squirming under Hecuba's quelling stare. "Lady Montaigne White, may we present Madame Daphne Bernard?"

"How do you do?" Hecuba said as the Frenchwoman, confused by His Imperial Highness's obvious agitation, sank into a demibow.

The Prince Regent all but hauled the Frenchwoman to her feet. "We are well pleased you have come. We believe dinner is soon to commence. We will converse with you afterwards, Montrose. Lady Montaigne White. Lady Catherine." Prince George beat a hasty retreat.

Thomas was grinning widely when he turned.

"What did you do?" Cat asked, rounding on Hecuba.

"*I* did nothing. The Prince Regent, on the other hand, has done a great deal. As have all his disreputable cronies. A guilty conscience, Catherine, is a sinner's worst flail."

"Are you calling the Prince Regent a sinner?" Thomas asked in mock horror.

"We are all sinners, Mr. Montrose. All of us, whether king or commoner. And we all have freely chosen our course." Hecuba fixed Thomas with such a penetrating look that, for the second time in as many minutes, a grown man squirmed.

Cat looked around for a timepiece. The dinner started promptly at six, fifteen minutes from now, and Thomas had disappeared. So, too, had Daphne Bernard. Hecuba was involved in a heated debate with the elderly Lady Brent. The two of them unceremoniously waved Cat off when she offered to fetch them a refreshment.

"Lady Cat. How *au courant* you are!" Cat knew the owner of those oily tones.

"Milord."

Hellsgate Barrymore pouted his lips. "So formal. So reserved. Such hauteur. I find it intensely . . . stimulating. Particularly in this gown." He motioned to the daring décolletage of her new gown, his fingers fluttering a hairsbreadth away from her exposed bosom. She stepped back. With a nasty smile, he followed her retreat.

"M'dear," Hellsgate said in a low voice, "you are now in my milieu. There are no stodgy matrons to impress here." He gestured around the room. Leaning toward her, he trailed his index finger along her exposed collarbone. She wanted to recoil from his outrageous touch, slap his leering face, but knew that to do so would only provoke a scandal. A scandal that would reach the ears of Lord Strand and thereby destroy her plan. Her sensible, necessary, abhorrent plan.

"No stiff-necked defenders of pedestrian morality here!" Hellsgate said. He licked his lips. "You may indulge yourself to whatever extent you wish.

We are all guilty here; therefore, all unaccountable. In the Prince Regent's circle, no one hears. No one sees. No one cares . . ." he whispered.

"How unfortunate, Barrymore, that age and disease have deprived you of whatever sense you once claimed," Thomas' voice drawled from behind Cat. "And most arrogant of you to surmise that the rest of us share you disabilities."

Thomas reached out, catching Hellsgate's wrist as it hovered inches above Cat's skin. The blood fled from Barrymore's already pale hand, leaving it deathly white. Thomas smiled, a slow baring of his teeth, and dropped Barrymore's hand.

"I hear. I see. And I can assure you, I care," Thomas said.

"Montrose," Barrymore hissed, rubbing his wrist. "The mastiff whelp has grown into a dog. I'd thought you to be running in French kennels. Tiresome that you are here. I didn't realize you were once more in your old haunts, nor that your attention had been fixed."

His eyes darted behind narrowed lids at Cat. One side of his mouth lifted in a sneer. "Not your usual fare. But perhaps you've taught her a few—"

Thomas was suddenly inches from Barrymore, his eyes glittering dangerously, his own upper lip curled in a snarl. But it was Cat who spoke from beside him. Her voice was cool, composed, detached.

"Thomas, thank you for offering to escort me to view the Prince Regent's menagerie. But I infer it to be a pitiful, raggedy, noisome lot—I distinctly hear the braying of an ass—and it no longer amuses me. Might we not, instead, proceed in to dine?"

Lifting the hem of her gown, Cat scanned the faces of the assembly, looking directly through Hellsgate Barrymore as though he were not there. Thomas laughed, suddenly, loudly. Several people nearby turned to see what so amused the tall, elegant man and found themselves instead viewing the angry, sputtering Earl of Barrymore. The venom in his face caused not a few to shudder; Barrymore's hellacious temper was well-known . . . and feared.

Thomas offered Cat his arm. They left the earl standing there, having cut him quite dead.

"Well done, m'dear," Thomas said as they gained the dining hall. Hecuba, in respect for her title, had gone in earlier on the arm of a decidedly uncomfortable-looking duke.

"Yes?" Cat asked as Thomas seated her. "The man scares me, Thomas. He is so utterly loathsome."

"He is standard for the breed. Dangerous, but eminently predictable. I doubt he'll trouble you again. His consequence could not afford another setdown. His intimates shall be dining out on that little episode for months."

"But shall he seek redress?" Cat asked as Thomas prepared to leave her to go to his preassigned seat.

"Only if a perfect opportunity presents itself. Barrymore and his ilk have not the energy or imagination to pursue revenge. Don't worry, Cat." He bent his dark head close to hers. "I would never allow Barrymore near enough to cause you any unpleasantness."

It was not so much a vow as a promise of continued concern. Cat's heart constricted painfully in her chest as she watched him take his chair. A small, unbidden hope sprang up at his words. Their kiss might have been nothing to him, but his concern for her was obvious, his regard genuine. She would swear to it. Perhaps regard might become affection, even love.

                        *   *   *

Dinner was the long, drawn-out affair common at
the Pavilion. Luckily, Barrymore was seated some
distance down the table from Cat, between an
unknown blonde and the dainty Daphne Bernard.
The Frenchwoman's titters could be heard the
length of the table. At one point, Cat chanced to
find Daphne staring at her with open speculation
as Barrymore whispered in her ear.

Cat had been placed between a duke's younger
son and an older military gentleman. They were
well within her league, the duke's son attempting
to impress her with his worldliness, the older man
with his East Indian experiences. She found she
merely had to arrange her mouth into an occasional moue of appreciation to satisfy both.

Thomas, seated a short distance up from her,
appeared to find more enjoyment in her performance than the one being acted out by the ladies
on either side of him. He listened politely to a
plump, bejeweled woman and made appropriate
noises of assent when the curly-haired girl on his
right paused for breath, but the lift of his dark
brow was reserved for Cat alone.

She was having fun. Not because of her dining
companions, but because of the amused expression
on Thomas' face when she put to test all the arts
they had practiced. It was to him she looked after
lowering her eyes in maidenly modesty, or pouting
in feigned intellectual consternation, or sighing with
rapt attention.

By the end of the three-hour meal, Cat was deli-
ciously happy. The duke's young son begged to
escort her to where a sextet had been assembled
for the guests' dancing pleasure. But seeing Thomas
go off with the Prince Regent and several other
men, she demurred, searching for Hecuba. Her
great-aunt was looking a trifle pale, not surprising

considering the warm, heavily scented room and
quantities of rich, spiced food she'd eaten. Cat was
immediately solicitous.

Helping Hecuba to a chair by an open door, Cat
spread her fan and wafted the air gently over
her great-aunt's face. Hecuba gratefully sank back
against the plump cushions.

"Don't fuss so, Catherine!" she said querulously.
"It is nigh hellishly hot in here, and your hovering
about so closely isn't doing anything to alleviate
the problem. Go off and get me an ice!"

Cat was hurrying to do so when Daphne Bernard
appeared before her, blocking her exit.

"Lady Catherine, *n'est ce pas?*"

Cat nodded.

"We must talk. I am intrigued by you. You set
milord Barrymore a nasty knock and lead *le grand
homme* Montrose about by the nose. How so?"

"I don't know what you're talking about, Madame Bernard," Cat said chillingly.

The other woman laughed. "But, *ma chère!* We
are both women, is it not so? Of two different
styles, *oui*, but *certainement*, we can . . . how shall
I say? Compare notes?"

The speculative, knowing look in the petite beauty's face was unpleasant in its avidity. Distracted,
Cat said, "Compare notes?"

"But yes! You are so different from Thomas' usual type."

"And you are more representative of that 'type'?"
Cat asked stiffly, hating herself for being drawn into
this vulgar conversation, but compelled to find out
what this woman meant to Thomas.

Again Daphne laughed, unfurling her ostrich
feather fan and languidly caressing her décolletage.
"Oh, I think that is a reasonable assumption. We
share a certain history, certain affinities, certain . . .
tastes. But you, so English! So naive and fresh . . .

like a glass of milk! And yet you have handled milord Barrymore most adroitly. There are depths to you, no?"

Daphne wrinkled her tiny nose. "It is a conclusion foregone!" she continued. "So demanding, so virile a man as Thomas would not be satisfied with less. But you are white, Lady Catherine! It is something I have said! Ah, me! *Pardon moi*! I do not mean to offend."

"I doubt that very much, Madame Bernard. And now, if you will excuse me?" Cat lifted her head, determined not to let this tiny woman and her insinuations upset her. Thomas had shown not the least interest in the Bernard woman. Cat swept from the room, a soft snicker following her.

Chapter 11

"We would like to be in your shoes, Montrose." His Royal Highness, Prince George, winked as he placed the crystal decanter back on the ornately carved sideboard.

The small chamber off the dining room was reserved for the chosen male guests presently in His Highness's good graces. Tonight, however, those men present were not the Prince Regent's boon companions, but his political advisors. After some desultory conversation, Colonel Seward had led Thomas to Prince George's side for a personal interview.

"Well, what's wrong with you, man? Lovely little foreign dovie and all . . . What say you?" Prince George asked affably.

"Mr. Montrose is finding his conscience uncomfortable," Seward said in response to Thomas' silence. "He is still considering Sir Stuart's request to meet with Daphne Bernard."

Prince George, the perpetually adolescent product of puritanical parenting, scowled. "The foreign office fellows tell us that they have always paid the Bernard woman well for her information. In fact, we believe we heard that she originally approached us. We did not seek her."

"Your Majesty, Mr. Montrose is not concerned

with Madame Bernard. He is bothered by the . . . moral implications of this meeting."

"I can speak for myself, Seward," Thomas said, his gaze remaining respectfully fixed on his future monarch.

The Prince Regent looked from one of his agents to the other. "Is this so, Montrose? Do you withhold aid to your country from some pedestrian notion of morality? We are disappointed, Montrose."

The look the Prince Regent spent on Thomas was chill in the extreme. Colonel Seward's expression remained a habitual bland, emotionless one.

"It is morality which has made this country the mightiest in the world, Your Highness," Thomas answered evenly. "It is the very foundation of your realm, the gift of greatness which we, your loyal subjects, humbly offer you, our sovereign."

George was silent a moment before clapping Thomas on the shoulder. "Begad! Well spoken, Montrose. We find ourself sympathetic to you. What is it then? The redheaded chit? Dashed lovely! We will see that she is well away from the 'field of battle.' 'Field of battle,' must tell Skeffington that one!" he chortled.

"Your Highness, is there no other person whom Mme. Bernard might negotiate with?" Thomas said with a hint of desperation.

But Prince George was now bored with the proceedings. In light of his munificent assurance to Thomas, he simply could not comprehend any further impediment to the proposed meeting. Prince George retreated to imperial disdain.

"We do not know. We find your attitude most unbecoming. Be guided by the knowledge that we have trusted you. Good God, man! Lady whoever she is, shan't know a thing about it!"

"But I shall, Your Highness," said Thomas, aware he trod close to arousing the mercurial royal temper.

Rather than anger, George responded with unconcealed impatience. "You will do what you must. It is ultimately what each of us do . . . some with less choice than others." His pudgy face fell into doleful lines before he was led away by yet another military attaché to yet another advisor.

"Thomas," Seward said, watching the retreating form, "I have delivered a message to Madame Bernard informing her you will meet her in your suite at the Old Ship at eleven o'clock."

"You presume much," growled Thomas.

The elegant, slender man shrugged. "You are here. I took that as acquiescence and have done what I deemed necessary. The Bernard woman demanded you act as courier. It was part of her price." A little frown marked Seward's bland countenance. "I find your ingratitude unfathomable. Has not the Prince Regent himself assured you that your Lady Catherine will be otherwise occupied during the pertinent time?"

"Why have you forced my hand in this sordid affair?"

"Have I forced you?" asked Seward. "You are your own man, Montrose. More so than the rest of us, to whom this is a career. In the past, had you ever been captured in your 'fact gathering,' you might have sustained some embarrassment, some discomfort, but ultimately you would have been returned to your comfortable Devon. In your unofficial capacity, you have avoided the hazards that others face; you have never put more on the line than your sexual prowess or your intellectual vanity."

"Considering how you feel, Seward, why did you press so hard for my recruitment?"

The other man held his gaze. "You were useful. You were certainly much more useful in your youth as an immoral opportunist than you are now. If

I have a distaste for you, it is primarily for that reason: Your conscience—or code or whatever you will call it—has rendered you useless to us. The foreign office, and I, begrudge you that." Seward scowled. "I have no doubt you will comply with this request. It is part of your code, is it not? How pleasant to have the luxury of a code."

A quarter of an hour later, after Thomas left, the Prince Regent had Seward brought to him.

"Will he meet with the Bernard woman, do you think?"

"Most assuredly, Your Highness. Montrose's sense of duty is unimpeachable. Whether he will be able to bring himself to secure the information"— *rather, if he will be able to once again play the gigolo,* thought Seward—"once the meeting is in progress, is subject to doubt."

The Prince Regent pouted. "Can you do nothing to encourage his cooperation, Seward? We are too involved with other matters of state to bother with the details. That is your function, is it not? But the Bernard woman has proven useful in the past. Or so Sir Stuart implies."

Seward nodded. "True, sir, in the past her information has been accurate. But now . . . ? We have no way of knowing, Your Highness. Unfortunately, Montrose is as aware of this as I. It will be hard to convince him to compromise his integrity for an untested bit of disclosure."

Seward was aware of his unfortunate choice of words as soon as he uttered them. It was rare he bobbled so badly. The Prince Regent's face immediately assumed a mask of imperial outrage, reddening the heavy folds of his jowls.

"We do not ask our subjects to compromise their integrity! We assume the integrity of loyal Englishmen is above reproach! If Thomas Montrose ascertains any information through an informal meeting with a foreign adventuress, we gladly welcome it. But he is in no way to be coerced into doing anything which belittles him in either our eyes or his own! Is this understood, Seward?"

Seward bowed, low, so the tightening lines of his face could not be read by the enraged Prince Regent. He kept his eyes firmly fixed on the floor until His Highness, in a melodramatic fit of pique, stomped off. Only then did he raise them, his own face flushed with emotions he seldom gave voice to: Even to himself.

Too often lately, Seward felt constrained by the atrociously naive moral niceties of aristocrats playing on the fringes of political subterfuge. Their power to affect the course of nations rubbed him raw. Dilettantes dallying, trying to make the game of politics conform to rules of etiquette, and in doing so, risking the lives of men and women who knew this game had no rules.

Seward was tired unto death of pandering to the vanity of dabblers. He had tried to beg off from this particular assignment, knowing the parties involved would not be objective, pragmatic, acting for one purpose and one purpose only—the advancement of England as a world power. They would be acting for England, true, but always in tandem with their own motives, motives tied up in nebulous, shifting concepts of moral, racial, and class superiority. But Sir Stuart had ordered his compliance, deeming the curiously respectful animosity between Montrose and himself a viable tool in the proceedings.

And now the Prince Regent further tied his hands, just as he had found the chink in Montrose's armor, found the raw nerve on which to press. Even before the disastrous affair with the Leons woman, it had been obvious for several years that Thomas

Montrose's considerable skills were being lost to them. His distaste for his function had grown with each passing week. The foreign office had managed to keep him on only through the judicious use of his skills: Nothing outre was assigned him. He only worked with the most blatant conspirators, those whose sole motivation had been greed.

Seward had cannily ascertained that Montrose was too aware of his own convoluted motives to destroy weak, self-deluded conspirators with their own frailties. He simply had lost the stomach for pulling the wings from flies. And now only his sense of honor compounded by his sense of guilt forced him to agree to this meeting with Daphne Bernard.

Seward remembered from years past the tortured expression on Montrose's face when he'd handed in his resignation and blithely announced his intention of buying a commission. Seward had seen a mirror of that pain tonight.

Still, it would be best for Seward to remind himself that Montrose was no fool; he knew his strings were being pulled. It was Seward's job to make sure the strings were strong.

Thomas stared out of the dark hallway window overlooking the enclosed garden at the back of the Pavilion. His knuckles grew white with the force of his grip on the sill. There was no relief from this damnable web. He would meet with Daphne Bernard later in the evening.

If nothing else, the meeting with Seward and Prince George had brought home some hard truths. Truths he had been running from ever since Cat Sinclair had ordered him to her side in a Devonshire pasture. He braced his arms against the sill.

Hopes, Thomas had learned, die hardest in those unused to them. They were a novelty. And novelty, Thomas thought, smiling bitterly, had been the main pursuit of his adult life. It had all been very well to eschew morality for the good of England. But hadn't the danger, the pitting of his skills and intellect against the collective ones of France, been the real reason he had bartered his honor? Wasn't England a ready excuse for reckless, self-gratifying titillation?

True, his tenure as an officer at Salamanca had been honorable. Some would say heroic. And his horror at the cruel, stupid, tragic reality of war had been genuine. He found he would do much to prevent the senseless waste of life, even barter what little remained of his personal honor by "meeting" with Daphne Bernard.

But even if the desire to circumvent war was what now motivated him . . . those motives had been the unforeseen by-products of his initial reasons for entering the seedy, nefarious world of espionage.

No, he couldn't absolve his history in the light of belatedly discovered principles. He couldn't absolve himself at all. And, certainly, he could not offer himself to Cat. Cat, who assumed wickedness to be a matter of décolletage.

It wasn't even that she was too good for him. He was too much a realist to spend his life as a martyr or waste it in a hairshirt of useless self-recriminations. No, he was simply too old for her. Not in years, but in lifetimes of self-indulgences, unpleasantness. Shadowy, tawdry years of excess and debauchery.

It was immaterial that he no longer pursued those courses. It was immaterial that years ago they had ceased to be factors in his life. They had been once. They had molded and affected him, whether to the good or the bad. Even were he to swear an oath of eternal chastity—which he would not—he could not offer for her. He could not wait tensely through the weeks and months, wondering which figure from his past would rise up and disclose to her, in graphic detail, his history. Perhaps even tell her the pitiful tale of Mariette Leons and her son.

And it would happen. The world, his world, was too fully populated by eager whisperers.

He could not be there to see the distaste, perhaps even the horror, the stories would nurture. He could not be there to see her pull away, to feel the first coolness, the gradual distrust, to intuit the first, unspoken thought, "A leopard can't change its spots."

He could not. He could not spend the years growing increasingly to love her, and have her grow to love him, only to watch that love die. And *that* was the damnable, gut-wrenching part of his horrifyingly selfish near-courtship. The knowledge he might have won her heart. He was well punished for his impertinent hopes; he had a small taste of what her love might have been.

Because, against all reason, she was growing to have an affection for him. He was too well versed in the language to miss the subtle, telling signs: her delight with his company, the way she looked around a room for him, the intimate smile when she found him.

He dared not—no, he must not—think of the feel of her in his arms, her intoxicating response to his kisses. Instead, he must do her a kindness. Was he not growing to be an altruistic penitent? He must dissuade her of her affection before she had a chance to discover it. Perhaps he was developing a taste for masochism.

Thomas swung away from the dark vista before him. His face was pale, his eyes obsidian shards. But first, he thought desperately, a dance. Just a dance. Just one more small memory to add to the others. Another lesson he could surely bear to learn. A dance was no great thing.

He was walking too quickly. His haste opened him to comment, but he could not rein in the need to see her, to talk to her, to touch her. He stopped at the entrance of the room, his great height allowing him to look easily over the crowd. She was there.

She was bending over her great-aunt, who was shooing her away with one hand. Looking patently disgusted, Cat straightened, setting her hands on her hips.

As though she felt his gaze, heard his voice whisper in her ear, she turned. Their eyes locked. He moved toward her, once more too quickly, too obviously . . . like a dog to his mistress's side. It would never do to draw unwelcome attention to her. He stopped short.

"Is it really all that much fun, standing about with a group of men and drinking brandy?" she scolded. Her calm, slightly disapproving tone was balm to Thomas' tightly stretched nerves. She was so matter-of-fact, a perfect contrast to the years Thomas had spent in near theatrical high tragedy.

"I think this new custom boorish in the extreme," she continued. "If men want to be alone, let them go to their clubs . . . but to invite a woman to dine and then summarily abandon her! Nothing short of rude!"

"I swear never to abandon a lady again for the questionable pleasure of brandy and snuff." *Fool*, thought Thomas, *mask your delight.*

"Oh, Thomas. You didn't take snuff. Disgusting habit. People, perfectly nice, well-dressed people, ending up looking like sugar-sprinkled seedcakes."

Thomas lifted his brows. "Now I must forswear not only the company of men, but also snuff. You demand much for the pleasure of your company."

She laughed. "I know."

"If I am to forfeit my harmless indulgences, you must forfeit your time. They have struck up a waltz," he said, holding out his hand. "I warned you that you must dance. And, as your instructor, I am compelled to sit judgment over your abilities before I loose you on the rest of these pitifully hopeful males."

Looking over to Hecuba, Thomas mouthed his request.

Hecuba muttered under her breath and querulously snapped, "Yes, yes, yes. Take the chit away and keep her there so she ceases her irksome hovering."

Thomas led Cat out, placing one hand at her waist, the other enveloping her much smaller one. She set her hand atop his shoulder, looking happily to him for his nod. And then they were dancing.

He was not a dance master, but his performance on the floor was more than adequate. As a rake, it was only to be expected. And yet, it felt so perfectly fluid, so effortless, dancing with him. The slight pressure of his hand directed their movements, dipping in and out with the swaying rhythms. A full, quick twirl and she was laughing with the sheer delight of it, closing her eyes against the distraction of colors and lights, concentrating on the pull of the heady music, never questioning the direction of his lead.

"Are you not afraid we draw perilously close to an open window?" Thomas teased.

"No! Were I to dance out onto the air, what harm could befall me? For I swear I am already flying!"

He drew her closer. She knew less than the proscribed twelve inches separated them. Cat did not care. Opening her eyes, she found his gaze avid upon her. His eyes, burning with unbanked fires,

bent close to her. She leaned in to meet his nearly
imperceptible advance. He was close enough now
that she could see the dark mahogany of his irises,
the tiny lines fanning out from the corners of his
lids. The warm sluice of his breath moved across
her cheek.

And the dance ended.

Thomas was breathing too hard, even considering the rigors of the dance. But he could not tear
himself away from the promise in her fern green
eyes. Her lips were parted, her color high. And
then he saw, reflected in her dilated black pupils,
Colonel Seward. *So it begins*, thought Thomas. He
stepped back from her and bowed.

"Lady Catherine," a male voice said from behind
Thomas.

In confusion, Cat looked to the slender, unknown
man addressing her. Thomas' face had become
shuttered, an impersonal mask, and she felt an
odd tension emanating from him. His hands were
curled into near fists at his sides. A vein beat in his
temple.

"Colonel Seward, Lady Catherine," Thomas
introduced them. "Attaché, sometime secretary
to the Foreign Office. Presently temporary social
aide to Prince George."

It was a gross breech of manners to relay the
history of a gentleman's employment to a lady, and
Cat looked at Thomas in shock. But he was studying Colonel Seward intently. The man returned
Thomas' gaze with bland indifference, only the
dusky hue of his throat betraying any emotion.

"Lady Catherine, I regret to inform you that Lady
Montaigne White has been taken ill and requests
your presence. Megrim, Mr. Montrose. I assure you
'tis nothing serious and completely unforeseen,"
Colonel Seward finished with odd emphasis.

"Of course," said Cat worriedly. She turned to

follow Colonel Seward to the chamber where her
great-aunt lay on a red chaise. Hecuba's face was
pasty and damp, her eyes closed.

"Please arrange for transportation immediately,"
Cat said, gaining her great-aunt's side and taking
up one wrinkled, beringed hand.

"Of course." Colonel Seward beckoned a footman forward and was on the point of instructing
him when Thomas broke in.

"I shall take Lady Montaigne White back to the
hotel, Seward. Have the coach brought round in five
minutes," he said. His tension was palpable. "There
is no reason for you to leave, Lady Catherine. I shall
see your great-aunt settled with Fielding and return
for you."

"I couldn't enjoy myself knowing that Aunt
Hecuba—" Cat started to protest.

"Oh, for God's sake," Hecuba grumbled, adding
as a repentant aside, "and sweet Jesus too,
Lord bless and protect us—I have the headache,
Catherine. I am not dying, not yet, and your fussing
and fidgeting will only exacerbate my discomfort.
Please *do* stay."

"But—"

Seward cleared his throat. "His Royal Highness
would, I am sure, be most disappointed if you
leave, Lady Catherine. Were you to consent to stay,
he would extend his royal person as chaperone,
with myself as surrogate, for the duration."

"That is very kind of you, Colonel Seward. But,
Thomas, don't you think . . . ?"

Thomas' beautiful eyes were blank, deadened
beyond recognition. "I think you are making a
great deal too much out of a situation which
does not warrant it," he said in a soft voice.
"I will return for you. You have nothing more
to do than enjoy yourself for a short while. You
can do nothing at the hotel but be underfoot. I

beg you to stay, Cat," he finished, an edge to his last words.

Colonel Seward was watching them intently, his gaze flickering back and forth. The undercurrents were too strong. Unspoken words hovered between the two men. Cat could find no reasonable way to demur. She nodded.

Thomas supervised Hecuba's loading onto a litter that had been brought into the room. A pair of stalwart footmen lifted her, preceding Thomas through the door.

"It is very nearly eleven, Cat. I will be back by midnight. Seward, you will see Lady Catherine is well occupied until then?" Thomas asked tightly.

"Yes." The two men's eyes held an instant longer than was necessary, and then Thomas was gone.

Colonel Seward smiled at Cat. For the first time, she noted he was a handsome man. He was not so very slight; it was just that his rapier-slenderness and breadth of shoulder were lost when he stood near Thomas. His hair was the color of old gold, neither blond nor brown, and his eyes were long, tilting up at the corners.

"Now, how shall we keep you entertained, Lady Catherine?" he asked pleasantly.

A derisive laugh issued from near the doorway. Hellsgate Barrymore leaned against the jamb, his arms crossed over his chest, a sneer on his leathery visage.

"Isn't this interesting? Montrose flown. The lady-bird still here—at least one of the ladybirds—and the ubiquitous and useful Colonel Seward raking his imagination for entertainment. Perhaps I can be of assistance? Let me see . . . I have it! Let's tell stories."

Chapter 12

The air in Thomas' suite was thick with perfume, an exotic combination of musk and roses. Thomas looked around the room, unwilling to play a juvenile game of hide-and-seek. Daphne's shawl was draped over a chair, her shoes beside it. Hanging opposite the entrance door was a tall beveled mirror. He could see the entire shadowy room reflected in its length.

"Daphne?" He started to close the door but, after a second's hesitation, left it slightly ajar, hoping to dispel any sense of intimacy, and create instead a situation where she would be anxious to deliver her information and be gone.

"Patience, *mon cœur*." The husky accents purred from behind a painted screen partitioning the room.

"You have some information you wish to sell," Thomas said, deliberately ignoring the assumption in her tone. Going to the sideboard, he poured himself a full glass of brandy.

"Sell?" Daphne's voice took on a pouty note as she emerged from behind the screen. She had undone her elaborate coiffure. Her dark locks hung in rippling disarray upon her bare, sloping shoulders. The sheerness of the muslin clinging to her slender thighs revealed a shadowy apex.

"I thought we were old friends. What is this 'sell'? In the course of our . . . conversation perhaps I will be less than discreet. What woman would think to guard her so foolish female tongue when engaged in other activities? Later, perhaps, I am given gifts. But what is more apropos from an admirer? 'Sell' is so vulgar, Thomas."

"And we must never be vulgar, no matter how base," Thomas murmured, downing the brandy in one long draft.

"Exactly!" Daphne said, holding up her own glass to be filled.

"Daphne," Thomas said carefully as he filled both their glasses to the brim, "we are, as you have said, old acquaintances. Can we not be frank with each other?"

Daphne wrinkled her small nose. " 'Frank' is sounding too much like 'honest,' Thomas. When have such as we ever concerned ourselves with such pedestrian notions? 'Honest' is ugliness, hurtfulness, illness. I am thinking it is better not to be frank."

Seductively she smiled up at him, reaching out and delicately scoring his lean cheek with one long nail. His expression remained impassive. She glanced over to where the door stood a few inches ajar and narrowed her eyes. She sighed.

"If you must be honest, by all means, be so," she said.

"You are a rich woman, Daphne. The English government has been responsible for much of that wealth. Your associations with Bonaparte's military have proven useful in the past." Daphne smiled with smug satisfaction before he continued. "But Napoleon is no longer in power. I have some doubts as to whether any information you have to impart can be sufficiently useful to justify your presumed fee."

Her eyes flashed. She set her glass down hard upon the table. The brandy sloshed over the sides, staining the lace scarf.

"How ugly, this 'frank'!" she hissed. "No, I do not like it at all. And you, *mon beau raffin*, you are unrecognizable!"

Visibly upset, she spun away from him. The clock ticked upon the mantel, chiming the quarter hour into the silence. Finally she turned back, her small, white teeth glinting between her bloodred lips as she smiled.

"Come, let us begin again. You are no gentleman to doubt my . . . 'veracity' is the word? But it was never your gentlemanly attributes which appealed to me. So see? I am not angered. I tell you openly, Bonaparte is not so toothless as you English wish to believe. Are not the number of cannons secreted in the countryside awaiting Napoleon's return a matter worthy of your time?"

"How many? In what part of France?"

She laughed. "Ah, so intense! So patriotic! So determined and single-minded!" Silently she opened her hand, patting the fingertips of the other against her palm in a parody of applause. He continued to regard her stonily. "But I am not. I wish to renew our friendship before I entrust my secrets to you. You have, as I have pointed out, changed, and I do not feel quite sure of you any longer. Come, Thomas, prove to me you are the Thomas Montrose I have known."

His mouth became a hard line, but his voice was quiet as he said, "And how am I to do that?"

She crossed the small distance until she stood so close, her thighs bracketed his knee. She pressed against him, rubbing her hands up his hard, flat stomach to his chest.

"Intimately," she purred.

*   *   *

"Lord Barrymore." Seward bowed his head in recognition, his gaze never leaving the other man's small, bloodshot eyes.

"Seward. Don't you have some pressing diplomatic endeavor to attend to? I will be delighted to keep Lady Catherine entertained for the nonce," Hellsgate drawled, pushing himself off the doorjamb.

Neither man missed the fleeting expression of entreaty on Lady Catherine's face. She masked it quickly, Seward noted with approval as she turned a cool expression of appraisal on the dissipated earl.

"That won't be necessary, Lord Barrymore," Seward said. "Though delightful in and of itself, my duty as Lady Catherine's escort is just that. A royal directive. Mr. Montrose has kindly seen fit to escort Lady Montaigne White to the hotel, and His Royal Highness has asked me to attend Lady Catherine in his absence."

"Lady Montaigne White?" Hellsgate sneered. "The man is incorrigible. *I* certainly wouldn't have abandoned youth for quite *that* much experience . . ."

Cat could feel the tremor of revolt that shook her body. He was disgusting. She would have swept from the room had he not been blocking the door. Her only recourse was to stand mutely and ignore him. Seward moved forward to stand beside her.

"Your choice of words is interesting, milord. I doubt whether I can decipher your meaning, but I am, as you well know, hardly one of your intimates. Perhaps Prince George can translate for us?" Seward said coldly.

Barrymore laughed, a dry, harsh sound. "Is that a threat, Seward?"

"A threat? Merely a thought, Lord Barrymore. As the Prince Regent's insistence on good manners

is well-known, I doubt your statement is as coarse
as it appears to be. I merely look for someone to
interpret."

Again, Barrymore let out a bark of laughter. "Very
good, Seward. Very good, indeed." He sketched a
mocking bow. "I was only trying to be amusing;
apparently I have failed." His avid glance darting
between Cat and Seward, he lifted his hands palm
upwards.

"Let me explain," Hellsgate said. "Anyone who
knows Thomas Montrose's reputation would be
entertained by the comical notion of him involved
with anything less than a young, comely, and
willing consort. The beauties do flock to him so."
Hellsgate turned one hand over and examined a
nail. "And he is ever obliging. Why, one season
he is reputed to have satisfied most of the *tonnish*
female population. In a purely 'social' way, of
course," he finished sarcastically, his eyes on Lady
Catherine's face.

She would not serve herself up for his amusement. Her expression remained detached. She
turned to Seward. "I do not wish to know this
person, Colonel Seward," she said, a slight quaver
belying her apparent composure.

"But this person wants to 'know' you, Lady
Catherine . . . in all ways." The drawl had fallen
from Barrymore's voice; the hard edge of anger
was distinct.

She tried, God knows she tried, not to look at
him, but Hellsgate had moved to stand directly at
her side.

"Lord Barrymore, you are a—" Cat heard Colonel Seward grind out, and she knew Seward
was going to offer Barrymore irreparable insult.
As an untitled functionary, Seward could ill
afford to alienate one of the Prince Regent's
most notorious friends. Seward had been kind

in a remote, civil way. It was not possible for Cat to repay that kindness by allowing him to chivalrously intervene in this battle she had begun with Barrymore. She acted an instant after the words rasped from Seward's lips. Placing her hand on his arm, Cat drew the colonel's attention.

"Please," she said, "I would like to go back to the hotel. I feel my place really must be at my aunt's side."

She forgave herself the lie. It was to Thomas' side she wanted to go. To his arms, his reassuring presence, she wanted to fly. Only with him would she feel safe from the sordidness named Hellsgate Barrymore.

Her request worked better to redirect Seward's attention than she could have imagined. Abruptly Seward stopped, caught short as if by an invisible rope. His head swung toward her.

"That really isn't necessary, Lady Catherine," he said tensely.

"I think it best," she answered.

"We could go in to dance. The Prince Regent has provided excellent musicians . . ." He bent a most winning smile on her, and her intention wavered. Perhaps, if they left Barrymore behind . . .

"Yes, excellent. Perhaps I will beg a waltz," Barrymore interjected.

Cat knew then. Hellsgate would hound her. She had pricked his overweening conceit, and now he would see that she paid. Cat shook her head, her eyes intent on Seward.

He was watching her in consternation. "Lady Catherine, this isn't necessary. The Prince Regent would be most annoyed—"

"Mustn't annoy Prinny," Hellsgate cut in.

"I wish to leave, Colonel Seward. Please see to it that transportation is procured for me," Cat insisted, desperate to be away from Barrymore, desperate to seek Thomas' sheltering presence.

"Lady Catherine, I beg you to reconsider," Seward said.

As Barrymore listened to the pleas on both sides of the odd, ongoing argument, his eyes narrowed. The haughty russet-haired bitch was hot to be off. The royal cat's-paw was equally hot to have her stay. He knew Montrose and Seward had an enduring relationship, although friendship had never seemed an aspect of it. Montrose had obviously asked Seward to keep the wench here. And noting the interest Montrose had been unable to hide, Barrymore suspected Seward's commission was to somehow protect Lady Catherine. Hellsgate snickered to himself. *He* had no such wish. In fact, strictly the opposite was true. The proud bitch would come down.

"Come along, Seward," he said tauntingly. "The lady wishes to go. No gentleman would insist she stay. I'll take her back myself." He smiled as Cat's eyes widened in horror.

"No," he continued in a gross imitation of concern. "I'll go one better and prove to Lady Catherine that I am, in fact, a gentleman. I'll order up my own coach. Don't pale like that, dear lady. I won't annoy you with my unworthy self. I shall stay here. I have two healthy footmen who will deliver you safely."

"I wouldn't presume . . ." Cat murmured, anxious to flee but disliking to avail herself of Barrymore's favors.

Seward sighed in relief, but Cat heard and now she looked at him, her eyes hard with determination, confusion evident in her low voice. "Colonel Seward, I wish to leave. I will be at the front door in five minutes. If Lord Barrymore's coach is there . . . unoccupied—" Cat looked meaningfully at Hellsgate "—I will make use of his offer. However, I prefer to have my host make the arrangements for my transportation." She slipped past Barrymore, heading from the room, intent on finding Thomas.

"Damn it to hell!" said Colonel Seward.

Thomas took hold of Daphne's wrist, wrenching the small hand from his chest. She twisted closer, brushing her barely covered breast against him. There was nothing appealing about the open lust in her expression. The difference between her groping and Cat's untutored exploration was brutal. The memory of Cat in his arms caused his body to harden. Daphne purred triumphantly, rubbing one leg up between his thighs.

"You are a beautiful woman, Daphne," Thomas managed to say in civil tones. "But our association can no longer be of an intimate nature. I would not insult you by suggesting that we start at a point where we left off four years ago." Thomas downed the second glass of potent spirits and set the empty glass aside.

She laughed, squirming closer, her free hand pulling the shirttails from his trousers. "You do not insult me, Thomas. Or, if you do, it is only because you take so long to disrobe. Come, *mon homme*, I wish to see if you are still the magnificent animal I remember!"

He watched her little tongue dart out to wet her small red lips. He remembered the full, lush curves of Cat's wide, warm mouth and closed his eyes.

"*Oui*," Daphne purred, freeing her hand and working the stays of his shirt loose. He attempted to brush her busy fingers away, but she only laughed. Catching her shoulders, he gave her a little shake to gain her attention. She looked up at him, still undoing his shirt, still licking her lips.

"I do not wish to be intimate," he said tersely.

"Your body says different," she said, her hand trailing down the front of his pants to press against him. And his body, whetted by unbidden images of Cat, and stimulated by her hand, betrayed him, becoming hard beneath her stroking.

"I am just a man," he attempted to explain as she looked up at him triumphantly.

"Not just," she vowed.

"Daphne, listen to me. In all honor, I cannot do this, no matter how tempting you try to make it." He finally had her attention. The movements of her hands stilled. A line appeared between her thin, arched brows.

"In all honor? Try?!" Daphne squealed. "Is it this big-breasted English girl? Oh, it is too, too obvious. She is oh so proper. So cold. So British. And so? You are to be cold and proper, too?! *Mon Dieu!*"

Her eyes narrowed, her voice dropping to a throaty cadence. "But I know different! Or do you not remember the Palace Royal? I will refresh your memory. Three of the *fille de joie* complained their patrons were weak little men, with no stamina, no movement. You offered yourself to satisfy them. And when one of them said they would do it for free, you laughed. I remember, Thomas, you laughed! And you said since you would be servicing them, they ought to pay *you*. Oh, you were quite obliging, taking each in turn and saying, 'Bring on the next.' " Her voice dropped huskily. "The management should have charged to view such . . . So big, so powerful. *Mais oui! Très, très* satisfying."

Her tone hardened, but the lustful light stayed in her eyes. "Does your so proper English filly know this? Is she so good?"

"Shut up," Thomas growled.

"No! Do not say she is a virgin! What would you do with a virgin? You would rend her apart!" Passing her hand down his trousers, she closed on him greedily through the cloth. "She would end screaming, were you to cover her."

The image of Cat beneath him as he taught her body the lesson of passion froze Thomas. He felt Daphne's hands upon him but was impaled by a combination of alcohol and the picture her words had evoked. Cat, who regarded his body as a massive curiosity. Cat, who had trembled beneath the slight passion he had allowed himself. Cat, who could never even imagine the restraint he had shown in the conservatory. Cat, who must never know the dissipation he had courted, nor the physical appetites he had indulged.

"It is better that we debauchees stay amongst our own kind for our pleasures," he heard a voice coax. "Why court pain? What good is honor when she will find some scrub-faced count to bed her, fully clad, once a month? I can better satisfy your dark nature, Thomas, for my nature is equally dark. If she should love you, she will survive ... Others before her have."

His shirt was open now, and Daphne was stroking him with hot hands, pausing to work the buttons of his trousers free, until the cool air met his bared flesh. He heard the sharp intake of her breath, felt the eager rake of her nails low, on the hard plane of his belly, felt her hands stroking him. But her words had mesmerized him.

Cat. Loving him. It was too much. He clamped his teeth together, willing the sensual image of Cat away. She would not leave. He envisioned the warmth in her eyes, the smile of welcome as she opened her arms to embrace him. The scenario rolled inexorably forth. Her anticipation, her soft skin pressed to his, the force of his own passion, aroused, ignited by her. With agonizing clarity, he saw her anticipation recede before his growing ardor, turn slowly to trepidation and finally to fear as the control he strove to maintain in daily, innocuous meetings gave way before his ultimate need of her. He would never be able to dish out his passion in palatable doses. He wanted her too much. And desire made him dangerous.

Daphne was right. He would not court pain. The wet touch of her tongue trailed with sensual deliberation through the thatch of hair on his chest. He opened his eyes to discover his trousers unfastened. Her hands were encircling him and she was groaning. He clasped her shoulders to drag her away. Already, deprived of Cat's image, disgusted with the animal moans Daphne made, he was growing soft.

A movement caught his eye, and he looked up. For the breadth of an instant he thought his mind had willed Cat's image there. But he would never have willed her awful pallor, the horror in her sea green eyes, the hand raised trembling, in supplication or denial, out in front of her. Cat's figure was caught, reflected in the mirror, as she stood in the opened doorway. By the time a groan of pure pain had erupted from deep within his chest, she was gone.

Chapter 13

He had been set up. Even in his fury, some analytical part of him searched fruitlessly for a reason for the vicious betrayal, the depraved impulse that had driven Seward to send Cat to his room. This went beyond a mere difference in ideologies; this was personal hatred, vindictive and cruel. Thomas was even angrier with himself; he had been grossly negligent. He should have recognized hatred so intense, even had Seward tried to mask it. Thomas' life had so often depended on his ability to clearly sense the motives and impulses that drove other men. But he hadn't read Seward, not at all.

The list of "shoulds" unrolled like a damning litany in his mind. He "should" have recognized Seward's hatred and thus "should" have been prepared for his betrayal. He "should not" have trusted Seward to keep Cat at the Pavilion. He "should" have realized that his suite's open door would have acted as a challenge—perhaps even as titillation—to a woman like Daphne. He "should" have walked from the room at Daphne's first suggestive overtures.

His carelessness had made him an accomplice in his own betrayal. But, by God, he still held Seward accountable. He still intended to thrash the man to within an inch of his life. Perhaps rending Seward's flesh, as Thomas felt his own heart had been rent, would help assuage the unremitting pain that racked him, ever since he had seen Cat's horror-stricken face in the dim mirror and flung Daphne from him.

Daphne had cowered on the floor, recoiling in fear from the enraged animal he had become, fleeing when he heaved the heavy chair against the wall, splintering it apart. It was well, for had she remained, he would have added the crime of murder to his sin-encrusted soul.

He spent the rest of the night in darkness, hunched in a wing-backed chair by a long-dead hearth fire, the scent of brandy and the chill sea air his only companions. The hours grew immeasurably long, the killing rage superseding his growing despair. He had lost Cat. Not merely her physical presence, but all of her affection . . . her respect.

Oh, he knew she could never be to him all he so desperately wanted. But he had thought, God help him, to keep some small portion of her regard. To be able, in the years spread before him, to comfort himself with the notion that should they ever chance to meet, Cat would smile. No more than that. He closed his eyes, unaware that the brandy glass had shattered in his hand.

Cat's face haunted him. Innocent Cat, so intent on acquiring sophistication, she had blindly transgressed its ultimate law: Trust no one. And yet she had trusted him: a roué, a debauchee, a spy. A tortured sound rasped from his throat. There was nothing he could say to Cat, nothing that would erase that tawdry exhibition from her mind. He only knew he had to see her, to feel the lash of her scorn, to offer her a voice for the pain he had caused. Hopefully, in allowing the pain expression, its poison might be diminished.

He waited, feeling damned beyond recognition, until he heard the first clattering of the hotel's maids bringing chocolate and toast to the guests. He went to her room and knocked.

Silence met him. Again he pounded his open palm against the paneled door. She did not answer; of course not. The thunder of his hand against the oak door reverberated into the enveloping predawn hush.

"Shouldn't I answer it, milady? Maybe it's just the girl come with a spot of tea. Oh, ma'am, you could use a touch of something, please," he heard Fielding say from the other side of the door, the worry in her voice making her words a plea.

He could not hear the reply, so quietly was the answer voiced.

"No, I won't. I promise," he heard Fielding soothe, "but you must let me fetch you something. I'll just slip out—"

"*No!*"

Thomas heard Cat clearly that time. He closed his eyes, tormented by the panic the thought of seeing him caused her. His lips parting in a feral grimace of pain, he pushed himself off the door, his anger once more white-hot and lethal.

In his room, he splashed water from the basin onto his face, raising it to stare with red, sleep-deprived eyes back at the lined ruin the cursed mirror reflected. He saw her face instead. With an oath, Thomas grabbed the coat he'd earlier hurled into a corner. He would find Seward. He hoped it had amused the man greatly to send Cat to his room hard on the heels of having arranged Daphne to be there, because it was going to cost him. Dearly. Every entertainment had its price.

A giant stood on the front steps leading to Colonel Henry Seward's rented Brighton town house.

His legs were braced apart, arms hanging loosely at his sides. His slate-streaked locks fell forward, unkempt, upon high cheekbones. A rumpled, black coat stretched in deep wrinkles across his broad back. His pose was preternaturally still.

The footman who'd sleepily answered the thunderous banging backed away from the black-eyed brute's intimidating figure. The dark man's gaze scoured the interior of the hallway before finally coming to rest on the footman.

"Fetch Colonel Seward." His quiet rasp was a frightening contrast to his ravaged appearance.

"Colonel Seward is not receiving visitors," stammered the footman.

The big hands curled at the giant's sides. "If I do not see Colonel Seward within the next five minutes, I will find him. Do I make myself clear?"

The footman gulped, bobbing his head. Uncertain whether he would be able to choke any words past the constriction in his throat, he ushered the towering man toward the morning room. Carefully he closed the door before running to get Colonel Seward, praying his master would be able to deal with the madman.

Fixing his eyes on the mantelpiece clock, Thomas silently willed the promised five minutes to pass that he might have the pleasure of ripping the room apart. Four minutes and ten seconds elapsed before the door swung open.

Seward looked done in. Warily regarding Thomas, he finished knotting the silk dressing robe around his waist. His hands, Thomas noted with detached disappointment, did not shake.

"I am going to beat the bloody hell out of you, Colonel," Thomas said softly, almost conversationally. "I only tell you so you might call for assistance. I welcome the opportunity for further violence."

Seward raised his chin. The flesh around his aquiline nose became white. "I am not going to call for reinforcements."

Thomas sighed, genuinely weary. "You needn't bother to simulate integrity. It isn't necessary. I am even willing to admit my own hand in the little scene you orchestrated last night. You see, I had judged you incapable of such gross duplicity." He laughed. The sound was frightening. For the first time, Seward realized how very, very dangerous Thomas was.

"Amusing, is it not?" Thomas said in the same frighteningly calm tone. "You have so often pointed out my jaded skepticism, and yet I was so easily gulled."

Thomas walked until he stood within easy reach. The man looked drunk, or drugged, thought Seward. He could not tell which. And then he had it; he remembered men with that peculiar gait, the abnormal calm, those fevered eyes; Thomas Montrose looked like the survivor of a massacre.

"I hope the enjoyment you received was worth it," Thomas said. "Despite what you think you know of my history, I really am well acquainted with . . . discomfort. Perhaps knowing I would certainly thrash you was part of your satisfaction. Are you that diseased? Well." A nearly gentle smile curved Thomas' lips. "I shall not disappoint you.

"Come, Seward," Thomas said. He stood in a relaxed pose, nay, more nearly an exhausted one, only his size and the promise in his soft words threatening. "I will amuse you further by admitting an unwillingness to strike the first blow. Pathetically proper, isn't it? *You* should have no problems, though."

"I won't rise to the bait, Montrose, though I doubt I would be as easy an opponent as you think," said Seward.

"Try; we shall see," Thomas said, and now his smile was gentle. He closed his eyes, swaying backward. Seward instinctively reached out to steady him, but before he could touch him, Thomas' lids opened a slit, and Seward saw a feral light gleam. He snatched his hand back, as though it were burned. With a gentle smile and soft words, Thomas Montrose would break his neck.

During the course of a highly hazardous career, Colonel Henry Seward had dealt with many types of men. He knew the most dangerous, the most unpredictable opponent, is the one with nothing left to lose. Thomas Montrose looked like such a man.

"No, not before you listen to me," Seward said, surprised he wanted to ease Thomas' despair.

"I am not interested," Thomas said, taking a step forward. Seward held his ground.

"I do not know what occurred last night," he said. "I can only surmise that, whatever it was, it had something to do with Lady Catherine's early return to the Old Ship."

Immediately Thomas caught Seward's lapels in his fists and jerked him forward. "I am credulous only once. Do you ask me to believe you didn't plan this as some sort of warped retribution? And retribution for what? My social position? For my leaving the Foreign Office? Do you ask me to believe that Daphne Bernard did not run to heel as soon as your plan had been carried out?" His voice was a whisper.

"Did you laugh, Seward," Thomas continued, "when she described the revulsion on Cat's face? Or was she too busy at my body to attend? How disappointing for you." He gave Seward a violent shake and, suddenly, casually, flung him away.

Seward stumbled backward; he reached out a shaking hand blindly to stop his fall. Montrose was incredibly strong. But it was not his physical strength that caused Seward to blanch. It was his words.

Seward had not known. But he'd guessed. Daphne Bernard had arrived, disheveled and shaken at two o'clock in the morning, demanding money as she scribbled down what she knew. When asked why she hadn't given her information to Thomas, she flew into gutter French epitaphs, swearing to return to Paris as soon as possible.

Seward had spent the rest of the night trying to convince himself there had been no real betrayal. His concern was pointless; Lady Catherine had had an uneventful return to her suite. He had sneered at what he considered Montrose's ethical affectations. But maybe, Seward conceded darkly, what he had really been sneering at was his own inability to embrace a code of honor. Any code of honor.

Because behind the rage that made the huge man facing him seem a lethal animal was an all-too-human anguish. In a moment of intuition, Seward suspected he was incapable of such feelings. That sudden knowledge filled Seward with self-loathing. Like an angry child who cannot ride and thus proclaims to hate horses, he had fashioned his character from his very inability to understand such concepts as honor, integrity, and morality.

Seward had never sought to justify himself to any man. He did not do so now. But he felt the need to educate Thomas Montrose as to the extent of Lord Barrymore's hatred.

"I am not your enemy, Montrose." Seward's last word was cut off by his own gasp as he doubled over in excruciating pain. He had not even seen the blow coming, so lightning quick was it delivered. Thomas stood still, once more relaxed, his arms at his sides, his breathing even.

"Once more, I have misjudged you, Seward. I congratulate you. I never suspected you to be a coward, too."

Now Seward's own ire was inflamed. Aiming his blow at Montrose's jaw, he attacked. His fist was caught, the impact halted inches from Thomas' face. It was an act of monumental strength and reflex, and yet the expression on Montrose's face stayed blank.

"Thank you," Thomas murmured, and Seward felt the bones in his hand grind together as Montrose twisted his wrist back, bringing Seward to his knees. He clenched his teeth against his groan, knowing his hand was being broken.

"Too easy," muttered Thomas, releasing him. "Tell me again you are not my enemy."

"Bloody hell!" Seward snarled, kicking out his foot, slamming it into Thomas' kneecap. Montrose stumbled back. Surging upward, Seward drove his elbow into Montrose's jaw before dancing back.

Thomas' head lowered; blood appeared in a line from the corner of his mouth. He looked up from beneath his dark brows, and Seward saw the evil fire, unbanked.

"Once more, my thanks," Thomas said, moving slowly toward him.

"Damn you, Montrose! You will hear me! If only to save your Lady Catherine!"

Now there was nothing casual or deceptive in Thomas Montrose's expression. Pure rage, lethal and focused, emanated from his soulless black eyes.

"Do you think to threaten her? Her?!" he roared, lunging forward. But Seward was ready this time. He flung up his arm just in time to ward off the blow. His forearm took the impact, transmitting it to his shattered hand.

"Not I!" he gasped, the lights of pain exploding before his eyes, the ground heaving beneath his feet. "Barrymore!"

"Barrymore?" Seward dimly heard Thomas ask, unaware Montrose even held him up until he felt himself released. Seward staggered unsteadily on his feet.

"Aye, Barrymore. 'Twas he who hounded your lady from the Pavilion. He leered and badgered and dogged her, making no attempt to disguise that he would make a spectacle of her with his gross attention. She fled," Seward ground out between his teeth. "In this I am at fault. I should have stopped her. I had promised you. I was wrong to order the carriage she demanded. I did not foresee her flying to your side. Again, I misjudged. But I did not send her there!"

Montrose's eyes narrowed. "Do you lie?" he snarled. The blood was flowing freely from his split lip, staining the open collar of his shirt.

"Why should I lie?" Seward asked. "In all the years we have been associated, when have personal feelings colored my actions? Whatever I have done, whatever I have ordered others to do, no matter how unsavory or abhorrent, I have done for the sake of my office. What reason would I have to alienate you? Hatred? You give me too much credit, Montrose. That is a human emotion." His voice was rife with self-contempt.

The passion slowly receded from Thomas' eyes as he considered Seward's words.

"Does he threaten her?" Thomas asked.

"Yes. But only if it is convenient." Seward held his broken hand cradled against his chest. "As long as she does not put herself in his range, I judge her to be safe enough. His actions are unfocused, small and vicious, but given the chance . . . he would destroy her. She made

him look a fool, something he will not forgive."

"Where does he stay?" Thomas bit out.

Seward shook his head, smiling bitterly. "He is a
friend of the Prince Regent's. You will not be able
to find satisfaction there."

"Oh, aye," promised Thomas, "I will."

"Don't be a fool, Montrose! What will you gain
by indulging in revenge?"

"Always so pragmatic, Seward?" Thomas
sneered.

"Always."

"I might make her life more comfortable."

"More comfortable? By making her name a
byword for scandal? What then are her chances?"

Thomas ran a hand through his hair. "You are
more clear-sighted in this than I," he finally said.

"Just less involved. I am good at that, too,"
Seward said.

Wordlessly Thomas started toward the door. He
paused only when he saw the blood on his cuff.
Staring at the stained white material in surprise,
he paused before mopping his mouth with it. As
if in an afterthought, he turned back to Seward.

"I will have your man fetch a quack," he said
tightly.

It was as much as the situation allowed. Seward
recognized the implicit generosity in the gesture.
He became aware of a faint, long-ignored need to
respect and be respected, a need for comradeship
in a life singularly devoid of it.

"Thank you," Seward said. When, once more,
Thomas would have left the room, he stopped him,
saying, "I am not blameless here."

"I know."

"I cannot unmake the situation. I can think of no
way I can offer my assistance. But I can apprise you
of other situations, situations which, I personally

assure you, you will no longer be called upon to resolve. And I will follow Lord Barrymore's course, most closely."

There was no answer. Seward was aware of being scrutinized and weighed. He did not know how he had been judged, but Thomas nodded once before leaving the room. It was a beginning.

The urge to act impulsively died by the time Thomas arrived back at the Old Ship. He had glimpsed the emptiness last night had purchased. He could not go to Cat and he could not leave her to Barrymore's tender mercies. While he believed Seward—he would have killed him had he not— he did not trust him to adequately protect Cat from Barrymore's attentions. But, he added sadly to himself, there was no one he would trust with Cat's care. He toyed with the idea of arranging for Hecuba, Cat, and himself to leave immediately for Devon, then abandoned it as impossible to carry out. Cat would not even see him, let alone agree to ensconce herself for a daylong carriage ride with him.

Dismissing Bob from his responsibilities, Thomas spent the remainder of the morning in his suite, trying unsuccessfully to find a way to protect Cat without attending her.

Finally, in frustration, he rang up the maid for a basin of fresh water. After giving himself a quick sponge bath, he pulled on fresh linen and a newly laundered coat. If Cat would not see him, Hecuba would. Perhaps he might enlist her aid. He knew Hecuba would not intercede for him— he was not such a fool as to believe all possible repair beyond hope—but he might persuade her to keep him apprised of Cat's activities. He vowed not to offend Cat with his physical presence, but with a few well-placed words he could save her the unpleasantness of Barrymore's badgering.

He rapped at Hecuba's suite, well aware it connected directly to Cat's chambers, but hoping nonetheless that he might find the older woman alone. His knock went unanswered.

Steeling himself for the revulsion he would see on Cat's face, he proceeded to her door. He told himself 'twas better to get this first, awkward meeting over with, but desperation drove him. He needed to see her beloved countenance, to see for himself how deeply the wound went, hoping there was more disgust than pain there, knowing it would not be so.

Once more, silence met his knock. A sudden, horrifying intuition caused him to raise his voice, calling out to her. Not the slightest rustle sounded from the other side of the door. His fear uncoiled in thick waves. Standing back, he kicked, shattering the thin oak door. It swung in drunkenly on broken brass hinges, the creak of its swaying the only sound. Thomas stepped into the suite.

It was empty. The bedclothes had been neatly folded onto the foot of the canopied bed, the windows raised to admit the soft sea air. Still, Cat's scent, illusive, evocative, teased his senses. He threw open the wardrobe. A single piece of string pooled on the floor. An amber bead winked at him from a dark corner.

He stood staring down at it, vaguely surprised his body was trembling. His gaze traveled the room; it was bereft of her. He heard the sea beating against the shore from far out beyond the window. Seabirds added their keening song to the inexorable rhythm. The sun outside seemed too bright.

He did not know how long he stood there, drinking in the dying fragrance, but slowly his eyes, which had never ceased moving over the room, began to recognize what they saw. A single sheet of creamy white paper lay folded on the mantel.

Reaching out, he took it up, as a man would take up dangerous blade. He unfolded it, wondering how Cat, with her pretty manners, would consign him to hell. He needn't have worried. It wasn't from Cat at all.

> Sir,
> I have been offered, and have accepted, employment elsewhere. My prorated wages can be sent to Bellingcourt Manor, Yorkshire.

The elegant, incisive scrawl, as well as the terse, imperious phraseology, gave Lady Montaigne White away as the author. But beneath the writing were more phrases, the much-blotted chicken scratching of an untutored hand.

> I dont no wat you dun to make Lady Cat so sad. I promisd her I wont tell as how she crys and so I wont. You wer a good mastr, I wont say otherways. But Lady Cat is qwality and awfl hert. I need to do for her.
>
> Tansy Elizabeth Fielding

Lucky Fielding, thought Thomas, carefully refolding the single sheet, *to be able to have what you need.*

Chapter 14

February 1815
Devon

Marcus Horatio Coynager, Viscount Eltheridge, drummed his fingers nervously against the arm of the chair. Recognizing the fine grained leather of the wing-back, the polish on the large library table, he weighed the furnishings of this room against the ramshackle collection in his own home. As was his habit, he promised himself some day Bellingcourt would be as properly cared for.

After traveling two days from his beloved home to reach here, he was uncertain whether the trip had been necessary or even advisable. His letter, asking for an account of Cat's unusual behavior, had gone unanswered. With uncharacteristic impulsiveness, Marcus had thrown together some clothes and taken the mail coach, all but bankrupting his family's monthly budget.

His arrival at the prosperous-looking estate was greeted by a tight-lipped, disapproving housekeeper. He enviously regarded the layout of orchards, gardens, and pastures before the housekeeper ushered him in to stand, hat in hand, in a spacious foyer. Only after he'd informed the sharp-faced old shrew of his relationship to Cat did she gasp and all but push him through the door leading to the library before scurrying off.

At eighteen years, Marcus was only now filling out the promise of his long frame. He had a youthful countenance. Thick, ash blond hair tumbled over a clear high, forehead. His mouth was tender, his hazel eyes clear. But his expression, far from being adolescent, was old beyond his years. Worry, not an unusual expression judging from the fine lines bracketing the bridge of his high nose, sat comfortably upon him.

Hearing the sound of heavy footfalls coming toward the door, Marcus leapt to his feet that he might face his unknowing host from no disadvantage. It was a pointless gesture. The man coming in topped Marcus' more than average height by half a foot. The man's dark head was bent over the packet of letters he held in his hand, reading their inscriptions. It gave Marcus a chance to observe him.

So this was Thomas Montrose: profligate extraordinaire, rake, gamester. The man Cat had sought to teach her all the wiles a young woman would need to catch a blade of the first rank. Marcus had a hard time reconciling his concept of the man with the reality.

Montrose was large: tall, broad, and lean. But it was not his size that discounted his reputation; it was his age. Montrose was an old man; he must be nearing his mid-thirties. And elegance? Marcus knew he was ill equipped to judge the town bronze of anyone, and yet even he could see the man was beyond unfashionable. Thomas' face was tanned nut brown, the slight hollows beneath his high cheekbones stubbled by an afternoon growth of beard. The small fans of white lines radiating from the corners of his eyes were an indictment against squinting into a winter sun. His hair, more than an occasional smoke gray strand lightening its darkness, hung so long that it coiled upon his shoulders.

Even as Marcus watched, Montrose frowned at one of the letters he held. Instead of opening it, he slowly turned his great head without lifting it, his raven black gaze impaling Marcus from a sidelong slant.

"What are you doing here?" The deep voice was curiously rich and, at the same time, discordant, nearly hollow-sounding, as though a magnificent instrument were being played by an amateur.

"I was asked to wait here by your housekeeper. Did she not tell you?" Marcus asked.

"I came in through the kitchens," Montrose explained dismissively. "Who are you?"

Marcus drew himself up, coming close to clicking his heels together. Something in his bearing must have moved Montrose to amusement; the corners of his mouth twitched.

"I am Viscount Eltheridge."

Montrose answered this pronouncement with a lift of one brow.

"Marcus Horatio Coynager."

Thomas' dark brow rose higher.

"Catherine Sinclair is my half sister."

The faint signs of humor died as though they had never been. A shutter deadened Montrose's features. He spoke not a word.

The silence stretched on uncomfortably, and Marcus shifted his feet, uncertain where to begin. Finally he blurted out, "I want to know what happened to her."

"What do you mean? What's happened to her?!" Montrose immediately rasped out.

Marcus replied to the tension underscoring the words, stammering, "Nothing . . . that is to say, no physical hurt. That is, that I know of."

The tautness seeped from Thomas' body. Sighing, he waved Marcus to a chair at the library table.

When Marcus had been seated, Montrose hitched his hip onto the table's edge, folding his arms across his chest.

"Now," he said, "what exactly *do* you mean?"

"Cat . . . Lady Catherine . . . is my half sister."

"So you have said."

"But she is more than a half sister." Marcus raked a hand through his heavy hair. "She has always been the head of our family. Our mother has been wed three times, four since she married your brother. Catherine and Enid were the offspring of her first union, I was born from the second, and the twins, Simon and Timon, and Marianne were the results of the third."

"Quite a menagerie," Montrose murmured.

Marcus nodded vigorously in agreement. "Well, as you can imagine, what with the quick succession of fathers, we have been at a loss as to how to go on. You see, none of my mother's husbands were deft hands at financial management. Quite the reverse. They were all miserably poor.

"Mother is no better. Her idea of remedying our financial difficulties has always been to fly off to London and round up another spouse. Unfortunately, in spite of her good intentions, she always chose to wed the most charming flats and gulls in town. Quite frankly, we rarely see Mother. She always seems to be either in mourning black or bridal finery." The boy's candor was disarming. Apparently, thought Thomas, he bore his profligate parent no ill will, but a strained, indulgent affection.

"Cat, being the oldest and quite the most intelligent, took over the household management in Mother's absence. Even later, when Mother *was* in attendance, Cat just sort of kept up the role. She was so much better at it than Mother. And then, oh, some five years

ago, after my third cousin died, leaving his title
and estate to me, she took over the management
of that, too."

The boy must have seen some sign of the anger
Thomas felt at the atrocious unfairness of the
situation. Steward, land manager, housekeeper,
accountant . . . Was there no role that hadn't been
foisted upon her young shoulders?

"I was only turned thirteen," Marcus said.

"And she was what? All of fifteen? Sixteen?"

"I could not afford to retain someone to manage
the land. My relative ran true to form. He had borrowed against the estate until there was nothing
left. Nothing but the people who were dependent
upon it. The situation might have been unfair to
Cat, but to ignore it would have been more than
unfair to the people who depended on me."

"On you. Now, there's an interesting choice of
words."

Marcus felt himself flush hotly under the decep-
tively mild words. "Cat has been teaching me. I
have taken more responsibility with each passing
year. Indeed, I am pleased to say that, within
another year or so, I shall have paid back all debts
incurred on my estate."

"How does all of this involve Cat?"

Marcus' moment of triumph dissolved under the
reminder of his errand. He leaned forward earnestly. Unknowingly, his very openness, his obvious concern for Cat, did much to redeem him in
Thomas' cynical eyes.

"When Mother wed your brother, we were,
as you can well imagine, overjoyed. Finally, it
seemed, she had found a suitable, and suitably
set up, husband to help bail us out of dun
territory. Our joy was premature. Mother and
Philip, having embarked on this extraordinarily
long tour of theirs, left no money for us."

"What?!" The word exploded, causing poor Marcus to wince.

"You didn't know?" he asked.

"Of course I didn't know! I thought you had merely run through your readily available funds. I had no idea. Let me see if I have the right of this," Thomas said, obviously trying to leash his temper. "Do you mean to tell me Philip and your . . . mother . . . have been toddling about the world for four years without having left you any monetary provisions *what so ever*?!"

Marcus numbly nodded his head in response.

Thomas took a deep breath. "Why the hell didn't you petition them for funds? Philip, while not the richest man in England, is still quite wealthy."

"They never stay long enough in one place to have any letters catch up with them," said the boy in such a tone that Thomas knew the situation had long ago ceased to anger him. "And if they are in one place, it is usually some godforsaken, undiscovered country. Oh, we have had reams of curiosities shipped to us: fertility gods, animal hides, exotic statuary. Unfortunately, there is not a huge market for gazelle horns or we should be rich."

"Continue."

"Well, two years ago Enid was supposed to make her bow. There just wasn't any money for it. The only reason Cat had a come-out was because Great-Aunt Hecuba sold off a few pieces left her by her paternal grandmother. Anyway, when Enid couldn't make her bow, Cat was fit to be tied. I'm sure she felt it more grievously than Enid.

"And then, last year, the twins were, er, dismissed from school for, ah, unpaid tuition. Simon wanted to embark on a naval career, Timon to further his education. There was, of course, no hope for either." Marcus looked up, embarrassed at having to relate his family's pitiful history, to find

Thomas staring out the window. A vein bulged in the side of his throat, but he only blew out a deep breath in a long, controlled exhalation.

"There is more," Thomas said.

"Yes," Marcus replied hurriedly, lest he lose courage. "Cat decided to solve all these problems in one fell swoop. By getting leg-shackled."

"I had no idea she fancied herself a martyr."

"Oh, she didn't! She doesn't! She isn't!" In any other circumstances, the over quick disclaimer would have been amusing. Thomas could only look askance at the boy's hurried denial.

"She's practical," Marcus explained. "Cat is, above all else, practical." He sighed. "Extremely, relentlessly practical. She didn't propose to wed the first rich ne'er-do-well she could find. She researched the situation thoroughly. Found herself the most likely candidate, interviewed his acquaintances, friends, associates—all very surreptitiously, of course—and arranged an introduction."

"I know I must appear, beyond reason, lacking in understanding, but allow me to clarify this in my own mind. Cat set her sights on a man she had never even seen?"

"Yes," Marcus answered. "She thought it best not to cloud her judgment with first impressions or aesthetic considerations."

"And do you happen to know her criteria?"

"Not all of it. But I do know he had to be very rich; intelligent, so as not to bore her; sophisticated, so as not to interfere with her; and not given to emotionalism, so as not to demand too much of her."

"And Lord Strand measured up."

"Admirably. Rather too well, if you must know. He was so sophisticated and unemotional, Cat despaired of ever getting him to the altar. That's when she thought of you."

"God help me," muttered Thomas.

"And that's really why I'm here. You see, when she first came to you she wrote us every day. Her notes were brief but sharp, amusing. Like Cat. You know."

"Yes."

Marcus barely heard the soft reply. "And regular. Regular as clockwork. You know Cat. 'Twas her duty to write, and so she did. Every day. We quite looked forward to them. Kept dinner conversation lively. And from what she wrote, we surmised her, er, education was going well. She seemed happy. Until Brighton. Since she left Brighton, we've had only a few letters. Long, prosy, brittle things, they are, too. And now that she's in Paris with Great-Aunt Hecuba, we've had nothing. We are worried about her. *I* am worried about her. And so I thought, seeing how she was . . . seeing how she and you . . . seeing how your repu—" Marcus broke off.

Thomas continued for him, his voice dangerously level. "Seeing how she was under my protection when this uncharacteristic change in her habits occurred, and how my reputation regarding young ladies is unsavory at best, you thought I might provide some direction as to the why and give you my opinion as to its import."

"Exactly!"

"I understand. As to the first, I have a fair idea as to why she is behaving thus. It's none of your business. As to the second, I do not know. I bloody well wish I did. There." Thomas pushed himself off the table.

"Next time you require information, I suggest you take pen to paper and save yourself a tedious journey." It was a dismissal, but Marcus, staring miserably at the hands he twisted in his lap, made no move to go.

"I did. You did not answer," Marcus said quietly. "Mr. Montrose, Cat is, for all she is only my half sister, fully that and more in my heart. She is my friend. I cannot be satisfied with your answer."

Marcus looked up at the tall, rangy form towering above him. His hazel eyes did not waver from Thomas' black ones, though his gulp was audible.

Thomas measured him for a long moment. "Your sister is safe. As safe as I can make her, which is considerable. I have friends who guard her welfare by all the means at their disposal. Her every movement has been watched and attended. Physically she is in no danger. There, boy," Thomas said with finality, a world of weariness creeping into his tone, "I have given you all the information I am going to. Go home and see to your crops. Cat is my concern."

The possessive statement made Marcus look up with filial suspicion. "How so?"

"How so, indeed?" Thomas echoed in a low, considering voice. "It does not matter. It is a fait accompli. It will always be so."

Thomas crumpled the piece of paper, swearing as he threw it against the grate. He had waited until he had heard the click of the outer door and Mrs. Medge coldly bidding the boy adieu before reading the post from France. He had unwittingly lied to Marcus. Cat was not safe.

The message he had just read outlined her danger. Seward, true to his word, regularly reported any information pertinent to the French situation as well as Hellsgate Barrymore. This message from Seward was succinct. Rumors, as yet unsubstantiated, were rife concerning an alleged plot by Napoleon to retake his lost country. Apparently, Thomas thought without satisfaction, his apprehensions concerning the little emperor were to be validated. The accuracy of his intuition afforded him no pleasure. Cat was in Paris.

There had to be some way to extricate her from the potential danger. He knew a letter from him, demanding she come back to England immediately, stood no hope of being obeyed. She probably wouldn't even read it. Besides, how could she feel endangered with every titled fool in England parading through Paris? Why, the whole bloody world was in Paris!

God help him, he would have to go himself and fetch her back. There ought to be enough time to make the journey. Convincing Cat to go with him would prove the greatest challenge.

He had thought himself done with Cat. Or, more to the point, he admitted with harsh humor, he'd thought to allow her to be done with him. It had been with masochistic pleasure that he'd read the accounts posted him by the friend he'd set to watch over her. The friend had written nothing suggesting that Cat was hurt. Perhaps Thomas had, after all, done her some small service. Perhaps she would abandon her scheme and find herself some smooth-cheeked boy to beguile.

She was so damn young. She would mend. As would he. And if the long, hollow days that each morning threatened to devour him showed no signs of relenting, well then, the numbness had kept pace with the emptiness. It would be interesting to see if that kind opiate relinquished its hold when he had to see her, talk to her, persuade her to come with him.

Thomas sat at his desk, penning a terse note to another well-placed and influential friend, outlining his requirements. After ringing for Bob, he barked out orders for immediate travel arrangements.

Ever since Thomas' return from Brighton, Bob had watched his employer grow more and more remote, cold, and taciturn. He'd seen Mr. Montrose drive himself to near exhaustion overseeing the estate, coming in from the fields long after the supper hour. Any attempts to persuade him to eat or rest were met with short, polite refusals. Thomas Montrose was a gentleman.

But an underlying tension seemed to simmer just beneath the surface of all that careful control. In truth, Thomas frightened Bob, like a chained wolf he had once seen at a fair had frightened him. Though Bob had known the beast couldn't get free, the wildness in its eyes promised danger. In Bob's not-so-humble opinion, Thomas needed a bit of merriment. And Paris, Bob thought with a grin, was a good place for that.

Chapter 15

March 1815
Paris

God, she was a desirable woman.

Giles Dalton, Marquis of Strand, watched Cat circulating through the crowded ballroom of Merton's rented Parisian town house. Yes, indeed, Catherine Sinclair, "Lady Cat," as fashionable society had taken to calling her, was well on her way to becoming the reigning toast.

She caught sight of him, and her full lower lip bowed out in plump invitation. Or was it a smile? He'd be damned if he knew. There was a lot, apparently, he did not know about the fascinating Lady Cat. And he'd been so sure he'd taken her measure during the past few seasons. So sure that he had been on the very precipice of bowing to convention and marrying the girl.

Lord Strand was finally growing weary of all the well-rehearsed lures cast his way. It had been fun for a while, but as with anything too easily attained, it had begun to pall. A practical, unsentimental man, Strand had turned his attention to a careful consideration of the candidates for his future marchioness. He had taken several seasons to study his choices, finally fixing his attention on Lady Catherine Sinclair.

She seemed perfect: lovely, amusing, pragmatic, and serene. He had even thought he'd sensed the potential for more than pure expedience in their marriage. He'd even thought it possible he might come to love her. And then she had appeared in Paris, changed.

But was it change, Strand asked himself, or playacting? Or even something else? Had the girl he'd thought to offer for simply matured into a woman? He could not tell, and ever a careful man, he waited until he had a better grasp of the situation before acting.

Because, were he not so cautious, he admitted wryly, he would have had her to an altar—or a bed—some time ago. She was enchanting, delicious, and if her bon mots were occasionally a bit sharp, the barbs were most often self-directed. He did not understand her, and he was wary of that which he didn't understand. Meanwhile, she would probably drive him mad; though it was an enjoyable madness.

With increasing frequency, Cat allowed his touch. Her lips were honey-sweet, her body lithe. Yet Giles did not detect a trap baited with her willingness. Nothing she did or said hinted at marital expectations. On the contrary, if anything, her reaction to his caress held a hint of impatience, a frisson of desperation, which manifested itself as a readiness to learn lessons he was afire to teach. If only he were not certain she was, in spite of her sophisticated veneer, her come-hither eyes, quite unimpeachably, regretfully, a virgin.

A young woman on the marriage mart had two things to recommend her: wealth and a maidenhead. As Cat Sinclair hadn't the first, he wasn't going to divest her of the second. Besides, Thomas

Montrose, being obstinately oblique on all other matters, had been crystal-clear about Cat going to the altar in her untouched state.

Characteristically enigmatic as to his own motives, Thomas had been explicit in his request: Strand was to set himself up as sentry over the physical well-being of Lady Catherine Sinclair, protecting her from any would-be assailants, including those who would try her virtue. Little did Thomas know, thought Strand with an inner sigh, he'd set the seducer up as guard.

If Giles hadn't such a profound respect for Thomas, he'd have suspected a scheme hidden in the request. The betting books at White's had Giles withstanding yet another season of Lady Catherine's siege. Anyone winning the wager stood to gain a large some of money. Giles knew the bets were based to a large degree on the lady's own orchestrations. It seemed all of society knew Lady Cat had set her cap at Lord Strand. Except, lately, Lady Cat herself. She had ceased pursuing him with the single-minded and amusing determination that had distinguished the previous seasons. It was beyond puzzling.

Giles' obligation to Thomas was deep, his friendship deeper. As a military attaché to Sir Stuart, Giles had been introduced to Thomas. He had been surprised to recognize Sir Stuart's premier agent as his school companion. They had rekindled their childhood friendship. Later, at Salamanca, Thomas had risked his life to save Giles'.

So Giles complied with Thomas' written request, never mentioning to Lady Catherine his association with Thomas. In turn, he never heard Thomas' name pass her own lovely lips. It was simple, attending Lady Cat; the job merely asked Giles to follow his own inclinations. Only the gutter-mouthed Hellsgate Barrymore threatened Cat's new, urbane composure, and he was easily avoided. Except at the larger parties, such as this.

With that in mind, Giles looked around the milling crowds. He saw Hellsgate at once, his whip-thin figure clad in black, his pale countenance turned with snakelike fixation on Cat. There was nothing for it, thought Giles with a quick grin. He would have to remove his negligent seductress from Hellsgate's too interested gaze.

"Lord Strand," Cat answered in reply to Giles' formal bow.

"Would you care to dance, Lady Cat?" he asked.

Lord, he does have pretty manners, thought Cat before saying, "A week ago I would have sent you over to my great-aunt for permission, as we have already been partnered once. But the last time I sent someone to her with a like petition, she fixed the poor fellow with the most disgusted look and said, 'Why the deuce don't you ask the gel, you ninnyhammered pup!'

"Sir Hale will never recover," Cat added sadly. "He didn't know whether to flush with delight or outrage. He is, after all, but ten years Aunt Hecuba's junior."

Strand joined in the laughter of the other bucks and ladies surrounding Cat.

"You are making this up," a young man protested.

"Just embellishing a bit . . . Sir Hale is quite fifteen years her junior," Cat said. She curved her mouth into a teasing smile, a smile that never reached her eyes.

For four months, Cat had dined out on her social triumph. It tasted of ashes. She continued with the charade because she knew no other course to follow. It still was the most direct way to her goal. A goal, Cat reminded herself with increasing frequency, that was still essential—providing for her family.

She could have kicked herself any number of times. She almost asked Fielding to do so last week. Strand had been so close to proposing. With just a small bit of encouragement . . . but no. The moment his careful, smooth expression took on a serious, intent aspect, she had divined his intent. And, like the fool she was, she had smiled, blinked, tittered, and fled. Idiot!

She didn't recognize herself. Indeed, everything—everyone!—she had been so confident she knew seemed to be changing. Even Great-Aunt Hecuba.

A fortnight ago, Cat had gone to fetch Hecuba for the evening's entertainment. Her great-aunt had come to the door, not in her usual endless layers of black bombazine, but in a gown of cerise satin with jet beads embroidering what looked suspiciously like a décolletage. Only the heavy crucifix, half-hidden beneath a layer of lace, told Cat it was Lady Montaigne White and not some impostor. Tonight the crucifix had disappeared altogether . . . along with another three inches of bodice.

Cat peered over the shoulder of one of her companions, searching for her great-aunt. By heavens, if Hecuba wasn't smiling! And her cheeks were rosy with more than the powder Cat had glimpsed her furtively applying with a rabbit's foot. Hecuba was positively glowing at the wizened old Marquis de Grenville, who dogged their footsteps! Cat gnawed her lower lip in consternation.

Giles' voice recalled her from her speculation. In a trice her forehead smoothed to bland serenity.

"Shall we risk Lady Montaigne White's considerable ire, and dance?" he asked.

Cat nodded. Placing her hand in Strand's outstretched one, she moved forward, catching the first movement in the intricate steps of the quadrille. Giles was an accomplished dancer. His trim length perfectly suited the graceful motions. As he bent his dark blond head toward her, she remarked anew the fine texture of his clear, pale skin, the silky wealth of waving hair.

There was no intriguing break to the faultless conformity of his features. His almond-shaped gray eyes were perfectly spaced above full lips and a square jaw. His ears lay flat against his well-molded head. His throat was strong. He was a purebred through and through, she thought as the dance ended and he escorted her to one side.

"Merton is quite proud of his newly acquired paintings. Would you care to see them?" he asked.

Again? Cat thought. She paused a second before agreeing. It was becoming an open ploy on Strand's part. Cat had spent an inordinate amount of time viewing statuary, paintings, and book collections during the past few weeks. She was disappointed Giles was so obvious. She was certain Thomas would never . . . Damn! With an effort, she kept her smile in place.

Giles led her to a gallery running off the hall's open stairway. True to his word, he pointed out a few desultory, poorly lit paintings hanging on the wall. But Strand was always true to his word.

"This is by Jacques David. He handles the modeling of light on the torso superbly, don't you agree?" His voice was intimate, low.

"Yes," Cat replied, feeling the warm blow of his breath caress her neck. He stood behind her, delicately trailing his fingers from her wrist to her upper arm. Willing herself to respond to his expert touch, she stood still beneath the familiarity.

Leaning forward, Giles laid his lips gently on her neck. She turned slowly, reaching up to embrace him. His kiss was a sigh on her lips, sweet, tender . . . controlled. In frustration, she moved her own mouth more fully under his. He answered her unspoken request, deepening the kiss, splaying his hands across her back to press her more fully to him.

His pulse quickened with the weight of supple femininity yielding so meltingly in his arms. With a ragged breath, he recalled himself. She was a warm promise, compliant in abandonment. She was also a virgin. And she might still be brought to his bed that way . . . as his wife.

Putting his hands on her shoulders, he held himself back from her just a little, and was surprised when she did not contest his drawing away with so much as a frown.

"You make a man forget himself," he said by way of explanation and apology.

"And here I thought you had remembered yourself," she answered evenly.

Once more, she perplexed him, her reactions not at all what he'd expected. He tried a smile.

"You are right, of course. Let us say I remembered my obligation as a gentleman."

"I know enough of the breed to realize if that were your only consideration, then indeed my situation would grow dire," she replied flippantly.

He did not know what drove her, but his own frustration was growing in the face of such blatant teasing. Taking her once more into his arms, he traced his forefinger over her lower lip. Thinking to shock her, he said, "Would you really like to experiment, m'dear? Because I could not deny a lady's request."

The heat in his eyes alerted her to the underlying promise in his bold query. She found herself nodding mutely, hoping his passion would set her afire, freeing her from the memory of another's touch. His brows drew together for the space of a heartbeat, and then his mouth was on hers, the tip of his tongue gently prodding her lips apart. She opened to him, and his tongue delved quickly in, plying hers with lavish expertise.

His arms pressed her closer, and with damnable detachment she heard his sound of pleasure muffled against her mouth, felt the increased tempo of his heartbeat.

The subtle tightening of her muscles, a drawing away of the spirit more than the flesh, pierced Giles' own pleasure. Being a man well attuned to the nuance of physical pleasure, and more, being a gentleman, he released her.

Her hands fell abruptly to her sides. Her eyes shone, awash with tears, deep green in her pale face.

"And now, it appears, an apology *is* required. Allow me to escort you back to the ballroom, Lady Cat," Giles said, concerned that her ardent response had frightened her.

Cat came close to weeping. The handsome, the refined, the elegant Marquis of Strand had just had his tongue in her mouth, and now he was using her formal title. He had wanted her. If only her own wayward heart hadn't refused to comply with the demands of her mind. She had spent months throwing herself at him, seeking to gain his undivided attention.

Oh, he was intrigued right enough. But she was not. In her frantic efforts to purge from her mind the memory of Thomas' firm mouth, she had allowed Giles a few overly warm embraces. Each new liberty only pointed up how his caresses failed to elicit an answering heat in her.

He was still a paragon amongst his countrymen, still as slender, elegant, and refined as in previous years. His gilt masculine beauty was as startling, his urbane wit as amusing, his manner as cosmopolitan. And yet, Cat found, to her growing dismay, Lord Strand's mouth was cool. His arms, though sinewy and strong and quite willing to pull her close, did so with measured determination rather than need. No amount of his fondling would awake in her the fire kindled by Thomas' restraint.

No, any tears she might shed were those of frustration, for his touch left her apathetic. Not provoked, or frightened, merely . . . pestered.

Nearly wincing, she laid her fingers lightly on Giles' proffered arm. Damn her memory. Damn her stupid heart. Damn Thomas Montrose!

Chapter 16

Hecuba looked up from her conversation with the old Marquis de Grenville, her eyes bright, her cheeks as pink as a maid's. The smile faltered on her lips.

"Back already, are you?" she grumbled at Cat and Giles.

"Oh, I think you can bear my company a short while, Aunt. Lord Strand has offered to fetch us a refreshment," Cat said, as Strand bowed himself away.

Hecuba, having spent as much time on Cat as she felt common courtesy demanded, turned back to her companion, ignoring her niece completely. Looking around the ballroom, Cat recognized many of the same people she had spent the past four seasons with in London.

English society had invaded Paris. In closed company, the English strolled the streets of Paris, exclaiming over Napoleon's artistic embellishments to the fabled city. They adopted French dress, savored French foods, and drained stockpiles of French wine.

Though the recent war had left the defeated French officers sullen, the tradesmen were delighted with waves of rich foreigners, hungry for the styles, the flair, the savoir faire, of previously forbidden Paris. There, were unfortunately, "difficulties" with

189

the discharged French officers. The English treated them with barely concealed contempt. Only the dispossessed French aristocracy, many of whom had familial ties to England, were treated with any respect.

The situation had degenerated to a shocking state; reported confrontations between French and English were becoming common. Increasing numbers of young men, ignoring the laws against dueling, were left bleeding to death on the grassy verges just outside of town. In order to traverse the great, dirty, dark network of twining alleys that was Paris, armed guards had to be hired to protect private coaches.

France no longer felt so safe to Cat. There were rumors Napoleon had escaped from Elba and was planning a march on Paris. Most of her countrymen sniffed at the suggestion. The little emperor's back had been broken; he would not soon come to the site of his ignominy. Cat was no longer so sure.

But the thought of returning to England, the small, though real, chance of encountering Thomas, caused Cat to extend her stay. She was a coward, she acknowledged bitterly. Her lengthy visit had, however, an unforeseen boon. She had received a letter from her erstwhile parent. Her mother and Philip proposed to be arriving in Paris in a few days. Because the missive had been posted some time ago, it had found its way to Cat with England's latest diplomatic attaché, Colonel Seward. Perhaps, she found herself hoping, she would not have to wed at all, at least not yet, not until the memory had faded.

Cat made her way to a withdrawing area for the female guests. Tilting her chin in recognition of an acquaintance, she settled herself in front of a mirror. A maid offered her a small sachet, which she dabbed on her throat. After her unproductive encounter with Strand, she needed a few minutes in which to gather her resolve.

The gentle, polite murmurings of refined beauties closeted together without the benefit of friendship was interrupted by a sharper voice breaking through her preoccupation.

"Sinjin will have to look to his laurels. He won't have the ladies fawning over him quite so easily, now that some real competition is here."

"Oh, surely *Monsieur Ruin* is a bit too old to cause much fluttering amongst the current flock of chicks," a bored voice drawled.

"You haven't seen him yet, have you?" came the openly amused reply. "A great, dark, dangerous-looking animal, he is. Beautiful, not in the languishing, self-aware manner of Byron, but beautiful like a bold, blooded steed. Oh, I assure you, he is quite capable of causing a stir amongst the youngest chicks . . . as well as the older hens."

"Why did he quit the *ton*?"

" 'Tis said he found it too tame. I know he was rumored to frequent the more dissolute circles of Europe. It stands to reason naughty Paris would charm him. I am not at all surprised to find him here."

The voices faded as the two ladies left. Cat stared, unseeing, at her own image. Desperately she told herself she was growing obsessed with Thomas. There must be any number of large, dark males in Paris. The overheard remarks need not be about him. She smoothed the gleaming cap of her hair, fidgeting with the escaped tendrils. After all, when she had found him, Thomas had been in Devon firmly planted in his pasture, not in the corrupt courts of foreign princes.

Noticing how pale her lips were, Cat applied a bit of the bright red salve Aunt Hecuba had secreted in her reticule. The color was a dark slash in the dimly lit room, but as Cat stepped out into the ballroom, brilliant with taper, oil, and chandelier, her mouth glistened like a ruby enticement.

At once she saw Thomas Montrose standing across the room. It seemed both inevitable and as though she were seeing him in a dream. The shift and pulse of moving figures obscured him momentarily. Craning her neck, she stared, sure this was some vision.

It *was* Thomas. But Thomas as she had never seen him. He was clad in close-fitting dark evening dress, his shirt flawless white linen, his cravat a snowy foil to his swarthy complexion. He was listening politely to one of his companions, but his eyes traveled the occupants of the room in a slow perusal even as he bent from his great height to catch the words of a jewel-bedecked beauty. He looked thinner and taller, darker and more dangerous. It was impossible to tell whether he had shed a camouflage or adopted one, so smooth and assured was his address, so polished and graceful his movements. An image of a Roman statue, a centaur, came unbidden to her mind. All muscle and sinew, power and grace. Flustered, Cat turned, seeking escape. Her heartbeat was suddenly too fast, her breath hard to catch.

Thomas listened with feigned interest to the unblushing invitation of the woman at his side. To be once more in Paris, listening to feminine French voices speaking overly familiar words, raised specters Thomas would have just as soon left buried. He had looked around, a tiny frisson of desperation in his scrutiny, searching to see if Mariette Leons was there, knowing she wouldn't be. Instead he had seen Cat.

She laid his ghosts. There was simply no room for specters when Cat was nearby. Even though all he had was a brief, tantalizing glimpse of gleaming blue and satiny pink flesh, immediately lost in the crowd.

With scintillating results, Cat had wholeheartedly embraced the French styles. No anemic little muslins for her. She wore a shimmering silk gown in an iridescent peacock blue. Her skirt was festooned with ribboned flounces. Her deeply cut bodice was adorned with brilliant gold embroidery.

Atop her gleaming nutmeg-colored curls, she had perched the most elaborate headpiece, a ridiculous construction of lace and huge feathers that dipped gently in time to the sway of her hips as she walked. On most women, it would have looked absurd, but Cat had in her eye something that acknowledged the absurdity, making it, incredibly enough, provocative.

Thomas left the woman in midproposition, with no more than a cursory bow. Cat was simply irresistible. He was drawn to her, regardless of what her reception of him might be. He was as unable to withstand her attraction as he was incapable of denying it.

The crowd shifted as he passed, an occasional hand laid upon his arm, familiar voices calling his name, all seeking to delay him, all ignored. And then he was behind her. The curve of her neck, the jut of her shoulder blade, the gentle indentation of her spine cloaked by the transparent purity of her skin, were all infinitely tempting to him. He wanted to reach out a single forefinger and trace her jaw.

"Lady Catherine."

She spun about, and, he clearly heard the hiss of silk settle about her feet. There was something of tears, the tiniest shadow of joy, before he saw it: distress so intense that his own sad smile became an acknowledgment of her pain as well as his own.

In this, at least, they were companions. And then it was gone.

The brilliance of that one brief moment of honesty was lost. Her lips reworked themselves into some acceptable expression. She jerked her chin up haughtily.

Ah, he thought wearily, *at least now I know my lines.*

"You'll get a crick in your neck doing that, Cat. Besides which, it has been done too often. Didn't I teach you that allure relies on the novel, not the hackneyed?"

A spark of anger flashed in her incredible eyes. Her chin climbed higher.

Better fire than ashes, Thomas thought.

"And, Cat, I fear you have given Fielding rather more of a free hand with your toilette than her talents warrant." He stepped back and perused her bejeweled, laced elegance with doubtful appreciation. "You look like some divergent form of a particularly gaudy butterfly."

There was no reply.

"And this silence. Very effective in creating a momentary mystique, but I fear you've overdone it a bit."

A young man in uniform approached from behind Cat, obviously intent on speaking to her, but Thomas could not let it end here. The look he shot the boy was deadly and proprietary. The lad veered sharply away.

Cat closed her eyes. Unwillingly Thomas reached out a hand. Her lids snapped open, the green fire dancing in smoky depths.

"What are you doing here?" she asked under her breath.

He turned to her in surprise. "I find I have a yen to indulge myself in . . . society." His eyes glimmered roguishly. This was, Cat reminded herself, his special milieu. He was acknowledged king of this very sort of innuendo. He was a rake; it is why she had sought him out. It was why Daphne Bernard had sought him out.

She raised her head determinedly and, smiling vivaciously, walked away. Only when she had gained the outer corridor leading off the ballroom did she discover that Thomas had shadowed her and was standing next to her, a tall, broad silhouette against the backlit glitter of the ballroom.

"So, Cat," he said, "how goes the game? Has the estimable Strap come up to scratch yet?"

"*Strand!* His name is *Strand!*"

"Ah yes, Strand. And has he?"

"No!"

She did not see his relief. The darkness spared him that.

"But he is at the precipice?"

Cat mistook the relief for amusement. "Yes!" she shot out. "Was I not a star pupil?"

"Oh, methinks there is some honing that might be done yet," Thomas answered. "And I, of course, in the spirit of true gamesmanship, humbly offer my services."

"Are you mocking me, sir?"

"Yes, ma'am, I believe I am," he said suavely.

She glared at him, unaware how bewitching she looked, her hair gleaming like burnished bronze in the lamplight, her green eyes as mystical as a woodland pond, her breasts rising and falling in fascinating agitation. He was content to devour her with his eyes, unsure why he needed to goad her to anger, only aware he had been transfixed by the fear that her bid for Strand might have worked.

Suddenly Cat was before him, a beguiling smile on her lips, her arms about his neck, tugging him down to her. Momentarily startled, he allowed himself to be drawn toward those parted lips. He felt the soft, warm wash of her breath over his mouth. Reflexively he sought her lips with his. But she held him back. Her eyes danced wickedly, triumphantly, into his own dazed ones.

"Caught you off guard, Milord Libertine? Mayhaps you have been too long from town, and 'tis *I* can offer *you* some instruction?" she suggested sweetly.

But he was master of himself once more, and he only leered down at her, straining forward over her. "Whatever lessons you wish to bestow, I am all aquiver to receive," he countered, daring her with the velvet of his voice to continue the contest.

She stepped back from him, away from the fear their intimacy aroused, away from the danger of his offhanded bid for her, knowing the same bid had been made and accepted by Daphne Bernard so few months ago.

"Damn you for being so good at this!" she spat.

When all was said and done, Thomas was a gentleman. If his impulses were punishing him with a need to continue his mouth's descent, he was well aware that impulse was misplaced. He stepped back from her.

"Well, after all, Cat, I have been at it much longer than you."

"Oh, then I can look toward my dim and distant future years with the hope of being able to play at seduction with the same sure-handedness that you do?"

"If you so wish," he said quietly.

"Why are you here, Thomas?" she asked once more. "And no double meanings now, if you please. I am not a prospective conquest. I would you did not treat me as such."

He shrugged in feigned hopelessness. "I cannot help it, Cat. It is an involuntary reaction I have whenever I am in the vicinity of a well-favored dame. My cross, but I bear it as well I can."

To his chagrin, he found her opinion mattered to him. Thomas awaited her words with more concern than he had known in a lifetime of imprudence and self-indulgence. He cursed as he watched faint color stain her cheeks.

"Excuse me, Cat. You do it so well, I forget this is only a cloak you have donned and not real. I fear old age has made me forget appearances are, after all, deceiving."

She was angry she had blushed. His soft words, ringing with patronage, goaded her to speak the first words she could think that might shake him from his benevolent complaisance.

"I have been here a fortnight, Thomas, and have put into practice what you have taught. I am well on my way to becoming in fact the fiction we authored. But silly me, here I was studying for advanced degrees when I had not even mastered the rudiments. There simply is no teacher in Paris who can offer me all of your experience and expertise. There is nothing for it, *Monsieur Ruin*; you shall have to take me back under your wing and become the *newest* of my lovers."

His face leeching of color, Thomas staggered back a step as though she had struck him. He raised a hand and, finding it shaking, let it fall to his side. He stared at her a for long moment before bowing stiffly. "I congratulate you." Turning blindly from her, he strode through the door.

He did not see the tears that slipped unchecked down her cheek, nor hear her soft litany after he had gone.

"Damn, oh damn, oh . . ."

Chapter 17

Thomas made it to the Mertons' library, feeling as though the hounds of hell themselves were on his heels. He shut the door with exaggerated care before bracing his arms on the back of a convenient chair. Dragging great breaths of air into his lungs, he shut his eyes against the image Cat's words had invoked. Cat and her "lovers." A new wave of pain gripped him.

An unseen hand rapped against the door. He turned with a feral snarl. Another applicant for his favors? Yet another forward little filly eager to see if his reputation stood the test of time? Eager to try his oft-tried body and see if his finesse, or dimensions, or staying power, or whatever the hell they sought, justified the reports?

He prowled to the door. He ought to throw the unknown woman's skirts up and take her against the wall. But, for all his sins, Thomas had never taken pleasure in causing pain, or found the idea stimulating in any manner, and so he threw open the door with nothing more than words to protect himself from any rapacious petition.

Giles Dalton, Lord Strand, lounged against the doorjamb. The quip died on his tongue as his discerning eye took in the caged quality of his friend's stance.

199

"Why didn't you tell me?" Giles asked quietly.

"Tell you what?" Thomas shot back.

Strand entered the room, his usual casualness absent. Some people said Thomas' self-possession bordered on the cold-blooded. In the many years Giles had known and worked with Thomas, only once had Strand seen him lose that self-control. The much-tortured and abused body of a French informant, not much more than a boy, had been dumped outside the inn where they waited. The perpetrators had paid. Thomas, with his bare hands, had beaten one of them to near death. His expression now was similar to the one he had worn then: rage and indescribable grief.

Strand closed the door behind him. "You should have said she was important to you."

"I thought it was clear."

"You implied a brotherly concern. You did not say you loved her."

Thomas didn't bother denying it. Not to Giles, one of his few close friends. "And what difference would that have made?" Thomas asked. "Would your vigilance have been any less? Besides which, the lady had set her mind on *your* own seduction long ere I met her. Who am I to stand in the way of love's true path?"

"Lady Catherine doesn't love me," Strand said uncomfortably.

"She might."

"She might already be in love."

"Not with me. My God. She has just gone to considerable pains to tell me she has had *lovers* since arriving in Paris. I know she was hurt, but I never knew her hurt had turned to hatred. And hatred is the only emotion I know of strong enough to make my little pragmatist imperil all her plans for a spot of revenge."

"She was lying," said Strand.

Thomas wheeled about, his expression sardonic. "I know she was lying. And I also know why. She wanted to draw blood. Lord, she must despise me to risk her reputation so! Any number of people could have overheard her! Thank God, I do not think any did."

Strand's nonchalance was tested by his own concerns for both Thomas and Cat. He had no solace to offer Thomas. He did not know what had caused Lady Cat to make such a dangerous claim, nor why she felt she must torment Thomas with such a patent, easily discovered lie. Strand had watched, unobserved, the moment of their meeting. Invisible strings had drawn Thomas headlong to Cat's side. His course to her had been unerringly direct, his attention concentrated.

All of Strand's plans to marry Cat had dissolved as he had watched Thomas' rapt progress. And he could not help but mourn her loss.

"One could wish you had informed me of how things stood, Thomas."

"There was nothing to inform you of. Nothing has changed. The lady sought my expertise in the matter of seduction. You were, and are, the motive for the request. But you know that. Good God, man, all society knows it! She ain't the most subtle thing." Thomas' smile was bittersweet.

"Thomas . . ."

"No. Cat has elected you as best fitting her designs. You'd be a bigger fool than I if you turned your back on such a gift. Marry her, Strand. Marry her now, and take her out of Paris. Tonight. It isn't safe to stay."

"I cannot." Strand's mobile face was fixed.

"What, then? You needn't fear I will spend the rest of my days littering the halls of your family manse, languishing heartfelt sighs each time the lady passes. Too embarrassing for everyone involved. Cat would probably stir me up an emetic should I indulge myself thus. No, I will take myself out of her scope until I can attend her with the most passionate disinterest."

Thomas was unaware his hands trembled nearly indiscernibly at his side. But Strand saw the betraying motion and turned his back on Thomas to study the titles of the myriad books lining the walls.

"I would," Strand said after long minutes. "It doesn't particularly please me to acknowledge it, but I would marry her. It seems I am forced to acknowledge that at heart I am an overindulged child. Because, having grown accustomed to thinking Cat was mine for the asking, I am most discomforted to find that which I took for granted is, after all, no sure thing.

"There is nothing so sweet to the juvenile mind than that which might be denied," he went on. "And so, in hindsight, Lady Cat is not merely a comely chit who dresses well. She is a paragon of womanhood. Her wit is sharper, her intellect keener, her beauty more stunning . . . all because it might be refused me. Or perhaps I simply see her more clearly. Or perhaps you see her most clearly, and I have borrowed your eyes. I cannot say. But I would marry her. If I could."

Strand did not turn. He did not want to see the contempt on Thomas' face.

In the charged silence, the door once more opened silently on well-oiled hinges. Strand composed his features to bland indifference before turning. Colonel Henry Seward entered, his light frame clothed in a military uniform.

"I'd thought you would be gone by now," Seward said in surprise.

Strand did not answer him, addressing Thomas instead. "And that is why I cannot. His Majesty's intrigues, once more, take precedence over my own. I am sent south."

"Why?" Thomas demanded.

"Napoleon has escaped from Elba," Seward said quietly. "Already there are blockades being set up in some of the outlying villages. He is accumulating an army with each step he takes."

Thomas wheeled on Strand. His tone was frigid. "And you would have left her here?"

Strand's chin snapped up. "I have admitted to some unpleasant traits. Ignoring my obligations is not one of them. Seward will accompany Lady Catherine to Dieppe."

"Impossible," Seward said. "I have arranged her passage on a packet out of Brighton, but I cannot see her to Dieppe to meet it. Napoleon is reported to have mustered nearly seven thousand men. I cannot leave Paris now."

"Bloody hell," growled Thomas.

"You'd best leave now, Strand, while the roads south are still open," Seward said, the alarm in his voice adding impetus to his words.

"Of course. Thomas." Strand turned, and his gaze locked with Thomas'. "I would have found some way of guaranteeing her safe conduct."

"I know," Thomas replied gravely. "Safe journey, my friend."

A smile, of relief and amusement, broke over Strand's features, returning them to their more accustomed expression of careless charm.

"After you see her home, you can always come back and play," Strand suggested, and then was gone. Seward, following behind, paused.

"The packet leaves in four days. I don't know when there will be another."

"Confound it, Catherine!" Hecuba said, flopping down on the bed beside her great-niece. "I'd thought you were over these self-indulgent histrionics. Of all the dratted times to come down with a case of weeps!"

Cat answered by burying her face deeper into the pillow. Hecuba sighed and scowled at Fielding, hovering ineffectually at the foot of the bed.

"Go away, Fielding. All that compassionate fluttering is only encouraging the gel. Go fold my dresses, or flirt with the doorman, or . . . oh, just go!" Fielding bobbed a curtsey and fled.

"Now," Hecuba said, reaching out a beringed, veined hand to stroke the silky tangle of Cat's hair, "tell me what this is about. And none of your gulping disclaimers this time, m'girl! I spent a fortnight listening to you muffle your sobs—and a bad job you made of it too—and I've no time to waste. Now, out with it!"

Cat lifted her face. Her tears had streaked her cheeks with little rivulets of gummy face powder. The skin beneath was splotched red. Her eyes were wounded, stricken.

Hecuba paused in divesting her bodice of wads of stuffed cotton, "bust improvers" she had lately begun using in order to augment her figure. Once more she sighed.

"It's Thomas Montrose, ain't it?"

Cat's lower lip trembled.

"I knew he was trouble the instant I laid eyes on him. Far too dangerous-looking. The sort who excites the reckless quality in a woman, makes her want to take a peek at the black side of her nature, to embrace the untamed impulses which . . ." Hecuba's eyes had glazed over in enthralled speculation. She dragged herself back to the matter at hand.

"Whatever *did* happen in Brighton, Catherine?"

"He . . . he . . . I can't say!" Cat said tearfully.

"Did that scoundrel take advantage of you while

you were under his care?! That blackguard! There are rules that all men, no matter how base, must attend to, and to take advantage of a young, chaste girl—"

"He didn't take advantage of *me*!" Cat wailed.

"Oh." Hecuba withdrew the last piece of padding from her gown; the bodice hung limply on her withered chest.

"And is *that* the problem?" Hecuba asked.

Cat thrust her head back under the down-filled pillow.

"Oh," Hecuba said once more.

The word spurred an instant reaction from Cat. She bolted upright, her eyes flashing. "I wouldn't want him. He's depraved."

Incredibly, Hecuba smiled. "I would have said Thomas Montrose capable of a good many things, but depravity isn't one of them."

"But he is!" Cat nodded vigorously.

"Tell me."

"I saw him, Aunt Hecuba. The night of the Regent's fete. After he escorted you back to the hotel . . . he arranged an assignation with that . . . that . . . French . . ."

"Whore?"

"Yes!"

"And how do you know this, Catherine?"

"Because I saw them!"

Hecuba lifted a brow in question.

"I went to his room . . . to thank him for helping you," Cat said.

"Such manners! Prompt, as well as pretty," Hecuba murmured sardonically.

" 'Tis true! His door swung ajar when I started to knock on it, and I just looked in. Aunt Hecuba! That woman was twined about him, and he was naked to the waist. She was kissing his bare chest, and his head was thrown back! Oh God! He opened his eyes and saw me in the mirror standing there!"

"Oh!" For the first time in Cat's memory, Hecuba looked flustered. Her great-aunt cleared her voice repeatedly before asking, "And what happened next?"

"Next? I ran back to my room, of course."

"And Thomas?"

"He came in the morning, and thundered at the door. I couldn't face him."

"Catherine, that hardly seems the act of a debauched satyr. Could you have misconstrued the situation?"

Even though Cat's face was puffed and tears still trickled from the corners of her eyes, her mouth twisted in caustic disbelief.

"I am still unconvinced," Hecuba said in reply to the volumes Cat's expression spoke. "I have always felt Thomas held you in no little esteem. He has always been most careful of you. Far more so than you, a sheltered, unwed woman, could ever hope to realize. To have him so blatantly . . . It just don't fit. Unless . . . Catherine, you weren't toying with him, were you?"

"I don't understand," Cat said, but her eyes refused to meet her great-aunt's penetrating gaze.

"Catherine, a man has certain bodily functions which he is at the mercy of. Certain women do, too. When the natural inclinations of men, and those certain, fortunate women, have been provoked, they seek a means of expressing them. If their initial impulse is denied them, for whatever reason, they naturally seek another means. Do I make myself clear?"

"No."

"Cat, if you teased the poor man into physical pain, he might have sought a willing piece of flesh to act as a substitute for that which societal and ethical codes forbade him. You."

"Oh," Cat said in surprise. Then, after a moment's consideration, she added, "But that doesn't make what he did right."

"We aren't talking *right*, Catherine. We are talking expedient! Believe me, when the itch is upon you, a self-encouraging clap on the back ain't going to scratch it! My advice to you is to simply ignore the whole episode."

A fresh battery of tears spilled from Cat's eyes.

"What now?" demanded Hecuba in exasperation.

"I can't ignore the whole thing! Not two hours ago, I told him that I had taken lovers!"

"Oh, Cat! *Lovers?* Whatever possessed you? Don't answer. I already know. And how did Thomas react?"

"Oh, Aunt Hecuba, he looked disgusted! I could see it. He might as well have shouted out that I lied. And then he just turned and walked away."

"Well, at least someone managed to keep his head," snorted Hecuba.

"I wanted so to impress him with my sophistication, my social triumph. I wanted to prove to him he was not the only one who was attractive. All I succeeded in doing was making myself look like a complete idiot."

"Thank God your mother will be here in two days. These are subtleties I cannot afford to deal with now. Your mother will know what to do," Hecuba muttered to herself.

Hearing the fretful note lacing her great-aunt's tone, Cat was reminded of how old and frail she was. Immediately Cat was sorry for having dumped her problems into Hecuba's aged lap.

"I know what to do, Aunt Hecuba. I have set

out to become a sophisticated woman, but have forgotten the practical aspects of my lessons. One must accept what one has no power to change. I cannot erase that French whore from Thomas' history, but I needn't align myself with her ilk. I shall apologize to Thomas on the morrow. Even if it kills me."

Hecuba was still twisting her hands together in her lap.

"Catherine, you really are the most sensible woman I have ever known."

"Thank you."

"But pragmatism is not always satisfying. Sometimes, Catherine, we must allow ourselves to fly in the face of convention. We must embrace the opportunities we are presented in order to find fulfillment. I will not say happiness—I know your views on that emotion—but I must say love. If I ever had the chance to try once more for love, I would take it. I would have to. And I would expect nothing less from you.

"Cat, I have had a long history with that emotion. Sometimes mere approximations. Sometimes illusively near. Once in a very great while, wonderfully, painfully real. For a time I had forgotten that, whatever the cost, even the mere chance of loving and being loved is worth everything we own or are or aspire to be. Don't let practical considerations rob you of it. I won't." Hecuba said the last words as though making a vow to herself. Then, looking as surprised with herself as Cat obviously was, she leaned down and placed her cool, papery-thin cheek next to Cat's hot, damp one.

She kissed Cat, wrapping her arms around her young body, hugging her tightly.

"For all my brave words, I am still a bit of a coward," Hecuba whispered, releasing her. She stood up, collecting the pieces of padding that littered the wrinkled counterpane.

"Your mother will be here in a few days, and all will be well. And really, Catherine, leave off the bawling . . . Your nose runs."

Chapter 18

Cat woke with a very cold nose. She burrowed under the cashmere blankets Fielding had heaped on her and squinted out from beneath the piles. It had to be very early. The brocade drapes were still shut against the tall window; only a faint ghostly light illuminated its outline in the dark room. It was odd no maid had arrived to stir the coals in the hearth to life, chasing the predawn chill from the dismal room. Odder still, Fielding was not up fomenting some new scheme to glamorize Great-Aunt Hecuba.

Fielding's allegiance had become fixed on the elderly duchess with a fierce, unexpected loyalty. With Hecuba's reentry into the world of fashion, Fielding's latent talent as a lady's maid had achieved full expression. She worried, fretted, and stewed over the tiniest detail of Hecuba's toilette. It wasn't that Fielding ignored Cat. It was merely that "gilding the lily ain't never so challenging as forcing a bloom on old wood."

Far into the night, Cat had listened to their muffled voices as Fielding administered to Great-Aunt Hecuba's headache. She had spent those hours trying to think of some way to approach Thomas and still retain her dignity. As she had finally fallen asleep, the image of the quick, derisive curl of Thomas' lip before he strode away had chased her into her dreams. With morning, the image returned to haunt her.

Finding it impossible to fall back asleep, Cat dropped her feet onto the cold floor. Wrapping a blanket about her shoulders, she went to ask Fielding to fetch her a cup of chocolate. As she tapped lightly on the door adjoining their suites, she glanced over at the clock on the mantel. It was nine. Far past time for Fielding to be up and about. Frowning, Cat rapped harder until finally, in concern, she opened the door.

The room was in havoc. Dresses, undergarments, shawls, and gloves were piled atop every available surface. A few pieces of jewelry were tangled with fans, ribbons, and pots of face powder, paint, and perfume. The armoire doors stood ajar, disinterred of all clothing. Trunks, half-packed, sat open on the floor.

Cat entered slowly, a feeling of unreality settling over her as, in growing confusion, she looked about the room. A letter stood propped against a vase of fading flowers, her name scrawled on it in her great-aunt's elegant hand. Shivering slightly in the draft, Cat opened it.

My dearest Catherine,

I have taken Fielding. She insisted, and as the slight enhancements I have adopted require a sure and youthful hand, I have agreed. I am sure your dear mama will be willing to share her maid's services with you when she arrives. Quite simply, I have eloped with the Marquis de Grenville. I have no desire to be badgered by the well-meaning but erroneous hand-wringing of either you or your mother.

Affectionately,
Hecuba Montaigne White

There was a postscript:

The pendant is, of course, paste, but a fine enough facsimile to fetch a pretty sum should you need it.
Burn the black bombazines.

Cat shook the envelope. A large, multifaceted gem slithered into her palm, trailed by a simple filigreed gold chain. Even in the dull half-light, it gleamed brightly. Cat stared at it. Slowly a bemused smile replaced her concerned expression.

Hecuba had flown the coop with that old rooster! Cat imagined the frantic packing, the hasty departure, the headlong flight from Paris, putting as much distance between themselves and her mother's ire as a twenty-four-hour head start allowed. Hecuba hadn't wanted to be dissuaded, or patronized, or stopped. There was still a bloom in the old wood after all. Cat laughed outright.

The old fake! Four years of sermons on base physical unions, self-restraint, and the evils of self-indulgence, all thrown over for an antiquated, spindle-shanked marquis with a twinkle in his rheumy old eye.

Cat's smile turned tender. Last night's uncharacteristic kiss made sense now. Hecuba had been saying good-bye. Cat stared down at the bright bauble in her hand, Hecuba's parting gift.

"Godspeed," Cat said softly. She sighed and padded back to her room, to dress as best she could.

After struggling into one of her warmer gowns, Cat jerked open the drapes, promising herself a word with the management regarding the lax manner in which the maids conducted themselves. They should have attended the room hours ago. The sky outside was leaden, heavy with low, scuttling clouds. Icy pellets skittered against the window-pane, borne by a rising wind. Few people braved the ugly-looking weather on the street below her.

Cat turned away from the depressing scene, hoping Hecuba had managed to outrun the weather. There was nothing left to do now but stay out of society's eye until her mother arrived. It should be simple enough. No one need know she was alone, unchaperoned by so much as a maid, for twenty-four hours. If they did find out, she might as well kiss good-bye any social aspirations she entertained.

Unfortunately, she was growing hungry. Her stomach growled in response to her thoughts. She had missed the late supper at Merton's last night, having fled directly from her disastrous encounter with Thomas. The memory brought back the wave of unhappiness Hecuba's elopement had momentarily displaced. She would avoid any future meetings with Thomas *after* she proved her integrity by offering him an apology for her outrageous words.

But she could not deny a frisson of anticipation at the thought of seeing him. He had looked so masculine, so intense, so darkly beautiful. He had lost weight. His big, lazy, bull-like strength had been pared down to pantherish leanness, his skin burnt dark, making the pewter streaks in his black locks gleam brighter in contrast. She refused to think of his expression of stunned incredulity at her scandalous words. But she could not rid herself of the image of him, his head rigidly upright, his shoulders squared with contempt, as he put distance between them as quickly as possible.

Well, she thought impatiently, she couldn't just sit here staring out the window for the rest of the day, particularly as the chambermaid seemed to have gone on holiday. She would have to get something to eat. Surely a midmorning repast would not provoke comment. Afterward she would arrange to have the rest of her meals sent to her room.

Cat looked down at the paste pendant she had been absently toying with. Pocketing it, she draped a shawl around her shoulders and left. When she reached the main lobby, she was pleased to find there were few people there. A small queue, everyone garbed for travel, was gathered at the doors. They were surrounded by traveling equipage: Trunks, cases, boxes, and portmanteaus were unceremoniously heaped into piles. Voices throbbed in a low, collective hum of murmured conversation.

One of the ladies, an acquaintance of Cat's, raised her head. Seeing Cat, she leaned close to her husband and whispered in his ear. His head shot up. Scowling, he broke away from the group. Forcing down her uneasiness, Cat schooled her features into polite recognition.

"Lady Catherine," the gentleman said, "has Lady Montaigne White been able to procure passage from the city?"

Cat didn't know what to say in response to this odd question, but unwilling to draw attention to herself, she nodded.

He blew out his breath in what seemed to be relief, bobbing his head in approval. "Good. I told my wife she undoubtedly had, but one must take every care. Lovely young lady like yourself. Where will you be heading? Near Rouen, I expect. Seems everyone is heading that way. Well then, good. Best of luck, Lady Catherine, and to your great-aunt, of course."

He bowed before returning to his anxiously waiting wife. Cat frowned. *Luck?* What on earth did luck have to do with a journey? She considered following the man and demanding an explanation, but then he might discover Aunt Hecuba was not upstairs drinking a treacly cup of tea. Instead, Cat strolled past the group, offering the worried-looking lady a reassuring, if confused, smile as she entered the hotel's small café.

Something was not right. Even at this early hour, there should have been more people here, mulling over last night's party, dissecting both the elaborate arrangements and their hostess's social prowess. There was only one other couple in the large room, their table drawn close to an exterior window. They bent over their plates, speaking in hushed voices as they stared out into the street.

The maitre d' arrived, breathless and distracted, to seat her with bare civility at a table in front of the far window. It was a full twenty minutes before a young man arrived, a stained apron tied around his skinny waist. He sloshed tea into her cup and slipped a plate of cold toast in front of her, hurrying off before Cat could frame a request for heartier fare.

Bewildered, she turned in her seat. She craned her neck, looking out the window to see what so riveted the attention of the other couple. Three men stood at the bottom of the hotel's steps, their arms raised in emphatic gestures, their faces contorted with anger as they shouted indiscernible words to the driver of an open landau. Cat could not believe they were arguing over so patently unacceptable a vehicle. The sleet had iced the tarnished rails and sides of the carriage. The ragged top, stuck a quarter of the way up, did nothing to shelter the torn leather benches from the elements. The seats shone slickly, soaked wet beneath the driving wind. And yet, incredibly, the men seemed about to come to blows over its hire.

The laconic-looking driver sat motionlessly, only

his eyes flickering with avaricious interest. Finally one gentleman tossed a weighty-looking purse up to him. The driver's hand shot out, grabbing it as he jerked his head toward the rear of his carriage.

Immediately four women and three other men, including the couple from the lobby, skittered down the icy stairs. The women scrambled, unaided, into the carriage while the men tossed trunks and cases pell-mell into the back. The driver shouted something above the raucous complaints of the outbid men, and abruptly the four men hauled themselves up and over the handrails, squatting on the floor between the benches, as there was no room for them to sit.

The landau jerked forward. One of the women pointed at something left amongst the boxes and trunks still piled on the side of the street, tears streaming down her already wet face, her mouth framing a silent plea as the carriage lurched drunkenly around the corner and was lost to sight.

Cat sat back, confused and anxious, as the remaining men, their shoulders bowed against the rain, retreated back into the hotel.

Fear, insidious and gnawing, stalked Cat's thoughts. She hailed the waiter and was ignored. She lifted the now cold tea to her lips but set the cup down when she noted the amber liquid shiver in response to her trembling hands.

"Lady Cat, *oui*?"

Cat jerked her head up. Daphne Bernard stood beside her. The Frenchwoman's dark head was raised, her eyes darting nervously around the nearly deserted room. Tiny lines of dissipation showed clearly in the unkind, flat gray light. The corded muscles stood out in her too slender neck. Her lips, which Cat remembered as being so red, were thin, bloodless lines. Only her eyes glittered as she continued her survey of the room. She looked down at Cat and tried a smile.

"Lady Cat, am I not right?" she said brightly. "But how could one forget *la belle Anglaise?*" She spread the dark skirts of her traveling gown and sank gracefully down.

"I sit."

Cat felt her mouth tighten with disapproval. "I would prefer not."

Daphne's eyes shot toward her, briefly arrested in their eerie continuous movement. She stared at Cat in genuine surprise. "But why not? You are the victor! You have the so masculine Thomas securely beneath your English thumb. Why would you not accept your victory with graciousness? How rude, you English!"

Daphne frowned, twin lines appearing between her thin brows. "*Ma chère*, we are in no place for groundless animosity. *I* am the injured party. After all, Thomas threw me out. Certainly he has told you so. Why else would a man throw out a woman who was offering him pleasure if not to relate so heroic a deed to his *amour*? Yet I, I who am most offended, I take no offense! I forgive! I am munificent!"

"He threw you out?" Cat asked before she could stop herself.

Daphne's eyes opened even wider. "He did not tell you? Oh, Thomas! Not only noble and heroic, but stupid! Bah!" Daphne laughed, but hearing the amplified echoes in the silent room, suddenly stopped, quickly turning her head once more in her unnerving search.

"Yes," she continued quietly. "He threw me out. Oh, not bodily. But he raged so, breaking much furniture. I decided it is advisable for me to leave. I leave."

"I do not believe you."

"No? Oh." Daphne shrugged. "What difference to me that you do not believe? None. Do not believe. Stupidity is an English trait."

Calmly claiming Cat's cup of tea, Daphne quickly drained the fluid before settling back in her chair. She rested her palms flat against the table and looked over at Cat, for all the world as though they were dear friends discussing the latest acquisition at the lending library.

"So Thomas has procured you passage out of this accursed city?"

"No, he has not. I am waiting for my mother and her husband to arrive."

"Then you shall be waiting a long, long time, *ma chère*. There is no way into the city now. And soon, as you well know, there will be no way out."

"What?" Cat asked in astonishment.

"The city, she is closed."

"What?!"

"*Tiens!* Surely you have heard." Daphne frowned at her. "The Russians, the Prussians, they have been leaving the city for days. How could you have not noticed? Ah! I forget how insular you English are, so unwilling to associate with foreigners, even when you yourselves are the interlopers. But surely, last night . . . your baronet, Lord Arbothnut, he rode from Cannes with the news."

"What news?!"

"Napoleon. He has escaped. He has landed in France and leads an army to retake Paris. Everyone is leaving. Fleeing. I would leave too if but I could," Daphne finished softly.

"Why? You are a Frenchwoman."

Daphne's mouth twisted into a wry smile. "You do not know this man who loves you very well, do you? You do not know what he is. I tell you.

"You see, I was much admired by many of Napoleon's advisors. Much admired. An acquaintance told me that certain things I had heard during some—how shall we say? romantic meetings?—could benefit your country. As my so beloved sister is now married to one of you *Anglaise*, I feel I have family obligations that superscede any national ones. Too, I am well paid for the risks I take.

"Your Sir Stuart arranges I give my information to someone it is not suspicious I meet. Someone with a reputation as . . . interesting as mine. Thomas. *Voilà!* Oh, I asked to meet with him more often, but I was told he dealt in more, how you say, tactical areas. So others of your *Anglaise* I meet. Yes, I know many, many of you aristocrats."

Thomas had been involved in espionage. Cat was stunned even as the odd bits and pieces of information about Thomas' past fell into place; his sudden, unaccountable retirement from society eight years ago, his perfect French accent, his military "friends." Thomas had been a spy.

Daphne's next words came to Cat as if from a long distance away. "But now my so good friends are gone, and I am left here. And Napoleon, he is not so very kind to those he feels have betrayed him. I dare not go to my house to even fetch my moneys. It is watched."

Daphne toyed with the empty cup of tea, her long fingers playing in tireless agitation. "Have you ever seen a person tortured, *ma chère*? I did not think so. It is very ugly. Much pain. Much screaming."

"What will you do?" The horror of Daphne's words produced an unexpected knot of concern in Cat's stomach, momentarily displacing her shock over Thomas' past.

"I do not know. I have a cousin outside of the city who would see me safely to Russia. There is a man there who does not forget me. But . . ." The lines deepened between her eyes. "I have nothing to offer the men guarding the blockades. They will never let me out without a bribe."

Daphne's eyes once more darted around the room and then settled, curiously blank and empty, on the tea leaves at the bottom of her cup.

Cat felt the lump of the pendant pressing against her leg. No one deserved to be tortured. Withdrawing the gem, she slid the bauble across the table in front of Daphne. It glittered and blinked, trapping the pale light and returning it as brilliant, dancing radiance. Cat heard the sharp intake of Daphne's breath.

"*C'est magnifique!*" Daphne exclaimed.

"*C'est* fake."

"Really?" Daphne held the pendant up to the window, studying it with a practiced eye. "Ah, yes. But such a good one!"

"If you are willing to risk having it discovered as paste, it's yours," Cat said.

Daphne's eyes held Cat's for the briefest of seconds before her fist closed in a tight knot over the sparkling glass. She rose at once, as though, having gotten from Cat what she wanted, she had no further use of her.

She looked down at Cat and found the Englishwoman's selfless act called forth a need in her to respond, just once, in kind.

"I did everything I could to seduce him. Everything. But he was already seduced far beyond my ability to compete. By you."

Cat made her way out of the café, her heart pounding painfully in her chest. She was alone, and no one was going to be coming for her. She was trapped without money, family, or friends. Fear worked on her, causing her legs to shake beneath her gown. She forced herself to walk calmly through the vacant lobby and up the stairs to her room.

She had to think. She couldn't give in to unproductive hysteria. She wiped her wet palms against the soft wool of her skirts. There had to be a way. There had to be. If only Thomas were here.

Her surprise at discovering he had been a spy had ebbed. It made so much sense in light of what she knew. But other things the Frenchwoman had said worked torturously on her. She wanted so much to believe Daphne's avowal that Thomas had resisted her.

And yet, Cat admitted to herself, it did not seem to matter to her heart what Thomas had done, or not done. The Frenchwoman's words gave justification for something her heart needed no reason for. She did not love Thomas more now than when she had been convinced of his amorality.

Even as she thought of him, her spirits fell. She did not know where he was; she only knew something must have kept him from her side. Thomas saw her as his responsibility. He would never willingly turn his back on such an obligation. She must have faith in him. She must believe he would be all right. To do otherwise was to court madness.

It was nearly eleven. She had to face facts: She was the only one who was going to get herself out of Paris. And there was no time to lose. If what Daphne had implied was correct, blockades were being set up even as she stood here in stupid immobility.

She went to Hecuba's room. Her aunt must have left something of value behind. Cat hastily rummaged through the abandoned piles of clothing and boxes. Fifteen minutes later, she sank onto the bed, her shoulders bowed in defeat. A pair of gold ear studs, a tourmaline brooch, a poorly made paste choker, a small cameo, and an emerald chip clasp lay pooled in her lap. She stared at the small hoard. Altogether they weren't worth as much as the paste pendant she'd given Daphne Bernard.

Tears blurred Cat's vision, and she dashed them away with the back of her hand. She would sign away her future if she wasted valuable time crying. She picked up a lump of something and worried it with her fingers, forcing herself to think. A sharp pin pricked her thumb, and she dropped the lump, sucking at the bead of blood. What the devil was the confounded thing, anyway? It was one of Aunt Hecuba's many "bust improvers." There were dozens of the things scattered all over the place.

Cat's eyes narrowed and she swiveled her head toward the vanity on which stood half-full pots of creams, lotions, and paints. Without a sound, she started to undress.

Monsieur Lebouef, manager of the hotel, watched the old lady hobble unsteadily down the grand stairway, her hands clutched around a small but heavy-looking portmanteau. So Lady Montaigne White has rededicated her life to God, he thought sardonically, noting the thick swathing of dark wool around the stout, bowed body, the heavy veil, and the iron crucifix. Well, he sighed, it was as good a time as any to befriend God. Soon the dispossessed would arrive, and they would not be friendly to those they considered traitors. God might not be such a bad idea.

Lady Montaigne White had reached the front door of the hotel. She was pulling her voluminous cape tightly about her. Perhaps the old girl was trying to fly without settling her considerable account with the hotel. Were the young and delicious Lady Cat with her, Monsieur Lebouef feared he would certainly have had to stop them. But Lady Cat had disappeared after breakfast. Irresolute, the manager stood, wondering if he should go after the ancient dame.

A sudden ear-shattering wail turned his attention toward the green baize door leading to the kitchens. One of the chambermaids, the one with a penchant for handsome English lordlings, was screaming that Napoleon's returning armies would surely kill her. They should be so kind, Monsieur Lebouef thought as, his course decided by this imminent crisis, he started for the kitchens.

He glanced over at the front door just in time to see the badly hemmed black skirts swish from view. He let her leave with a shrug of indifference. Where could she possibly run to, anyway?

Chapter 19

Seward's approximation of forty-eight hours before Paris heard of Napoleon's march had been wrong. Not long after Thomas had left Merton's, Peter Arbuthnot had arrived from the coast, breathless and disheveled. His garbled exhortations quickly deciphered, the other gentlemen had raised him onto their shoulders, from where he shouted, "Napoleon is in France! He marches on Paris!"

In the morning, a tidal wave of Englishmen flooded the streets trying to secure any means out of the city. Thomas rose late and, determined to confront Cat, went to hire a hack. There were none. Every available means of conveyance was occupied. Hay wagons pulled dukes and their duchesses. Drays carted lords and their ladies through the cold drizzle.

Thomas hurried the short distance to the Mertons' address, seeking Cat and Hecuba's location. The mansion was abandoned. Only a handful of servants remained gleefully, if fearfully, scavenging the treasures, toys, and pretties abandoned in the Mertons' haste to leave. Thomas pulled the French valet to his feet and demanded to know where Lady Cat was staying. The valet shook his head. Angrily Thomas flung him away. He went on to the next servant and then the next even as the minutes ticked away with brutal regularity: ten-thirty, three quarters past ten, and then eleven o'clock.

Finally a tweenie, the glint of greed sharp in her pale blue eyes, beckoned him forward to demand payment for her information. Wordlessly Thomas pressed a stack of sovereigns into her hand, and she spat a name at him before darting away.

Fontaine. He swore viciously. The Hotel Fontaine was miles across town. He left the house, the sharp pellets scoring his face as he jogged down the deserted streets, heading toward the river.

He had gone nearly two miles when he saw the horse. A small group of rough-looking men surrounded her as she danced at the end of her reins, made nervous by the press of the crowd. She was a big, ugly-looking nag, her eyes rolling in her great slab of a head.

Thomas was by her in a trice.

"How much?" he demanded of the men in their coarse patois. They eyed him suspiciously.

"You aren't going to turn around and sell her to some stinking English dog, are you?" one of the men asked.

Thomas flashed his teeth in a violent grin. "No. No. This horse carries me."

Another man stepped forward. "And what would a patriot want to run away for?"

Thomas grabbed him by the collar of his shirt, dragging him until he stood bare inches from Thomas' snarling face. "Who said I was running away?"

The other men shifted uneasily on their feet. Sweat and sleet had plastered Thomas' hair to his head and down his neck. His eyes burned in his workman-dark face. He appeared a true devotee of the cause.

"I go to join our general!" Thomas flung the man from him, flashing another fierce smile at the group.

"How much?!"

"What have you got?" a voice asked. A burly, potbellied man stepped forward.

Thomas fished into his pockets and withdrew a small leather purse. He untied the jesses and dumped twelve gold coins into his palm.

"This is what I have. Therefore, this must be her price." He grabbed the burly fellow's hand, forcing his fingers open, and pressed the gold into his palm.

"For Napoleon!" Thomas shouted, jerking the reins free and leaping onto the mare's broad back. He wheeled her around, rearing away from the little group.

Spurring her forward over the icy cobblestones, he pushed her hard, praying he would find Cat. A church bell tolled the noon hour.

Her shaking was due more to fear than the cold, Cat knew. Hecuba's "bust improvers" and her own dress worn beneath Hecuba's gown kept much of the biting wind from her flesh. She had thought the hotel manager was going to stop her; she had seen his eyes narrowing as she hobbled slowly past him. But she had made it. She was on the streets, committed to her plan to find a way out of Paris, away from Thomas. She forced herself not to think of him: where he was, what danger he was in.

The few carriages that passed hadn't even slowed when she hailed them. Cat fought down her panic. Her own resourcefulness was her only hope of exiting the city, and that virtue was being quickly depleted.

A wagon pulled by a pair of plow horses clattered around the corner. A group of English, eloquent in their rigid silence, was crowded onto the hay-covered bed.

Cat dropped her bag and jerked it open, fishing frantically for a piece of jewelry. Her hand closed on the paste collar and she thrust it over her head, shaking it so its glass prisms would catch the driver's eye.

The wagon was almost even with her now, and after a quick glance, the driver was once more clucking to the horses, urging them past her. An older gentleman, his face red and set, directed his angry gaze on her. His fleshy lower lip trembled before he lifted his walking stick and rapped the driver sharply on the shoulder. He said something to the man and—merciful heavens—the wagon pulled to a stop.

"It will be a fine day when an English gentleman abandons a lady!" the gray-haired man sputtered, reaching down for Cat.

"I can get much more than that *pauvre* necklace from someone else," grumbled the driver.

"I have more!" Cat gasped fearfully as she passed her portmanteau up to one of the men in the wagon.

"Now, now, m'dear. Do not concern yourself." Her savior patted her hand. "Come now, lads, help the lady!"

Three pairs of hands reached over and swung Cat up over the wagon's sides. One of the middle-aged women offered a distracted smile. The other ignored her. The little company retreated into silence as the wagon started forward.

Only the man who'd spoken revealed any emotion. His face, Cat surmised, was not red from the cold, but with barely restrained anger. He muttered to himself in sharp, vehement barks before noting Cat's stare, obscured though it was by the heavy veil.

"Excuse me, ma'am." He inclined his head in an abrupt, military nod. "Gerald Leades, of His Maj—"

"Gerald!" the woman who'd smiled at Cat gasped.

"Damnation! Am I to skulk about like some whipped cur while that miserable little, trumped-up—"

"Gerald!" the woman implored, laying a restraining hand on his arm. The couple's eyes locked. Abruptly the rage seeped from Leades' face, leaving on his florid countenance an odd combination of misery and tenderness.

"For you, Sally. Only for you," he whispered. He turned back to Cat. "My wife, Sally Leades."

"Lady Hecuba Montaigne White," Cat rasped.

"Honored, ma'am," the older woman said shyly.

The group fell into silence. A young English dandy appeared, panting breathlessly at the side of the wagon as he kept up with them. Wordlessly the men reached down to lift him over the side. He shook his head and pointed to several trunks piled on the curb some yards behind. As silently as hands had been offered, they were withdrawn, leaving the youth staring, openmouthed and astonished, in their wake.

"Fool!" said Leades, rage once more coloring his face.

"Lady Montaigne White, how is it you are alone during this crisis?" Sally Leades seemed to ask more to distract her husband than from any real interest.

"My footmen ran away. My maid was French," Cat answered, aware her words sounded curt, but afraid conversation would give her away. She knew the *haute ton*, comfortably reviewing her actions in London, would find no situation dire enough to justify an unchaperoned state.

The driver suddenly pulled the horses to a stop, pointing to a huge crowd gathered at the end of the street. "The blockades are up. We go no farther. Get out."

Stunned, the occupants of the wagon struggled to their feet, fear and uncertainty robbing them of argument. Except for Leades. His jowls quivering, he grated out, "How much?"

The driver shrugged, eager to be off and haul more passengers from one point of entrapment to another.

"There is nothing I can do. See? Blockade. Soldiers."

Leades pulled a purse from his greatcoat. It swung heavily from its leather thong. The driver watched its hypnotic movement as his hand slowly reached up toward it.

"Not yet," sneered Leades. "Not until we are past the blockade."

"You are too many," whined the driver.

"Take the women, then."

"*Oui, oui!* I will take the women."

"No!" Sally Leades cried out. "I won't go without you!"

Leades smiled, love and satisfaction equally mingled. "But you must, Sal. I shall be much better use to His Majesty with you safely on your way to England."

Gently he brushed his blunt fingertips across her cheek. Unfolding her hand, he placed the purse in it.

"Not until you are past the barricades. If he should try anything, scream for the soldiers. They would not like to be left out of any transaction he's made. I will see you in London when this situation has been properly resolved."

Leades heaved himself out of the wagon. Wordlessly the other men followed. Clipping one of the horses on its rump, an expression of anticipation on his solid face, Gerald Leades watched the wagon roll away.

A few minutes later, the driver stopped the wagon on a quiet back street.

"Soon you cover yourselves with straw. Be quiet. Maybe we get you past," he said, his eyes on the purse Sally Leades was tightly clutching.

"I will not cover myself in these filthy weeds," the other woman said, the first words Cat had heard her voice.

"Then you get out," said the driver. "These soldiers will look away from a wagon of hay, but I do not bet my neck they not see Englishwomen."

"All right." The woman stood up, dusting off her sodden skirts. "I will get off."

"Please," implored Sally, "you mustn't. You can't."

"Oh, but I can," the woman retorted, every inch the grande dame. "I shall go back to the hotel. Someone there will, no doubt, procure *proper* transport to England. One must have standards."

Cat wanted to laugh. Ridiculous, foolish woman! Acting as though this were some game she no longer wanted to play.

"Sit down!" Cat hissed. "Your misplaced sense of decorum will find you a permanent guest of Napoleon's!"

The woman sniffed. "I can understand this sort of behavior from a soldier's wife but would have thought better of you, Lady Montaigne White."

Than you don't know Hecuba, thought Cat grimly. "There is a time and place for insisting on purposeless niceties. This is neither."

The woman sniffed and clambered over the side of the wagon before Cat could restrain her, dragging a jewelry case after her. The driver, obviously eager to leave the troublesome woman behind, snapped the leads on the horses' rumps, moving them forward into a trot.

"You must stop!" Cat called to him.

"She stay!" he said without turning.

Cat stared at the diminishing figure, standing stiff with offended dignity.

"Make it back to the hotel!" she called, the wind sucking the words from her mouth and scattering them in the frozen alley.

"Now, you women give me your purse and cover yourselves with hay" the driver said a few minutes later. He had fetched the wagon up behind a stack of crates, a few yards from the barricade. A couple of shabby soldiers huddled next to a muddy quagmire encompassing most of the street. Apparently they were guarding the road.

"Give me the purse, I say!" the driver hissed, his eyes sidling back and forth between Sally Leades and the rough plank he used as a footboard.

"Don't give it to him, Mrs. Leades," Cat whispered, burrowing into the hay. "Remember what your husband said."

The driver's cruel eyes shifted toward Cat. "Husband gone. Give it to me now or get out!"

Sally, her expression tortured with indecision, looked pleadingly at Cat.

"Mrs. Leades," Cat said, "listen to me. Give your purse into my keeping."

With a sigh of gratitude, Sally shoved the bag into Cat's frozen hands. "Yes, milady!" she breathed.

"Bah!" The driver swung down from the seat and stomped unhurriedly over to Cat's side of the wagon. She shrank against the back of the seat. Once more she was struck by the apparent negligence of the guards. There was no possible way they could have failed to notice them.

"Maybe you should give it to him," Sally said in a quavering voice.

"Give?" Cat said. "He's going to take it. Look, Mrs. Leades. No muddy tracks exit the far side of the mud. Those guards aren't blind or deaf. They know we are here. They are simply waiting for their share of what this man robs us of."

Cat's mind raced, looking for a way out. "Whatever I do, Mrs. Leades, just hang on to the sides of the wagon."

"You women, give it to me!" The driver had reached them now, his dirty face twisted with frustration.

"No!" Cat yelled so loudly that even the guards lifted their heads.

"Than I take!" the driver snarled.

"Take?" shrieked Cat. "I should say so! You have taken from every person unfortunate enough to have hired you!"

A cruel smile twisted the driver's face. "So. You discover my little game. Fine. You are one smart old bird. Now . . ." He held his hand up, and Cat rose, intentionally wobbly, to her feet.

"Guards! I demand you arrest this man!" she shouted.

The guards, roused by her strident screeches, hesitated a moment until finally heading toward them. Sally was staring at Cat with wide eyes. The driver had started to laugh, a wicked, humorless sound.

"She is crazy. A lunatic!" he told the guards.

"Arrest this man!" Cat demanded, forcing her breath to wheeze between her lips, praying her plan would work. Her body needed no encouragement to shake convincingly.

"All right, *grand-mère*. Get down now," one of the guards said impatiently.

"You must arrest this villain. You must arrest this—" Suddenly Cat clutched her stomach, doubling up and falling forward over the driver's seat.

Seizing the plank footboard, she yanked, praying her guess was correct.

It was. As the board was wrenched free, a treasure trove of gems, gold sovereigns, fat purses, and shimmering jewelry met her eyes.

She thrust her arms wrist-deep into the hoard, lifting pearls and pendants, strands of diamonds and gold chains, high above her head. She heard the guards' indrawn hisses, the driver's violent swearing.

Using all of her strength, she hurled fistfuls of treasure into the center of the mudhole and reached immediately for more handfuls to fling.

"He steals from you, too!" she yelled as the driver started to scramble up over the side of the wagon. A guard seized him by the collar, dragging him back. The other guard pitched himself into the mud, sifting desperately in the freezing black muck for the riches he knew it contained.

"You hold out on us, Gaston?" The one guard gave the driver a violent shake. He whined pitiably.

Taking advantage of their momentary distraction, Cat grabbed the reins. She snatched up the whip and brought it down with a ringing crack over the heads of the horses. The team reared in fright. The faces of the three men swiveled in the cart's direction. For one agonizing moment, Cat was sure the beasts would do nothing more than rear and buck in their traces. And then the front quarters of the two horses came crashing down, their haunches gathered, and they bolted straight at the guard half-buried in the mud.

With a yelp, he lurched from beneath the wheels of the careening wagon.

"Shoot them!" Cat heard the driver shriek. She squeezed her eyes shut and bent low, waiting for pain to find her.

"Shut up, filthy cheat!" she heard the guard answer. "I could as soon shoot my own grandmother!"

Cat's legs were cramped with cold. Her fingers in the inadequate leather gloves were numb, scored red from handling the heavy traces. Her teeth chattered with each gust of wind. Long hours had passed since the freezing rain had soaked through her clothing. Longer hours since the barricade where Sally, a combination of fear and respect on her chafed face, had sobbed her thanks.

The raw wind howling at their backs blistered Cat's neck where the wet veil lashed her skin. Sally had retreated into a miserable lump, her eyes red-rimmed.

What dim light there was bled from the sky as night fell. Still the icy blasts of wind snatched their breath away. Frigid fingers burrowed under their clothes. Their journey seemed at once timeless and as if each moment held its own torturous eternity. *Silence and cold*, Cat thought numbly, *the final circle of hell*. She squinted into the darkness, her tired gaze scanning the road ahead. She still hoped that somehow Thomas would appear there, strong and safe and warm and . . . She shook the lulling image off, afraid she would soon topple from the seat if they didn't find a place to stop soon.

"Lights!" Sally suddenly yelled. Cat turned. Sally was on her knees, pointing at a pale glow appearing and disappearing behind a stand of wind-lashed trees.

"Can we stop?" Sally begged. Cat snapped the leads on the horses' rump in answer.

Soon they were entering the crowded yard of a ramshackle building where a score of horses huddled together, tethered at a post. A motley assortment of carriages loomed in the shadows to one side. The smell of frying onions, garlic, and unseasoned wood smoke permeated the air. A plump young woman opened the door, tossing out a pail of slop, raucous laughter spilling out after her. Nothing had ever looked more inviting.

Cat crawled tiredly over the side of the wagon. When her feet touched the ground, her legs buckled beneath her. Grimly she clasped the side of the wagon and hauled herself upright.

Sally was faring far worse, unable even to clamber from the bed. A man, a thin cigar clamped between tobacco-stained teeth, strode from around the side of the building and stopped short when he saw them.

"Help her to the door," Cat gasped.

With exclamations of concern, the man leapt forward. *Thank God*, Cat thought, *he's an Englishman.* Quickly he lifted Sally from the wagon, supporting her round her waist. Cat stumbled gamely after them. The man shouldered the front door open and gently settled Sally onto a bench just inside.

Cat looked about the crowded room. Several young Englishmen were seated at a table, apparently content with the innkeeper's cellars, their voices raised in a strident attempt at bravado. Others were scattered around the smoky room, conversing in uneasy tones.

"Sally?" a tentative voice asked.

Cat looked up at the thin, middle-aged gentleman approaching them. His brown eyes were filling with tears. He held his arms out.

Sally Leades rose to her feet. "Frank!"

Enfolded in his arms, Sally set her cheek against the man's chest. Cat could see the concern drain out of Sally as she rested there. And in that moment, Cat knew a greater envy than any she had ever experienced. To be able to put aside all one's worries, to know that stronger shoulders bore the burden, keener minds solved the riddles. Unfortunate, she thought, that she had always been so damned good at riddles, and that her shoulders were unfashionably strong. Unwillingly she thought of Thomas. She said a brief prayer, asking only that he be safe. Nothing else.

"Ahm." Sally cleared her throat.

Cat blinked up at her, exhausted. Water dripped from her veil as the ice melted in the warm room, yet she dared not remove it.

"Lady Montaigne White, may I present my brother Frank Grisham?" Sally said.

"Lady Montaigne White," the man said, a world of awe in his voice. "You have been a legend since my boyhood. How gratifying to see your resourcefulness and spirit have only grown with age. The story Sally has related is beyond wondrous. Madame, you have my eternal respect and gratitude."

Grisham was staring fixedly at Cat's face, avoiding looking at any other part of her person. In confusion, Cat looked down. Her hands! Horrified, she stared at them. The dye from her gloves had bled, staining her hands a vibrant shade of blue. A wondrous model of aged propriety she must look: soggy, veiled in a soaking rag, and with blue hands!

"Frank has a room," Sally was saying softly. "He says there might be a carriage leaving for Rouen in the morning."

The innkeeper scuttled up to them, his hands raised in an expression of failure. "Pardon, monsieur, mesdames," he said. "I look, but it is no use. There are no rooms available. The English 'bucks' have already doubled themselves to accommodate! There is nothing."

"Then I will give the ladies my room—"

"No!" Cat interrupted, afraid her masquerade would end if she were forced to share lodging with

Sally. "I simply will not share a room," she said, knowing she sounded as absurd and haughty as the woman they had left at the barricades in Paris.

"But, madame! There is no choice!"

"I will stay out here, then."

"Wait!" The innkeeper touched his fingertips to his temples. "If you are willing to sleep in the, er—how you say? loft?—it can be arranged. If you will pay."

"Payment isn't the problem," said Frank Grisham. "There is no loft, Lady Montaigne White. It is likely a filthy attic corner, no doubt where the scullery maid sleeps."

"Mr. Grisham, would you be so kind as to make a loan to me?"

"Of course! But, Lady Montaigne White—"

"How kind. And now, innkeeper, if you would show me to my quarters?" Cat said with as regal an air as she could muster. It was hard, draped as she was in a freezing cold, soaking wet dress, "bust improvers" slipping down toward her already soggily bulging waist, her blue hands shaking on the handle of her portmanteau. It was hard, but necessary.

Chapter 20

The jackals were in Paris. As occurs during all political upheavals, human scavengers masquerading as patriots took the opportunity to roam the city, hunting in packs. Thomas, protected by his great size, camouflaged by his perfect French accent, traversed the twisting corridors of the great, dark city unchallenged.

At the Fontaine, the harassed manager had sworn to him that Hecuba Montaigne White had left the hotel by herself before noon. Lady Catherine had breakfasted earlier and disappeared upstairs. Thomas raced up to the suite and tore open the door. Empty. The room looked as though she might return at any moment; even her undergarments were still neatly folded between scented sheets of tissue in the drawers. He went through the adjoining door to Hecuba's apartment.

These rooms bespoke a hasty and tumultuous departure. It was a shambles of clothing, powders, and personal belongings. A few huge trunks were the only traveling equipage left behind. Hecuba was gone. As was Cat.

Thomas hammered on every apartment door of the hotel, asking the few remaining guests for any information about Cat's whereabouts. No one knew where she was.

He left the hotel and headed north, knowing Hecuba and Cat were most likely to follow the steady stream of English people trying to escape to the Channel. Too often during the long search, Thomas saw aristocrats paying the price for their self-satisfied superiority. Stripped of their belongings, in many cases their very coats, they were sometimes beaten, sometimes merely driven in front of jeering crowds, always humiliated.

One young beauty was being thrust from the filthy embrace of one guard into the waiting arms of the next and back again as her parents stood at bayonet point, rage and terror indelibly printed on their faces. A harsh, barked command in French military cant ended the sordid scene, but Thomas knew similar scenes were being enacted throughout Paris. Perhaps with Cat as the victim.

His pulse pounded in his throat. He would find her. He must.

In a little-used side street, a beaten, battered man staggered across the cobblestones, looking back over his shoulders as he stumbled along.

"Lady Montaigne White! Lady Catherine Sinclair!" Thomas called to him.

The man stopped, squinting through one puffy eye up at Thomas; the other was swollen to a purple slit.

"The army is very eager to find these two," Thomas said, hopelessness washing over him. The man could tell him nothing. He was probably some pathetic traitor escaping from a mob.

"What is in it for me?"

"Maybe a reward," Thomas answered. Cynically he prepared a few easily tested queries. There were always those willing to lie for a quid.

"Bah!" The man suddenly spat, a thin stream of saliva and blood. "I do it for nothing. The bitch has gone north, through the Rue Ange barricade."

"Who?" Thomas demanded.

"The Montaigne White. The one responsible for this." The man pointed at his bruised and broken face.

"And the other?" Thomas asked, unaware he held his breath.

"I do not know that one's name. It might have been said, but her name, I did not hear. Timid little rabbit."

"They escaped?"

"Yes, curse them!"

"Unharmed? Untouched?"

The man eyed Thomas suspiciously before shrugging. "Yes. Who would want anything more from those hags besides the coin which they carry? Now, Monsieur, about that reward—"

"When?" Thomas shouted.

"This morning. This noon. Now, I have rethought this reward—" The man looked up. Thomas had already gone.

Blessedly there were only a few main thoroughfares the departing English could take from this route north to the coast. Thomas stopped at each coaching house, each inn, each farm along the way, looking for them.

He was more frightened than he had ever been in a career rife with frightening situations. Images of Cat tortured him, spurring him on beneath the pitch black veil of the evening sky.

Everywhere his tense query met with the same answer. No old lady traveling alone. No young lady. The sky was black, empty. No stars or moon offered the slightest illumination; the wind and cold were his only companions on his search. He was tireless, the lengthening of the evening hours bringing no sense of imminent exhaustion, only a terrible impetus; he had to find her.

He nearly rode past the little tavern, hidden as it was behind a knoll. If Cat was not there, he had to give his horse a brief rest before she dropped beneath him. And he must get some nourishment.

Sliding from the back of the rawboned horse, Thomas walked his mount into the fenced yard crowded with horses. Unbuckling the bridle, he set the horse free, scooping up a quarter bucket of oats and setting it on the ground. He rubbed the heels of his hands into his eyes as he walked toward the front door of the inn. Half an hour. No more.

Though it was well past midnight, the public rooms were still crowded with men. Many slept propped up on benches, their heads fallen forward on their chests. Still more were awake, calling for the owner to refill their cups.

"An older Englishwoman and a young lady," Thomas said in French to the innkeeper when he finally found him. The short, rotund man, hailed by several men at once in the overcrowded room, replied, "Old, young, man, woman! There are many English here. Look yourself!"

Thomas took quick notice of the interest of a thin middle-aged gentleman warming his hands around a steaming mug. He was a stranger. Furrowing his wet hair back in a despairing gesture, Thomas searched the room for a familiar form.

"What do you want with an elderly gentle-woman?" a quiet voice asked.

Thomas was beside the man in an instant, tow-ering over him. "Do you know where she is?"

"Where who is? What is the name of this wom-an? And why does a Frenchman seek an English lady?" the man asked suspiciously.

Thomas had to restrain himself from pulling the thin man to his feet and choking the information from him. In English he said, "I am looking for one of two women. Lady Hecuba Montaigne White or Lady Catherine Sinclair."

"You are a friend?" the man asked.

"Yes! Do you know where either of them is?"

The man studied Thomas, a frown creasing his forehead before he muttered, "Distressing times, most distressing, and I strongly disagreed with her insistence on staying in that garret alone, but she would have none of it."

"Who would have none of it? What garret?" Thomas demanded.

"Lady Montaigne White. She and my sister managed to escape here together. Lady Montaigne White insisted on sleeping in the maid's quarters by herself."

"And the younger woman?" Thomas asked, desperation clear in his voice.

The older man shook his head. "There were only the Lady Montaigne White and my sister."

Thomas' heart pounded in a thick, dread-drugged rhythm. The man was pointing to a rackety flight of stairs rising from the corner of the small room. Thomas ascended them quickly, fearful of what Hecuba might tell him, impelled by his need to know where he could find Cat. Another flight of stairs, no more than a steep, encased ladder, rose from the end of the hall. He flew up them and heaved open the trapdoor at the top.

It was dark inside. Only a candle, guttering in a cold draft, danced light on the low ceiling, failing to cast its golden pool into the corners of the room. A small cot stood on the floor, a chair enshrouded with dark drapery at its head. The slow cadence of deep, exhausted breathing reached Thomas' ears.

He made his way across the room, bent over so his head would not bang against the thick beams. Kneeling beside the cot, he placed a gentle hand on her shoulder, sorry to have to wake her, yet unable to waste valuable time. She moaned as he lightly shook her.

"Wake up!" he whispered, "Hecuba, you must—"

She turned. The dim light revealed Cat's face. Her cheeks was blotched with runnels of black dirt, and filth smeared her flawless skin. Her hair was a mat of tangled gingery gloss. Her eyes were pressed shut, her lashes a golden sweep on the high curve of her dirty cheek.

"Oh, God!" Thomas breathed.

He slid his arms under her, lifting her gently, slowly, up against his breast, careful not to wake her, powerless to deny himself. He leaned against the wall, bracing his back, carrying her with him, until she lay across his lap, her head tucked beneath his chin. He raised his head high, squeezing his eyes shut, opening his mouth in a wordless expression of agonized relief. Only now did the terror that had ridden with him from Paris find voice, and his legs and arms shook uncontrollably as he tenderly cradled her to him.

She shifted restlessly in his arms, and he stroked the long, disheveled locks away from her face, brushing his fingertips over the shadowy contours. Like a blind man, he read the shallow indentation of her vulnerable temple, the silky flare of her brow, the delicate jaw, the slender throat. Breathing in the warm exhalation of her breath, he counted the beats of her heart. And he knew, with unwavering certainty, that he was bound to her as inexorably as the tides to the moon.

He reviewed his actions—the flight to France, the desperate search, the agony of fear—and came to an unassailable conclusion. Where Cat was concerned, he had no choice. His heart was constant, immutable. It didn't matter how many scapegraces she chose to charm, how many husbands she ultimately had; if he perceived her needs, he would meet them. No other union, sanctioned by church or state, would supersede his heart's obstinate claim. He loved her.

Thomas smiled, the hollowness of the preceding months vanishing with acceptance. He laid his lips on the silky tangle of her hair. He would be to Cat mentor, guardian, rake, confidant, fool. He would be anything she wanted or needed. And if she needed him gone, he would even do that. But he would no longer try and convince himself that his heart was a spurious betrayer. As long as he lived, Thomas conceded, he would love Cat Sinclair.

The cold was finally gone. Cat nestled deeper into the encompassing warmth, lulled by the deep tempo beneath her ear. She started to stretch, but her movement was stymied.

"Cat."

God, she was dreaming! Half a nightmare of flight and exhaustion, cold and fear, and half undiluted fantasy. For it was Thomas' voice: tender, exasperated . . . whispered. She was being cocooned in heavy, warm layers; lifted, enfolded.

"Love." His voice again, a welcome sanctuary in the black, threat-riddled night. She wasn't surprised. So many nights he waited just beyond slumber's door, to hold her just as he was doing now, to whisper the word he had just spoken. She ignored the trace of sadness she felt. She did not care if it was just a dream.

Wrapping her arms around the hard warmth, she refused to relinquish him to consciousness. Strong arms tightened about her as hands winnowed through the hair at the nape of her neck. She turned, and her mouth pressed against smooth, warm skin. A phantom heart beat beneath her lips. She smiled.

In her dream Thomas cursed . . . or was it a prayer? It was impossible to say. She wiggled closer, pressing her length more fully to his. He shuddered, and her body answered.

Even in her dreams, when she was chased by terror and danger, he had the power to ignite her senses, to call from her body the shivering response that only he could. Her hands slowly measured the breadth of his shoulders, palmed the slope of his chest, tested the hardness of the ghostly arms that held her. She sighed.

His breath sluiced over her closed eyes; his heart was a thick, mesmerizing rhythm beneath her ear. His unyielding embrace was so at odds with the shivering brush of unseen fingertips. Something velvety and warm trailed across her forehead, over her cheeks, and down her throat. A languid, yet somehow fervent movement. He was kissing her! Cat purred in delight, unwilling ever to wake up, and snuggled closer still.

"Cat, wake up. We have to leave soon!" Thomas said in soft, urgent tones.

Twisting beneath the thick eiderdown, Cat blinked rapidly, trying to accustom her eyes to the blackness. Abruptly the bed shifted beneath her. She bolted upright, banging her head painfully on some overhead projection.

"Damn!" a voice muttered from close by in the dark.

Confused, Cat struggled in the bedclothes and, becoming more entangled, pitched forward. Strong hands caught her, hauling her back upright. He was real. Thomas was safe!

She spun around, her hands reaching of their own volition to touch him, to reassure herself he was no exhaustion-induced fantasy. "Thomas?"

"Your hardheadedness is no longer open to debate, m'dear," he said, rubbing his chin.

His voice dispelled the lingering enchantment of her dream. But even his impassive tone could not erase her joy.

"How did you find me?"

"First things first," he said. She heard the scrape of a flint. The sudden light caused her to squint.

"Thomas?" She could not see his face beyond the flame. He had gone very quiet. "Thomas? What is it?"

"Ahm. You have, I take it, been . . . excuse me, hm . . . masquerading as your aunt?" He was laughing! The damned, great beast was laughing!

She went rigid with offended dignity. "So?"

"Cat," he said, and now she could see he was grinning. "Take a look."

He nodded at the large, broken triangle of mirror propped against the wall next to the bed. Flinging the end of a quilt over her shoulder, Cat leaned over from the waist to see what had caused him so much amusement.

A hideous, filthy hag stared back at her. The greasepaint she had applied that morning had frozen, melted, and thawed. Oily dark streaks bracketed her nose and encircled her eyes. Straw and hayseeds had become fixed in the thicker layers of paint, pebbling one cheek in a bizarre approximation of a beard. Her hair hung in long, snarled ropes. In horror, Cat lifted her hands to her mouth. They gleamed bishop's blue.

She turned to Thomas, her eyes wide. "There wasn't a water basin or a cloth, and I was too tired to do more than rid myself of those sodden dresses, and I never so much as realized there was even a mirror to look into, and I . . ."

His expression was patronizingly encouraging, near to bursting with amused smugness. She shook her head, inwardly seething, refusing to let the tears, which had unaccountably filled her eyes, escape.

"I . . . I will be damned if I explain why I do not look as though I were about to attend some cursed musicale when I have spent the entire day banging along in an open wagon while the skies poured ice on me!" She was so angry, and relieved, and embarrassed, she could find only one outlet for all the emotions bubbling inside her. Reaching out her hand, she braced it against Thomas' chest to shove him backward off the chair.

She might as well have tried to push an oak tree over. He looked at her hand pressed open on his now-stained shirt and captured it in his own. Turning her hand over, he bent his head and placed his lips on her palm in a warm kiss.

"You are intelligent, brave, courageous, and resourceful, and I am filled with admiration for you," he said softly.

She pushed her other hand against him, the threatening tears spilling over, leaving glistening tracks in her ruined makeup.

"I am not! I am none of those things!" The words tumbled out. The words she had to say. Ridiculous now to even think them, but they were impossible to contain. They had haunted her throughout the entire terrifying, horrendous day. "I am a liar! I lied to you, Thomas! I haven't had any lovers. None!"

He didn't seem to know how to respond. He stared at her.

"Not a one," she insisted.

"I know," he finally said, smiling slightly.

Her perceived sins loomed in front of her, making confession a necessity. "And I ran, Thomas! I fled

like the most base coward! I could not think where
to . . . I left without . . . Oh, Thomas! I didn't know
where to find you!"

He was stunned. Even as he gathered her to him,
rocking her gently in his great arms, the impact of
what she had just said overwhelmed him. No other
woman he knew would have had the ingenuity to
escape past the blockades. But more astounding
still, no woman he had ever known would have
then tortured herself for having left behind an
unrelated man of twice her size and experience.

Foolish heart, he chided himself, to read something in that. It was just Cat, who, having assumed
responsibility for the welfare of so many, had
unthinkingly added him to her long list.

"It's all right, Cat." He withdrew a square of
linen from his pocket and carefully daubed at her
messy face.

" . . . and Hecuba!" She gulped, trying to gather her composure. "I haven't the least idea where
she is!"

"Ah, yes, Hecuba. I admit, I expected to find
her beneath that pile of blankets, and be back to
chasing you to ground by now. Where is the Lady
Montaigne White?"

"Eloped."

"Pardon me?"

"She eloped, and I swear, Thomas, if you start
laughing again . . . !"

"Forgive me. It is merely the result of extravagant relief."

She eyed him suspiciously.

"Really," he assured her. "Now, do tell me the
details. Some pretty young French cicisbeo, I expect.
Well, she's a canny old thing. She'll protect her
assets well enough."

"Not at all! She eloped with the Marquis de
Grenville."

"Grenville? You're gulling me. I thought he'd died of the French pox a decade ago!"

Cat disengaged herself from her comfortable position tucked under Thomas, chin and threw her hands up in mock surrender. "You're right. I am teasing you. Sitting here, freezing to death in this drafty hole, without a guinea to pay the landlord, not knowing if you were alive or dead, or if I should ever see you again, I got bored. So I thought to myself, 'If perchance Thomas should reappear, however shall I entertain him? I know! I'll tell him some Banbury tale about Hecuba and a diseased marquis!' "

Thomas grinned at her sarcasm, relieved to have the despair gone from her eyes. This was his Cat. "Point well taken."

She fidgeted a second before settling herself once more against him. He pushed her upright.

"Sorry, Cat. We haven't time for you to take a nap. We have to be off before the other guests awaken and bribe, buy, or steal their way out of here."

"Do you have a carriage?" she asked.

"No. Just a farmer's plow horse. At this point, worth more than any of the blood at Tattersall's. I rode astride. We will have to find something to hitch her to."

"I have a wagon."

Thomas stood up, carefully lowering Cat to her feet. "Why doesn't this surprise me? Well, then, we'd best be off. Our most pressing concern now is getting you back to England with your reputation intact."

His eyes grew tender as he watched hers widen. "Did you think that your mother's marriage to my half brother would sanction our unchaperoned trip across France? No matter what the circumstances, my notoriety would negate far more than so dubious a family connection."

"What will we do?" Cat asked quietly, reading pain in the gently offered self-condemnation.

"Hecuba's elopement suggests a plan," Thomas said thoughtfully. "I shall be your French 'companion,' and you shall be my rich, elderly benefactress. Not only will we protect your identity, but we also stand a better chance of making it quickly across the country. The French are a nationalistic, but practical people. They won't be averse to helping an unthreatening old woman, even if she is English, and her opportunistic French lover. For a fee."

"And you think you can give a creditable performance as a French 'companion'?" Cat asked, openly doubtful.

"I have some experience at this sort of play-acting," Thomas replied.

"Ah yes, your foreign service, no doubt," Cat said dryly.

Thomas looked at her, startled. "What do you know of my foreign service?"

"Only that you were involved in some information-gathering capacity here in France."

"And who told you this? Daphne Bernard?"

"What difference does that make?" she asked.

Thomas took a deep breath. "Pray listen, Cat. My past is not a particularly savory one. I have done things unfit for your ears—"

"Your past found you in Brighton, Thomas," Cat said, trying to meet his eye and failing. "Daphne Bernard is part of that past. Whatever your relationship with her, no matter how unsavory, I know it was necessary. But please, I don't want to discuss it any further."

Thomas watched her closely, reading the telltale stain rising beneath the greasy smears on her cheeks. If only Daphne were the most sordid piece of the history he could have related to her. If she caused Cat's cheeks to flame and her eyes to dart away from his in embarrassment, how would she react if she were to hear about Mariette Leons and her son? He refused to think of it.

Unhappy that Daphne Bernard had managed to spoil their reunion, Cat frowned. Dropping the blanket from her shoulders, she lifted the hem of her shift, scrubbing at her cheeks.

Her form beneath the thin muslin was silhouetted by the candle. The sway of her full breasts as she bent over was a sensuous motion revealed in tantalizing clarity by the backlighting.

Thoughts of Daphne and Mariette and every other woman he'd ever known slowly dissolved as Thomas stared at Cat. He felt his blood pound to his loins in instant appreciation.

Damn! he thought. He might as well be a sixteen-year-old virgin himself instead of a man on the brink of his middle years, she affected him so potently. She wasn't even aware of it; her actions were without calculation, utterly unselfconscious. And why should she fret over his avuncular presence? How could she know he fought his body's urgency as he stood, seemingly relaxed, beside her?

"I have to get dressed," Cat said patiently, misreading the absorption in his gaze as woolgathering.

"Yes."

"Thomas, you were the one who was exhorting me to speed a few minutes ago."

"Ah, yes. Yes. I'll meet you down in the public room in—what? quarter of an hour?"

Cat sighed as she picked up one after the other of the still damp bust improvers.

"Better half of an hour," she said.

Chapter 21

Thomas, waiting outside the inn beneath the ebony sky, had already hitched one of the horses to the wagon by the time Cat appeared, slipping from the shadows at the back of the inn by way of the maid's exit from the attic, a stout pole ladder leaning against the window. She fretted a moment over leaving Sally Leades and her brother, but Thomas reassured her in a hushed voice, telling her they were safe with their countrymen. Safer than he and Cat were likely to be.

He waited until she nodded, his greatcoat billowing in the wind about his broad shoulders, his dark head bare to the elements. Wordlessly he handed Cat into the cart, his black eyes scanning the horizon as he tucked her under the blankets and lap rugs he had somehow procured.

As they traveled slowly northward, the rain gave way to sleet. Buffeted on relentless winds, the wet snow churned in the air until the difference between the thick, white sky and the frost-rimed ground became negligible. The wind made conversation impossible.

Cat, wedged onto the narrow seat, was conscious, even through the layers of wool, of the press of Thomas, leg against hers. She squeezed her eyes shut, willing herself to adopt the casual familiarity that came so easily to him.

She could not. He had come for her. He had searched until he had found her. He meant to insure her safe passage through this suddenly hostile countryside. All of his actions spoke eloquently . . . of duty and responsibility. There was nothing of the relieved lover in his manner; no lingering glances, no concentrated worry, no passionate declarations. Her dream faded in his practical, self-possessed presense.

The occasional smile he flashed at her was sympathetic, encouraging . . . nothing more. An honorable man, honor-bound to see to her protection, he would ever be subject to his own rigid code of obligation.

The incongruity of it! Cat thought. Her knowledge of this "libertine" was so utterly incommensurate with society's. And yet an image of a woman, her hands on Thomas, his head thrown back in sensual ecstasy, was burned in Cat's memory. Hiding her face in the woolen scarf, she could feel her cheeks redden.

She wasn't even certain what she had seen, nor what "intense pleasure" Thomas had denied himself, nor even why he had ordered Daphne Bernard from his room. Cat had no reason to trust Daphne's assurance that Thomas had rejected her. Yet she had no reason to distrust it. Cat only knew she wanted more than anything to believe the Frenchwoman.

It did not matter, she realized. Whatever Thomas had done, or chose to do, he would always be to her more than some notorious title. He was Thomas: onetime spy, libertine very likely. But, more important, honorable, kind, clever, and a thousand other qualities that defined him, setting him apart from and above any other man. Whatever experiences had fashioned Thomas, Cat could not be repelled by them. She would change nothing about him,

not a word or a deed, that had shaped his singular
character.

It was well past dusk. They had watched the sun
breach the low hills and climb to its apex in the
winter sky and then watched its slow, remorseless
descent. Cat shuddered on the seat of the wagon,
her lips turning an angry blue in her pale face. Her
lashes fluttered with agitation against the bruised
flesh encircling her eyes.

"Cat!" Thomas said urgently. "Cat, wake up!"

Her eyelids opened, and she stared at him for a
moment, her gaze without recognition.

"Damn!" Thomas cursed, stopping the wagon.
He pulled her from the seat and buried her in the
hay, piling the blankets on top of her. Snapping the
lead on the mare, he drove her toward the light of
a farmhouse tucked between two hills. He had to
get something hot into Cat.

Fear for her made him careless. He tucked another
blanket around her before vaulting from the seat.
Mounting the steps, he pounded his fists against
the farmhouse door.

"What?" a voice called from within.

"Open, monsieur! I have a sick woman outside!"
Thomas shouted back.

"Go away!"

"No! I cannot! She must get warm!" Thomas
called, on the brink of kicking the door down.

A crack appeared in the solid portal. A small, aged
man peered up at him. "Be you English?" he said.

Thomas quickly dismissed the idea of him and
Cat impersonating a Frenchman and his aged mistress. He was unsure of what Cat would say in her
present condition. And also, he could not allow her
to suffocate beneath those awful veils. One look at
the beautiful purity of her face, and their lie would
be discovered.

He threw himself on the old man's mercy. "Yes, English. Please, you must help me. I will pay."

The old man slammed the door shut Thomas could hear muttered voices behind the barrier. He leaned his forehead against the wood, praying the old man would not make him use force, knowing he would if necessary, if Cat needed him to. Turning, he looked over to the motionless heap of cloth and hay in the wagon bed.

The door swung open. The old man stood grinning up at him. Sighing in relief, Thomas breathed a word of thanks before turning to get Cat.

He did not see the old man's two sons appear like thick, black shadows from the corner of the house. He did not hear their footfalls over the howling wind. But he felt the blow that caught him viciously behind the ear. He felt the ground rise up to meet his collapsing form, and his last despairing thought was that he had failed Cat, after all.

Thomas shook his head, willing the dizziness away. Blinding lights streaked fireworks through his eyes each time he tried to open them. Cat, he thought. His eyes shot open, and his head swam in pain-filled waves. She wasn't in the room. Only two beefy farm lads and the wizened old man kept him company.

"Up, are you?" the ancient man said in French. He limped forward to stand in front of Thomas. "Thought to do us, did you?" he continued. "Bah! Nothing in that rackety thing but a pile of blankets. What's your game, m'lad? You're no more English than my boys here!"

Experience had taught Thomas never to offer information, so he sat quietly, waiting, every nerve straining to detect some sign of Cat.

The old man suddenly snarled, and his hand

swung out, catching Thomas' cheek in a savage backhanded blow. "Out with it! If you're English quality, where's your money? Why, you're as dark as a gypsy!"

The old man bent low, his face inches from Thomas'. He lifted his hand again. This time it held a short leather strap. His sons watched impassively. Thomas struggled against the ropes that twisted his arms painfully behind him, and the old man laughed. From outside a dog started barking. The old man's head snapped up.

"Jacques, go and see what that fool dog is barking about." One of the hulking, speechless men left.

A sudden intuition caused Thomas to shut his eyes. Please, God, let her not do what he thought she was doing. A moment ticked by, then two and three. The old man grew agitated, cursing as he paced the floor.

"Go and find your brother," he finally spat. The other son rose and lumbered from the room. Thomas' prayers increased.

The old man spun on Thomas, bringing the leather strap slashing down across his face. Thomas' head snapped back in pain. "Who is out there? What have you done?" he shouted. Again the leather strap cut across Thomas' cheek. He gasped.

The door swung open. The old man's two sons filled the frame. As silently as they had left, they entered, their eyes shifting uneasily in their round faces. A pitch-colored figure detached itself from the blackness, gliding into the room. From head to toe, the feminine figure was cloaked in inky darkness, even down to the black gun muzzle projecting from the wide folds of her skirts and trained on the old man.

"Untie him," she said in a soft, melodious voice. No one moved. "Untie him, *old man*, or I will shoot you." If the words had been a demand, loud and anxious, the elderly farmer might have called the black-shrouded woman's bluff. But the very colorlessness of the words made them all the more credible. With a snarl, he complied.

Thomas rose unsteadily. The black muzzle of the gun remained fixed on the old man. Taking up the heavy ropes, Thomas jerked the hands of his captors behind them and, one by one, secured them there.

He saw Cat sway slightly and said, "Just a moment more."

Hurrying upstairs, he snatched a heavy eider-down blanket from a bed. At the bottom of the stairs, he found the kitchen and sloshed soup, hot from the hearth fire, into a big mug. He returned to Cat just in time to catch her as she started to fall forward.

Once outside, Thomas lifted her tenderly onto the wagon seat and spread the warm, thick blanket about her, placing the hot mug in her trembling hands. She raised the life-giving liquid to her lips, sighing with contentment as he moved the mare forward out of the farmyard.

When they were well away, Thomas cast a worried glance at Cat and was relieved to see her face did not look nearly so waxen as it had before.

"You simply *had* to be a hero, didn't you?" he said.

"I don't know what you mean."

"You scared the bloody hell out of me!" Thomas roared, the terror of the long minutes when he had thought Cat was intending to physically assault the two brutish brothers returning to him in full force.

"*I* scared *you*!" Cat shouted back, her fatigue and fear forgotten in her indignation. "I am having a nice little nap when you start yelling my name at me. When I finally feel up to having a conversation, I look up to see you lying on the ground with two hulking monsters standing over you! And *you* were scared!"

"Oh God, Cat. I thought you were going to try and hit them as they came out."

"Now, that *would* have been stupid. Whatever have I done to give you such little respect of my intelligence? Those things outweighed me by twelve stone. I believe they even outweighed *you*!"

Thomas found Cat looking at him, a teasing smile starting a dimple in one flawless cheek. Covering her hand, he dragged it up to his lips. "I don't mean to sound ungrateful. I was so damned worried. Wonderful, intelligent, resourceful Cat, wherever did you find a firearm?"

"I didn't."

"All right then, a pistol or whatever you want to call it."

"It wasn't any sort of weapon at all. It was a piece of pipe I found in the shed. Honestly, Thomas, however do you think I would conjure up an expensive firearm?"

"You didn't have any weapon at all?!" Thomas roared.

Cat decided any further attempt at conversation was pointless.

Chapter 22

The sky above was a pitch-colored canvas. The small coastal town of Dieppe, however, was ablaze with lights. Englishmen and women crowded the village, waiting for some transport to cross the Channel. Many, hearing ships were few and costly, had ridden to larger Bologna, hoping to find a way back to England there. But many had stayed.

On entering the town, Thomas had hailed a workman and, after engaging in a short conversation, whistled up the tired mare, guiding her through the streets to this unlikely address. He halted the cart in an alley behind the inn where he planned to stop.

Cat's clothes had dried for the most part, but the padding around her waist was still damp and uncomfortable. After rummaging in her bag, she carefully applied powders and greasepaint by the weak light coming from the inn's back window. Satisfied, she covered her face with a light veil and donned every piece of jewelry she'd brought. She rechecked the mirror. With all of the paste jewels winking from wrists, ears, and throat, she was certain she looked every inch a wealthy, crude old woman.

Thomas handed Cat down from the cart and bid her to follow him closely, saying nothing. She was more than happy to oblige. The heat of the interior room worked its way through the stiff, cold bombazine. She slumped against the wall, holding her freezing fingers to her mouth and blowing on them while Thomas spoke to a fat, swarthy man, presumably the manager.

Thomas did not look as though he had spent hours in a freezing, open cart. He radiated Gaelic goodwill. His teeth flashed in overt bonhomie, and his laughter was loud, nay, booming.

He swung the heavy greatcoat from his shoulders. Cat felt her lower lip go slack with surprise. She would never have thought it possible for Thomas to look as he did. His long, muscular legs were gloved in obscenely form-fitting black pantaloons. His broad shoulders sported a ridiculously tight, wasp-waist black coat. Lace appeared at every conceivable point of exit from the atrocious garment; it dripped from collar and cuffs; it sprouted above the snug, garishly embroidered waistcoat; it erupted from pockets.

His long, dark hair was tied back in an old-fashioned queue, but he had brushed some of it forward onto his face à la Byron. Rings, set with huge, semiprecious stones, bedecked most of the fingers he was waving in agitation at the innkeeper.

There was no way of disguising Thomas's size, but every other aspect of him was alien to her. He languished and pouted as he talked to the innkeeper; he slouched and tapped his toe; he patted his curls. He looked like a great, vulgar imitation of an English fop.

He turned as though he felt her amazed gaze, and his eyes lit up. Grabbing her gloved hand, he pulled her forward.

"Ah, this is she! *Ma petite chat!* You would be so unkind as to endanger her so enchanting life?" he said in loud English, and then, lowering his voice, he added in French, "The old hen doesn't hear very well. And she isn't in the best of health. I have got to get her back to England quickly before she bellies up on me and I'm left without even coach fare back to Lyons!"

Cat, though not conversant in the patois Thomas spoke, understood the gist of what he said and, accordingly, gasped.

The innkeeper shot her a sharp look. "She speaks French?"

Thomas shrugged. "What French she speaks is the schoolroom French of the English bourgeois, but I doubt she can even hear what we say without her horn. She says she is a rich merchant's widow. Humph! I think she was likely a rich merchant's trollop from some decades past. She has the appetites of a brothel-bred cyprian! But what matter to me, eh? The coin, from any hand, buys the same bread."

Again, Cat could not refrain from making a choking sound. The innkeeper watched her suspiciously.

"I think she understands us better than you suppose."

"Nonsense!" Thomas grabbed Cat around the waist and dragged her forward, pressing her close against his side. "She just wants attention, don't you, my precious cat?"

Thomas eloquently rolled his eyes at the innkeeper before turning Cat and lifting her veil. "Now, now," he said in heavily accented English, "there is no need to be so eager, *ma petite chat!* Tomas, he will kiss you."

Bending his head, he captured her mouth with his. His breath hissed warmly against her lips. "For God's sake, behave!"

He abruptly lifted his head and flipped down her veil, casually patting her rump as he turned her back around. She went rigid with indignation.

"Insatiable, these old cats. About that room . . ."

The innkeeper snickered. "And why should I rent you a room for half the price some others would be willing to pay?"

"Come now," Thomas said, reverting once more to the coarse French dialect, "you have made yourself a handsome profit on the English *putin*. Would you deny your countryman a few of the same coin? Look at her! She is an aging hag with nothing more to do than buy herself a slap and tickle. Now she wants to be slapped and tickled in England. *Voilà!* I send her back. She pays me well for this last night, to touch a young man's body once more. You will deny her? You will deny me? I tell you, my friend, I have much need of the money this night will bring."

The unmitigated gall of the insufferable brute! Playacting or not, he could not get away with his infuriating charade unchallenged. She clawed at his arm.

"Tomas! Tomas, I'm hungry," she complained.

He patted her hand. "Yes, my sweetings, my adored, *ma chat*."

"And I want more kisses! Not that puny little peck you just gave me. You'll have to earn your keep with more heat than that, m'lad! You pretty Frenchmen, always bragging about *l'amour* . . . pish! Thin-lipped lot of bandy roosters. More strut than stuff!"

Thomas stared at her.

"All those boasts you made!" Cat continued, warming to her role. "I should have realized with that much smoke, there would only be ashes! Ha! If last night is any example of what I can expect tonight, I'd be better off with a randy sailor. Something with a bit of bottom, and not all wind."

The innkeeper sputtered, his eyes bulging from his round face.

"Yes, my little dove, my lamb, my . . . cat," Thomas said, reaching out to tweak her cheek through the veil. It was just a little bit too much like a pinch to be affectionate. His eyes gleamed with some indecipherable light.

"And I don't want to stand here anymore," Cat whined. "My legs are tired. I want a cup of chocolate. I want a nice pillow to sit on. You arrange it. Do it now! I don't wish to stand here all day while you mumble with this fat man! Might as well make yourself useful in *some* capacity! I want you to—"

Suddenly the innkeeper snorted, clapping Thomas on the back. Rapidly he said, "Take the room, my friend. Whatever you make off this old witch, you will more than earn!"

"I don't know whether to applaud or blush for you," Thomas said as soon as they were in the small chamber the innkeeper had directed them to.

"Blush?! If you even have a memory of embarrassment, it would come as a shock! How could you tell him such—"

"As easily as you. 'A bit of bottom,' indeed!" he said.

"I overheard the phrase on the Paris streets," Cat said saucily.

"I should hope so!" The beginnings of a smile hovered on his lips.

"Although I might as well have heard it from you. You aren't very good company for a virtuous woman to keep." She tapped his chest with her forefinger.

The teasing light dimmed in his eyes. Hoping to provoke him into one of their enjoyable verbal battles, Cat continued. "A woman would have to be beyond naive to allow you to exercise any influence over her. You are far too bad. Dangerous for a decent woman to be with. No, indeed, you needn't sound so self-righteous! I may just as easily have heard the term from you . . . *Monsieur Ruin!*"

Something had gone badly awry. Her attempts to draw him into a bit of wordplay had failed miserably. His humor had died. She could see that, even though his mouth still wore something like a smile.

"You are, as always, correct. It was a bit of a farce I was attempting to divert you with. Lessons in unimpeachable behavior given by the crown prince of degeneracy."

She had not thought her careless words could wound him. But it was there, a shadow of pain hidden in his level gaze. She reached out a hand.

"Thomas, I did not mean what you think. You aren't like that!" she said earnestly.

Suddenly he understood. And understanding was like a curse. Cat's almost miraculous acceptance of his debauched past, the way she ignored that despicable scene with Daphne, the blushing allusion to his foreign intrigues and his "necessary role"; it all made a sort of bitter sense. She had made him into some sort of hero! She had sanitized his past, carefully constructing illusions.

God, he thought humorlessly, *such an imagination might even be able to account for Mariette Leons' little son*. It was a pity he had to punish such an achievement.

He did not want her sympathy, or the ridiculous, maddening fantasy she was trying to erect about him. He wanted her to see him as he was, as he had been. He did not want her to make him into some misunderstood paragon on a pedestal. He had no head for heights.

And so, his gaze locked on hers, his arms held rigidly at his sides so they mightn't betray him by gathering her to him, he said, "You are correct. I am unfit company for young girls. Happily, I favor women. The titter of untried chits is quaint, but I appreciate a great deal more other, more intimate sounds women make."

Each word was enunciated calmly, his casual tone at variance with his erect stance as he awaited her inevitable reaction.

"Thomas, no," she said, so softly he could just hear the denial. A denial of his past. Of him. She would detest him if she fully understood. Darkness flowered inside him.

"Oh, yes, Cat," he said sadly, desperately. "Yes. Did you think because I played at being a rustic, all the stories were just rumors? Society might embellish a few details, but embellishments do not negate fact."

His self-condemnation was painful for her to witness. His anguish was nearly tangible. She hated it, hated that he caused himself such pain. "Don't," she said.

Thomas heard her. She must be pleading for him to retract his words. Why else would she sound so wretched? He drew his breath in deeply through his nostrils. She didn't even want to hear that small truth about him. The darkness expanded.

Each "no" she said was a toll, knelling the death of his too fervent hopes, his too extravagant dreams, goading the blackness, forcing him to continue. Each "no" built higher the already unscalable wall that separated them, the wall he had been futilely hammering against. Better to kill his hope now, even if it meant destroying her pretty little illusion. At least, if nothing else, they would have honesty between them.

"Do you know why I was recruited to serve His Majesty in France? It really is an amusing, if naughty, anecdote. But you have chosen to embrace the slightly outré in your role as temptress and should hear it. No, I insist. It will further your instruction.

"I didn't quit society, Cat. Nor were any doors closed to me. I am, for all my sins, discreet. No, Cat. I chose to leave London society because it did not allow me to—how shall I put this?—explore my most base impulses. 'Twas too restrictive, by half. Yes, Cat, the netherworld of the *ton* did not offer me the recreation I sought." The words were choked from him. His voice had dropped to a hoarse whisper.

"Thomas, don't—"

"Don't? But, Cat!" A horrible parody of amusement issued from his mouth. "My dearest! Best beloved! That's just it. I did. I was twenty-four and bored. Don't stop me, Cat; the story is just getting good." She had reached out a hand to arrest his recitation. Angrily he shook it off.

He didn't have to do this; to try and shock her, repulse her, warn her. She loved him just as fervently as she hated his past. Hated everything he'd done, every horror he had witnessed. But only because it had wounded him so deeply, had injured his soul so grievously.

She had to make him understand, make him stop hurting himself so much. Proud Thomas. Worldly, sophisticated Thomas, wanting so much to forgive himself. He would laugh at her if she were to suggest he was his harshest judge. His only judge. Damn! She could not think of any words to convince him!

He fixed his gaze over her head, taking her silence for shock. He continued. "I went to France. I had spent enough time in so many, varied beds in France that, coupled with a natural aptitude for languages, I had grown more than proficient with any number of dialects. I had great fun eluding Napoleon's agents. That's when Colonel Seward approached me. Such God-given talents mustn't be allowed to go to waste.

"Isn't it a quiz, Cat, my angel? Uncurbed promiscuity recommends one as a spy? That's what I was, a spy. What, nothing to say? Let me finish. Do you know what a spy does, Cat? He uses people. He wheedles information from them. He works on their weaknesses, their secret vices, to get things from them. To exploit them. I was very good at it."

He was talking about Daphne Bernard. He had to be. Cat seized on the memory of Daphne's avaricious eyes, her hand grabbing the paste pendant. Desperately she sought a way to combat his self-loathing.

"Women like Daphne Bernard are not innocent victims," she said. "They make choices. They know what they are doing."

"Daphne Bernard?" Thomas frowned, looking befuddled for a second. "Ah, yes, Daphne. True, she knows what she's about. But what about women like Mariette Leons?"

"Who?" Cat whispered.

"Mariette Leons. The pretty young wife of a deputy in Napoleon's cabinet. An ambitious man, André Leons. Ambitious and stupid. He neglected his wife and little son. He never paid attention to them unless it was to boast of his privileged position. The rest of his time he spent currying favor with his superiors."

Thomas stared at her, haunted. Cat knew he wasn't seeing her then. He was seeing another woman, a specter from his past. She held her breath.

"I saw I could make use of this most fortuitous situation. I paid her court. She was so young, Cat. Not much older than you. She tried so hard to be a respectable, virtuous wife. But I couldn't have that now, could I? I hounded her. I pursued her. I pushed, and pleaded, and pressed until I finally wore her down.

"She agreed to meet me at a park, early in the morning. To avert any suspicions, she brought her son, Emile. I was angry she'd brought the lad. He was young. Three, I believe." Thomas's voice was soft. He lifted his hand to brush a lock of hair from Cat's face. The gesture was distracted, automatic. His hand shook.

"We sat on a bench surrounded by a nice, thick screen of bushes, and I proceeded to . . . seduce her. She was excited, nervous, and I was . . . intent. Then I heard horses on the bridle path. An early morning race. I looked around and noticed the boy was gone. And I knew.

"I tore through the hedge. I ran faster than I had ever run, and I was still too late. But not too late to see him. He was playing in the path where it curved sharply around a bend. I would like to blame the riders, but I can't. There is no way they could possibly have seen him. He died instantly."

"Oh, God, Thomas," Cat whispered in horror.

Poor little boy, all his potential, all his might-have-beens ended in a tragic instant. Poor mother, all the smiles she'd never see, the tears she'd never dry. His little clothes put away, never to be out-grown, never to be worn out. Sobs choked Cat. Tears flowed down her cheeks.

"Yes. God," murmured Thomas. "I bought a commission and went to Salamanca after that. I was even given medals for my proficiency in kill-ing. Eventually that diversion palled. I resigned my commission and went to Devon. That is when you arrived, Cat, my own, to rescue me from inevitable ennui. I thank you."

So much bitterness. So much hate. So much guilt.

Her head was bent forward in misery, the fall of her hair obscuring her features. But he could see the flash of a tear catch the rounded curve of her chin.

"How could you foresee his death, Thomas? It was a tragic accident." She sounded so sad, and yet there was no censure, no hate. It could not be. He was investing her tone with the things he yearned to hear. He shook with unchecked anger at his own heart's stubborn refusal even now to relinquish its claim.

"Damn it, madam!" he ground out. "What can I say to convince you? I am not some misunderstood Byronic ass, unaccountable for his own actions. My parents were decent people, my youth unexceptional. I chose my course. I was not forced to it!"

She could not speak for weeping. She struggled for mastery. She lifted her eyes to his. White lines scored the grim set of his mouth. Dark shadows hung beneath his burning eyes. Tears fell unchecked down her cheeks.

She made one last attempt, raising a shaking hand and laying it on his arm. "Thomas! To me you are never—"

Her words seemed to shatter his harsh restraint.

"Damnation!" he said again, and this time his curse was a groan. "I was never what? Vulgar? Forward? Salacious? And you thought since I had never pressed you, I could not be those things and worse? Have you not be listening? Ridiculous child! Imprudent chit!

"You thought since you had never seen me wink and leer and caper, I was incapable of base action? I'd thought I'd taught you better than that. Subtlety, *ma coeur*. I am ever subtle."

He grabbed her wrists, dragging her forward, bending his face inches from her bowed head. "I undressed you even as you sat drinking tea in my

morning room. I wetted your mouth with mine
each time you nibbled a piece of toast. I ravished
you every damned time you entered a room! My
God, woman, in my mind I have had you a thousand times since we met!

"There! Does *that* disabuse you of any little mis-
conceptions you might have concerning my character? What? No? Well, maybe this will!"

He caught her to him, intent on taking her
mouth and punishing her with his kiss, forcing
her, once and for all, to reject him. She did
nothing to stop him; no hand was raised to
fend him off; she did not plead with him to
release her.

He could not do it. For all that he was, he had
never forced himself on any woman. And this
woman was Cat. He could not take from her in
anger, not even a kiss.

Abruptly he released her, and she stumbled back,
bracing her hand on a chair. He lifted both hands to
his temples. She was shaking, agitation fluttering
the lace covering her décolletage.

His gaze traveled haphazardly about the room,
entrapment expressive in the erratic movement of
his eyes. He looked older, tired; deep lines scored
his lean cheeks; his jaw was stubbled with a gray-
black beard. Cat wanted to brush the strand of
glossy, dark hair from his forehead, wanted to tell
him his kiss could never frighten her. She would
welcome it. His anger was too great an obstacle.
She had to try.

"Thomas."

He stepped back, opening the door behind him.
"Forgive me," he said, and was gone.

Thomas did not see the black-clad gentleman
lounging in the wing-backed chair before the host's
fire. A seamed countenance turned with rapacious

interest as Thomas crossed the room and disappeared into the night.

"Monsieur." The thin Englishman beat his ebony cane against the tabletop, calling the manager to him. "Monsieur, I see you have staying with you Mr. Thomas Montrose."

The innkeeper frowned in consternation, more than willing to avail himself of this oh-so-rich English aristo's whim. The man had paid excellent well for the use of his last room, and he was polishing off bottle after bottle of the house's cheapest wine in order to, he said, "carry me through any damned embargo."

"No Mr. Montrose is staying here, milord."

"Curse you, man! I just saw his monstrous form leave!"

"That? That was no Englishman, milord. Just a French *putin*, trash what makes his living off of servicing rich women."

"Damn you man, that was no Frenchie. 'Twas Montrose, I say!"

The innkeeper wrung his hands, unwilling to disagree with so rich a guest, yet not wanting to encourage a potentially embarrassing encounter.

"I am sorry to say, but you are mistaken. He has brought his English keeper with him. She is upstairs even now. No doubt she has sent him off for some exotic toy to entertain her. She is very much the bawd." He winked as he leaned over to fill the gentleman's cup.

"I still say 'tis Montrose. Who is this English doxy?"

The innkeeper shrugged. "Some rich merchant's widow."

"Does she have a name?"

"No name was given, monsieur."

"Come now, you fat jackanapes, he must have called her something!" the man demanded angrily, leaning forward on the table and slamming a fist down.

The innkeeper rifled his memory to oblige. His face broke into a smile. "Cat!" he said triumphantly. "He called her his 'little cat' many times.

"Now," the innkeeper continued as the gentleman eased back in his chair, an expression of surprise quickly supplanted by malicious satisfaction, "can I get you anything else, Milord Barrymore?"

Chapter 23

Thomas returned a few hours before dawn. Cat was waiting for him. Her face pale and, still wearing Hecuba's awful gown, she rose shakily from the chair and came to him.

She looked tired unto death, and his mind could not fight his heart's need to comfort her. He could punish her with his history no longer.

"Thomas." It was a single word, but enough. Taking her into his arms, he cradled her against his chest.

"Thomas, please—"

"Shh, now, *enfant*. It's all right."

"It isn't! You must understand!"

"Yes, yes. I understand," he soothed, stroking her hair back, kneading the tense muscles in her shoulders. "I am a great beast to have subjected you to a self-indulgent litany of my past. Forgive me."

"It is the past, Thomas. It is a tragedy, but it was an accident. An accident!" she said into his chest. His arms tightened. It would be all right. She pulled her head up to look into his eyes and found him smiling tenderly at her.

Her words sounded so intent, so determined. A pity he could not believe them. She was exhausted and frightened and alone with a man whom all members of society would call a monster if they had the information he'd just given her. Of course she must make herself believe in him, if but for a little while longer. The accumulative effect of all the fears she'd endured in the past two days had blunted her ability to appreciate the enormity of his guilt. That had to be the answer. Sighing, Thomas regained his hold on her, forcing himself to be content with these few embraces, this torturous, tentative intimacy.

"Of course, child," he murmured into her silky hair. "And now, we must be off. The packet unloaded an hour ago, and it's in our best interest to have you secreted aboard before anyone else divines your presence."

Child. Enfant. She rebelled against the innocent appellations. He was deliberately putting distance between them. She felt as though she stood on one side of a vast chasm, and he on the other, and while she tried desperately to breach the distance, he did all he could to widen it. She was tired and exhausted and terrified of the remote look in his eyes.

She didn't deserve to be summarily expelled from the ranks of adulthood. She didn't deserve to have her words, nay, her heart, dismissed. And yet what could she do? How could she help him to forgive himself? How could she breach the gap that each of his kind, detached smiles widened? She retreated into frustrated anger. If he did not want her, so be it! But it was cruel to reject her love as childish infatuation.

As she pushed herself away from him, anger animated Cat's wan face. "You may choose to distance me by calling me a child, but naming me thus does not make it so," she said with dignity.

Thomas wanted to believe her. God knows, he wanted to trust her words, her faith, but other lessons, learned long ago, whispered to him. *She has convinced herself*, he thought, *and that is why she is so convincing to me. And I have the added liability of wanting to believe.* He did not think he was strong enough to withstand her revulsion when facts presented themselves to her in the guise of an ex-mistress, a rumored story.

All this, he thought in the space of a breath, while her eyes met his directly. And love, he admitted, had made a coward of him. He knew any wound dealt her would be a fatal one to him.

"No. Of course not, Cat," he said patiently. "But we really need make haste."

Lifting her cloak, he wrapped it about her shoulders, pulling the drawstrings closed about her neck, his warm fingers moving impersonally against her flesh.

She jerked away from his touch, tears threatening once more. He was as removed from her as if they inhabited different worlds. He was utterly inaccessible to anything she might do or say.

"Damn you!"

"Quite," Thomas returned sadly.

The Channel crossing was rough. The waves mounted high in front of the cold March wind, and the packet ship lurched into watery gullies, climbing temporary precipices only to crash down into deep chasms. The sea churned, and the air boiled with thick clouds; rain was the only constant.

Cat was sick. Horribly sick. Thomas had spirited her to the tiny cabin well before daybreak and left her there. She refused to let him see how ill she felt, nodding tersely in reply to his comments, not trusting herself to speak.

The intensity of her nausea didn't abate with time. She ended the voyage lying on the narrow plank bed, shaking uncontrollably as each receding wave of sickness promised an immediate replacement. Several times Thomas had knocked on the door. Cat mustered enough strength to tell him to go away or reply that she was fine.

Even after docking in Brighton, she wasn't allowed to leave the cursed ship. Thomas, finally realizing Cat was not going to see him, sent a note via the cabin boy. She must wait until the other passengers had disembarked, and then another hour for good measure, before leaving the horrid-smelling little hole.

By the time Thomas came for her, Cat was feverish and weak, her stomach empty of anything more to expel. She was only happy the darkness of the night masked her sickness. She would show Thomas no weakness to support his concept of her as a juvenile. She stumbled as she made her way down the gangplank. Thomas caught her arm. Hailing a coach, he lifted her bodily inside, shouting an address at the driver before swinging himself on top.

Within a quarter of an hour, they had arrived at the Castle Inn. Only then did the irregularity of her situation occur to Cat. And so she looked for support where support had always been given, slipping her hand in Thomas'. Exhausted and weak as she was, her voice sounded plaintive to her own ears.

"All our careful schemes are sure to be for naught now, Thomas." She tried a sophisticated smile. "Someone is going to remark my unchaperoned condition. Even if it's the manager, or a chambermaid, my reputation shall be in shreds by dawn. Ah, well, 'twas an adventure."

She was so brave, so unbelievably game, he thought, drawing her up the stairs through the doors of the fashionable hotel. The skin beneath her eyes was purple with dark shadows. Her pale forehead gleamed with moisture, and her fingers trembled in his clasp. She was terrified, nearly sick with fright.

He shouldn't have been surprised; most young, unmarried girls would have succumbed to hysteria days ago. The future of any unmarried woman hinged on the good opinion of so few. And yet to see Cat so overset by the chance that someone might see her unchaperoned, that it made her quite literally ill, did surprise him.

"Don't fret, m'dear," he said. "It's been taken care of."

He led her into the lobby and seated her in a deep velvet settee before going to the front desk. A liveried youth scurried up the broad staircase, and Cat clasped her hands in her lap, waiting for . . . a bath.

The image of a steaming tub beguiled her weary mind. Closing her eyes, she swayed back against the thick, tufted cushion, allowing herself to let go of the anger, the sickness, the hurt.

"Cat!" a familiar voice exclaimed.

Her eyes flew open. Her half brother Marcus stood before her. His amber-shot green eyes were alight with joy. "Marcus!" Cat cried, holding out her hands. He grabbed hold of them, gripping tightly, and settled himself next to her. "What . . . ? However did you . . . ?"

Marcus' grin turned wry. "I've been sitting here in Brighton, twiddling my thumbs for nearly a week. Montrose sent word I was to meet you and Great-Aunt Hecuba. He couldn't give me an exact time but urged me to be here to meet any incoming ships from mid-month on."

"He did, did he?"

"Yes. Quite adamant he was, too. Must have sent the damned—excuse me, Cat—dratted thing before he even left the country. Good heavens, Cat, I *am* glad to see you," he ended fervently.

His obvious joy warmed her. Of all her variously sired siblings, Cat had always been closest to Marcus. Most probably because she fretted so over him. He seemed to feel the irregularity of their family, as well as their financial situation, so keenly. He took his responsibilities so seriously. There was too little time in his young life for the pleasurable pursuits of most young men of his age and station. So typical of Marcus, to fly from Bellingcourt to make sure he had fulfilled the letter of Thomas' edict.

"I thank you, Marcus," Cat said, her obvious pride making him blush.

"Not at all, Cat. My pleasure," he said stiffly. "And now, where is my great-aunt? Preaching to the serving girls already?"

"Not exactly . . ."

Marcus sobered immediately. "Is she all right? A strenuous journey such as you have just undertaken might well render the heartiest physique ill—"

"No, no," Cat said hurriedly. "She's fine. I think."

"You think?" Marcus' brows rose. "Oh Lord, Cat. Don't tell me she remained in France to carry the Church of England's word to Napoleon's hordes!"

Cat laughed. "Oh, Marcus! Quite the reverse. Hecuba has eloped with a French marquis. She had hied herself off to the border when last I heard." Her giggles erupted anew as Marcus' expression became one of stunned incredulity.

"Never say!"

"I swear to it." Cat attempted to keep her lips from twitching as she solemnly raised her hand.

He stared at her a moment and then threw back his blond head, laughing. "The old faker!"

"I believe that is exactly what I said."

They smiled at each other in approval before Marcus said, "But you must be done in, Cat. You look . . . that is, I admit, after hearing all the reports of your social success in Paris, I am a bit confounded to think French mode insists on that black wool thing sagging around you."

Cat haughtily tilted her chin, staring at Marcus as though through a lorgnette. "The reports of my success were, no doubt, *under*emphasized. And this is bombazine, not wool, and it is about to be revived as the epitome of *au courant* fashion."

"You're quizzing me, Cat."

"A little, little brother," she said gently.

"Sounded a bit of a peacock, did I?"

"No more than I a peahen," she said. She looked down at her dress. Soaked in perspiration from her bouts with seasickness, it had wilted. She became distinctly aware of an unpleasant aroma. "I am a fright."

"Yes." The fondness of his tone robbed it of insult. "And I am a boor to keep you hanging about a public lobby while a bath waits for you in your suite upstairs."

"A bath? A suite? How?"

"I heard Montrose ordering the manager to see to it immediately. The suite has been held in readiness for four days."

Cat's head swung to where she had last seen Thomas. He was not there.

It had been a harmless, vicarious pleasure, watching Cat's reunion with her brother. Her humorous animation, so absent from her during the past twenty-four hours—no, Thomas corrected himself, so absent from his own life for nearly seven months—had reappeared. Her eyes gleamed with a teasing light. Her laughter rippled like low, throaty music across the lobby.

She had looked thus any number of times in the few short weeks during which he had instructed her. *He* had made her laugh like that; *he* had provoked the devilish gleam in her eyes; *he* had drawn out the quick wit, the naughty observations. It had all been for *him*.

He was jealous of Cat's gangly eighteen-year-old-brother. If it weren't so damned laughable, it would be sad. As sad as watching her slip from his scope like a woodland sylph disappearing into the dawn mists, leaving only her laughter to taunt her mortal lover with a taste of eternally denied pleasures.

Well, he sighed, turning to sign the various registration papers the manager had slipped beneath his hand, he had done his honorable, chivalrous, damned duty by her. She was properly delivered to the inexperienced hand of her brother, the Viscount Eltheridge. She could sail about Brighton under the perfectly acceptable auspices of his protectorship . . . such as it was.

What matter if Marcus was even more a boy than Cat was a girl? The two of them ought to have a grand time of it, tweaking society's nose. *I am acting like a sulking schoolboy*, Thomas thought. He forced himself to amend his evaluation. The lad did not seem the nose-tweaking sort, and Cat? Well, Cat was circumspect. Practical. Canny.

In point of fact, Cat needed male guidance and protection less than any woman Thomas had ever known. It had taken an impending war to offer him a chance to be of use to her, and even here he was not at all certain she wouldn't have escaped and made it back to England quite as well without his aid. Cat was self-reliant, independent, and wholly desirable. He would go mad if he pursued these thoughts.

She deserved to find herself a real hero, a "parfait gentle man," with no dark past to threaten her happily-ever-after. Seldom had Thomas indulged in regrets, considering them to be emotionally destructive. And, he told himself fiercely, he did not regret his past now, at this far too late a date. He never had. He had always accepted what he had been.

Damned if he could figure out why his objectivity had deserted him now. Why now his past taunted him with details he had thought long forgotten.

No, any excuses he came up with for hanging about Brighton were fabrications he built for the single purpose of being near her.

The manager broke through Thomas' absorption, asking if he, too, required a room. Thomas looked back to where Cat sat, her hands closed tightly about one of her brother's, her head tilted at an inquiring angle. How could he leave her? However could he stay?

Chapter 24

Thomas' hand was evident in the alacrity with which the staff of the Castle Inn sought to make Cat's stay as pleasant as humanly possible. A maid and a footman were miraculously employed by the following morning. Her suite was the most opulent the hotel had to offer. Exotic, out-of-season hyacinths and roses perfumed the air. Fine-textured linens were daily replaced on the huge canopied bed. A driver of a private hack stationed himself at the entrance to the lobby, her destination his sole concern.

And Thomas had disappeared.

Over the next several days, he sent a few notes, as often addressed to Marcus as to Cat. They were brief, impersonal inquiries as to their health and requirements. These notes so infuriated Cat with their remote politeness that she tore them up, consigning them to the flames in which she wished to send their author.

Cat knew Marcus had seen Thomas. There was no other explanation for her brother's knowledge of her escape with him. Marcus advised her to claim she had been accompanied by a loyal French maid—whom she had left happily enriched at Dieppe—when she recounted her adventure. The suggestion sounded like something Thomas would have concocted. She did not question it.

And then, a day later, Marcus returned with a thick packet of bank notes, his young countenance troubled. Thomas had insisted on making them the loan, he explained. Cat's first impulse was to send the money back, along with a bouquet of his bloody roses. But practicality forbade so dramatic, albeit noble, a gesture; she couldn't go about Brighton dressed in Hecuba's sorry outfit.

Her sojourn in France having sharpened her eye, Cat assembled a wardrobe of extravagant chic. Madame Feille, only too happy to get word of the most *à la mode* fashions, promised to dispatch a few of the simpler gowns within a day.

By the end of the week, Cat and Marcus had rejoined society. Cat's thrilling if mysterious flight from Paris secured them invitations everywhere. Forthwith, she became a minor celebrity. With each laurel, Cat inwardly cringed. Each commendation brought a denial to her lips. The *ton* considered her modest reticence further grounds for tribute. Accordingly, she was courted, her adventure the main course at many a fashionable meal. Each time she was asked to relate the tale, she was afraid she would look up in mid narration to find Thomas watching her in mock admiration.

He never was.

If not for the flowers, the notes, and Marcus, occasional, unexplained absence, Cat would have thought Thomas had quit Brighton altogether. She decided to ignore him as thoroughly as he ignored her. But, God help her, she missed him.

And then, suddenly—inexplicably—it was over. The invitations stopped with humiliating abruptness. Women who had clutched their hands together in open admiration not twenty-four hours before averted their eyes in confusion when Cat entered a room. And men, with sad smiles, turned from her without uttering a word.

Cat knew what social ruin looked like. She had seen it from the fringes several times. It was not always ugly, vicious. It could be sad, inexorable, apologetic . . . like this.

She half suspected—and God forgive her, she more than half hoped—Thomas would come to her now. But wishing did not make it so. Even poor Marcus was undone by Thomas' apparent defection. She knew her brother had finally sent a note to Thomas' address. She knew, from the pale, strained expression on his far too-youthful face, that it had gone unanswered.

There were many things to be taken care of: details to be ironed out, documents to be secured, debts to be called in. Thomas handled them all with grim resolve.

The reports sent by Marcus had not exaggerated; Cat's reputation was destroyed. And Thomas was going to find the root of the evil rumors. He made the rounds of places he had not been in years. The gaming hells, the houses of pleasure. His ears open, his eyes watchful, he spoke with men he had not passed words with in half a dozen seasons. Nothing much had changed. Some familiar faces were older, but younger ones had surfaced. The expressions, sly, knowing, rapacious, were the same. Winks greeted Thomas, arrival at Raggert's clubhouse on the Steyne. Allusions to "exotic pleasurable devices" were pitched loudly enough to ensure he overheard them. The disreputable companions of his past clapped him on the back as he passed, welcoming him back to the fold.

He endured it all, preoccupied with allaying the worst of the consequences, seeking the source of the gossip. After he found it, Thomas went to London. To find Hellsgate Barrymore.

Thomas ran Hellsgate to ground at a cockfight ten miles outside of London. In a dim, smoke-filled arena, Barrymore was surrounded by his cronies, a coterie of drunken highborn devils made surly by the repeated failure of their birds to win. He was lounging in an incongruously ornate sedan chair, his long, black-clad body emphasizing the death-white pallor of his face, his thin lips smiling with satisfaction as he watched the violent dispatch of yet another gaming cock.

"Blood sports, Barrymore? I would have thought you'd be interested in more participatory pleasures," Thomas murmured.

Barrymore's deep-set eyes flickered sideways, his surprise at Thomas' appearance immediately masked. His companions paused in their raucous encouragement of the birds, their attention diverted by the more interesting play now unfolding.

"Hmm. Yes, Montrose. Usually," Barrymore said.

"Something which forces you to extend yourself, no doubt. Really test your manhood?" The corner of Thomas' mouth curled, though his voice remained soft.

"I'm accounted fair in a number of 'manly' pursuits, as, I believe, are you." Hellsgate sneered, looking around to acknowledge the appreciative snickers of his followers.

"Oh, I wouldn't feign to place myself in your company. I never pulled the wings from flies, like some boys did, to establish my masculinity."

The smile died on Barrymore's face.

"I hear there are any number of wingless flies in your filthy lair," Thomas continued calmly.

The snickers grew more pronounced as the surrounding men, like a pack of jackals eager to exploit any weakness, turned their attention toward Hellsgate.

"They say that causing pain is the only thing that can excite you enough to make you of any use to a woman. There are even rumors you carry a bottle of flies about in your pocket in case you find some poor female desperate enough to accept coin to endure your attention," Thomas said.

He continued. "But you know what filthy things rumors are, don't you, Barrymore? You'll be pleased to know I severely remonstrated the talebearers . . . I promised them bugs alone would never coax you to readiness."

The thin nostrils at the end of Barrymore's long nose became pinched and white. His eyes narrowed.

"Satisfaction." Hellsgate hissed the single word.

"Not from what the doxies in Five Dials say."

Barrymore uncoiled from his seat, his wiry frame tense with anger. "I demand satisfaction, you trumped-up cur!"

A beatific smile curved Thomas' lips. "Yes."

"When?"

"Now."

Barrymore frowned. Though he was known for his hot-blooded rages, some fundamental instinct urged him caution in dealing with this tall, preternaturally quiet man.

"Impossible," Barrymore blustered in contempt. "There's no place where we can meet safely for swordplay."

"Safe?" Thomas queried softly. "Oh, but this won't be safe. Not at all. And swordplay? I believe as you issued the challenge, your code as gentleman binds you to comply with my choice of weapon. I have been too long from my country home and have a whim to bury my hands in manure. Fisticuffs."

Barrymore's head spun around, looking to his companions for the support he needed to deny this nobody his ridiculous demand. But the bloodthirsty crowd, eager for sport, nodded in vigorous agreement with Thomas' assertion.

"Where?" Barrymore demanded.

"Here. Now. Outside."

"You'll be sorry for this, Montrose. I'll break your bloody neck!" Barrymore promised, leading the way past Thomas' mocking bow to the field outside.

Ripping his coat off, Hellsgate flung it at one of a growing number of men who had given up the spectacle inside for the one without. A drunken gent raised his hand, waving a fat coin purse above his head.

"A hundred quid on Barrymore!" he shouted.

"Fifty on Montrose!"

The voices rose to a din, the shouted bets met and raised as the crowd jostled one another, ringing the two men, pressing closer.

Thomas shrugged out of his coat. A hand snatched it from his grip. He turned to look at his opponent.

Barrymore shifted back and forth on the balls of his feet, his body oscillating restlessly, his hands clasping and unclasping at his sides, his head moving in a snakelike motion as he evaluated Thomas. Hellsgate was an acknowledged whip, a fearless swordsman; his sinewy physique bespoke dangerous speed.

Thomas was motionless. His pose was relaxed, his shoulders slouched slightly as Barrymore took his measure. Thomas' hands hung open. He looked too lean for his great height and breadth, a starved bull being sized up for dinner by a bush wolf. With lightning rapidity, Hellsgate feinted forward to deliver a wicked blow to Thomas' jaw.

The blow never landed. Barrymore pivoted on the balls of his feet, his head swinging as he looked around in confusion to where Thomas had gone.

He stood, still relaxed, his expression watchful. Barrymore threw another punch, and then a series of vicious, sharp blows which glanced off arms raised in near-negligent self-defense.

The crowd shouted at the combatants, eager for blood, impatient with the awkward, one-sided fight. Hellsgate flung himself at Thomas, seeking to batter him low in the gut. It was like pounding his fists against corded leather. There was no give to the man. Thomas deflected Barrymore's most powerful blows, knocking his fists down just as they were about to make contact.

"Dog!" Barrymore panted, winded by his fruitless efforts. The howls of derision rising from the mob incited him. Fury—mindless, murderous rage—eclipsed his capacity to think. Spying a thick prod on the ground, Hellsgate snatched it up and wheeled around to bring the stout pole crashing into Thomas' ribs.

Its deadly arc slammed into Thomas' lean side. But Thomas only wrenched the pole from Barrymore's grasp and hurled it over the heads of the hooting mob. For the first time, fear tickled Barrymore's self-confidence. Thomas still stood. His eyes gleamed black in his bronzed face. His eyes alone seemed alive, mocking.

Barrymore roared and flew at Thomas, determined to knock him to the ground. And then, as if in thick, slowed motion, Barrymore saw Thomas raise one large brown hand. Hellsgate tried to twist clear, but he felt the impact of the open-handed blow catch the side of his face. His legs buckled as his head snapped backward with an audible crack.

Thomas caught Hellsgate as he fell and pulled him upright. He steadied him, one hand twisting into the dirty white linen of Hellsgate's shirt. With the other hand, Thomas slapped Barrymore brutally across the face, first with his palm, then with the back of his hand, then with his palm again. And then again, and again, and still again. The violence took on the savage cadence of a drumbeat as the rhythmic smack of knuckle against flesh echoed through the suddenly quiet crowd.

Clawing at the man holding him, Hellsgate sought to gouge the merciless black eyes impaling him with cold-blooded joy. His nails scored the dark face above his. He saw the blood running in ruby rivulets, and yet Montrose did not seem to notice. Barrymore's mind clouded as the relentless blows rained down on him. He struggled in the implacable grip. Even more than the pain, he was aware of the humiliating spectacle he made, held upright and slapped nearly insensate by the silent man. As one might beat a dog or a servant.

"I'll ruin you for this, Montrose! You won't be accepted into the lowest fringes of society when I'm done with you!" he choked desperately.

The upraised hand halted in midmotion. Barrymore felt triumphant glee well up inside. He had won! His position as Prinny's confidant enabled him to make good the threatened social blackmail. Montrose would cease or be destroyed . . . and Barrymore wielded the power to bring the swarthy giant to heel, like the cringing cur he was.

Hellsgate's lips twisted into a smile. Blood dribbled down his chin from his torn lip. He blinked, wanting to clear his sight to better enjoy Montrose's helpless capitulation. He looked up.

A chilling smile split Montrose's face. Disbelieving, Barrymore heard the man laugh, a sound bereft of amusement.

Thomas leaned toward Barrymore, still dangling from a single fist, until their faces were inches apart.

"You fool!" Montrose said in a low voice. "You bloody ass! I am a *war hero*, for God's sake!" He made the tribute sound like a curse. "Do you think society will rally round you, you swine?! You, who skulked drunkenly in carnal houses while I played the bloody hero for them! I severed heads for them! I butchered Frenchmen for them! For the Regent. For the bloody empire! Do you think now, with Napoleon gathering forces, the *ton* is going to give a rat's ass about your whims, your offended consequence? They'll look at the beating I give you and be delighted I am still in fighting trim!"

Like cornered vermin, Barrymore fought for his survival, kicking his legs out, spitting and twisting in the merciless hold. It was useless. Another blow, and Hellsgate felt the blackness swallow him.

The crowd was silent, stunned by the cold-blooded vehemence they had just witnessed. With machinelike motions Montrose had battered Barrymore insensible, seemingly impervious to the vicious attack Barrymore had made with the staff. Montrose hadn't even flinched when the rod had cracked into his side. Such passionless violence seemed unnatural, even by their standards.

Thomas slowly scanned their number. His intensity made them uncomfortable, unnerved.

"You may take your 'friend' away now," he finally said. "And bear in mind that I am *not* one of you. I am unconcerned with your censure or approbation. But I will answer any future intimations concerning my wife with a savagery you can't begin to imagine."

Chapter 25

There was nothing Marcus could do. He was simply too young, too inexperienced, to deal with the tons disapproval. A single week ago, it had looked as though Cat were destined to be one of the favored stars in their shifting firmament. Today she was excluded with chilling finality. A few brave, foolish souls risked their own censure to whisper surreptitious words of greeting to her. But they dared venture no closer toward the thin line of expulsion.

Cat seemed oblivious to the slights. She was as serene as if she were a novitiate in some cloistered order. Only Marcus understood the cost of the pretense and saw her distress in the telltale quiver of her hand as she took his arm for their daily stroll in the park. It fed his burgeoning sense of insult. As did Thomas Montrose. Thomas had apparently yielded them to society's tender mercies after hearing, from Marcus' own pen, of the disgusting insults being heaped upon Cat's head. And all Marcus could do was silently escort Cat.

Of Thomas Montrose, Cat would not say a word. Daily, Marcus' mood grew more taciturn. Therefore, it was with unaccustomed suspicion that Marcus told Cat about her visitor one morning, two weeks after her arrival in Brighton.

"Giles Dalton, Marquis of Strand, is down in the lobby, Cat," Marcus said. He watched her carefully, uncertain how the arrival of her erstwhile suitor would affect her. Though she did not lift her eyes from the book open in her lap, she stopped reading.

"He begs an audience. I have told him you are not receiving visitors, but he insists."

"Show him up, Marcus."

"Cat, I don't think this is wise—"

She lifted her eyes and smiled with a teasing hint of genuine amusement. "I believe there is some adage about a barn door and an already absent horse. I confess, I am eager to hear why Giles ventures where others are loath to tread. No doubt it adds to his reputation as a dangerous man. On such banalities is notoriety founded."

"I won't leave you here alone with him," Marcus said gruffly.

"Pish. You may lurk outside the door if you so desire, but you haven't my leave to embarrass me with your protective posture."

Cat did not look overset by the prospect of an interview with Strand. Marcus wavered at the door, unwilling to allow her to open herself unsuspectingly to yet another wound. But after reading the determination in her posture, he finally went to fetch Strand.

Cat looked down at the book in her lap. Absently she noted she was still on the first chapter of the dratted thing, even though she had opened it over two hours ago. She closed it, a small frown between her brows.

She was glad Giles had safely made the trip from Paris. But she had never doubted he would. His financial resources and social connections had all but assured his safe passage.

It was this unfathomable visit that interested her. She could see no reason for it. She hadn't believed her own flippant comments to Marcus. Strand was too much of a gentleman to use her fall from grace to further his own reputation and too much of a stranger to upbraid her for her indiscretion. Indeed, Cat had been candid in telling Marcus she was curious. Nothing more.

If it were Thomas who had come . . . but he hadn't. His desertion robbed her of more sleep than any of the snubs she daily encountered. And, too, she was worried about Marcus. He was changing, his sweet nature eroded by his introduction into society. Poor Marcus. He so keenly felt her own presumed distress at these petty slights. He would never understand that her pain had been orchestrated by an altogether different maestro: a giant black-eyed one.

Cat could hardly admit it to herself. She was nearly as confused by Thomas' disappearance as she was wounded by it. It was the last thing she would have expected of him, so unlike everything she knew of him.

Giles Dalton, Lord Strand, entered, interrupting Cat's thoughts. His usual elegant saunter was replaced by a hurried gait. His linen, always so flawless, was crumpled. The cravat at his neck was pulled together haphazardly. His gray eyes lit on her immediately. He turned, speaking a few curt words to Marcus, who hovered at the door before closing it.

Strand came to her side, stopping to plant his lean legs apart, clasping his hands behind his back in a military attitude of respect.

"Lady Catherine," he said, his voice clipped.

"Lord Strand," she acknowledged. "I am pleased to see your return to London was a safe one."

"Yes. Ah . . . yes. I arrived yesterday."

"How precipitous of you to visit me so soon after your arrival," Cat teased gently. "Such haste must be exhausting. Won't you please be seated?" She motioned him to a chair.

He seemed taken aback by her cajoling tone, his eyes widening. Taking a seat near hers, his back stiff, Giles cleared his throat. "I trust you are well?"

"I enjoy unremarkable health, yes." Cat was increasingly amazed by the change in the man. His usually impeccable groomed hair was tousled. Tension tightened a physique she had become used to thinking of as slack, indolent. His lazy, bored expression had become sharp, focused.

"Good," he said. "Your well-being is important to me."

"You are kind."

"No." For the first time a familiar look of amusement appeared on his lean face, his sardonic humor colored by self-deprecation in his tone. "No, 'kind' is a word few would apply to me. Including myself. 'Tisn't kindness which prompts my visit."

Cat questioned him with a raised brow.

Giles took a deep breath before continuing. "Lady Catherine, er, Cat . . ."

"Yes?" she prompted.

"I know this is sudden on my part, but these things are often understood between two parties before any public awareness is necessary . . ." Giles trailed off, muttering a soft epitaph.

A sudden explanation for Strand's extraordinary behavior horrified Cat. Giles had heard the rumors about her. It should have been amusing. All of her well-laid plans, her carefully thought-out stratagems, her lessons with Thomas, had never garnered her the intense interest with which Giles was now watching her.

Her goal of becoming an irresistible seductress had finally been achieved. It had taken the malicious tongues of society to pique Strand's interest and bring him to the point of making an offer. But not the offer she had sought. Giles, Cat suspected, was going to offer her carte blanche. And it was not amusing.

Cat knew her face had become as white as the unseasonable snow melting against the windowpane. "Please, Lord Strand, do not—"

Lifting a hand to forestall her, Giles smiled wryly. "Besides, what with your erstwhile parent gallivanting about the world, I might well be in my dotage were I to await a personal reply to my suit."

Cat stared at him, now utterly confused.

Her shocked expression dismayed him. He ran a hand through his tangled golden hair. "I'm going about this badly, ain't I, m'dear? I would look as shocked myself if some disheveled brute burst into my sanctuary spouting inane chatter. Let me begin again."

My God! Cat thought in a daze. Giles Dalton, Marquis of Strand, was going to offer for her hand. His brilliant silver eyes were alight with tenderness, his hesitancy suddenly explicable. She knew she should be fair swelling with triumph, delight, joy—even as she knew the only emotion she felt was . . . pity. What did she know of Giles Dalton? She had pursued him with as little regard for his thoughts, concerns, or future happiness as the most hardened of social roués. She was ashamed.

He was saying something else now. She had to stop him. Bursting into his soft recitation, she said, "Lord Strand, speaking in a purely hypothetical manner, I could not imagine a greater honor than to have you circumvent convention on my behalf. But I can also not conceive of any situation in which you might wish to do so."

She waited, her heart in her throat, praying he would understand and relinquish his as-yet-unvoiced suit.

His eyes narrowed slightly in his handsome face, and his silence lasted a long heartbeat. "Well done, m'dear. Well felt." They were by far the most intimate words he had ever spoken to her. "Is it Montrose?"

Unprepared for that name coming from Strand, Cat brought her head up. For an instant her heart was clear in her eyes. She sat in numbed silence.

Giles rose. "I thought as much. It is hardly unexpected. Thomas alone seems able to surprise you into candor. I have seen you all but yawn at some of the most celebrated wags, but say Montrose's name and you fair blaze with emotion. You have never even spoken my given name, and yet you are no end filled with exclamations of 'Thomas.' "

"Surely you overstate the case, Lord Strand," Cat said, openly distressed.

"No," Giles said thoughtfully, "I think I state it very plainly. To society you are Lady Catherine Sinclair. To Montrose you are 'Cat,' and 'Lady Cat,' and any number of possibilities. And to you, Thomas Montrose is not merely a rusticating peer bored with the *ton*. I never stood a chance against a mentor, a co-conspirator, a playmate, a friend . . . a lover."

Her chin rose at that.

Giles smiled grimly. "The ultimate physical act is, when all is said and done, merely that. It is not essential, though desirable."

Seeing Cat's blush, Giles hurried on. "Forgive me," he said. "I have been unconscionably forward. Thomas would call me out if he knew I had caused a stain on your lovely cheeks. Regardless of his reputation, he is the most doggedly honor-bound man I have the pleasure of calling friend."

His own heart aching unfamiliarly, Strand was impatient to be gone from her and the possibilities she represented; potential that could only tantalize him. He missed her jerk of surprise, the astonishment in her gray-green eyes.

"Are you saying you know Thomas? How long have you known him? Do you know him well?"

"Well?" Strand asked, cocking his head. He gave a short laugh. "I would have said so. We were at Salamanca together. It was he who asked me to keep an eye on you in Paris."

"In Paris? Thomas asked you to be my escort? He *arranged* it?"

Strand noticed the color flushing her cheeks. "Of course. He told me not to leave you unattended under the direst of penalties. Not that I needed much persuasion. I confess, I was suspicious he had been trying his hand at matchmaking. I know better now."

"Do you?"

"Yes. I know Thomas very well. But then, I had thought I knew you, Lady Catherine. You have saved us both from a grave mistake. You would make a delightful marchioness, if Montrose were only a marquis."

He saluted her and, bowing sharply from the waist, took his leave of her.

Thomas fair flew to Brighton, pushing his gelding to a punishing pace, desperate to outdistance the rumor of his claim. Claiming her as his wife was the only thing he could have done, he told himself. Cat—practical, systematic Cat—could be convinced it was the only sensible course to follow. A part of him was enraged because, through no fault of her own, she was forced to this pass. But the intoxicating joy that surged through him at the thought of making her his wife left little room for noble sentiments.

Stopping at his rooms only long enough to change his linen and rid himself of the travel dust, Thomas sought Cat at the Castle Inn. It was still early. Few people were about. Thomas took the stairs two at a time in his eagerness to find her. In his haste, he nearly knocked over Marcus at the top of the stairs. Thomas nodded, intending to hurry past the boy, but a terse voice stayed him.

"Well. Cat's all sorts of popular today. How kind of you to deign to visit her, Mr. Montrose."

"Marcus?"

"Yes, indeed. Marcus. 'Tis kind of you to recall my name. Do you remember anything of my family? An older sister called Catherine?"

"What the bloody hell is this?" Thomas asked impatiently.

"You do remember. How splendid and miraculous. For no one else does! No one else remarks her very existence!"

"I haven't the time or the inclination for this now, boy. Your outraged sense of family honor is very commendable, but I won't be offering you any explanations," Thomas said, leaving the angry youth behind him.

Rapping on the door, Thomas felt his heartbeat quicken in response to Cat's voice, bidding him enter. She stood before the window, the soft light lining her voluptuous elegance with incandescence, touching her dark locks with a mahogany sheen. She held a small silver shear and was ruthlessly beheading the blossoms in an enormous vase of roses. He smiled at the picture she presented. Though she adopted an attitude of regal composure in society, he well knew that the private Cat was an active one, given to very physical displays of emotion.

"Something has not gone well?" he queried softly.

Cat stiffened at the sound of his voice.

"Why should you say that?" she asked without turning. Her voice was collected, even.

Here was no vaporous miss lying prostate with the horror of social ignominy, Thomas thought with amusement. "The grim testimony is scattered about your feet."

"These spent blooms merely take up room," she said meaningfully.

He heard the gravity of her tone and dropped his own cajoling one. "Oh?"

She turned at last, and Thomas saw the anger in her hard eyes, in her tight lips.

Cat's gaze flew to the livid wounds scoring his dark cheek. For an instant her anger at having learned Thomas knew Giles Dalton and had schemed for her marriage without apprising her of his plots was forgotten in her undeniable concern. "What has happened to your face?" she demanded stiffly.

"My face?" He furrowed his brow in obvious confusion.

"Yes, your face. The thing that looks as though it has been attacked by a drunken chef with a fillet knife."

Thomas briefly touched the painful wounds. "A mishap with a headstrong horse and some low-hanging branches."

"Pish."

"I swear, Cat, I have grown to loathe that expression with an unparalleled passion." A smile started to tilt the corners of his broad, mobile mouth. Cat found the sight too captivating by half. She wasn't going to be distracted by his handsome face.

She stepped back from him even as he stepped forward. "Strand has just left."

"Strand?" Thomas repeated dumbly.

"I applaud you on finally pronouncing his name correctly. How timely of you, Thomas. But timing is a rake's milieu. And that is what not only society but your own words assert you to be, is it not?"

He narrowed his eyes, attempting to discern the cause of her obvious ire.

"Is it not?" she demanded.

"I do not give a damn what society chooses to call me," he finally said.

"How happy a circumstance for you. Would that I were so fortunate as to disregard an entire community, to serve my own whims." Cat held up her hand to stop whatever he would have said. "So, society be damned. Do you not claim the title seducer? Libertine? Debauchee?"

How quickly those words killed what had been the first stirring of hope in his jaded heart. How ridiculous he must be: the lecher thinking regret could change the mold in which he had been cast. And how conveniently he had forgotten that those very titles she now flung at him were the same ones she had first sought him out for. But she had not forgotten, nor lost sight of the purpose that had led her to his home—and into his heart—months ago.

Aye, Thomas thought, he was certainly ridiculous, a source of amusement for even himself, reaching for that which his past so blatantly forswore.

Cat saw Thomas pale as he listened to her inventory. His lips stretched in a slow, grim, and ghastly parody of a smile.

"What is it, Cat? Has our association impeded one with Strand?" He came toward her, his advance slow, deliberate, until he stood before her, his size obstructing her view of the rest of the room.

It was more than his size, she realized in despair, impressive as it was. Even when he was not present, he still eclipsed other men. She could not see other men, for her mind's eye was constantly fixed on him. She loved Thomas. Even now, even knowing that he had only been entertaining himself, she could not deny her love.

Close behind her anger came confusion. Duping women seemed too juvenile, too tame a diversion for a man such as Thomas. And yet the evidence was undeniable. He knew Strand, and yet he hadn't told her. He had arranged to have Strand all but live in her pocket, orchestrating their courtship from afar even though he must have known that she cared for him, not Strand. She clenched her jaw in confused agitation.

Thomas saw the gesture and mistook its cause. His smile became a sneer. "Or is it more? Has Strand had the temerity to suggest that you and I—"

"That we what? Are lovers?" Cat broke in, tilting her chin defiantly.

"I would have thought better of him," Thomas murmured, adding, "There will be no further misunderstanding. I will see that he retracts his suggestion." He turned to leave, but she reached out suddenly, and he was held fast by the sight of those elegant fingers on his wrist.

"Strand has proposed."

So she has finally gotten what she wanted, he thought. It was good that he was looking at her fingers. It was good, because he was not sure what he would do if he saw the triumph in her eyes. Yes, much better to see her hand. How pale against his darker flesh. How elegant and yet curiously strong.

"It is deemed bad *ton* to congratulate a prospective bride. But in your case, m'dear, I can think of nothing more appropriate." He was relieved the words sounded so even.

She snatched her hand from his arm. He didn't care, she realized. He thought she'd accepted Strand, and yet not a ripple of emotion showed on his dark face. It meant nothing to him. There was no reason to disabuse him of his mistaken assumption. "I do not want your congratulations!"

Still he did not look at her. "My best wishes then."

"Nor your best wishes!"

His smile was tender, sad, and wise. "But I have nothing left to offer you, nothing I have not already given."

And then he was gone, and his absence was more tangible than any other man's presence.

Chapter 26

"**B**loody cold, isn't it, Strand?" Thomas said without turning from the window overlooking the street. "Last year the Thames froze over. But God, this seems as bad! I cannot remember a more brutal winter." He heard Bob promise Strand a hot cup of tea, and the door click shut. Thomas stared out of the window. There was no sound behind him.

"Napoleon chose a damn chill time to escape Mediterranean climes. I hear Castlereagh has sent for Wellington. The wisest choice. Surprising that he's capable of wise choices. After all, he precipitated this altogether avoidable situation." Still Strand did not answer him, and Thomas sighed. Strand had not come to discuss Wellington's command of the allied forces being mustered.

"I hear you offered for Cat," Thomas said as evenly as possible.

Strand replied tersely, "This morning." He tossed his hat onto an inlaid desk and yanked off his gloves. "That's why I've come to see you."

"Really? I never would have taken you for the gloating sort, Giles. I really do not think I can stand here and listen to an enactment of that tender tableau," Thomas said quietly.

"Tender?" snorted Strand, obviously overset. "In

307

a way. Tell me, Thomas, why haven't you offered for the gel?"

Thomas turned and scanned Strand's urbane figure. Giles looked nearly angry. Thomas shrugged tiredly. "I don't believe even our friendship allows you that intimate knowledge."

A sharp expletive rasped from between Strand's lips.

Thomas' gaze met and held the slender, blond man's. Strand was one of the very few men whom Thomas trusted, whose judgment he valued, whose friendship he revered. Thomas answered his unvoiced concern. "She has certain knowledge of me that precludes any possible attachment."

"Thomas." Strand's smooth brow furrowed in consternation. "I have known you since we were at school together. There are chapters in your past which are displeasing, but a summation of your history could be termed no less than noble. The offenses you committed in your youth were just that, a matter of youth. Many of the proclivities of our peers are far more onerous. Surely Cat would have forgiven you your past?"

"Perhaps," said Thomas, almost to himself, "if the past had not intruded on the present."

"What do you mean?"

"Cat had the misfortune of witnessing the culmination of a little seduction between Daphne Bernard and myself."

"Bloody hell," said Strand in a low voice. "How could you?!"

"Fool that I am, I thought the coin of my flesh worth the information it garnered. It isn't the first time I bartered myself for a 'cause,' though it will be the last. I didn't even get the bloody information.

"And too, there are certain things in my past that

might just be unforgivable to someone like Cat,"
Thomas murmured, his thoughts on Mariette Leons.
Giles was scowling at him. Giles knew nothing of
Mariette and her son.

"You see, Strand," Thomas went on, "with dross
goods of my body I also bartered away something
irreplaceable: the right to declare myself to Cat
Sinclair. But I would have done it anyway, had
you not beat me to it. I was going to." Thomas
fell silent, battling his inner anguish. Purposefully
he gathered his resolve.

"Tell me, when are the nuptials to take place? No
doubt I'll be called upon to give the bride away."
His voice was laced with pain. "Those whom the
gods would destroy, first make mad."

"For God's sake, Thomas," Strand said, snapping
his gloves into his open palm. "Cat refused me. I
know my proposal was precipitate. I would never
have rushed my fences were it not for the situation
you have gotten her into."

Thomas stiffened, scowling at Strand.

"It is all over London, thanks to that degenerate
Satan spawn, Barrymore. Her name is being ban-
died about everywhere. I had even purchased a
special license in hopes of staving off the majority
of the tattle mongers. I had hoped to be allowed
the honor of protecting her," Giles said bitterly,
the feeling that he, too, had had something irreplaceable within his grasp and had lost it making
his voice sharp. "I swear, Thomas, if you allow her
to be ruined by this, I will call you out myself. You
are a bloody fool, but it appears you are the bloody
fool she wants."

Snatching up his hat, Strand strode from the room
with no further word.

Thomas lifted his eyes, seeking divine guidance.
Unquenchable, inappropriate elation warred with

frustration as he found his voice. "Bloody, bloody hell!"

There was no other situation that could have conspired to make Thomas offer Cat his tarnished name. No other set of circumstances that would allow him to beg for her hand. That it had occurred nearly made him believe in a benevolent and merciful God. He might have an opportunity to protect her, shelter her—bloody hell, he would not lie to himself—*love* her! It was a boon so munificent, it staggered him. And it really was her only "practical" recourse. She would simply have to wed him. He grinned.

He hadn't the least idea why Cat had let him think she had accepted Strand's proposal, or any clue as to the reason for her all-too-obvious anger. Perhaps it was his neglect, an inner voice teased him. Perhaps she had missed his company. Anything seemed possible right now.

He thrust the provocative idea away. Whatever the reason for her reception of him, he would have to address it later. Right now he had to formulate some convincing speech, some immutable argument, to persuade his enticing pragmatist to become his wife.

Slumping down into a wing-backed chair, Thomas steepled his fingers in front of his lips, considering the tack he might take. Hope, insidious fraud that she was, uncoiled within him.

A soft rap broke through his concentration.

"Yes, yes, Bob, do get on with it! The marquis is gone, and there's no one here to impress with your redoubtable valeting."

The door swung open. Cat stood framed there, her chin thrust out belligerently. Her arms were straight at her sides. Her bosom swelled as she drew in a long breath.

"Why?" she asked in a voice that was a full octave higher than her usual one. "Why didn't you tell me you knew Giles Dalton?"

"Cat," Thomas breathed, unable to contain his delight at her unlooked-for appearance.

She took a few steps into the room. Her color was high, her eyes sparkling like dew-shimmered leaves.

"Don't you dare 'Cat' me!"

Thomas strode toward her, his hands rising as he approached her. She shifted sideways. His hands dropped.

"I reiterate, why didn't you tell me you knew Giles Dalton? That he was a confidant of yours?" Cat demanded.

"Strand?"

"Why is it each time today I have mentioned his name, you echo me, but for the past seven months you were unable to choke out even a *near* approximation of his name? How you must have laughed behind your hand at me."

He studied her in silence for a moment. Cat would never be satisfied with half-truths and unctuous verbal salves.

"Well, yes . . . I did," Thomas admitted slowly. This must be the reason she had allowed him to believe she'd accepted Strand. She thought he'd been mocking her.

"I knew it!" Cat stomped past him, kicking out the flounced hem of her gown as she went. Abruptly she wheeled around. "Well, sir, I think *that* was unspeakably caddish of you!"

"I can see how you would consider it so."

"Anyone would!"

"Cat . . . Lady Catherine, might I send Bob for some tea? You appear somewhat overset—"

"Bob?" Cat scowled, bewildered. "What the devil are you mumbling about?"

Thomas jerked his head toward the door. "Bob. The cur with the overlarge ears and wriggling nose. The fellow lurking about in the shadows of the doorway. I'm sure he would be only too happy to fetch you some refreshment. I would even hazard to wager he gets it in record time . . ."

A hoarse clearing of a throat drew Cat's attention to the doorway.

"I brung the tea for Lord Strand already, sir," Bob said equitably, walking into the room with a silver platter laden with a china pot of tea, a toast holder, and various containers of jam, butter, sugar, and cream.

"Lord Strand!" Cat exclaimed in a shrill voice. Apparently she divined some sort of conspiracy.

"Yes, ma'am," Bob said as Thomas groaned. "He must've gone then, sir?"

"Yes, Bob. Gone. Like you should be," Thomas growled.

"I'll just go into your bedchambers then and tidy up a bit—"

"No, Bob, you will not. You will go away. Far away. Now."

Cat stood in barely contained anger as the foiled Bob sketched her a bow and retired, grumbling, from the room. She counted to ten. There was no perceptible lessening of her anger. She tried twenty. No good. So she shouted.

"Of all the callous, manipulative, deceitful and . . . and .... childish things I have ever heard! Tell me, did you and Strand keep a daily correspondence concerning my amusing presumptions?!" Cat stomped her foot. The delicate china service jingled on the table.

"Cat," Thomas said.

He was approaching her slowly, warily, as though she might at any moment launch herself tooth and nail at him. *And well I might*, thought Cat grimly.

"Cat," Thomas repeated soothingly.

Did the blackguard actually sigh in relief when it became obvious she wasn't going to indulge herself by physically attacking him? She must consider that particular option. He motioned for her to take a seat. Wavering but a second, Cat flopped down. Merely, she told herself, to see what further horridness he would own up to next.

He poured her a cup of tea, liberally ladling in cream and sugar before handing it to her. "It will take more sugar than the world presently produces to sweeten my estimation of you!" Cat muttered, snatching the offered saucer and sloshing tea onto her skirts.

"Damn! Damn! Damn!" she exclaimed. It was the final straw. Tears welled up in her eyes. Angrily she tried to blink them away. Jumping up, Thomas grabbed a napkin. He knelt before her and industriously began to blot away at her lap. She slapped ineffectually at his large hands so impersonally at work. A wave of pure physical longing defeated her. She wanted nothing more than to feel those strong hands upon her, holding her, caressing her. Gazing helplessly down at his dark head, she noted the bright tracery of silver woven among the silky black curls. Her tears fell.

Finally flinging the soaked towel away, Thomas sat back on his heels and peered up at her from behind his ludicrously thick black lashes. He reached out his strong brown hands and captured her own. She tried to pull away, but his grip, though gentle, was intractable.

"When you first came to me," he said, "you were no end filled with the exemplary qualifications of Giles Dalton as a potential husband. You were also bursting with ill-concealed doubts concerning my own qualifications as a desirable . . . ah, suitor. It . . . pricked my pride, Cat."

She sniffed, half in misery, half in contempt.

"And because of that, it was simply irresistible to tease you." Thomas grinned, his teeth a white gleam in his dark face. It was a smile that invited her to join him, without derision or mockery. A beautiful smile.

"Because I was insolently unappreciative of you?" she said. "And what about the conniving you did in Paris? Setting Strand up as my beau!"

"Your beau?" Thomas' expression was one of comical confusion. "I did no such thing. I knew, because of my connections with the foreign office, that Paris might be on the brink of another occupation. I asked Strand, as my friend, to watch out for you."

"Why didn't you tell me?"

"I did not think, at the time, that you would read any letter I had written. And I knew you had certain hopeful expectations of your relationship with Strand. I did not want to further intrude on your life," he finished quietly.

Cat, however, seemed heedless of her destroyed prospects regarding Strand. "At that time, I would have consigned *any* missive from you to the fire," she admitted.

Thomas laughed, rocking back on his heels, though his hands still clasped hers firmly.

How could she not return his humor when so much of it was self-deprecatory? She would look a churl if she did not offer him at least something of a smile.

Thomas caught his breath at the transformation of Cat's face. Devilment and high spirits glittered in her warm gaze. His hands tightened on hers.

"And later," he hurried to continue, lest he lose track of his explanation, "I simply forgot. And in

Paris, the subject of Strand, and whether or not I knew him, could not have been further from my mind. There were other things I felt I needed to tell you."

"Mariette Leons?" Cat said urgently. "How long will you flay yourself for that tragedy, Thomas? You were in a war. War does not ask which of its victims deserves to die and which does not. It is indiscriminate. Innocent as well as guilty fall before it. You were trying to make sure that fewer of the innocent felt its deadly touch."

All at once he realized that her support of him hadn't been merely a matter of her fear-dulled perceptions or her wishful thinking. It had been long enough for her to have gone over in her mind every bitter detail of his past. She did not forgive him. It was far better than forgiveness. It was understanding.

Hope and joy surged through him.

"My dearest," he said.

Something cold and tense, something that had begun to thaw when Thomas mopped the spilled tea from her skirts, melted completely in Cat's heart.

Thomas saw the opportunity. He was, after all, a strategist. "Cat, I would never *knowingly* hurt you."

Just as she began to believe in his sincerity, a new doubt sprung up to eclipse the brief communion Cat felt. "You have avoided me," she said.

He shook his head in denial, his eyes never leaving hers. "No. I deemed it best not to hover."

"Hover?" she exclaimed. "Well, you made a right good job of that! No one could accuse you of 'hovering.' "

"Cat, my reputation is such that a young, unmarried woman of unexceptional birth could not associate herself with me and go unscathed."

"But last summer you had no such qualms . . ."

"Last summer I labored under the ridiculous assumption that I'd been absent from society long enough to assuage a long-spent notoriety. You yourself encouraged that particular delusion."

Cat frowned, perplexed. Turning over her hand, Thomas rubbed Cat's soft palm with his thumb, an unconsciously comforting gesture. It did not comfort her. It excited her.

"You went on, ad nauseam, I might add, about my agedness. But while I am not in my first flush of youth, I have not yet attained the years necessary to distance myself from past transgressions. That realization was borne in on me acutely when we arrived in Brighton, and almost immediately the snickers began. I had hoped to save you from the gossip mill."

He could not tell her all of it, that it had been impossible for him to be with her; him, a perverse uncle figure, lusting after her even as he watched other men court her as he so wished to do. And yet his care had not stopped the gossip—or the desire.

"Cat, you must listen to me. It is essential that you not allow emotions to overrule your good sense." His tone was serious, compelling. "Barrymore has sought to ruin you. He has somehow found out you were with me, unchaperoned, overnight in Dieppe. He has spread tales which no one, no matter how blameless a face they presented, could hope to overcome."

Anger burned in Cat's green eyes. Not fear, not even consternation . . . but pure outrage. She pulled free from his clasp, clenching her hands together in her lap.

Thomas stood up. If he remained this close, he would gather her to him, and frighten her, thereby relinquishing this one opportunity to make her his own. He must appear reasonable, sober, moderate, not a man governed by a passion that might alarm her in its intensity.

"The damage is done. It is now up to us to decide what to do about it." He picked up the teapot and poured her a fresh cup. Handing it to her, he dragged a chair forward, seating himself on the edge, facing her. "Have you any suggestions, Cat?"

She had obviously considered the problem. Her answer was quick, incisive. "I have thought I might join my mother and Philip on their travels. I see no reason why they shouldn't continue on as they have been for some years before finally coming back to England."

Thomas leaned forward, offering her a piece of toast. "And what of your siblings?"

A crease appeared between her dark brows. She accepted the toast, absently staring at it. *Aha!* thought Thomas. He had found her Achilles' heel.

"Well . . ." she said slowly, "what with Great-Aunt Hecuba gone, that has been a concern. But Marcus tells me cousin Emmaline is happily dug in and hasn't been too much of a trial." She bit into the toast, crunching thoughtfully. "And really, I am most impressed with how Marcus has matured. He seems able to take over the reins of management. Though I would have wished I could have set up a few of the newer husbandry techniques reported in last month's—"

"Yes, yes," Thomas broke in gently. "I am sure Marcus is well able to handle the estate, and your cousin is probably capable enough to handle whatever it is she handles. That is not, however, what I was referring to, Cat. You have two sisters, am I correct?"

She nodded.

"And neither of them has yet made her bow?"

Cat stopped chewing in midbite. Her eyes widened as she finally understood his direction. She choked the toast down.

"They wouldn't . . . No one could hold my sisters responsible for—"

"It isn't only your sisters, Cat. It's your brothers, too. Particularly Marcus. He has been a hairsbreadth from a duel for the past fortnight. It is only a matter of time before he, or one of the twins, is provoked into one."

Thomas felt like a brute, even though what he said was true. Cat's anxiety was palpable, her eyes stricken.

"Oh, God!" she breathed.

"Cat, this next question is very important. Please, trust me here, and answer as honestly as you can."

She nodded mutely. Her failure to rail at him for the suggestion that she would be anything less than honest testified to the extent of her distress.

"Why did you refuse Strand?" Thomas asked.

"I . . . I do not . . ." Cat trembled, on the brink of disclosing to him all that was in her heart. But pride, and fear, forbade her to tell him the simple truth, that she did not love Giles Dalton. She loved Thomas. She gave him half the truth. "Lord Strand does not love me. It was obvious his offer was made from a sense of chivalry. I could not allow him to sacrifice himself on my behalf. It wouldn't be honorable. He is innocent of any involvement in my present situation."

Thomas watched her, oddly dissatisfied with her reasoning but unable to criticize it. In a similar situation, he would act much the same.

"I *am* involved," he finally said.

She had no reply to this ridiculously obvious statement.

"I want you to hear me out before you make any

decisions. I suggest we follow the most obvious and reasonable course open to us. As I am the correspondent of any allegations concerning your morals, I am clearly the most logical choice to be your husband." Holding up both hands to stem the protests he knew were coming, he sought to forestall her. Cat remained unnaturally still, watching him intently.

"I propose we wed," Thomas hurried on. "By doing so, most of the outraged matrons will be assuaged. Those sticklers who are not will, over the course of time, slowly readmit you to their circle. After a while, you will be seen as an overly emotional, impulsive girl, who was seduced by a seasoned roué who finally had the decency to own up to his culpability and marry you. I realize it is not what one would wish in the best of circumstances, but neither is it the worse possible scenario. At least, any assault on your honor will become *my* responsibility. Indeed, it would only further provoke scandal were your brothers to involve themselves after our marriage."

Thomas realized he had rushed through his proposal. He was breathing quickly. But she had not interrupted him to laugh or scorn him, and he took heart. Gulping down a bit more tea, he continued. "And too, Cat, this would have the benefit of providing you with just the sort of marriage you originally sought with Strand. In spite of what you believe, I am quite, quite wealthy. I can easily afford to bolster up your family's fortunes without feeling any pinch. I am sophisticated enough to allow you to go your own way. I would make an undemanding spouse.

"We have the added bonus of actually getting on well together. The boredom many wives feel when they are forced to their country estates does not affect you. We might . . . work together to improve the productivity of the home farm." It might work. He could see she was considering his words. He pressed on, convinced he was taking the right tack.

"We will have a magnificent estate. I am certain of it. Together we will raise the most prime merino wool. What a nice flock of sheep we could have! Your input as a land manager will be invaluable. I can promise you, Cat, a perfectly civil, mutually beneficial union."

He sat back, well pleased with himself. To his mind, he had just sweetened the pill considerably. How could Cat fail to respond affirmatively?

"You think we will make a good team. Produce good wool."

He nodded vigorously. "I have no doubt about it."

"I see."

Thomas beamed at her. He knew what would appeal to Cat. "It all makes perfectly good sense, does it not?"

He could not read the emotion gleaming in her moss green eyes. Though her features were composed, there was something tense in her posture; a frown of—what? concern?—marred her smooth brow. Thinking he knew what caused it, Thomas quickly tried to form words that would be truthful, yet unthreatening. There was no way it could be done.

"Cat, I cannot tell you what you doubtless want to hear. I will not gloss over a subject which so intimately involves you, nor allow you to go into a marriage with me with unreasonable expectations," Thomas said gravely. "While I am willing to offer you a marriage free of many impediments, and the chance to live as you would like, I will not divorce you."

His gaze sought hers, but Cat's head remained bowed, a troubled expression on her face as she studied something of interest in the bottom of her teacup.

Thomas took a deep breath. "It is a convenient marriage I propose, but not a marriage of convenience. I expect to have children."

He was aware he was holding his breath. If he were made of nobler material, he would have given her the sanctuary of his name without making any demands on her body. But he had never lied to himself, and he would not start now. There was simply no possibility he could be married to Cat without loving her . . . in every sense of the word. If she accepted his suit, she would have to know that.

He waited while she considered his words. Nothing in his entire life had been as important as her answer. And yet there were no other words of persuasion he could employ. His fingers ached to touch her vulnerable throat, the silky down at the nape of her neck.

Finally Cat lifted her head, her gaze direct.

"All right," she said.

Chapter 27

For all the haste and confusion that marked the two days between Thomas' proposal and the wedding, the service itself was curiously tranquil. The midafternoon sun streamed through the high stained-glass windows, dancing jewel-like prisms across the centuries-worn slate floors of the nave. Their small group was clustered around the altar, dwarfed by the huge, nearly empty edifice, their voices hushed by its cavernous proportions. The air within was chill with early spring capriciousness, and their breaths turned to shimmering vapor as they spoke.

All right, Cat told herself with a steadying breath as she mounted the shallow steps to the altar. *It is time to be honest with yourself.* For all the logical, judicious, irrefutable reasons why she *should* marry Thomas, the pure, unadulterated truth remained. She was marrying him because she loved him. She wanted to be with him, converse with him, touch him. Thomas' ridiculous reasons for marrying her may satisfy him, but they merely offered Cat the opportunity to have the one thing she wanted above all others; to be with Thomas for the rest of her life.

Aching with hurt, Cat had come close to throwing Thomas' abhorrent proposal back in his face.

Luckily, prudence had urged her to wait, delaying her imminent eruption of temper long enough for her to notice the slight quiver in Thomas' hand, the plea in his eyes.

It was enough. Whether she saw Thomas' love or merely his desire, she did not know. But it was more than she had expected, enough to throw herself at the mercy of her own want and agree to this marriage.

Now, standing at the altar, Cat was conscious of Thomas' tall, broad form, acutely aware of each unintentional brush of his black-clad arm against hers; of the low, even cadence of his breath as he listened to the words the bishop spoke; of the calm, level tenor of his answers to the ritual questions.

When it was over Thomas turned, tucking her hand into the crook of his arm, and bestowed a look of heart-twisting tenderness on her. Cat answered him with a smile, hoping he might see how much he meant to her. How much he had always meant.

Only Marcus brought a jarring note of skepticism to the ceremony. He had spent the preceding night questioning the wisdom of the marriage. He told Cat she need not offer herself for society's sake, promising he would defend her honor. Cat had tried to assure her brother she didn't feel she was sacrificing herself at all. She wanted the marriage, she told him. She and Thomas would deal very well together.

She could not bring herself to tell Marcus she loved Thomas. She had too many memories of wiping his nose to suddenly reverse their roles. And, too, she was unsure of Thomas' feelings. If it became obvious that he did not return her love, she did not want Marcus to add pity for her to his litany of grievances against Thomas.

Marcus left immediately after the service, nodding curtly to Thomas before silently bowing to Cat. She felt guiltily relieved.

Afterward, Thomas took her to a fashionable café for dinner. He ignored the stares that met their entrance, but Cat could not prevent the warmth from creeping up her cheeks under the openly speculative glances.

"My wife and I require a table. Preferably near the window, well away from the inquisitive proletariat," Thomas said, his voice pitched to carry.

Excited, murmured conversation immediately arose in response to this interesting news. Thomas disregarded the hushed whispers with imperial disdain. Over the course of the meal, he put himself out to entertain and charm Cat. He pointed out many of the room's occupants, relating pithy, and often farcical, anecdotes about the rudest of starers until he had Cat laughing, her discomfort forgotten.

Finishing a nonsensical tale about a would-be toast and her refusal to eat her hostess's shrimp because their color clashed with her gown, Thomas leaned back. Entering the spirit of the conversation, Cat said with feigned hauteur, "I understand the poor lady's dilemma. You'll recall I was quite the mode in Paris, Thomas."

"So I saw."

"Indeed," she went on, "Lord Brent named me a diamond of the first water."

Thomas smiled, his fathomless eyes gleaming as he caught her hand. "You, m'dear, are a veritable lake." His gentle tone robbed the words of sarcasm, and he carried her unresisting hand to his mouth, pressing warm lips to the inside of her wrist. Cat nearly gave in to the impulse to touch his polished dark locks as he bent over her hand. The sudden hush of the room awoke her to the spectacle they were making of themselves.

Thomas seemed to know her thoughts, for he

raised his head and said, "Be damned to them, Cat. Courting their approval is the surest way to win their contempt."

She trusted him implicitly. Reaching across the table, she covered his large, tanned hand with her own and was rewarded by his brilliant smile.

"Aunt Hecuba always averred a woman should heed the wise and ever correct counsel of her husband."

"A font of knowledge, is Aunt Hecuba. I heartily concur."

They finished their leisurely meal and took a stroll down the Steyne, meandering slowly back to the Castle Inn as twilight stained the sky. They found themselves caught up in an exhilarating debate about the new Corn Bill, and were so involved in the conversation, they did not notice the stares of the gawkers and gossips.

When they arrived back at the hotel, Thomas escorted Cat to her room. For the first time that day, she was nervous in his company. Her agitation was in no way diminished by the subtle suspicion that Thomas, too, was becoming . . . apprehensive? tense?

"May I come in, Cat?" he asked.

She mumbled something that sounded affirmative, though totally unintelligible, as he reached behind her, pushing open the door.

What? thought Cat anxiously. Was it going to happen now? This minute? She cast about, looking for something to occupy her hands as she heard Thomas dismiss the maid. He strolled over to the hearth and stirred the embers. The room already seemed unaccountably warm.

Spying a piece of needlework lying on a chair, she snatched it up, plopping down and stabbing the needle into the silk stretched over the small hoop.

She knew Thomas approached but kept her eyes firmly fixed on the brilliant threads. His proximity was like a physical sensation.

With sudden, startling accuracy, she remembered the exact feel of his skin, its fine-grained texture, the satiny warmth of the flesh sheathing the hard, unyielding muscles of his chest. She wanted to touch him. Her cheeks burned.

"I did not know you numbered needlework amongst your accomplishments," she heard him say.

Cat loved Thomas. She wanted to be with him. She wanted to kiss him and she wanted him to kiss her. And she wanted everything else that marriage meant.

"I don't," she answered decisively, allowing the hoop to fall to her lap, the few uneven stitches she had poked into it glaringly obvious in the otherwise flawless pattern. "This must be the maid's."

Thomas grinned at her, delighted with her honesty, knowing she must be filled with no end of trepidation. Valiant little Cat. At least he could ease her mind on this point.

"Cat, let me be unchivalrously frank," he said. "I know I told you I want our marriage to be a . . . complete one."

She nodded, her eyes riveted on his face.

"But I am not some randy sailor." He teased her with the remarks she herself had used to provoke his embarrassment in Dieppe. Cat felt the corners of her mouth quirk in memory of her outrageous impersonation.

"I shall not force an intimacy on you with the first opportunity that presents itself."

"You won't?" she asked blankly.

He was all tenderness and consideration. "No, I won't."

He just stood there, smiling at her, while her

own mind stumbled about blindly for a suitable response to his statement. Was she supposed to *thank* him, for God's sake? He certainly looked as though he was expecting gratitude. But she didn't feel thankful. She felt disappointed . . . cheated!

"Oh," she managed to mumble.

"I shall be more than happy to wait until you feel sufficiently accustomed to our marriage before we consummate it," he said encouragingly.

"That's awfully good of you."

She did not sound particularly relieved. He tried again. "Not at all. I want you to be happy."

"Oh."

"I want you to be comfortable."

"That's nice." Her muttered responses sounded patently insincere. He was growing anxious in his quest to ease her anxiety.

"I do not want you to feel you are being coerced."

"I see."

"You must tell me when you feel ready," he finally said, bending down to press a chaste kiss on her forehead.

She wanted to raise her mouth and taste his lips on hers. He was preparing to leave, that peculiar smile pasted firmly on his devilishly handsome face. Turning away, he started for the door.

"I will send your maid to you directly."

"I'm ready."

He stopped. "I'm sure you are, m'dear. It's been a long day. She's probably just outside, or downstairs. Perhaps Bob knows where she has gone—"

"No. I mean I'm *ready*."

Thomas turned slowly, releasing the handle of the door, disbelieving the meaning of her simple words. But her face was serious, never more serious. In her expression there was something subtle, questioning, something that wrenched from him all of the half-truths he had built in order to contain his simple, essential need of her.

It was more than the longing to hear her voice, to keep her safe from anything and anyone threatening her happiness. It was more than just the hunger to be with her, talk to her, tease her, be instructed by her, debate with her. It was the culmination of all the years of need: his heart's final response to the joyless mounting of heated female flesh. It had all been but a precursor to the overriding need to make love with this woman. Cat.

In granting her a temporary reprieve, Thomas hoped to accustom himself to the giddying fact that now he could touch her, be with her, whenever she allowed. Time, he trusted, would blunt the intensity of this physical craving.

He had lied to her. No randy youth was as rife with urgency as he was right now. He was stiff and tight, full and engorged by her mere proximity. His hands shook as he came to her, placing two fingers slowly beneath her upturned chin to look into her candid gray-green eyes.

"Do you know what this entails?" he queried softly, afraid she would say no, afraid she would say yes.

"I . . . I lived on a country estate," was the only answer she could manage. His eyes were so steady, so intense, even though his touch of her chin was the smallest whisper of callused fingertips, less than a caress.

"I am not a stud. You are no breeding mare."

She did not understand the anger lacing his steady voice. "I realize that," she said.

"God, I hope so," he breathed, and reached down to capture her wrists, pulling her inexorably up until she stood before him, her eyes on a level with his tanned, strong throat.

"I would touch you," he said, trying desperately

to make the words sound debatable, knowing it was already beyond that.

"Yes," she answered.

Dropping his hands lightly to her shoulders, he brushed his thumbs along the creamy column of her throat. His fingers cupped her delicately molded head, testing the sumptuous texture of her hair: cool and silky and thick. He indulged himself with the small pleasure of drawing the pins from her coiffure. Her tresses fell in a rippling mass over the backs of his hands. He felt her tremble, and his own body suddenly felt too heavy, overburdened, saturated with overly intense sensations. He felt as though he might fall upon her like some ravening beast, his compulsion weakening his will, making it impossible to stand before her and be allowed the liberty of touching her so intimately.

He had no words to tell her. No way to explain how he felt, how the feel of her was as frightening as though he had been given some priceless treasure and told to balance it on the head of a pin. Her breath sluiced over his throat, forcing Thomas to note how hard she breathed and wonder if he was already alarming her.

"I would . . . Turn around, for God's sake," he said thickly, lest she suddenly note his extremity and become apprehensive. She is a virgin, he told himself, and unused to a man's response.

She looked at him questioningly, but did as he asked. Silently he reached for the back of her ivory gown.

His fingers felt unwieldy as he pushed each small hook from its clasp, slowly uncovering her slender back. Wide bands of satin encircled her from midback to waist; *zonas*, he vaguely recalled. He undid the hooks on these too, and the satin cloth slipped to her hips.

With a single knuckle, he followed the shallow

valley of her spine. He reversed the sensuous journey with his fingertip, his breath coming unevenly as he traced the flare of her shoulder blade, the sweep of her rib, to the vale of her waist and gentle swell of her hip.

"God, you are so lovely."

"Please, may I turn now?" she asked. He did not answer, and so she twisted, unaware her unlaced gown fell from her shoulders, gaping wide to reveal her tip-tilted breasts to his hungry eyes. He dropped his hands from her waist, freeing her, vexing her with his sudden withdrawal. But his eyes! She felt devoured by him, riveted by his scalding gaze.

Acting purely on instinct, she raised her arms, settling them around his broad shoulders. The quivering in his massive body increased, and her eyes widened.

She had no way of knowing how to go on from here. He was so near. The absence of his touch was nearly a physical discomfort. *Wanton*, whispered a voice within her, which she immediately ignored. She could not stop herself.

Her fingers fumbled with his cravat, and she tugged at it in frustration. "Can I? Please, I want . . ."

"Madam, I could teach lessons in hell on the subject of 'want,' " Thomas said, savagely jerking the cloth from around his neck. The studs on his shirt burst open, and her eyes fell on his chest, the heavy planes of his muscles rising and falling in a harsh, deep rhythm. He shrugged out of his coat, tearing his shirt from his body and casting it to the floor. "Touch me. God have mercy! Touch me, Cat!"

He was as superbly male as any statue of idealized virility she had ever seen. Everything about him bespoke mature strength, tempered and fine-honed, from the pale golden skin of his chest to the tanned, weathered flesh cloaking all of the hard sinew, tendon, and thew of him.

Her hands fluttered out, ungovernable in the need to feel his sleekness once more. He was as warm and densely plush as she remembered. With innocent luxury, she explored the mystery of his powerful male chest, sliding her fingertips to the long, hard bulges of his biceps.

He watched her study him, closed his eyes when he felt the first caress. Her touch was a benediction, a slow, barely endurable pleasure, scorching in its artlessness. He was confounded by desire and restraint. He had never before made love to a virgin. God! he thought despairingly. He had never before made *love*.

She lay her cheek gently upon his bare chest. The gesture was so luxuriously trusting, so intimate. She stroked her jaw over his naked flesh, a sound like a purr trilling from deep within her throat. He was undone.

His touch was sin. Dark, dangerous, irresistible, impelling her toward pleasures she had never dreamed existed, let alone experienced. Urging her toward things as real and dark and unsafe as anything she had known. Luring her to give herself over to the deed, to relish it, savor it, embrace it, and follow it. He peeled the sheer bodice of her dress down, allowing it to fall low on her hips.

"Thomas!"

"Yes, my love. And yes. Yes."

Her breasts tantalized him, their pink tips touching him briefly with each breath she inhaled. He cupped his palm high on her rib cage, on the silky vulnerability beneath her arms, his thumbs just brushing the heavy, full billow of her nether breast.

She made a sound like a sigh, and he trailed his hands lower and forward, gently cupping the feminine bounty, testing their weight, their texture, the nearly imperceptible jiggle of womanly flesh with each movement she made.

It was erotic, this intensely hesitant exploration of her. Moving his hands downward, he flattened them as he reached the shimmering slip of material draped low on her belly, crumpling the fabric in his fists, needing to slow down, needing to control himself.

She pressed more fully against him, and he dragged the dress and underlying petticoat down, past the full, curved mounds of her buttocks, dropping the cloth so that she stood naked in a pool of lace, muslin, and silk. He spread his own legs, widening his stance, urging her closer, so he could more fully encompass her with his arms and thighs. He laid her rich softness and silky texture against him that he might feel her soft belly beneath his hard one, her long, satiny thighs between his heavy ones.

Praying she would not draw away, Thomas cautioned himself to go slowly. But she didn't protest. Her fingers slipped through his hair. Her cheek rubbed sensuously against him. She allowed him this.

Cat hadn't known a man could be so exquisitely gentle, so tender and measured. She felt utterly precious, cherished by him. She felt rife, and luxurious, sensuous and completely feminine. Never before had she been so aware of her own womanhood, of the dramatic difference between her curves and his planes, her softness and his hardness.

Raising her mouth to the strong pillar of his throat, Cat opened her lips ever so slightly against his hot skin, slipping upwards, exploring the rasping slant of his beard-stubbled jaw, glorying in the salty taste of him, the warm, unmistakably male scent of him. She inhaled deeply, relishing the smell of soap beneath the heated masculine musk.

As if in a dream, she felt him bend down and swing her easily up into his arms. Awash in drowsy sensuality, she blinked up at him. His eyes were brilliant, black onyx rimmed by velvety brown.

He strode to the bed with her, following her down and bracing his forearms on either side of her. He did not say a word, his breath a quick, harsh sound close to her ear. He suddenly closed his eyes, the dark fringe of lashes lying upon his cheek. Slowly he lowered his head, resting his forehead against her shoulder. She stroked the broad span of shoulders enveloping her, feeling the muscles bunch and slip beneath his skin. How exotically alien he was, how perfectly in proportion his breadth and depth and long, clean lines. How fascinating the ripple of muscles along his upper arm, the flexing of his back.

It was too much for Thomas. He felt her body quiescent beneath him, felt her hands on him, and he was sure he would be lost in the flooding sensation of her. Reaching up, he bracketed her face with his hands and took her mouth. She opened for him, eagerly, instinctively, and God help him, he could not but take advantage of that sweetness. He answered her offer with his tongue, feeling the warm, sleek interior of her mouth, and groaned, delving deeper. He would suffocate her, he knew, but he could not tear himself away from her mouth.

His hands searched her arms, stroking her sides, catching the jut of her hipbone, sliding upwards to the plump roundness of her breast. He found her nipple, a hard pebble. He let go her mouth, and she tried to pull his head back down. He slid his lips across her collarbone, nipping the elegant line, trailing down to her breast. Opening his mouth over her nipple, he delicately sucked in the hardened bud. She gasped and arched beneath him, her hands fluttering over him.

Languor died instantly. The deep pulls at her breast were a sudden, ravishing stimulation. Writhing, Cat sought to escape the intense sensation, but his tongue and mouth promised too much, and she found herself pulling his dark head to her, seeking to find where such carnal pleasure could lead.

Thomas tried to pace himself, to go deep within, to distance himself from her, but it was too overpowering, the want too imminent. He was in danger of overwhelming her. Nothing had ever compelled him like this. Nothing in his many joinings had prepared him for this. His desire had a life of its own, an incendiary, scalding imperative. He licked the satin curves, the shadowed contours and gleaming swells, the velvety stroke of her flesh against him an urgent, driving force.

"Please," he whispered, laying his fingers against the down-covered mound between her legs, awaiting her gasped rejection, unable to promise himself he would stop. She moaned at that brief touch, her head swinging fretfully, her hands still on his body, still touching him, still moving with torturous fascination over him.

Sliding his hand between their bodies, Thomas found the silky curls. Parting her with a single finger, he was stunned to find her wet, a sleek moisture on his finger.

She shuddered and arched, a straining bow, the movement causing his finger to enter her more deeply. Thomas lifted his eyes to find her staring at him. Confusion, eroticism, and shame were mingled on her flushed face. Her mouth was parted, her breath shallow, uneven, frantic.

"Please!" The word echoed his plea. "Please . . .

oh, God, Thomas! Stop! Please, I . . ." she panted, her glorious breasts quivering.

He knew what she begged for, even if she did not. Here at last, his past could offer a boon. He could give her pleasure. Lifting his hand to her mouth, he rested his fingertips gently against her trembling lips, trying to quiet her fear. With his other hand, he stroked her, his finger pressed within her, his thumb circling with deep caresses the small, sleek nub pulsing at the apex of her thighs.

Her eyes glazed. Her breathing became deep, harsh. Frantically she clutched at him. He would not stop. He added to the exquisite torment, nipping the underside of her breast before closing over her nipple, drawing on it, in counterpoint to the rhythm of his finger.

She couldn't think. Twisting, her hips lifting and falling, Cat unconsciously sought the cadence of fulfillment. And the buildup of sensation swirling through her flesh, her breasts, centering where his thumb played, went on and on.

"Give yourself to me," Thomas demanded thickly, releasing her breast, his eyes determined, brilliant. "Give!"

"What?!" she pleaded. Anything to end the torment, to take her up over the edge, toward the extreme sensation tantalizing her, seeming just beyond reach.

He slid down over her, his rock-hard body an agonizing slide over sensitized skin.

He withdrew his hand, and she sobbed in frustration. Bending his head, he covered her with his mouth. She was beyond shame, beyond confusion. Arching to meet him, she pressed her hips forward in a quest for surcease.

"Give it to me! To *me*!" he growled, stroking his tongue flat against her and upward.

"What?!" she cried again, nearly frantic.

"Your body's first pleasuring! Your want!"

He felt her buck in her passionate search. Clasping her hips in his large hands, he held her still as he delved into her femininity. Suddenly she sobbed, bowing up, her legs straining rigidly, her hands clutching fistfuls of satin bed sheets, her head flung back. A sound like pain, but more like pleasure, ecstasy and effort, rasped from between her lips, and she hung for a moment, impaled on the physical pinnacle of her climax. Slowly she wilted, panting shallowly.

He wondered if he could leave her now, limp and drained, while his own sex, stiff and distended, throbbed. Feeling the brush of her hand, Thomas looked up to see an expression of amazement in her jade green eyes.

"Kiss me," Cat asked, shyness staining her cheeks and breasts a rosy hue.

He rose, found her mouth, devoured her lips with his own. "Want" was a living force now, rending his self-control to shreds. Her legs had fallen open, and he found himself cradled between them; he could feel her heat through the straining fabric of his pants.

Her hands roamed over him, down his ribs, touching with teasing hesitancy his buttocks, flowing up his back, holding his shoulders, urging him closer.

Pressing himself to her, Thomas deepened the kiss, crushing her breasts beneath him. His urgency was palpable. She recognized that the thing that had spurred her a short time ago now rode him. He wanted her with something akin to desperation. The controlled savagery of his passion was more stimulating to her than all that had gone before. Desire, so recently satisfied, erupted anew.

She felt an unfamiliar, hard bulge pressing against her sensitized mound. The flooding, building feeling would not be denied, and she rubbed up toward the pleasuring hardness.

Thomas groaned.

Cat's movements were devastating. Always in the past, women had been receptacles for his seed. He would satisfy them because it increased his own enjoyment. But in the ultimate act of penetration, Thomas was removed, ultimately alone, going deep within himself, an unconscious sexual being, insensate to the personality servicing him.

With Cat . . . God, with Cat, he could not forget for one instant that it was Cat's satiny skin beneath him, Cat opening her mouth for him, Cat's tongue meeting the thrust of his, Cat's legs spread now to encompass him.

He sought the usual oblivion, thinking to cool his ardor by disassociating the act from the actors, thinking in this way he might not frighten her with the intensity of his desire. He could not do it.

He tried. God knows he tried, as he fumbled to release himself from his pants. But the brush of his knuckles against her downy curls was impossible to discount. It was Cat's heat he lay against. He tried to slow his breathing, burrowing his face into the curve of her throat and shoulder, but it was Cat's scent invading his sense, so musky, so replete with satisfaction, so female.

With a shaking hand, Thomas positioned himself between her thighs, easing himself into her, trying desperately to ignore the unmistakable frisson of fear on her face. But it was Cat. He could not ignore, not for one instant, the trust and desire and uncertainty he saw there. So he drove slowly but deeply into her, to her maidenhead and beyond . . .

He saw her eyes widen in surprise, a brief flicker of discomfort. He stopped, impaled by contradictory needs. All of his great muscles trembled with restraint and hunger. Her arms pulled at him, her teeth eagerly sinking into his shoulder, and he knew with sudden grateful, awed certainty that Cat wanted this too.

He drove deeply, slowly, within the tight, velvety embrace, joyfully aware that her small fear had died before it had fully lived.

He felt the thickening pleasure of it, the erotic pumping, the thrust and retreat, and he rocked with the intensity of knowing he was within *her*, Cat! Grinding his teeth together, Thomas felt her legs strain about his hips, taking them both to the flash point. He lifted his head, baring his teeth with the exquisite driving sensuality of it. And so, his body pulsing, his thrusts culminating in a shattering release, and finding he could not lose himself while making love to Cat, Thomas finally found himself.

Chapter 28

"And you shall allow me to turn the library into a sumptuous Oriental pagoda," Cat said, catching Thomas' hand in hers. "I will strew the floors with pillows, and hand-stuffed, gilded cranes from the ceiling. I know, I'll have Bob affect a pigtail. Or maybe you." She was flirting outrageously, a saucy gleam in her eye as she tugged at Thomas' long hair.

As usual, he was confounded by the response her slightest touch elicited from him. Even here, in the circumspect confines of a fabric broker, in the full light of day, he felt his attraction grow. Gently he replaced her hand on his forearm, safely cloaking his skin with shirt and coat material. Or it *should* have been safe, he amended silently.

Cat frowned, disappointed he wouldn't join in her play, hurt for a moment by the gentle, unvoiced rebuke before hurrying off to join the Brighton merchant in exclaiming over his tables of brocade, satins, and silks.

Thomas felt like a satyr.

He had spent their wedding night cradling her love-dampened body close, watching her as she fell into deep, exhausted slumber. He had let his hand flow over her recumbent form, savoring the awesome luxury of being able to do so, telling himself it was enough. Liar, his conscience had

341

whispered, as excitement exploded amidst simple appreciation.

Thomas knew how keen a blade desire was. It cut deeply and mercilessly, paring away the veneer of discipline he struggled to maintain. And he could not control it, could not bring peace to the hunger that burned in him. God knows, he tried. For the past ten days he had tried.

For, he told himself, though he had wed Cat, he had yet to win her. Promising himself he would woo her tenderly, he set out to gain her trust, her respect, and ultimately her love. He had to. Having given his own heart absolutely, he could be satisfied with nothing less in return.

He escorted her to the various places he thought would interest her. He discoursed on Prinny's accumulated art treasures, on architectural marvels, on the *ton* and its members. They discussed Mr. Coke's progressive land practices, politics, economics. And during the day Thomas managed to disguise his craving, proving to himself he could be an undemanding suitor. It was a temporary reprieve.

He appalled himself with his need of her. He would force himself to leave her after dinner, stalking the darkened streets of Brighton for an hour, an hour and a half, two hours, before he would allow himself to return to her, striding with unseemly haste to her door, holding his breath as he waited. Would she welcome him as she had before? Would she greet him with the joyous smile, the shimmering, fully aware gaze of a lover? Could it happen again?

And each night had been a gift. Throughout the insufficient hours of darkness, Thomas made Cat burn for him as he burned for her, using every bit of his expertise to ignite within her the flames with which she so effortlessly seared him.

She would think him unnatural. She would come

to fear his unquenchable passion. She must. He was nearly afraid of himself. Always before there had been control: an appetite whetted and appeased, a casual union of bodies, pleasure piqued and satisfied. But this went beyond anything he had ever experienced in his all-too-experienced life.

Cat strode back to him, a victorious expression on her face. "The shopkeeper has promised delivery within a fortnight . . . at *my* prices!" she said triumphantly.

"As always, m'dear, you drive a hard bargain," Thomas replied, opening the door to the street and bowing politely as she passed, giving the gossipmongers no cause to turn their avid gaze on his self-possessed manner toward her. He could give Cat the days . . . as long as she allowed him the nights.

Cat twirled slowly in front of the mirror. The French maid, Annette, stood behind her, thin hands clasped, a smile of approval on her sharp-featured face.

"Madame looks *très jeune fille!*"

"Yes," Cat said doubtfully.

"Most ravishing!"

"Yes?"

A soft rap alerted her to Thomas' presence at the door between their rooms. He had made arrangements for the adjoining suites the day after their wedding. Cat had been delighted, eager to experience all the familiarities of marriage. She wanted to be allowed the intimacy of waking up and finding Thomas beside her, his long hair rumpled, the bleached white of the bed linen contrasting with the dark tan of his strong body.

Each night he came to her, and she felt she would expire in his embrace. He called forth from her body a pleasure that was devastating in its intensity.

The hours became a timeless maelstrom of explicit gratification. And each culmination was only a precursor to the next. Until, tender and swollen with his possession, her muscles exhausted with tension and release, she fell into a dreamless sleep.

But each morning she awoke alone, Thomas having left while she slept. Then, shortly after Annette had arrived to dress her, he would appear at her door, knocking softly, asking politely if he might enter. Thus began their day.

It was as though she had wed two different men. The daytime Thomas was controlled, amusing, reserved; the midnight Thomas was a hot-eyed lover who impelled her along the rapier-sharp crest of pleasure, demanding, spurring her to erotic action.

She had thought she knew Thomas. But in his role as her husband, he was nearly unrecognizable. And she felt awkward. She had always taken pride in her unblushing pragmatism, her hardheaded logic. But now she felt vulnerable. She was confused by his attitude and unwilling to broach the subject of his demeanor, at least until she felt more sure of his feelings.

That he wanted her body was obvious. But did he love her?

Cat wanted that. She wanted that hot-eyed lover to come to her door in the day, to watch her with his feral eyes, damning convention. She was certain that none of his other lovers had made Thomas forget himself, had pushed him past his perfect self-containment. Cat wanted that, too. For, as much as she gloried in his body's possession, she wanted his heart.

Just once she wished he would look at her with something other than considerate attention, damn society's eye and kiss her! *Bloody hell!* she thought irritably. Right now she'd be happy if he just would forswear knocking on the damned door every time he was about to enter!

She toyed with the idea of allowing him to stand there until he got tired enough to enter without asking her permission. Abandoning the notion, she sighed, calling for him to come in.

She smiled in greeting until she saw his startled expression. "What?" she asked worriedly.

"Your outfit, m'dear," Thomas said, "it is most . . . youthful."

Doubtfully, Cat looked down at the heavy flounces of white muslin gathered in tiny satin rosettes. The high, conspicuously modest bodice was inset with a pristine section of palest pink lace. Long sleeves ended in the same. Rosebuds peeked out of her carefully controlled coiffure.

"You don't like it," Cat said.

"It is very ingenuous."

Cat wrinkled her nose. "I feel as though the curate's lady is about to show up and give me lessons on deportment."

Thomas grinned.

"You are right, Thomas," Cat said, answering his thoughts as accurately as if he'd spoken aloud, "We have given society enough entertainment without now offering them a comedy." She turned to Annette, who was watching from nearby.

"I am sure your intentions are most laudable, Annette, but I am a married lady and cannot suddenly appear in a debutante's getup. It would only excite untoward comment. The bottle green dress, please."

Cat started to loosen the fastening at her neck.

"Would you like me to leave?" Thomas asked abruptly.

"No!" she burst out, caught unawares by the gentlemanly offer. "I mean, 'tisn't necessary. I will go behind the screen here."

Wonderful test of my composure, mused Thomas, *to be privy to a view of Cat's charms under the interested gaze of the dragon-like Annette.* The Frenchwoman was looking suspiciously at him, as though he were some half-tamed beast about to launch himself at her mistress. *She may well be right*, he thought grimly.

"Thomas," Cat called from behind the screen, "a footman brought up a note for you. It's on the mantel."

He picked up the envelope, glad of something to distract him from Cat's dishabille. He scanned the letter quickly and crumpled it in his fist.

Damn! He must learn to avoid Brighton in the future. Each time he was in residence, Seward managed to run him to ground. Thomas considered denying the colonel an audience before he remembered it was Seward's timely intervention that had led Thomas to Cat in Paris. Thomas always paid his debts. Besides, Giles Dalton was apparently going to tag along on the interview.

"Cat, I have some business to attend to this afternoon," he said.

"Yes?"

"Do you think you might take Annette and find a way to amuse yourself? The circulating library, Fisher's, is reputed to be well stocked."

Cat's head peeped out from the side of the elaborately carved screen. Her face was puzzled. "Yes, of course, Thomas. I shall spend my luncheon with Marcus. He leaves for Bellingcourt this afternoon."

"You'll have a pleasant time without me. I doubt your brother will ever forgive me the irregularity of our wedding," Thomas said as Cat emerged in a fashionable gown. Its low, square neck was unadorned except for the creamy white swells of her bosom.

Control, Thomas abjured himself sternly, offering her his arm and a polite smile. "And how shall we spend this morning?"

Seward and Strand arrived just before noon, well ahead of their proposed schedule. Giles looked tired. Seward, slender and unbending, appeared as he always did, remote and inhuman.

Strand drew a deep breath and stepped forward, extending his hand. "My congratulations on your marriage, Thomas."

A wry smile tilted one corner of Thomas' mouth. "Thank you, Giles."

Seward nodded, keeping the distance that had always been between him and Thomas a physical one. "I would like to add my sentiments to those of Lord Strand."

Thomas looked from one to the other. Both men seemed uneasy. Strand shifted on his feet. Seward became, if possible, even more rigidly upright.

"I suspect pleasant nuptial platitudes are not the only reason for your visit," Thomas said, motioning the two men to take seats before the table. It was still littered with the leavings of his morning tea. Cat's reticule lay abandoned on the floor. He smiled at this physical reminder of her reality in his life.

"No. I wish it were." Strand's voice recalled Thomas from his momentary preoccupation.

"Napoleon is on the march," Seward said without preamble. "Lord Strand gathered some information before leaving France that suggested Napoleon would be satisfied to retake Paris. That is why he was able to return to England so quickly. We thought the situation would remain static for a while.

"But now things have changed. Napoleon apparently seeks to use the present discontent amongst the allies to his advantage and gather a force while Wellington is in Brussels."

"And what has this to do with me?" asked Thomas, too gently.

"The men we will be able to muster to meet this challenge are not seasoned veterans. The troops in France are merely ceremonial ones. Even the allied forces are green, the soldiers who fought in the Peninsula having disbanded with Napoleon's removal to Elba."

Thomas nodded without saying a word.

"We have few qualified men available on such short notice. We need experienced campaigners to command the men," Seward said.

"Thank God you have Strand here," Thomas said sardonically.

"Pretty damn quick to throw me to the wolves, aren't you, Thomas?"

"Not as quick as you, apparently," Thomas replied obliquely, causing the color to flood Strand's clear complexion.

Seward cleared his throat. "Enlisting you was my idea, Thomas. I asked Strand the favor of using whatever influence he might have."

"I believe Wellington might be able to rout a few Frenchmen without my aid," Thomas said.

"That's just it, Thomas," Strand said. "They are not 'a few Frenchmen.' Reports come in daily that Napoleon is mustering a large force. The Royalist Fifth vacillated all of twenty minutes before swearing renewed allegiance to him at Grenoble."

"Damn, you say!" growled Thomas.

"Lord Strand is correct," interjected Seward. "Our need for leaders is pressing. In your own way, you command as much respect amongst the enlisted men as Wellington does."

"Being part and parcel of their untitled ranks?"

"As you say," said Seward smoothly "We might spend hours sitting here evaluating the merits of your reinstatement as captain. But you already know all the reasons why you should accept. It only remains to be seen if you will."

There was a long moment of silence. Duty, clinging jade that she was, would not be gainsaid. Thomas was not vain enough to judge himself more qualified to lead than others. He assumed he was merely one of the few *left* to lead. He was all too familiar with Napoleon's tactics: the feints, shifts, and thrusts of his military campaign. If Thomas did not go, he would certainly be responsible for avoidable deaths.

How could he hope to win Cat's love if he had no respect for himself? But to leave her! To make the grim wager he would return to her unscathed, whole of limb and mind?

What choice did he have? If he stayed, he would be consigned to offer Cat a pitiful excuse for a man.

"Yes," he said.

The two men were too well bred to be visibly pleased, but there was a lessening of tension in their stances.

"You might try to curb your rather indelicate and offensive relief," Thomas said.

"How will you tell Cat?" Strand asked quietly.

"I shall lay the fault at your door, Strand," Thomas said wryly.

Seward cleared his throat, drawing the attention of the two friends. "I must leave forthwith for the Continent. I wish to express my recognition of the sacrifice you make on behalf of your country, Thomas."

It was clearly a difficult thing for Seward to say, a tentative step toward breaching the chasm between them. Thomas found himself nodding, not yet willing to embrace the overture, but not totally discounting it.

"I am hoping to learn to accept that the worth of a man is not predestined by his social circumstances. My own included. Your servant, Thomas . . . Lord Strand." Seward made a sharply correct bow and left.

"The colonel had best watch these suspicious tendencies toward introspection," murmured Strand, "or he might yet discover he's human."

"You might be misjudging him, Giles," Thomas said.

"Misjudging him? He is so often already there, ahead of us all, misjudging others."

"He didn't misjudge me."

"No, he just knew what salt to use in what wound."

Thomas laughed. "Strand, your steadfastness is one of your few truly sterling qualities."

"And you have always had a conceited view of your own shortcomings."

"No," said Thomas, suddenly quieting. "I know myself well. As does the colonel. He had the right of it, Strand. All his speculation was founded on fact. I did enter his service for the most repellent of reasons. I was bored."

"You were of service to your country, Thomas."

"I was of service to myself. I know there were men who were willing to tolerate the excesses, the subterfuge, for a piece of potentially pertinent information. These men were motivated by patriotism, loyalty, and conviction . . . I was not one of their number.

"But my greatest sin was taking so long to appreciate that fact. Even an addiction would be preferable to what motivated me. For I was compelled by the thrill of it. When I finally awoke to what I had become ... it was too late to get out. Too much depended on my continued services. On my usefulness.

"God!" swore Thomas. "How I grew to loathe it! The dirty convenience of it. The necessary evil! How many did I cajole, threaten, browbeat, seduce, into betraying themselves and their country? How many silly women and foolish men believed my lies?" Thomas asked, knowing there would be no answer.

"It's an occupation that licks away at a man's self-respect, Strand, until one's very soul becomes a wound abraded by the rough tongue of deceit." Recalling himself, Thomas smiled apologetically. "Forgive my histrionics. Don't judge Seward too harshly. If he is discovering his humanity, and trying to atone for it, it is no less than I hope for myself. Can that be so bad?"

Strand shrugged. "For someone like Seward? A man who has spent thirty years trying to disprove the fact that he is a man much like other men, given to the same weaknesses, bigotries and failings? It would be nearly as disconcerting as it is to find one has a heart after years of failing to recognize it," he said blandly.

Thomas shot a sharp look at Strand.

"You needn't be concerned, Thomas. I shall not pant after your wife, trying to lure her out behind the potted ferns to steal a kiss."

"It doesn't worry me in the least, Giles," Thomas said.

"My! You have an overblown notion of my integrity. I don't know if I would be so trusting were the roles reversed." There was the faintest tinge of bitterness in Strand's well-modulated tones.

Thomas smiled. "First, while I do trust you, it is only so far as not to make an ass of yourself. It is Cat who is incapable of nefarious activity. You would find yourself fondling the fern and nothing more. Second, if by some chance the roles were reversed, I would not hesitate to pursue Cat relentlessly, everywhere and at all times.

"She doesn't love you, you see." Thomas' words were not said unkindly. "And the barest possibility that she might come to love me would be impetus enough to send me in pursuit of her, regardless of any sanctions state or church or society has devised." Thomas knew that what he said hurt Strand, but in this, even with Strand, he needed to make himself absolutely clear. There was no force in the world capable of making Thomas quit his claim on Cat.

It was still early yet, thought Cat as she slipped into her room. Thomas and his mysterious guests would not be here for another half hour or so.

The sound of male voices droning from beyond the door leading to Thomas' rooms alerted Cat to her mistake. *Ah well*, she thought, *I'll just find my wretched reticule and be off before they even know I'm here.*

She rummaged silently amongst her things, unable to discover the misplaced beaded bag. It wasn't beneath her fans . . . in the drawers. She had last seen it after breaking fast in Thomas' room . . . Drat! Well, she would just have to breach the walls of the masculine sanctum and apologize. She could not very well hie herself off to a café without a penny to her name.

She moved to the door.

"And now you would leave her?" It was Giles Dalton's voice.

"How can I not leave her? How can I not go when to stay would only breed the utmost contempt, if not in Cat then in myself?"

The words froze Cat's hand in the act of reaching for the handle. The words tolled a death knell.

They thundered in her ears, waves of hurt echoing in her mind. Her heart hammered upward in her throat. Thomas was leaving? she thought wildly, turning as if in a trance and retracing her steps.

Thomas was leaving! Why?! Sinking to the floor beside the bed, her shaking legs unable to support her any further, Cat buried her face in her hands. If she hadn't heard the words in Thomas' own voice, clear, imperative, unshakable in their conviction, she would not have believed them.

The days of companionable dialogue, the debates, the affability, the laughter . . . But he was so formal, his manners so impeccable. She had thought he was trying to forestall gossip. That was what he had been doing, wasn't it? She begged herself to answer yes. But another seed, one of black uncertainty, had taken root.

And in view of that dark, whispering fear, his formality looked like distance, his manners like politeness, his morning withdrawal from her like disinterest. But the nights! Surely such intensity could not be feigned. Surely here was a refutation of her doubts.

Feigned? the voice of idiot reason argued. *Why must it be feigned?* Thomas was a man much associated with all matters of sexuality. He was a rake. Was it so surprising he would make the best of the situation in whatever way he could?

Perhaps the care he took in pleasuring her was merely what all his other lovers had experienced. It made abundantly clear how he had achieved his reputation. For Cat could not imagine a more demanding, impassioned lover than Thomas.

Has he ever spoken of love? the voice continued. *Have I?* she countered.

Her mind became a tumultuous explosion of questions. Her perspective shifted with bewildering speed as she struggled to bring meaning to the meaningless words she had heard Thomas utter. A sensation of being suspended high above an eroding precipice overwhelmed her. It was her future, suddenly threatening, black and impenetrable.

I am not thinking clearly. I must think what to do. But how can I bring any logic or sense to this when I am with him? How can I confront him when I am in terror of his answers? I cannot stay waiting for him to take his leave, for him to abandon me. I cannot think here. Not with Thomas so close. I must go.

Marcus was departing for Bellingcourt in the afternoon. She would go with him. She would go home.

Rising unsteadily to her feet, Cat forced herself to straighten, to go to the small desk and pen a note, to ring for Annette and start removing her clothing from the wardrobe.

Oh God, she thought despairingly, the tears welling up in her eyes. A sudden thought finally caused the sobs to erupt, strangling in her throat.

She could go to Bellingcourt. But it wasn't home anymore.

Chapter 29

Well, thought Cat, *this was a stupid idea.*

She sat on the slipper chair next to her bed and pulled the thin satin ribbons from her hair, preparing for sleep. If only she *could* sleep.

After dinner, she had retired to her old bedroom. It looked unfamiliar to her, felt alien, as though some stranger lived there. It was filled with her youthful leavings and empty of those things that now defined her. She stared out of the rain-sheeted window, into the night.

For two days, Cat had been at Bellingcourt. It had started to rain the evening she and Marcus had arrived. And it had rained ever since. A relentless deluge, swirling from the leaden skies, buffeted by strong spring winds.

Absently Cat plucked at the fastening to her gown. She had left Annette in Brighton, unwilling to take the shocked, so proper maid to her family seat. Annette wouldn't have lasted a day here, anyway.

Her family had greeted her with all the enthusiasm her long sojourn merited. Only Timon and Simon were not there to greet her. Simon having purchased a commission in the Lancers on Thomas' moneys, and Timon enrolled at Oxford on a similar boon. Cat hadn't known. Thomas had never told her he had begun to bolster the flagging estate as long ago as last autumn. And he had sworn the rest of them to secrecy.

Apparently Thomas' aid extended to her sisters, too. Enid was to be presented this season. Thomas had persuaded a dignified matron to champion her. Even little Marianne was filled with tales of the wondrous generosity of Cat's husband.

Husband, thought Cat woefully. Thomas would be amused to learn her new title caused so much joy in her family. Even in cousin Emmaline.

Emmaline had received Cat at the door, expressing a patently insincere welcome home and immediately following the greeting with a query as to how long Cat intended to stay before she rejoined "kind Mr. Montrose." Cat did all she could to assuage the older woman's obvious fear of being shipped, posthaste, back to Wales.

Cat sank down onto her bed, wearily unlacing her boots. She was exhausted. For two days she had been at the tender mercies of her family. Two days of her sweet, good-natured sisters' heavy-handed interrogation. It was driving her mad.

This morning Marcus had taken her on a tour of Bellingcourt, pointing out through the pouring rain the various improvements he had implemented. Repairs that had been made to the home farm and were being done on the stables. He even made her sit for ten minutes while he proudly inspected a flock of—heaven help her!—dolefully dripping sheep on the lower field. Apparently Marcus had procured "a loan made by Mr. Thomas Montrose which is being repaid quarterly at a rate agreeable to both lender and borrower."

Cat unhooked the pearl choker Thomas had given her on their wedding day, feathering her fingertips over the satiny balls.

"Wear them close to the skin and they shall

develop a sheen as glorious as your skin," Thomas had said.

They were not the words of a man on the verge of abandoning his wife.

Other phrases, small gestures, arose as she finally drew the bedclothes over her tired body. Sleepless hour after sleepless hour, she tossed, his words haunting her to sleep.

"You shall grow bored with my company, Thomas," she had teased him at the end of one long, wonderful day. "You will need a rest from me."

"But, m'dear, the only ease I find is in your company. You are my own refuge, my sweet asylum, recompense for my ill-spent youth."

His voice gave way to his image. Shatteringly, the memories of their nights together pursued her. His body pressing into hers. His hands unquenchable in their search, harbingers of erotic, lush pleasure. His voice compelling her as she spiraled upwards toward the inevitable release his lovemaking brought.

"Give yourself to me!" he'd whispered as she arched beneath him. He had tantalized her with the climax he controlled, sating her only to reawaken the hunger within minutes of completion, bringing her again and again to rapture, exhausting her, draining her, and still demanding she experience more.

"What do you want of me?" she had asked dazedly as he sank his full, hard length into her, the muscles of his chest leaping with exquisite constriction.

"Want?" he had rasped, his midnight gaze riveting her until she felt she would be lost, translated by the intensity of his thrusts into a part of him, absorbed into his great body. "I want you! Your heart. Your thoughts. Your spirit. The very essence of you!"

Bolting upright, Cat dragged her hands through her hair, shaking as she tried to ignore the brilliant images. Confusion slowly replaced the pain. It did not make sense. He felt something for her. He must. No man who claimed to hate hypocrisy could breathe those words into a woman's ear!

But she had heard him say he was going to leave her! Finding no answer for the riddle upon which her future hung, Cat tried once more to make sense of it.

Perhaps he wanted the convenient marriage he had proposed. Perhaps he meant merely to begin the pattern of daily life he wished them to follow: he, going about his business; she, hers. Perhaps he meant for them to live apart to pursue their own course. Hadn't his proposal outlined such a plan? Hadn't he been clear? Had she misread or merely dismissed his plans because she so desperately wanted there to be something else?

Had he seen in her physical abandonment a future in which she clung to him with disgusting tenacity? Did he worry she would cause remark with her undiluted attentions? Was her love so obvious? So suffocating? So distasteful? She didn't know!

She knew nothing. Nothing except that she loved Thomas. Loved him enough to want his happiness. His life had been so bereft of it. He was hard on himself, so contemptuous of his past.

Crawling back beneath the blankets, Cat stared at the high, black ceiling. She knew it well. She had studied each corner for hours during the past two nights. There was no peace for Cat at Bellingcourt.

The rain had slowed to a fine drizzle, no more than a mist, by the next morning. Cat rose early, exhausted, unable yet to face the goodwill of her family. Unwilling to offend them with a spoken desire to be alone, she donned a heavy cape and slipped through the back door. Passing the kitchen garden and orchards, she wandered down toward the small creek that traversed the borders of Bellingcourt.

The air was thick and fragrant with the scent of moist soil, new grass, and budding trees. A heavy mist intensified the clarion call of birds, an unseen choir breaking the stillness of the early gray light. The dew saturated her half boots and clung to the thick wool mantle. She paused, experiencing the first real delight since leaving Thomas Bellingcourt. Perhaps it was no longer home, but it was still beautiful. A sense of calm overtook her.

She would give Thomas what he needed. She would not struggle any longer with questions for which she had no answers. He had said he would leave her. She would accept that. He had also said he would not divorce her and would want heirs. She would accept that. She would learn to welcome him when he appeared, content with whatever he offered. If she must learn to live with only a piece of Thomas, so be it. She would survive.

Taking a deep, clearing breath, Cat willed herself to appreciate the watercolor tints of the new leaves, the scent of spring earth and vegetation.

"You know, m'dear, I am growing deuced fatigued with these confounded notes."

Cat spun around. Thomas stood a few paces from her, leaning against the trunk of a burr oak, his arms folded across his broad chest. "And this onerous habit of bustling off leaving half your clothing behind works havoc with the servants. Annette has given notice."

The dew caught in his dark hair, turning the overlong, dusky locks into a tangle of wet strands, curling damply upon his tanned throat. His expression was composed, but his eyes burned in his handsome face.

Her gaze devoured his beloved figure. He was magnificent. His cravatless linen shirt was open at the throat. His greatcoat was flung back over his wide shoulders. His boots were mud-spattered and dull.

"Thomas, what are you doing here?" Cat asked, her voice faint.

"Why, I'm here with my wife, of course. She seems to have taken a notion to visit her family manse and unaccountably forgot to pack her husband along with the rest of her things. Really, my love, for someone known for her relentless practicality, you show a marked tendency for impetuous action."

"You are supposed to be gone," she said.

A frown deepened the lines bracketing his well-sculpted lips. He pushed himself off the tree, stalking toward her.

"Gone? Why?" he demanded.

"Because." Damn! How could he just stand there, so handsome, so masculine, so nonchalant, when she had been stretched on a rack of misery for three entire days?! Feeling her lower lip starting to tremble, she tried to compose herself. She began again, mindful of the promises she had just made to herself. "Because that is the type of marriage we are to have. You said so yourself. You are to go your way, and I, mine."

"And this means you can just up and leave me whenever the whim dictates?" he growled, leaning close to her.

"I . . . I left you a note."

"Oh, yes." He rocked back on his heels, his eyes becoming shuttered. "And a pretty, nice little bit of noninformation it was, too. 'Thomas,

I am going away. I will contact you later. Your wife, Catherine Sinclair.' Your name, madam, is Catherine Montrose!"

Cat shrank back, aghast at the anger with which the words erupted. Why would such a simple mistake enrage him so? She stepped back again, and he followed, closing in.

"Really, Thomas, I don't know what you are so angry about. I am giving you the freedom you outlined."

Once more, the fire of his eyes was banked behind a screen of inscrutable emotion. "What freedom?" he asked.

Cat was getting angry. She had tried to be sophisticated, unperturbed, munificent. But to have the blackguard stand there feigning confusion when not a few days ago she had heard him outline a plan to dissolve their marriage! Well, as good as dissolve their union. She wasn't going to allow him to play this ridiculous game any longer. To bloody hell with her good intentions!

"You! You pompous, egotistical, monstrous . . . *man!* I am referring to your convenient, practical, pathetic excuse for a proposal!"

Thomas' eyebrows shot up in a nearly comical display of offended dignity. Except Cat didn't feel like laughing. She felt like clawing him.

"You didn't like my proposal?" he asked stiffly.

"I *hated* your proposal! 'We will raise nice sheep together,' 'your input as a land manager will be invaluable,' a *'civil union'!* If you have need of a land steward—hire one!"

Unbelievably, horribly, the corners of his mouth began to quirk. Horrid man.

"But why should I hire one when fate has conspired to hand me wife and steward in one?"

"Oh!"

"Come along, Cat," Thomas said placatingly,

reaching out his hand. "We must bid your family good-bye before we leave for London. The season begins in a few weeks, and I have a desire to see you queen it over the *ton*."

Scowling at him, Cat sidled backwards, out of his reach. She tried to regulate her voice, matching his insouciant tone. She failed.

"I am not going with you!" she shouted.

"Yes, you are," Thomas replied with dangerous quietness.

"No, I am not! I have had enough of your polite inattention. Knocking at my door. Steering me about Brighton by the elbow as though to touch my arm would give you a case of the French pox. Avoiding my eye. Calling me 'madam,' for God's sake!" She felt the tears bubble over her lids and dashed them angrily away, "And . . . and after the exquisite nights! Oh, Thomas, how could you?"

"Exquisite?" he echoed.

She felt her cheeks grow hot. *Fine*, she thought wildly, *why not end this scene without any dignity left at all? Why the hell not?*

"Yes, exquisite! Rapturous! Wondrous! At least they were to me! *I* do not have the advantage of a past which dulls the impact of these . . . feelings. I am sorry I have not yet acquired enough experience to take them for granted. But yes, damn it! To me our nights were exquisite!"

Oh, God! He was grinning openly now, his wide, mobile mouth displaying a set of strong, white teeth.

"Cat, you are overset," he said, placing a calming hand on her arm. She shook him off angrily.

"Can you not understand the King's English? I am not going to put up with your diffuse courtesy during the day and your too intent lovemaking at night. 'Tis too great a discrepancy for a poor, simpleminded, naive little idiot like me!"

He reached out and, ignoring her waving arms, grabbed hold of her wrists, hauling her to him, wrapping her in his iron embrace. "Madam, you are coming with me. You are my wife, and I am not going to hear any more about my 'advantageous past'. I am sick unto death of my past and the hold it has had over my life—no, *our* lives!"

He was growing angry himself. She could hear it in the tight growl of his words.

He continued, "I am not going to spend my days scuttling about trying to avoid some tart whom I bedded a decade ago because she might remind you there were other bodies in my past! There were! Bodies! Nothing more! So be it!"

"Thomas," she began, but he gave her a little shake, his eyes burning with unbridled conviction, stilling hers.

"Listen to me, Cat. The past is done. Over. You said so yourself. You are my wife, my companion, and damn it, you are my love. The first and only love of my entire thirty-three years. I have waited a lifetime for you, and I will have you!"

Cat stared at him, once more opening her mouth to speak, but he would have none of it.

"If I promised you a marriage of polite recognition and accommodation—I lied! I lied, and you will just have to live with that. I want you with me. Now, tomorrow, tonight, and for all the rest of my bloody days! And you will be there if I have to follow you about the face of the earth, your little notes in one hand and the rest of your clothing in the other! Do you understand?"

She looked up at him, nodding mutely. Love burned, blazed, exposing itself with absolute clarity in his onyx eyes. Unguarded, direct, vulnerable. His love could be no less apparent than the sun burning brightly through the scattered remnants of the morning fog. Her arms crept upwards to pull his dark, beautiful face to hers. But he held her back.

"And you love me!" he shouted. "Damn it, Cat. You love me! Say it!"

"I love you, Thomas," she said.

"And as for inattentive politeness. I shall attend you, madam, until you are so sore, you won't be able to walk. I shall attend you from morning till night. Until we both burn to cinders with my attentions. Now say it again. I have waited a lifetime for your words."

"I love—" Her last word was smothered by his mouth.

Her lips opened under his, her tongue seeking a deeper union. She brushed the wet hair from his forehead and kissed the corners of his eyes, his high cheekbones, his temples, his jaw, and his mouth again. His hands moved to encompass her, and she burrowed into his embrace, knowing he needed her to be the aggressor, needed this first move from her, needed her to want.

And she did. Holding him as tightly as she could, Cat wrapped her arms about him, pushing her hip into the berth of his thighs, her mouth roaming hungrily, achingly over his face and throat and chest.

"I thought you were going to leave me. I heard you say so to Strand. I heard you tell him if you did not leave, it would be a hypocrisy you could not live with," she whispered raggedly against his heated skin. "I thought it was what you wanted."

"Never! They want a captain to play soldier for them. I agreed. I could not hope for your love if I let men die while I wooed you. I would not respect myself. How then could I hope to win your heart?"

"My heart? My heart is yours! My heart, my body, my very soul, are yours. I love you, Thomas!"

He rose, swinging her up into his arms and settling her against his chest. His mouth trailed liquid fire down her throat, sipping the moisture from her eyelashes. Frantically she tried to hold him closer, as though she feared he might disappear and leave her bereft once more.

"Hush, love," he whispered, rocking her gently even as he stood. "Hush! It's all right, now. There is no need for these tears. It is all right."

"No," she sobbed, lifting bright, shimmering eyes to his. "It's not! You are going away. You might be killed. Oh, Thomas, I would rather you didn't love me at all than have you die in battle. I do not care for your honor, your duty!

"Hate them as I do!" she begged. "Duty, honor, wretched words impelling you to leave me." His sad, loving eyes gave her his answer. She could not ask Thomas to be anything less than he was. It was her joy, and her misfortune.

"Oh, Thomas," she said, "please don't die! I'll find you if you die! I'll search the afterworld and hound you through eternity if you leave me now. I swear I will!" she finished fiercely.

"Cat," Thomas said, striding with her in his arms to the house, the dew sparkling a jeweled trail behind them. "All that your threats promise is heaven."

Epilogue

July 1815
Devon

Catherine Montrose was not in the best of moods.

For two months she had been in Devon, at her new home, waiting for Thomas to return. Two months of sweat-soaked night terrors, waking to endless day after endless day of wondering if Thomas lived or died. Thousands of men had lost their lives near two insignificant little farms at a place called Waterloo.

Finally Colonel Seward had gotten word to her. Thomas lived. Cat had spent the next two weeks waiting for a note in her husband's own hand. No message, in any form, arrived. Her relief gave way to anger, frustration, and finally dark conjecture. He could be wounded, maimed, or ill.

Refusing to give in to melancholy speculation, Cat sat in Thomas' library each evening, poring over account books, studying demographic sheets, reading the newest agricultural findings, anything to keep the horrendous images at bay. The estate was her pledge of trust to Thomas, trust that he would come back to her. Proof of her faith in him. And it was better than the dream-haunted nights.

Anxious and tired, Cat had picked up the mail

this morning and flipped through the correspondence. A foreign watermark caught her eye. Anxiously she ripped it open. Perplexed by the long,
elegant scrawl, she finally recognizing it as Aunt
Hecuba's. She had smiled before she had read the
first line. A smile that had quickly faded.

Aunt Hecuba was fine. Glowingly fine, wondrously fine, blooming under the concentrated
(she had actually underlined the word, the old
tart!) attentions of the marquis. Had Cat managed
to get that great, black, handsome brute to the altar
yet? Of course she had. Blood ran true. By the
way, Hecuba had run into that interesting Daphne
Bernard. It seems the young lady had managed a
daring escape from Paris!

As had she. Really, people are most odd. True,
her own flight from Paris had been exciting, but
she really hadn't outsmarted an entire regiment of
guards at some blockade, as some Sally Leades person was intimating. And she hadn't single-handedly
thwarted a criminal ring terrorizing their fleeing
countrymen in the northern French provinces. Still,
being a celebrity had its rewards. Of course, she
knew Thomas would be there to take care of Cat.
Her beloved niece had never truly been in any
danger.

But Daphne. What a resourceful woman Daphne
Bernard was. They had only met because "Daffy"
owned a large pendant, remarkably similar to the
one Hecuba had left behind. Of course, Daphne's
was real.

Of course, Cat had muttered to herself as she
read.

Perhaps they had misjudged the young woman,
Hecuba went on to write. Daffy had explained to
Hecuba that she had merely taken the opportunities *le bon Dieu* had thrown in her path to further
her own sorry little way in the world. Daffy hadn't

the advantages of so aristocratic and loving a family as the big English girl—Kitty, was it? (Isn't that cute? Hecuba had written.) They had become quite friendly.

Had Cat heard from her dear mama? Hecuba had. She and Grenville had stopped at a coaching house on the Prussian border. Fellow travelers had had a message to be delivered in London. Wonderful happenstance! It was from Cat's mama. By the way, Cat had best not expect her parent for some time. Philip had taken a notion to follow Hannibal's path.

Crumpling the paper, Cat pitched it into the hearth and stomped angrily from the room. On her way down the stair, she barked out orders to have the coach brought about. At least now she was in the proper mood to confront her wretched sister Enid concerning the chit's defiant demands regarding her coming-out wardrobe.

Enid, who was staying with Cat, as was only proper, was waiting for her at the local seamstress's. The girl was probably attempting to bribe, blackmail, and bully the poor woman into lowering the décolletage on Enid's many gowns, thought Cat. Enid, it seemed, wanted to be a seductress. Well, thought Cat darkly as she settled herself in the carriage, we'll see about that!

Cat enumerated on her fingers the many pithy things she was going to say to her sister as the elegant coach rolled down the lane toward town. She was staring out the window, green fire dancing in her eyes, when she saw a big, fat ewe standing frozen in the hedge separating the lane from the pasture. Leaning out the window, Cat called for the driver to stop.

Bob jumped down and worriedly approached her, asking if anything was amiss. Alphonse joined him from the rear of the coach.

Cat pointed at the sheep in the thicket. "There's nothing for it, we'll just have to get her out of there."

"Begging your pardon, ma'am, but couldn't I just ride back to the house and have one of the lads fetch a workman? I'm sure I haven't the sorriest notion on how one goes about disentangling a great, fat, fleecy thing like that."

Cat harrumphed. "Waste of valuable time. I'm promised at the seamstress in half an hour and shall be late as it is."

"Well then, couldn't we just leave her there, Mrs. Montrose? She don't look too uncomfortable like."

"No, we cannot," Cat said firmly. The farm, and everything on it, was her responsibility, and she was going to see everything was taken care of properly.

"Now, Bob, you go around and hold her middle while Alphonse grabs her legs and drags her out."

Dubiously the two men approached the sheep. The ornery creature bleated at them at the first touch of their hands, and the driver jumped back.

"Coo! She be a biggun!" Alphonse said, rubbing his hands together in preparation for the next assault.

"Lift her up as Alphonse pulls, Bob!" Cat shouted encouragingly.

"Easy fer her to say," Bob muttered, wrapping his arms around the ewe's impressive girth. He heaved her up, grunting for Alphonse to pull.

Alphonse gave an irresolute yank on one of the sheep's hind legs, causing the animal to twist in panic, her sudden movement pitching Bob backward into the hedge.

He sat there sputtering, glaring balefully at his lady mistress, who was, in turn, eyeing him with distinct disillusionment.

"For heaven's sake, Bob," Cat said as she descended from the carriage, "it's only a sheep! Now then," she said, striding over to where the ewe was trying to bury itself in the briar. She pointed her elegant ivory fan at its hindquarters.

"I suggest you, Bob, lift her so that her front legs cannot gain any purchase in the branches," Cat said. "At the same time, you, Alphonse, take hold of both her hind feet. Firmly. And pull for all you're worth. The sooner done, the sooner over. On my count, lads."

She was so intent on marshaling her ill-prepared troops, she did not hear the approaching rider.

Thomas had pushed his gelding to a lather in his haste to make it home. He had not paused at Brighton, or even in London, to rid himself of his military uniform and procure civilian attire. He wanted to see Cat. He *needed* to see Cat. He hadn't taken time to pen a note, certain he would beat any missive he sent.

Only as he turned onto the mile-long road leading to his home did he allow the poor horse time to cool down. His eyes had widened in pleased surprise as he noted the various and sundry improvements that had been made in his absence. The barley in the fields, the multitude of lambs and sheep grazing in the verdant pastures.

How like Cat. With what a deft hand she arranged and ordered things. She would have made a fine field marshal. The thought brought unwanted images of the massacre that history would call Waterloo to Thomas' mind. He had fought so fiercely so that there would be no further Waterloos. The waste of human life had sickened him.

He shook off the dark images, his mind's eye seeking an image of Cat, like a tern seeks the pure, free expanse of the ocean. Cat. Tranquil. Calm. Serene. Composed. Moderation in his havoc-filled world. Contentment and peace.

He rounded the sharp corner leading to the drive and saw a woman. Reining in the gelding some paces back, he suddenly recognized Cat.

She was standing in a hedgerow, her sleeves rolled up over her forearms, the luscious silk of her dress stained with grass, a mud smear on its lace-edged hem. Her hair had tumbled from some hat-like confection. She was railing at two red-faced, liveried men who all but scuffed their feet, their gazes fixed on the ground.

Cat. Tranquil.

" . . . and furthermore, I have never in my life seen two grown men incapable of acting in unison in such a patently simple maneuver . . ."

Serene.

" . . . I refuse to believe that one stupid sheep can so flummox three reasonably intelligent adults . . ."

Composed.

" . . . If I have to wade in there and wrench the bloody thing free myself, I will!"

Regal. His Cat. His own.

"You there, madam!" Thomas called. She turned, her lovely brow creased in a thunderous scowl. Her eyes, those impossible gray-green eyes, widened. Gladness spread through each feature, lighting her beloved face with a joy impossible to contain.

His contentment. His Cat.

She lifted up her skirts as he swung down from the saddle.

God, the woman could run!

Avon Romances—
the best in exceptional authors and unforgettable novels!

HEART OF THE WILD   Donna Stephens
77014-8/$4.50 US/$5.50 Can

TRAITOR'S KISS   Joy Tucker
76446-6/$4.50 US/$5.50 Can

SILVER AND SAPPHIRES   Shelly Thacker
77034-2/$4.50 US/$5.50 Can

SCOUNDREL'S DESIRE   Joann DeLazzari
76421-0/$4.50 US/$5.50 Can

MY LADY NOTORIOUS   Jo Beverley
76785-6/$4.50 US/$5.50 Can

SURRENDER MY HEART   Lois Greiman
77181-0/$4.50 US/$5.50 Can

MY REBELLIOUS HEART   Samantha James
76937-9/$4.50 US/$5.50 Can

COME BE MY LOVE   Patricia Watters
76909-3/$4.50 US/$5.50 Can

SUNSHINE AND SHADOW   Kathleen Harrington
77058-X/$4.50 US/$5.50 Can

WILD CONQUEST   Hannah Howell
77182-9/$4.50 US/$5.50 Can

Avon Regency Romance

Kasey Michaels

THE CHAOTIC MISS CRISPINO
76300-1/$3.99 US/$4.99 Can

THE DUBIOUS MISS DALRYMPLE
89908-6/$2.95 US/$3.50 Can

THE HAUNTED MISS HAMPSHIRE
76301-X/$3.99 US/$4.99 Can

Loretta Chase

THE ENGLISH WITCH 70660-1/$2.95 US/$3.50 Can
ISABELLA 70597-4/$2.95 US/$3.95 Can
KNAVES' WAGER 71363-2/$3.95 US/$4.95 Can
THE SANDALWOOD PRINCESS
71455-8/$3.99 US/$4.99 Can
THE VISCOUNT VAGABOND
70836-1/$2.95 US/$3.50 Can

Jo Beverley

EMILY AND THE DARK ANGEL
71555-4/$3.99 US/$4.99 Can

THE FORTUNE HUNTER
71771-9/$3.99 US/$4.99 Can

THE STANFORTH SECRETS
71438-8/$3.99 US/$4.99 Can

Avon Romantic Treasures

*Unforgettable, enthralling love stories,
sparkling with passion and adventure
from Romance's bestselling authors*

MY WILD ROSE *by Deborah Camp*
76738-4/$4.50 US/$5.50 Can

MIDNIGHT AND MAGNOLIAS *by Rebecca Paisley*
76566-7/$4.50 US/$5.50 Can

THE MASTER'S BRIDE *by Suzannah Davis*
76821-6/$4.50 US/$5.50 Can

A ROSE AT MIDNIGHT *by Anne Stuart*
76740-6/$4.50 US/$5.50 Can

FORTUNE'S MISTRESS *by Judith E. French*
76864-X/$4.50 US/$5.50 Can

HIS MAGIC TOUCH *by Stella Cameron*
76607-8/$4.50 US/$5.50 Can

COMANCHE WIND *by Genell Dellin*
76717-1/$4.50 US/$5.50 Can

THEN CAME YOU *by Lisa Kleypas*
77013-X/$4.50 US/$5.50 Can

*If you enjoyed this book,
take advantage
of this special offer.
Subscribe now and get a*

FREE
Historical
Romance

No Obligation (a $4.50 value)

Each month the editors of True Value select the four *very best* novels from America's leading publishers of romantic fiction. Preview them in your home *Free* for 10 days. With the first four books you receive, we'll send you a FREE book as our introductory gift. No Obligation!

If for any reason you decide not to keep them, just return them and owe nothing. If you like them as much as we think you will, you'll pay just $4.00 each and save at *least* $.50 each off the cover price. (Your savings are *guaranteed* to be at least $2.00 each month.) There is NO postage and handling – or other hidden charges. There are no minimum number of books to buy and you may cancel at any time.

***Send in
the Coupon
Below***

To get your FREE historical romance fill out the coupon below and mail it today. As soon as we receive it we'll send you your FREE Book along with your first month's selections.

Mail To: **True Value Home Subscription Services, Inc., P.O. Box 5235
120 Brighton Road, Clifton, New Jersey 07015-5235**

YES! I want to start previewing the very best historical romances being published today. Send me my FREE book along with the first month's selections. I understand that I may look them over FREE for 10 days. If I'm not absolutely delighted I may return them and owe nothing. Otherwise I will pay the low price of just $4.00 each: a total $16.00 (at least an $18.00 value) and save at least $2.00. Then each month I will receive four brand new novels to preview as soon as they are published for the same low price. I can always return a shipment and I may cancel this subscription at any time with no obligation to buy even a single book. In any event the FREE book is mine to keep regardless.

Name _____

Street Address _____ Apt. No. _____

City _____ State _____ Zip _____

Telephone _____

Signature _____
(if under 18 parent or guardian must sign)

Terms and prices subject to change. Orders subject to acceptance by True Value Home Subscription Services, Inc.

77550-6